The Glimmer Palace

The Glimmer Palace

BEATRICE COLIN

RIVERHEAD BOOKS
a member of Penguin Group (USA) Inc.
New York
2008

RIVERHEAD BOOKS
Published by the Penguin Group
Penguin Group (USA) Inc., 375 Hudson Street, New York, New York 10014, USA • Penguin Group (Canada), 90 Eglinton Avenue East, Suite 700, Toronto, Ontario M4P 2Y3, Canada (a division of Pearson Canada Inc.) • Penguin Books Ltd, 80 Strand, London WC2R 0RL, England • Penguin Ireland, 25 St Stephen's Green, Dublin 2, Ireland (a division of Penguin Books Ltd) • Penguin Group (Australia), 250 Camberwell Road, Camberwell, Victoria 3124, Australia (a division of Pearson Australia Group Pty Ltd) • Penguin Books India Pvt Ltd, 11 Community Centre, Panchsheel Park, New Delhi–110 017, India • Penguin Group (NZ), 67 Apollo Drive, Rosedale, North Shore 0632, New Zealand (a division of Pearson New Zealand Ltd) • Penguin Books (South Africa) (Pty) Ltd, 24 Sturdee Avenue, Rosebank, Johannesburg 2196, South Africa

Penguin Books Ltd, Registered Offices:
80 Strand, London WC2R 0RL, England

Published simultaneously in Canada

For a list of illustration credits, see page 403.

Library of Congress Cataloging-in-Publication Data

Colin, Beatrice.
The glimmer palace / Beatrice Colin.
p. cm.
ISBN 978-1-59448-985-3
1. Motion-picture industry—Fiction. 2. Berlin (Germany)—Fiction.
3. Berlin (Germany)—History—20th century—Fiction. I. Title.
PR6103.O443G55 2008 2008006835
823'.92—dc22

Printed in the United States of America
1 3 5 7 9 10 8 6 4 2

Book design by Michelle McMillian

For Veronica and Andrew

All that is transitory is only an image.

—GOETHE

The Glimmer Palace

The First Spark

Berlin, a word that chimes in your chest like a bell. Berlin, a place so bright it pulls down the stars and wears them around its neck. Berlin, a city built on the scattered sand of circuses and the scuffed floorboards of theater spectaculars. Roll up, roll up to see the living photographs. Max Skladanowsky and his brother Eugen, still wearing black around their eyes, out of habit rather than necessity, present their electromechanical effects. The spectacle of the year, the highlight of 1895, guaranteed.

The houselights dim, and the air is filled with the sour taste of hot celluloid and blue smoke from a hundred burning cigarettes. A blond girl looms up suddenly on a white sheet. She laughs, a flickery shiver on the taut cotton; she seems to speak but her voice is mute, until, quite unexpectedly, a black patch appears where her heart should be and she disappears into the burning hole in seconds.

The audience gasps, and one child chokes on his chewed-up ticket. The couple in the front row insist it is a trick with mirrors; a woman in a red hat peeks behind the sheet but finds no one there. And all the while, trickles of kohl from India fall down Eugen's ashen face as he comes to realize he'll never again see the girl he left behind in Lübbenau.

Lilly Nelly Aphrodite was born in the final moments of the last hour of the nineteenth century. She was caught in a dark blue handwoven cloth threaded with real gold instead of the obligatory white receiving shawl and was declared perfect by everyone around the bedside, including the landlady and the Bavarian lover. Unfortunately, the dye, though a beautiful shade, was not fast and the cloth stained her creased and slippery newborn skin.

"She's blue," her mother cooed. "How novel."

The Bavarian lover lit a cigar and looked at his watch.

"Happy New Year," he said through a mouthful of smoke.

As Champagne corks popped and strangers kissed, as the Bavarian lover started to sing and the mother reapplied her French cologne, the midwife, already packing up, suddenly snatched the baby back from where she rested serenely in her cot and began to spank her violently on the bottom. The baby was not just blue, everyone noticed at once; she seemed devoid of life.

And in that tiny eternity, while the bells tolled and a million glasses clinked, while the midwife swore and shook and smacked, and tears sprang to eyes so recently crumpled up with joy, the infant seemed all but dead. And then, as hope was fading by the second and the midwife's palm struck her chilled behind with full force for a final desperate time, she jerked twice and gasped. Air rushed into her brand-new lungs, a blast of cool with a hint of cigar, her eyes opened, and she stared straight into the face of a clock. It was one minute past twelve. She took another mouthful of air and let out a high-pitched scream. Her skin was still blue but no one could doubt that she was now very much alive.

Although the date of her birth was officially the thirty-first of December, Lilly Nelly Aphrodite's first breath was taken in the twentieth century. It was as if, the midwife said as she tried to console the child's mother, she was determined to wait. A certain willfulness was noted. And when in the coming months she screamed and sobbed and could not be comforted no matter what, her mother blamed that night, that midwife, and that handwoven cloth that she had been so stupidly sentimental to accept from her stuttering Bavarian lover and that, he eventually admitted, he had been given by a former mistress who had traveled to Constantinople and been locked in a sultan's harem for an entire year before she managed to escape with nothing but the dress she was wearing and a suitcase full of precious cloth.

Later, much later, while her parents finally slept, the new baby lay awake and stared out at the orange sodium night. In rings around Potsdamer Platz and all along the wiggle of the river Spree, a hundred thousand electric bulbs lit up in strings. Although it has been many places at many times, Berlin at that moment was a city not built but randomly piled around the provincial capital of Prussia. It was a metropolis where smokestacks exhaled and factories whistled, where telephone wires hummed and the tracks of the underground lines shrieked with excitement with each passing train. In 1900, Berlin was a place where workers flocked in their millions to live in crowded tenements in the newly constructed suburbs and commute by tram to work. It was a city where writers and artists rented garrets and starved themselves into shape. It was a city without memory, a city without tradition; in Berlin freedom came face-to-face with casual indifference and nobody minded what happened next.

Lilly Nelly Aphrodite was conceived in a *Wanderkino*, pitched in the Tiergarten, at a screening of Georges Méliès's film *Escamotage d'une dame au théâtre Robert Houdin*. Tantalized by the smell of canvas and libidinous clatter of this radical new invention, her parents watched the actress Jeanne d'Alcy turn from flesh to skeleton five times before they consummated their brief acquaintance in the darkened back row beneath his greatcoat.

The Bavarian lover claimed that he was a speculator about to invest his fortune in German topicalities. In fact, he had little interest in cinema and that day he had merely ducked into the tent to hide from a woman he had had an affair with a few years before. But fate, if you believe in it, had placed the man from the South in the seat next to the pretty young actress. And as the rain thrummed relentlessly against the fly sheet and the Frenchwoman disappeared into thin air all over again, it seemed suddenly as if death was much closer than either of them had realized and the moment, the flickering moment, was all either had to lose.

It was an illusion, of course, created within Méliès's camera using stop-motion photography. By the time the pregnancy was diagnosed, it was much too late to halt it. Although he initially suggested otherwise, however, the philandering Bavarian wasn't about to play the responsible father to his illegitimate offspring. Likewise, the actress wasn't ready to be a mother to anyone.

The baby's first home was a cramped apartment two blocks south of the Kurfürstendamm. Her mother, a writer, actress, and occasional member of a cabaret group in the vein of Munich's own Eleven Executioners, was seldom home by bedtime and seldom awake by lunch. When the two were together, her mother smothered her with kisses but had little patience for games of peekaboo or catch. At first she had tried to write the opus that had been sprawling in her mind for years while her daughter clambered on her lap and screamed for milk. Ink was spilled, manuscripts rendered illegible, and white dresses were ruined. And so in homage to all the creativity that had been wasted, and faced with a spoiled set of clothes, she decided to dye the lot and dress her baby in black. "I'm sorry," people would mutter as they passed her in the street, thinking the infant the victim of some awful tragedy or other. "Me too," replied the mother through the twisted corner of her crimson-painted mouth.

As for her father, his supposed speculations took up all week and most of the weekends as well. And so Baby, as she was known briefly, was taken to theatrical auditions and abandoned in the stalls. She rapidly perfected a high-pitched screech that nobody, apart from her mother, could bear for more than a minute. Eventually arrangements were made and Baby was cared for by the landlady or, if she wasn't available, the philosophy student on the third floor. The landlady had too much experience with infants and used to stick her in a high-sided clothes basket from which Baby could not escape. Once, exhausted from screaming, she fell asleep, was covered up with soiled sheets, was carried all the way to the laundry, and was just about to be thrown into a cauldron of boiling water laced with starch when someone noticed her faint but dainty snore.

The student, on the other hand, had too little experience and spent many hours pontificating on the pitfalls of humanism and dangling his silver watch chain just out of her reach until, intoxicated with the schnapps he drank to help him concentrate, he would fall asleep and leave her to crawl around his filthy floor and eat the crusts, cigarette ends, and single beads from ex-girlfriends' dresses that he had never bothered to sweep up. It was a miracle that she survived at all.

Her mother didn't. The Bavarian lover shot her when he came back unexpectedly and discovered her in bed with the philosophy student. The philosophy student, quoting Kierkegaard, grabbed the firearm and shot him back. Baby slept through the entire episode. She was one and a half.

Somebody from the cabaret group knew someone who knew someone else whose child had just been killed in a perambulator accident. Baby was the same sex, same age, same size—the same in everything, it was said, except in the color of her hair, which was dark instead of fair. And so, still dressed in black, which was now deemed appropriate under the circumstances, the child was shipped off to the suburbs to grow up in a dead girl's set of clothes and renamed Dora.

The new father worked as a foreman in a factory and, at forty-three, had waited until he could provide a suitable home for his wife before he would allow her to conceive. But only once, he had clarified at the time, for reasons of safety. The house was sparsely furnished, with just a few ornaments brought from another, poorer life, that had been rationed one to each mantelpiece. Stepping inside felt like trying on a coat a few sizes too large.

Dora's new room had a cot, a wardrobe, and a small, threadbare rug. Despite an almost tangible sense of sadness, it was always meticulously clean. Her new mother fought a daily battle with dust and the thick black dirt that was pumped out of her husband's factory and fell on every surface like gritty rain. Each morning, after fastidiously scrubbing the floors with scalding water, she was visibly satisfied when the newfangled carpet sweeper her husband had bought for her birthday failed to pick up a single mote.

Life as Dora was not bad, just uneventful. Nothing changed but the food they ate for dinner, and even that was on a weekly rotation. When Friday came again and her new mother placed a plate of mashed whitefish and cabbage before her, Dora did not even hesitate before she launched the whole lot onto the spotless floor.

It was not that her new parents were unkind to her: they gave her every form of sustenance they could, except one. Even as a toddler, Lilly Nelly Aphrodite was aware that something was not quite right. Why did her so-called mother sob when she brushed her long dark hair? And why did they look at her with eyes half closed, as if trying to see something or someone else dressed in her clothes? She knew instinctively that these people did not belong to her, or she to them.

It was not surprising then that her terrible twos started early and never stopped. She would refuse to get dressed, eat supper, have a bath, get undressed, get out of the bath—in fact do anything she was asked to do. She left sooty black finger marks on the pristine white walls and liked to run around naked whenever visitors came for tea. Her new parents took her to the doctor, who recommended a firm hand and a hard bed. When they told him that this only made matters worse, he looked at them with pity and a visible amount of scorn. Dora could not be sent back to the place she had come from. Or could she?

The new father wrote a check equivalent to ten percent of his earnings for the next five years and finally let himself and his wife grieve for dear little dead Dora the First. The St. Francis Xavier Home for Orphaned Children agreed to take Dora the Second at the end of the week. Lilly Nelly Aphrodite, as she was named on her birth certificate, stood on the main steps with a suitcase at her feet that contained nothing more than her personal papers in a brown manila envelope. The new parents, now former, had already walked away, just as she had insisted. She clutched a present that she had promised in a rare moment of sweetness she would open once she was inside. It was from her mother's cabaret group, who, following her fate and feeling just a little responsible—but not responsible enough to take her in themselves—had all chipped in and bought a doll with a wind-up smile.

Snow was falling gently on the blackened building. The organization was running on a skeleton staff of one elderly nun who was rushed off her feet. A seven-year-old had tried to set fire to the director's curtains. A ten-year-old had found the trapdoor to the roof and was encouraging as many as he could to follow him up the ladder. It was, in short, chaos.

After what seemed like hours, the new orphan gave up pressing her tiny finger on the large brass doorbell. A whistle followed by a loud bang came from somewhere nearby. She turned round and looked up. In the sky above the orphanage an explosion of light illuminated the falling snow. She didn't know it, as no one had told her, but she had arrived at St. Francis Xavier's on her third birthday, the thirty-first of December, 1903. Finally the main door opened.

"Don't just stand there. Come inside," said a nun in a grubby cotton apron. "Do you want to catch your death?"

Lilly Nelly Aphrodite paused before she stepped through the main door and into the darkened reception hall of the orphanage. Could death be caught, like a cold? At that point in her infancy, however, the dead were still very much alive. A trail of French scent or the drift of a Havana cigar triggered vivid memories of the kind that young children are not supposed to retain: a long-fingered hand, the graze of a newly shaved chin, a kiss on the top of her head. And somewhere deep inside her subconscious was a long-held conviction that she had merely been set aside, stowed away, put in storage for collection by her people at a later date. A snowflake landed on her bottom lip but immediately melted. She sniffed twice: cabbage and disinfectant. The nun picked up the suitcase and ushered her in with an impatient wave. Lilly Nelly Aphrodite tentatively stepped across the threshold. The main door slammed behind her with a long, low boom.

Die geschiedene Frau.
„Ein Domino in violetter Seide,
Figur und Köpfchen tadellos."
Gustav Matzner
Marie Ottmann
6686-3

Falling Light

Meet Oskar Messter, Germany's first King of Film. His hair may be gone and his mustache may look like two black slugs, but his eyes are filled with the kind of energy that can only be electric. He'll talk about his inventions without a prompt—the projector, the camera, the processor, and the reproducer. "I make moving pictures too," he'll say.

In Messter's new cinemas the seats are cheap and filled with loafers and losers, shopgirls and shovelers, pimps and peasants, and at the very back where it's so dark you can hardly see your own hand let alone anyone else's, the lovers. And on the screen? Well-turned ankles, arms and legs and vigorous exercises: Lydia Was Not Dressed to Receive Callers; Clara Forgets to Pull Down the Blinds.

Everybody thinks that Messter's cinemas are temples of ill repute and sin. And for now everybody is right. But there's nothing like sitting in the dark watching the world in all its shades of monochrome flicker through his spectacular invention, the picture sequencer. When Messter proclaims it the medium of the new century, it would be churlish to disagree. Long live King Messter. And long live his glorious, illustrious, magnificent screen.

There is a single photograph of Lilly Nelly Aphrodite, or Tiny Lil, as she was known then, as a child. Third from the right in the second row from the front, she wears a gray dress and her dark hair has been braided and arranged over the right shoulder. While many of the children's faces that surround her are rendered illegible by the smudge of movement, Tiny Lil stands perfectly still and stares out of the frame as if her name has just been called. Her enormous eyes are glassy clear and her mouth is resolutely closed. Her left hand clutches the pocket in her dress to hide its contents. Inside is a dead mouse that she has been trying, in vain, to bring back to life. You can just about see, if you look closely, that her knees are caked black from all the praying.

At the back, in the center of six rows of twenty children each, is Sister August. Her image is ghostly and transparent, the result of joining or leaving the group between the moment the photographer pressed his button and the twenty seconds later or so that the shutter fell. Through her chest, the open door to her office behind is clearly visible. It is filled with the pale dusty sunshine of childhood memory. The date, written in longhand in faded brown ink on the back of the print, is the twelfth of February, 1906.

"Useless," shouted the photographer. "Is there time for one more?"

But there was not. A bell rang and the children dispersed up stairs, down corridors and through doorways until none was left except one.

"Sister says I'm to show you out," Tiny Lil told the photographer.

He let the little girl look at his lenses while he packed up his camera. She held up a fish-eye and stared at the vaulted glass ceiling.

"Mind you, don't drop it," he told her.

The world was beveled. Golden light fell in wide shafts from the cupola and threw the rest of the hall into a rich, gilded darkness. Although she knew the reality was otherwise, it became the kind of space where angels and archangels or even the Virgin Mary with her beloved bundle might appear.

The photographer, a boy of seventeen who had recently set up in business and had offered to take the orphanage photo for nothing to add to his portfolio, held out his hand and waited for her to give it back.

"Everything looks different," she said.

He glanced around the main hall. The glass ceiling was cloudy with dirt, the walls were painted a dark, shiny green, and the marble floor was dull and streaked with the gray residue of industrial-strength disinfectant. It couldn't, he considered, look any worse.

"You can keep it if you like," he said. "What's your name?"

"Tiny Lil," she replied. "Want to see my cot?"

Noting his hesitancy, she continued.

"It's all right. They've all gone to Mass. I don't need to go, because I went this morning. And besides, it's on the way."

Tiny Lil led the photographer through the orphanage. The hallways and stairwells were so multiple and nondescript, so dimly lit and featureless, that the photographer soon began to suspect that he was being led around in circles, which he was. Years later he would be reminded of St. Francis Xavier's when, lost at Verdun in a maze of trenches, he turned left and right, then left and right again, as if led by a little girl wearing a gray dress. He did not hear the mortar launched by a mason's apprentice from Aberdeen a quarter of a mile away, and the last image that raced through his head was a memory of the afternoon sun streaming onto two dozen identical cots.

"Guess which one is mine," said Tiny Lil.

He could not. They were, you see, all the same.

After she had shown him the front door and the photographer had climbed upon his bicycle and ridden off down the driveway, Tiny Lil pulled the dead mouse out of her pocket and dropped it down a drain. Then she took out the photographer's lens and held it, heavy, in her palm.

The certainty that her parents would come and soon collect her had taken some time to fade. The doll with the wind-up smile, however, was stolen the day after she arrived by an eight-year-old girl with a harelip. After several inconsolable hours, she snatched a small brown woolen bear from a six-year-old who had also just been admitted after losing both parents to diphtheria. Earless and eyeless, with one leg coming loose, the bear was the only toy that the bereaved child had been allowed to bring. Hugging the substitute to her chest and finally able to sleep, Tiny Lil breathed in the germs that for some reason the toy bear's owner was immune to, succumbed to diphtheria herself, and nearly died.

The bear was burned and the doll was buried by its harelipped thief, who intended to dig it up later. Tiny Lil never saw the six-year-old again; she had been adopted by a distant relative from Hamburg who instantly presented her with a brand-new bear that he had bought that morning in Hertzog's department store. But Child 198, as she was labeled on her arrival, spent six weeks in isolation in the orphanage infirmary. There were times when it was proclaimed that she would not last the night. Last rites were read no fewer than three times. And yet, with what the doctor could only put down to constitutional irregularities, Child 198 recovered despite the odds stacked against her. As she recuperated she insisted on lemonade every day. When it was decided that tap water would be adequate, she lapsed back into a critical condition, forcing the doctor to prescribe her favorite drink on demand.

Later, all she could remember about her illness were the upside-down clouds that raced across a clean blue sky, the smell of damp cotton sheets, the sharp tang of lemons, and the sweetness of her own sick breath. It was here, however, that she started to suspect that the specters of her parents might never become fully realized again after all. If so, why hadn't they come when she cried for them? Where were their cigar-scented kisses and long-fingered, perfumed hands when she had needed them the most?

"What's an orphan?" she asked the nurse one day.

The nurse, a woman who had six children of her own and was unshakably unsentimental, explained.

"Am I one?" she asked.

The nurse pretended not to hear the question. That was answer enough.

When she was completely well again, Tiny Lil, as the nurse had named her, was led back to the dormitory and given a cot at the very end of the room, opposite the bathroom.

"Your friends will be glad to have you back," said the nurse with a pat.

She smiled and hoped it was so. But Tiny Lil did not have any friends. The other three-year-olds glanced at her with a mixture of schadenfreude and contempt. Who could forget the bear-snatching incident? And rumors about her lemonade habit had spread. Besides, everyone had a best friend—or the next best thing, a brother or a sister—already.

Tiny Lil lacked a partner for the compulsory two-by-two crocodile formation, she had no one to play with when the weather was fine, and she sat facing a wall at mealtimes. And so she spent much of her time alone or, if she was especially unlucky, paired up with a couple to make a threesome.

The thick black pipes rattled and gulped along the dormitory walls as she listened to one of the twins pretend to read the single book all three had been issued before bedtime.

"May I have a look?" she asked in her nicest voice.

"The Virgin Mary came to me in a vision and said only good girls are allowed to read the book," said Isa, the twin with the book on her lap.

"You're going to come to a bad end," said Ava, the other twin. "Everybody says so."

The first blow hit Isa smack on the nose; the second caught Ava across the cheek. Tiny Lil had both eyes screwed shut, was holding one thick blond plait from each twin in each hand, and was pulling as hard as she could when her fists were prised open by the nurse.

"That's no way to behave," the nurse said.

She opened her eyes. The twins were red-faced and yelling. The book was lying facedown on the floor. The nurse, with her cold hands and her soapy smell, was kneeling down in front of her, so close that the thought occurred to Tiny Lil that the rise and fall of the nurse's soft padded breast was the perfect place to lay her head, if only for a moment. The nurse, as if suddenly aware of what Tiny Lil was thinking, took her by both shoulders and shook her.

"If you ever do that again," she said, "I'll have to report it. Understand?"

Tiny Lil gulped a mouthful of air and leaned into the nurse's grip, willing her to not let go, not yet. The nurse stood up and clapped her hands.

"Lights out. And stop making such a racket," she told the twins.

Tiny Lil's shoulder's still felt aglow long after the nurse had strode out of the dormitory and switched off the lights. In the dark, the twins whispered their grievances to each other; three beds down, a girl climbed into bed with her elder sister; in the far corner, two teenagers sat up and shared a cigarette. And slowly the glow began to fade. Eventually, the "smokes" were stubbed out and the chatter stopped, but Tiny Lil couldn't sleep. By the time that the birds started to sing and the room lightened, she had a plan. She would pair herself with the only other female in the building who did not have a partner: the other new arrival, the nun, the tall one.

Sister August, real name Lotte von Kismet, was six-foot-two and had been so since she was fourteen. Socially marooned by her height and consequently rendered invisible to the opposite sex, her long limbs and large feet were invariably too big for the styles her mother had once ordered from Paris, no matter how many times they were altered.

"She looks like a man dressed up," her father had carelessly commented when he thought she was out of earshot.

Despite the fact that her skin was perfect, her face finely drawn, and her eyes the color of bluebells, Lotte's heart had been broken more than once by young men who simply failed to notice her. She began to believe that she was sexless, unfeminine, inelegant, and that she would never produce any children of her own. It wasn't just her own experience; several maiden aunts of a similar height had spent their lives stooping or permanently sitting down, dressed up in altered clothes, waiting.

When she reached the age of eighteen and despite the fact that she had been brought up as a Protestant, Lotte was struck by the certainty that she must become a Catholic nun. Looking back, she guessed it was partly an act of revenge against her father, a military adviser to the kaiser, who regarded Catholicism as an enemy of the empire. Against her family's wishes and after having learned, by letter, that she would inherit nothing, Lotte was admitted into the Sisters of St. Henry, an order based in Munich, whose mission included sheltering disgraced women and abandoned orphans.

It was a huge relief to take off her corset, throw away her stockings, and put on the novice's white shift. She wore men's shoes, which were comfortable and flat. She tucked her hair into her wimple and, because she wasn't obliged to twist it painfully in rags, slept well for the first time since childhood. And when she took her vows, she didn't feel subjugated but liberated.

After ten years in the convent office, stamping papers and stuffing envelopes, Lotte had been posted to Berlin. She started on the first day of spring, 1904, at the St. Francis Xavier Home for Orphaned Children. Before she arrived, she had visualized the institution situated in a leafy suburb. She had half imagined herself surrounded by an adoring crowd of pretty blond children, a ministering angel in a starched white apron. As she approached the blackened building with its gloomy wooden door and filthy glass, however, a dead swallow plummeted onto the gravel in front of her. A window on the third floor was wide open. Coming from inside, she could hear the sounds of adolescent laughter and the ping of rubber stretched and then released.

"You!" shouted Sister August as soon as a boy appeared at the window, even though she was not entirely sure that he was the one who had fired the makeshift catapult and killed the bird. "I want you down here—now!"

There was something in the tone of her voice, maybe directly inherited from her father, that demanded obedience. In under a minute the boy was there, with his head bowed and his cap in his hands. He was about eight, with huge ears that glowed red in the light and a ring of grime on his neck.

"I want you to bury this bird," she said. "And then I want you to find out everything you can about swallows and come and tell me."

The boy looked up at her in amazement.

"You mean you don't want me to say one hundred Hail Marys?" he muttered.

"Not today," she replied. "But first I want you to have a bath."

The memory of Sister August's arrival never left the child who was known as Tiny Lil. From the moment she had hung up her coat, the nun ruled over the orphanage with a bar of green carbolic soap in one hand and a bunch of keys in the other. The nun whose position she had been sent to fill had spent most of her time fretting and scolding in a tone of voice to which nearly all the children had grown deaf; any notions of discipline or hygiene had been systematically unheeded. Food had gone missing on a daily basis from the kitchen, there was never any soap in the bathroom, and anything that was small enough to fit in a pocket rarely remained in the orphanage for long.

Decades later, Tiny Lil could picture Sister August as she presided over bedtime. Scrubbed so clean their faces shone, with their hair combed and their prayers learned by heart, the younger children looked almost too good to be true. Likewise, with the pale northern sun framing her face and turning her eyelashes gold, the nun looked as if she were an actress playing a part.

In reality, as she marched up and down the hall with her key chain swinging and her face set into an expression that revealed that she would rather die than admit defeat, the new nun seemed to have more in common with the real Joan of Arc than the actress Renée Falconetti, who was to play the doe-eyed martyr in the film version in 1928.

Sister August was determined to stand against the complacency of the establishment and do what had never been done before at St. Francis Xavier's: put the children's interests first. Thus, to protect her charges from themselves, she introduced communal prayer time, installed locks on every exit and cupboard, and slept with the keys beneath her pillow. God and prayer had their place, she had privately decided, but so did propriety, a clean environment, and a decent diet. With all opportunities and temptations eliminated, the incidents of theft dwindled to almost zero, and the food budget of three hundred marks a month went much further.

And every single pfennig was desperately needed. St. Francis Xavier's was a holding bay for an ever-increasing number of children who were too old or unruly to be considered for adoption. Infertile couples in search of the child they desired but could not produce did occasionally come in for a look, but they all usually headed over to St. Mary's Hospital in Alexanderplatz, where the babies were new and untainted by tragedy or neglect.

Located just off the Altonaer Strasse, between the river Spree and the Tiergarten, St. Francis Xavier's backed right onto the elevated lines of the S-Bahn. Commuters shivered as they thundered past its sooty walls. Occasionally they caught a low-wattage glimpse of children lining up for baths or a meal and vowed to place a couple of coins in the box provided at the gate next time they passed on foot.

Five stories high and built on a swamp, the orphanage was squat and barrel-chested despite its size. Constructed for the purpose by an altruistic factory owner who had nowhere to put all the bastard children of his employees, St. Francis Xavier's was originally designed for a smaller number of children on a much larger plot of land.

Tiny Lil used to wonder why the garden stopped so abruptly only a few meters from the back of the building. Sometimes she imagined that it would almost be possible to leap from a window, land on a train carriage, climb inside, and be carried off to another life.

The reason for the S-Bahn's proximity, however, was that in 1878 Otto von Bismarck had given the go-ahead for the elevated railway, which would, he planned, run right across the factory owner's plot. He offered reasonable compensation and promised that the factory owner's name would be immortalized forever as a station. By the time the line had been built, however, Bismarck had changed his mind and the factory owner was dead. But his name lived on anyway, as a type of orthopedic corset.

The owner of the underwear factory had been a man of his age and, rather than staffing the orphanage with a motley crew of cleaners, laundry girls, and kitchen maids who might only end up adding to the problem, had installed brand-new appliances such as a sewing machine, an electric stove, and a wooden-tub washing machine.

And they worked—most of the time. No one would ever forget the night when the lights went out and all the fuses were found thrown in the garden. Or the day that the washing machine flooded and it was discovered that it had been filled up with newspaper. Even the electric range with its heavy black plates and greasy knobs wasn't immune. A series of baked toys was blamed for its tendency to malfunction. And one day Tiny Lil was caught urging Little Franz to climb in with a blanket.

"What would have happened," Sister August had pointed out, "if cook had switched it on?"

"He might have warmed up a little," she had replied.

Tiny Lil spent much of her first year at the orphanage sitting in a chair in silence as punishment for bad behavior. She ate hundreds of meals alone in the dark and had been beaten more than once with a leather slipper by the director. At night, as the light from the carriages of the elevated train, next stop Bellevue, lit up her face in flickering strips, Tiny Lil kicked off her blankets, shoved away her pillow, and lay shivering in the cold. Soon Sister August will come, she told herself; soon she'll come and find me dead. And then she'll be sorry. She didn't know it but she had inherited her father's temper and her mother's impulsiveness. Neither, however, had been subjected to the severity of Sister August's regime.

If the nun ever came and checked up on her, however, Tiny Lil was never awake to witness it. And if her blankets were tucked in the next morning and the pillow wedged firmly underneath her head, she never suspected that it was anyone other than her own sleepy self who had remade the bed and doubled up the layers to ward off the night chill.

It took some time but she learned that insubordination did nothing to further her relationship with Sister August. The tall nun's eyes would not meet hers or see the tears they spilled, and her voice contained no pity as she administered a series of increasingly severe punitive measures. And even when Tiny Lil had a fever and claimed she might not last the night, Sister August would do nothing more than place her hand upon her brow and say, "You'll either die or get better." It was always the latter. No one had died since she had arrived. The only way, Tiny Lil soon realized, was the one of least resistance, of compliance.

Eventually, the doctor from long ago was proven right: a firm hand and a hard bed had the desired effect. Tiny Lil became an ideal orphan, silent unless spoken to, polite and pious. She learned to read and studied the Bible in bed every night, could quote any rule when required, was never late for Mass, and—although she was not always meticulous about changing her pinafore—prayed so often for forgiveness that her soul, to outside eyes at least, was regularly laundered.

In the moments before the nun ushered the children into their beds, as the cold northern wind shook the glazing and the rain beat against trees, Sister August would let her hand rest just for an instant on each little head.

"You're never alone. God is all around," she would tell them. "He watches you every moment of the day."

Tiny Lil imagined that, at Sister August's instruction, God had punctured a hole in the sky and was training his eye on that patch of land between the river and the bright green park. And when she bowed her head and, side by side, all the orphans whispered the words to the Lord's Prayer, Tiny Lil's heart was filled with such hope and light that there was no doubt, no doubt at all, that the nun was right.

Sometimes Tiny Lil looked for God. She explored every inch of the orphanage, from the spaces between the eaves in the attic to a secret cupboard behind the coal bunker in the basement, for evidence of his presence that she could offer to Sister August. And yet she never found anything, nothing but dead spiders and single socks, balls of dust and small locked suitcases that former inhabitants had forgotten.

In the garden, between a yew hedge and the perimeter wall, where the air was a thick dark green and the sky above a strip of bone-white cloud, she laid out two fatty wax candles half burned down, a rusty hat pin, and a faded postcard of the Virgin Mary on a mossy stone ledge. Nobody ever went there. Nobody knew what was there but Tiny Lil. And God, of course. On the day that Tiny Lil gave up on the dead mouse, the day of the orphanage photograph—one of the coldest, incidentally, of 1906—she crossed herself and placed the photographer's lens next to one of the candles. And then she knelt down in the mulch and prayed for the mouse's soul.

"Hail Mary," she whispered. "Hail Mary, mother of Christ."

She stopped abruptly. Someone was coming through the undergrowth, someone who kicked his way through the leaves and roots, the roosting birds and small mammals, with sheer brute force. She dropped the lens, the candles, and the hat pin into her pocket just as Otto Klint, an eleven-year-old who had been left on the doorstep when he was just a few days old, stumbled out of the gloom. He started when he saw her but grabbed a handful of leaves to hide it.

"What are you doing here?" he asked, and threw the leaves at her.

"Nothing," she replied.

He examined her for a moment, her small face with its sharp little chin defiant in the half-light. But her eyes would not meet his.

"What's in your pockets, Tiny Lil?" he said, taking a few steps toward her. "I'll tell Sister August."

"Nothing," she said again, her voice rising in pitch.

Otto held her wrists together with one hand and emptied her pockets with the other. He looked through her things briefly, then handed them back to her again.

"Sorry," he said briefly. "I thought you might have a cigarette."

Then Otto sized up the wall. It was two meters high.

"I won't tell if you won't," he said.

Tiny Lil finally looked up at him. His fair hair had been shaved after a recent outbreak of lice and his thin face looked hungry. He smiled and it seemed too generous an expression for the pared-down proportions of his face.

"Right, then. See you later," he said. "Little Sister."

Otto turned, placed one boot on the ledge, and levered himself up. With a grunt of effort, he grabbed the top of the wall with both hands and crawled over. She listened as his boots hit the paving stones with a dull, hollow thud. On the other side of the wall the streetlights came on with a flicker and a buzz. The ground shuddered as an omnibus thundered past. A bell was ringing. The birds were settling back into their nests. Tiny Lil picked up the postcard of the Virgin Mary. The black imprint of Otto's boot covered her face. She tried to brush it off but the mud streaked and stained it. She licked her finger and rubbed and rubbed until there was only a gray smudge where the face had been.

Luckily the photographer gave the orphanage a dozen prints of his photograph, of varying quality. When one went missing and Sister August found it in the dustbin with a single hole in the middle of the image, nobody claimed responsibility. The proof of Tiny Lil's crime, if it had ever been found, was a grubby postcard of the Virgin Mary with Sister August's semitransparent face stuck on.

Seven Hundred Kilometers

"Y*our hat's in my shot, madam. If you would be so kind as to shift a little to the right.*" *On the zeppelin LZ6's maiden flight are forty passengers, six crates of* Sekt, *one moving-picture camera, and twenty reels of film. Hans von Friedrich ducks under the hood and starts to crank. Below, the world slowly unrolls: lakes like discs of glass briefly scored by the flight of a swan; a train crossing an elevated steel bridge, three ponies cantering, a girl on a bicycle who stops and waves hello, hello, hello.*

Hours later but right on schedule, here's Berlin. Charlottenburg; the Schloss, perfect as a jewel; the zoological gardens, where elephants, zebras, giraffes all look up at this long black blot against the sun. The Tiergarten, green and soft as velvet; ladies in their boats; a brass band playing in the Englischer Garten. Then the Unter den Linden, St. Hedwig's Cathedral, the opera house, and the university. Look there, and there. Hundreds, maybe thousands, have come out on their rooftops to watch the zeppelin's slow descent. The airfield comes close, and closer still. Men on the ground pull on the ropes. And here to greet the LZ6 is the empress herself. Three cheers for the rigid dirigible. "Is my hat in your shot?" the lady asks. "No, madam," says Hans von Friedrich, whose grasp of mathematics is rudimentary. "But I seem to have run out of film."

Tiny Lil loved Sister August. Although it was sinful, she loved her more than the Virgin Mary, she loved her more than Jesus. At meal-times she sat not beside her, as that wasn't allowed, but at the nearest possible table. At Mass she sang the responses in Latin, loud and clear so she would be sure to be heard. She hovered around Sister August's closed door, waiting to be asked to run an errand or pass on a message. And once, and only once, when she was sitting behind her in a special service for the kaiser's birthday, she leaned over, inhaled the clean almond smell of her, and ran her finger down the stiff brown slope of her habit.

Sister August noticed, of course she did, but she had so much more to think about than one little girl's attachment to her. According to the *Berliner Morgenpost*, the population of Berlin had risen to more than two million; it had doubled since German unification in 1871. Orphans were being deposited at St. Francis Xavier's at the rate of a dozen a week. Some were not even genuine, but the overspill of the large families who were leaving their farms in Silesia or Pomerania and moving into two-roomed apartments in Wedding or Rixdorf. An ever-increasing number of other babies had just been dumped on the doorstep in milk crates or cardboard boxes with no sign as to where they had come from or why.

The director, a distant cousin of the founder—a man who sat at a large, empty mahogany desk all day and never seemed to actually do anything—did not appear to think it was a problem.

"The more, the merrier," he sometimes said. Or, "Let them eat cake."

He was large and lugubrious, and suffered from excessively sweaty hands and chronic catarrh. He employed a series of women as secretaries whose only visible duties were to type his correspondence, hang up his coat on a polished brass peg, and make him coffee with exactly the right amount of sugar. Some days he looked deep in thought as he leaned back in his leather chair, with an expression that suggested he was mulling over the nature of philanthropy or the ethical problems stirred up by Fontane's new novel, *Effi Briest.* In fact, he spent much of his time wondering whether to make a pass at the women he had hired and, if he did so, if he could keep an affair on the boil without his wife finding out. It was a fantasy, fortunately for all concerned, that never got further than the brush of a damp hand on a well-padded bottom or a lingering Christmas kiss.

It was to him, in an attempt to involve him somehow, that Sister August brought the orphans who had gone way beyond the limits of so-called acceptable behavior. Uncomfortable with children, as he had only one son, whom he had sent to boarding school, the director would tell the children to lie across a piano stool and then he would beat them on the bottom with a slipper up to ten times, depending on their crime.

"It obviously works," he told the nun. "Just look at Tiny Lil."

However, the slipper, a Turkish shoe with fancy embroidery, was flimsy and soft. The director's aim was poor and his blows were feeble. It was not the physical pain that made the director's slipper beatings so distressing, but the unpleasantness of being beaten by a man whose hands dripped and who coughed loudly and repulsively after every stroke.

The sister regarded the director with notable and understandable disdain. He was scared of her and attracted to her in roughly equal measure. And when she spoke, it was not unusual for him to fail to hear a single word, so smitten was he by the bloom on her perfect virgin's cheek.

"So you'll do it today," she would say after suggesting once again that he write to the founder's family to solicit more funds.

"Of course," he would answer, although he didn't know what she was talking about, as he hadn't been listening. "I'll do it immediately."

And so it was left to Sister August to deal with the ever-increasing volume of children on a fixed budget while the director drank his coffee, stroked the shiny sole of his embroidered Turkish slipper, and contemplated a series of particularly becoming behinds.

New beds were ordered on credit and a dormitory was set up in the gymnasium. Boots had to be bought for those who came barefoot, and more food had to be prepared in the kitchen than it could realistically produce. God, the factory owner's widow—who was growing increasingly parsimonious—or, as a last resort, the Sisters of St. Henry would have to provide. If only, Sister August thought to herself when she was well away from the chapel, men and women would stop fornicating. The director was almost sixty. And once he had retired, she would take the seat behind the mahogany desk and quickly fill up the drawers with leaflets on abstinence.

Nuns joined her and nuns moved away, claimed by poor health, rheumatism, or nervous exhaustion. Few had the vitality or tenacity of Sister August. Her blue eyes were chipped with determination; her full mouth was a straight line unbroken by the exercise of smiling; and her hands, although often chapped and blistered, were long-fingered and dexterous. She had just one indulgence, just one: in the long, quiet afternoons, which she had set aside for paying bills and transcribing medical records onto thick green cards, her mind would start to drift and her index finger would slip down between her legs. She did not consider it a sin. She would always stop herself or, more usually, be interrupted by a crying child or a ringing telephone well before she reached the place her body longed to go. And so Sister August was often breathless and a little flushed, as if she had just run up a flight of stairs or been informed of some awful tragedy.

"Hello?" she would sob into the receiver. Without a word, many women would replace the handset, lift up the baby they could not afford to keep, and reconsider.

Tiny Lil had known for as long as she could remember that when they were fourteen, the children had to leave the orphanage. The girls went to work in the owner's underwear factory and the boys to a chemical plant or military service. Some, like Otto, left willingly with a round of kisses and a promise that he'd come back and visit. Others had to be forcibly removed and were led out after dark when it was thought that no one would hear their distress. But Tiny Lil couldn't imagine a life outside St. Francis Xavier's or a single day without Sister August.

By the time they left, most of the orphans could read and write. It was written into the factory owner's legacy. He had learned to his own cost that a workforce that could read the safety signs was preferable to one that could not.

Because of the rise in population, all the local schools and gymnasiums were full. The orphans were educated instead in a couple of large attic rooms. Sister August taught the younger children literacy and the elder ones elocution. They all learned to write using India ink and chancery cursive and could drop their guttural vowels when required and speak with the softer accent of Sister August's native Munich.

In 1909 the orphanage had half a dozen teachers on loan from the university. They had only one thing in common: they had fallen for Sister August's dynamic charm and agreed to teach at St. Francis Xavier's on an ad hoc, no-fee basis. Some immediately regretted it and secretly considered it unwise to educate the children and give them false expectations. Others were worried that they might catch an incurable disease, and opened the windows whatever the weather. But, despite their grievances, the orphanage did have one thing going for it: it was a place where they could practice lectures or just waffle on about their own particular passions without any scrutiny whatsoever. Sister August knew that the 1909 syllabus, which included the habits of the fruit fly, German poetry, and a minor German painting school that specialized in the portraiture of dogs, did not make a rounded education. But until she could offer an alternative, she wasn't in any position to rectify it.

One day in May, when the children were lining up to be taught about ammonites by a young geologist, Tiny Lil was summoned. Sister August was clutching a letter with a military crest as a letterhead. She turned and surveyed Tiny Lil, taking in the scuffed boots, the stained apron, and the plaits she had slept in for two nights running.

"Here's a clean pinafore," she said, and handed one to her. "Now go and wash your face, brush your hair, polish your boots, and be back in the front hall in ten minutes."

The pinafore was freshly laundered and stiff with starch. The nun had changed into a clean tunic and veil. Not a single strand of fair hair escaped from her wimple.

"The Number Eighty-two will take us there," she told Tiny Lil as she buttoned up her coat. "We won't have to wait long."

It didn't occur to the nun to tell the orphan where they were going. There wasn't enough time for Tiny Lil to ask. The streets outside the orphanage were quiet in mid-morning. A horse and cart piled with coal trotted past, followed by a lone dog with a bone in its mouth. No one else was waiting at the tram stop.

Of course, Tiny Lil immediately decided that she had finally been claimed. A parent with amnesia, a favorite fantasy of hers; a distant relative; a set of rich and kindly foster parents had recovered their memory or accidentally discovered her existence or chosen her from afar, and now she was going to meet them. Why else would she have been singled out and taken from class with no notice? It had occasionally happened to other children, so why not to her?

Sister August was staring into the distance, her beautiful long-lashed eyes fixed on a point where apple blossom was blowing across the elevated train tracks like snow. As if she felt the girl's gaze physically, the nun turned her head and glanced down at her companion. Tiny Lil grabbed hold of her hand and held it tightly. She was too old to have her hand held, they both knew that, but Sister August didn't pull away. Tiny Lil felt her cheeks burn and her heart beat faster. And so she lifted Sister August's hand to her lips and kissed it.

"I don't want to leave you," she whispered.

But the nun didn't hear. A tram was approaching and came to a halt right in front of them with a screech of brakes and a sigh of pressurized air.

"Right on time," said Sister August. The doors opened and the nun used both hands to propel Tiny Lil up the steps and onto the lower deck.

The tram was packed and there was only one seat. Several men immediately stood but Sister August would not take their place. Instead she sat Tiny Lil down and then grabbed hold of a leather loop that dangled from the roof. The heavy gold crucifix around her neck swung backward and forward like a circus performer.

As they sped away from the orphanage, Tiny Lil was struck by the difference between the city outside the walls and the one she had imagined. She rarely left the grounds and had become so used to the noise of trolley cars, the rattle of the S-Bahn, the regular rhythm of construction, and the thrump of military marches outside that she saw them in her mind as children's toys, tin soldiers, train sets, and toy men scaling building blocks.

But when she boarded the Number 82 to Schlesisches Tor, it was as if she had stepped right out of her childhood. The city they crossed was bigger, much bigger than she had ever imagined. They passed huge palaces, black stone monuments, and enormous parks. The tenements seemed to lean inward and block out all the sunlight. The road was wide but maybe not wide enough. Polished automobiles, horse-drawn carriages, and dozens and dozens of bicycles sped past them and occasionally seemed about to hit them until, at the very last moment, one or the other veered away.

The most shocking thing as they neared the center of the city, however, was the sheer number of people. Hundreds and hundreds of men in suits and women in heels were striding along the pavements and swarming at the intersections. It was amazing, she thought then, a miracle that out of two or even three million she had been discovered; she had been found at last. And she tilted her chin up as they sped through an orange light.

Almost everyone had a newspaper. Almost no one spoke. The tram smelled of cigarette smoke, warm leather, horse dung, and something unfamiliar, a sourness that stuck in Tiny Lil's mouth like a bad taste. One man with a huge curly mustache winked. Would her relative or foster parent look like him? She stared at him until he cleared his throat and went back to his newspaper. Another woman's eyes traveled up and down her length, took in her worn-out boots and darned stockings. Her eyes, heavy-lidded and shadowed with black kohl, finally settled on her face. Tiny Lil looked away this time.

As the tram turned the corner into the Kurfürstendamm, a large woman with a huge bag stuffed with clean laundry stood up. She joined the shoving crowd at the exit doors and then hauled herself and the bag down the stairs. The bell rang and the tram pulled off. Tiny Lil watched the woman pick up the bag from the pavement and heave it onto her head. As the tram sped away, the woman took a step into the road and the bag toppled and fell, spilling her laundry all over cobblestones.

Sister August and Tiny Lil rode down the boulevard to Charlottenburg. The bell rang again and the tram rapidly came to a halt. Sister August took her hand again and they climbed down onto the street. Almost at once they set off at such a fast pace that Tiny Lil had to run to keep up.

The street was lined with shops and department stores, each window more amazing than the one before: mannequins with floor-length fur coats and feathered hats; a toy monkey twirling a trapeze while a dancing bear spun to a silent waltz; a stack of satin boxes in reds and blues and greens topped by a single tray of chocolate-covered cherries.

"Murder in Berlin North!" shouted a boy on a bicycle, a huge bag of newspapers in his basket. "Man slays his whole family with an ax!"

"What did he say?" Tiny Lil shouted up at Sister August. But her voice was drowned out by a hurdy-gurdy that was playing outside a tobacconist's.

"Keep up," the sister commanded. "And jump over the puddles, don't wade through them."

Tiny Lil jumped, but her feet were already wet.

The music of the hurdy-gurdy overlapped with the wheeze of an organ. On the other side of the road, on a vacant lot, two girls of about her age rode round and round on the horses of a painted carousel. Maybe, she thought, she would do the same, maybe even later that day. Farther along, on a construction site, men with cloth caps and vests were digging sand and nailing wooden struts together. The rhythm of the hammer was briefly in time with a passing horse and trap. Everything seemed to be moving, escalating, rising. Even the new apartments, which were being constructed on the next block, seemed to grow an inch as she passed.

"Excuse me," said Sister August to the woman with a grubby hem who was strolling at half the speed of everyone else. The woman turned and by the look on her face it was clear she was about to say something rude. But then she saw the sister's habit and moved aside.

"God bless you," she muttered, and rapidly crossed herself.

They paused at an eight-sided green pillar covered in advertisements for theater shows, magazines, and exhibitions while Sister August checked her leather-covered notebook. Then she snapped the book shut, turned on her heel, and took the first street on the right. As a girl, the nun had been taught to march by her father, and now—even when she wasn't aware of it—she stepped to a strict one, two, one, two.

Halfway down the street was the garrison of the Third Grenadier Guards. Two flags on poles flapped in the wind. Men in uniforms with hats under their arms strolled down the curved marble steps in twos and threes, and from deep inside came the slow and uneven tick and ratchet of an inexpert typist.

"I'm expected," said the sister to an elderly man behind a small ornate desk.

He pulled out a fountain pen and very carefully made a note in a large gilt-edged book. Women weren't usually allowed entry to the garrison, only grieving mothers and, on special request, daughters under the age of twelve.

"The first floor," said the man. "And then straight ahead."

Sister August and Tiny Lil hurried up the steps and along a wide corridor. Here on the first floor, the walls were covered with portraits of tight-lipped generals, commanders, and captains of the Prussian army. At the end of the hallway a set of double doors was wedged open. A huge chandelier fitted with electric bulbs lit the room beyond. Cigar smoke drifted out, yellow and opaque. Tiny Lil noticed that Sister August's hands were moist. She paused to wipe them both on a white handkerchief she pulled from her pocket. Then she smoothed down her face and stepped through.

Three soldiers were sitting on gilt chairs while a fourth was reclining on a velvet daybed. He was in charge, that much was immediately obvious. The others perched, balancing cups of tea on their knees. They were talking about how much money a colleague had lost at gambling. The nun and the orphan stood in the doorway and waited, the girl looking from one face to the next to the next to the next and finally back to the nun again.

"Gentlemen, we have guests," said the fourth man. He stood up and the other three immediately followed suit. He took a step forward to shake the nun's hand. He was at least six inches shorter than she. The flicker of his eyelid revealed that she wasn't quite what he had expected.

"Do come in and sit down," he urged.

Sister August and Tiny Lil sat down on the gilt chairs and were offered cups of tea.

"Thank you, no," said Sister August, answering for both of them.

The three soldiers sat down again, on a desk, on a windowsill, and on the remaining chair. None of them, Tiny Lil suddenly realized, seemed remotely interested in her.

"Well," said the fourth man, who had remained standing. "Let's get straight down to business, then, shall we? To what do we owe the pleasure?"

The nun launched into the speech she had prepared in her head the previous evening. She started with facts and told them how the growing population had produced hundreds of unwanted children. She explained that despite increasing pressure on her resources, she had turned the orphanage around and was educating the children in her care to a much higher standard than before. She regretted that, although she had some money from the trust fund left by the factory owner, it was not enough.

"I know his name," said one of the three soldiers who perched on the windowsill. "Wait, let me think."

"I need more books," she continued. "So that I can truly implement a proper curriculum. I will use any money you may generously offer to donate for this purpose."

The fourth man rested one arm on the marble mantelpiece. His leather boots were polished a rich chestnut brown and his brocade tunic was covered with medals. As he listened, however, a bead of sweat appeared, then dripped down his temple. His finger tap, tap, tapped on the marble.

"You want us to buy you more Bibles?"

Sister August blushed despite herself.

"We have enough, thank you," she said. "No, it's textbooks we need."

"But really, Sister, what kind of education are you going to give these unfortunates?" he said. "The lives of obscure saints, no doubt. Fire and brimstone. Heaven and hell. Rather irrelevant, don't you think, in a modern world, in the twentieth century?"

"My superiors require that the school has a spiritual aspect, but—"

The general guffawed.

"But you know nothing of life, Sister. You know nothing of love, of passion, of loss. You are a woman and yet you are not. Is that not true?"

Sister August was so shocked she was momentarily rendered speechless. The silence was broken only by the dainty clink of three teaspoons on china.

"What's your name?" the fourth man said. Tiny Lil didn't immediately realize he was addressing her. Four sets of eyes gazed in her direction. "You, yes, you, girl."

"Lilly Nelly Aphrodite," she said very quickly. She glanced up and saw the puzzled looks on the soldiers' faces.

"Tiny Lil," she said a little louder, even though at eight she wasn't tiny anymore.

"Well, Tiny Lil," the fourth man proclaimed with a wave of his hand, "as my men know, I give to dozens of good causes: the poor, the sick, the dying. Even to poor little unclaimed and unwanted children like you. But although I deal every day with the mostly mundane, like our dear kaiser, I am an aesthete at heart."

He hesitated.

"You do know what an aesthete is?"

"No," she whispered.

"I am propelled by beauty. Moved by the sight of the first bud opening in spring. Inspired by the singing of a thrush. . . . I love the arts, painting, opera, horticulture."

He paused to check on the impact of his words. The three men were nodding sagely. Sister August's mouth was pulled taut. When his eyes fell on her, he smiled ever so slightly.

"And so, much as I am swayed by your wonderful work, Sister"—he picked up a letter from his desk—"August, I must . . ."

Sister August stood.

"I don't think I made myself clear," she said.

"I haven't finished," the fourth man said softly.

Sister August sat down again. There was a shuffle, a small general rearrangement of legs and bottoms and boots.

"Even though I am a Lutheran, a Protestant, as most of us are in the North, my dear Sister," the fourth man said, "I would like to offer you a rose garden, a rose garden for the enrichment of the souls of all those unfortunate children. For what can be more illustrative of the pain and the beauty of human existence than the juxtaposition of rose petal and thorn?"

"Textbooks," Sister August said, "would be a much more practical—"

"La Luna," he interrupted. "A beautiful tea rose, bred by a Frenchman, I think, Gilbert Nabonnand. As pink as a little girl's buttock."

Sister August started to breathe more rapidly.

"Chinas, Damask Perpetuals—now, there's a bloom. Cross the first with the second and you get the Bourbon Rose. You must have the Schneekönigin," he continued, "an interesting variety although hard to cultivate . . . the Snow Queen—all white, of course, but completely lacking in scent."

He looked pointedly at Sister August. Sister August looked back at him. Neither would look away.

"The Romans were fond, you know, of roses," he continued. "They imported them from Egypt. I wonder if our dear Lord wore a wreath of Gallica thorns around his head at Calgary. Or Albas?"

The fourth man suddenly took three short strides and bent down on one knee in front of Tiny Lil.

"What an interesting face," he said. "Let's ask the would-be recipient of my charitable donation: What would you like . . . roses or textbooks?"

The room grew silent. Tiny Lil stared at the scuffed toes of her all-too-rapidly polished boots. There was a discernible pool of dirty puddle water brought in from the street on the parquet floor beneath her feet. A rush began to well up behind her face like an approaching sneeze; her eyes burned, her mouth pulled taut, her forehead creased. She gulped a deep breath and blew it out, slowly, through her nose.

"Tiny Lil?" Sister August said. "Answer him."

The fourth man leaned forward a fraction. He was so close she could hear the almost inaudible clank of his medals jangling together on his chest. He was so close she could smell the extract of lavender in his soap. She glanced up. He was so close that she could see contempt only thinly masked in his eyes.

"Cat got your tongue?" he said, with just the tiniest hint of impatience.

Textbooks, textbooks, textbooks. Arithmetic and Latin. Literature and history. Sister August shifted in her seat and sighed out loud, as if this were only to be expected from an orphan. And Tiny Lil, who knew she wasn't tiny anymore, was suddenly filled with fury. How dare she make her believe that she was about to claimed, to be wanted? How dare she bring her all the way to this room full of men simply to humiliate her? How dare she still call her Tiny Lil?

She looked up and she stared in turn into every pair of the expectant eyes except one.

"I think . . . I think . . . roses," she said.

The fourth man laughed a short, mirthless little laugh.

"Orthopedic underwear," proclaimed one of the three soldiers as he leapt to his feet. "I knew I knew the name."

The Winter Garden

Glass film studios, sheer and clear and filled with sun, glazed edifices where beautiful women blossom and handsome men wilt. And the light floods in all day for free; all you have to do is catch it.

Asta Nielsen, Danish actress, eyes as round as saucers, hips as narrow as a wink, walking down a city street. All of a sudden—Hey there, stop him!—a handsome young ruffian steals her purse. He turns and runs but accidentally drops his misbegotten handful. And in that pause, that wafer-thin moment when he stoops and she grabs his sleeve, Asta's expression changes from indignation to recognition. He's her long-lost darling brother, fallen on hard times.

But by and by here's a policeman running down the street with a lady. He sees the brother beggar. The lady points her umbrella and says the words "It's him, it's him." Before he can run, the brother is arrested, and Asta can do nothing but plead with her hands, her mouth, her saucer eyes, to no avail. Her purse, still lying on the cobbles, is snatched up by some opportunistic street kid. And as if God knew the script, right at that very moment a cloud covers the sun.

"Cut!" the director shouts. "Cut, cut, cut!" The film was so nearly in the can, and now they'll have to shoot another day. Asta Nielsen swears softly in Danish and calls for coffee laced with something stronger.

Hanne Schmidt, flanked by her three younger brothers, stood on the doorstep of the orphanage and asked Sister August if she could speak to her in private. She carried the youngest boy on her hip and slapped the other boys' heads when they picked their noses or fiddled with their buttons. Her heels were high and she wore a hat with a feather on it, rouge, and a line of lipstick. There was a yellow bruise on her left cheekbone just beneath the eye. The nun led them in, gave the boys bowls of soup, invited the girl into her office, and closed the door.

The girl—who, despite the clothes, could not have been more than twelve—told the sister that her mother had leapt from the roof of the newly built apartment building in which they had been living for a low rent while the plaster walls dried. They had a couple more weeks to go, the walls were still damp, but the reason for her suicide was her husband's desertion.

The story was verified in the evening paper, although there was no mention of the woman having any children. Sister August prayed for all four of them and tried to take them up to the dormitories where she intended to place them, sardine-style, in any available bed.

"Oh, no," said Hanne Schmidt. "I'm not staying."

Nobody was really sure what Sister August had said to her, but the girl didn't speak again for six months. After washing off the makeup, she was given a patched-up orphanage dress, boots, and a pillow and instructed to share with the girl at the end, the small one.

Tiny Lil didn't object when the new girl started to take off her boots and then climb under her very own sheets. Most of the orphans in her dormitory had been doubled up already, and some even claimed that it was much warmer in winter that way. And so she shifted as close to the edge as she could and tried to ignore the air that whisked beneath the blankets and the pair of small, dirty feet that the new girl had tucked beneath her pillow.

Lights had been out for at least an hour but Tiny Lil couldn't sleep.

And she wasn't the only one. The liquid glimmer of the new girl's open eyes was clearly visible in the dark.

"I know you're awake," Tiny Lil whispered. "What's your name?"

But the new girl simply sighed out loud and turned over.

Her silence did not crack in the following days, either. She sat with her head upon the desk in the schoolroom and ate her meals quickly and furtively, saving her bread or her potatoes to pass on to her brothers when she thought no one was looking. At bedtime she climbed into the bed they shared, but if any part of her touched Tiny Lil, she would immediately shift away as if stung by a rogue charge of electricity.

Sometimes when Tiny Lil woke in the middle of the night, the girl would be gone. She would lie awake for as long as she could, waiting for her to return. But when she opened her eyes in the morning, the girl would always be back, with smudges beneath her eyes and her pale hair hanging in strands around her face.

Hanne and her brothers were the last orphans that St. Francis Xavier's accepted in 1910. There was simply not enough room for any more. As it was, some of the younger boys shared three to a cot. But the children didn't stop coming. They came in rags and muddy clogs, in pairs and alone, dragging blankets or holding screaming babies. When she had enough to spare, Sister August gave them food. When it was all gone, she gave them a few pfennigs and blessed their filthy heads.

The general sent a couple of gardeners to tend the roses. Despite the poor soil and the lack of sunlight, they did exceptionally well.

Tiny Lil knew when they left the garrison of the Third Grenadiers that she had done something unforgivable. All the way home, the nun stared out the window and did not react when strangers crossed themselves or genuflected. At one point she looked down at her with an expression of such incomprehension that Tiny Lil would have howled an explanation at her had they not been surrounded by commuters on a rush-hour tram. And so she struggled to keep her face composed. Sister August clearly did not realize what she had done; she had no idea at all. And this hurt far more than accepting that she was just one more unclaimed, unwanted orphan all over again.

As they sped through the Tiergarten and she thought of the man with the mustache whom she had stared at on the way, a drop of hot salty liquid landed on her lip. It was a tear, her own tear, which she had wept without realizing. And so she turned around and wiped her face quickly with the back of her sleeve so that Sister August would not know or see or feel obliged to feel even slightly sorry for her.

The nun stared at the back of Tiny Lil's head as the little girl wiped her face with her sleeve. Normally she would have chastised her for this, reminded her about the spread of germs and the cost of soap. But this time she said nothing. She was thinking about the general. She didn't understand how it could have turned out this way, how he had managed to turn Tiny Lil against her. Maybe he was right. What did she know of life? And why had she chosen Tiny Lil? When she examined her motives, she realized that the girl had in fact chosen her first: from very early on Tiny Lil had singled her out. And despite what had just happened, she was flooded with love of the kind that she knew was inappropriate. This, she decided, had to change. It was a weak spot, a vulnerability. Besides, she could never be the parent that the girl so desperately needed. The tram began to slow; it was their stop. They climbed off wordlessly and walked back to the orphanage with a visible gap between them.

The general's rose garden started an unfortunate trend. The economy was booming, and a number of wealthy benefactors followed his example. An industrialist bequeathed a full set of brass instruments. The director took up the French horn but could manage only the most rudimentary of Christmas carols. The rest of the instruments gathered dust in their cases; they couldn't afford a music teacher. The orphans were also given a miniature train, a set of child-size Shakespearean costumes, and several dozen crates of a new kind of sweetened drink. Sister August was privately exasperated. They didn't have the room for any more things. But after such relentless soliciting, they could hardly refuse them.

In December that year, a cabaret group came to St. Francis Xavier's to put on a Christmas show for the children. It was the very same cabaret group that Tiny Lil's mother had been a member of, the very same cabaret group who had sent her as a baby to the couple in the suburbs and who still felt vaguely responsible—the very same cabaret group who had sent her the doll with the wind-up smile that had subsequently been unearthed by one of the general's gardeners and taken home for his daughter.

The visit had been organized by an actor named Wernher Siegfried. He had long black hair, which he swept back with olive oil; a large, forceful nose; and a weak chin, which he hid, when he remembered, with his hand. He thought he had been in love with the orphan's mother and had once successfully consummated his infatuation in a boat hut on the shores of the Tegeler See in the early spring of 1899. While the rest of the cabaret group were drunkenly skating on the ice after drinking copious amounts of Liebfraumilch, he had coaxed the actress into the hut after she had twisted her ankle, not seriously, and was in need of sympathy and a shot of something stronger.

The Christmas show was a short musical play called *The Chocolate Sailor*. Set in a candy shop, its cotton-candy heroine was tied up with licorice laces by a greedy child. The highlight was a chase sequence, during which the cabaret group, dressed up as a box of chocolates, pursued the child—a small, middle-aged woman in a very short dress—with a huge candy cane through the audience.

Wernher cast himself as the sailor but spent much of the performance peering out at the audience and trying to work out which one was Lilly Nelly Aphrodite. His eyes fell on Hanne Schmidt, who looked about the right age. At the end of the show he marched down to the row she sat in and persuaded her to join him on the stage. He was unaware that Hanne Schmidt had not said a word since she had arrived and was less surprised than the audience when she took the stage, closed her eyes, and launched into the musical hit of a few years before, "Bower of My Heart," unaccompanied.

Standing on her tiptoes, Hanne waved the ghost of a feather boa. She had a strong voice but sang without any hint of expression at all. And, sung at half its usual speed, the song seemed to ring with melancholy.

"Safe in the bower of my heart," she sang, *"a place strewn in blossom just for you, where always and forever, for all time and a day, the love I feel will never fade or be untrue."*

One of her front teeth was chipped and this made her consonants whistle. Her voice was low and just a little hoarse; when she hit the high notes, it cracked and threatened to break. But not until she had reached the last lines, *The blooms may wither on the vine, but I know you'll always be mine*, did her voice trail off and her eyes open.

The applause was spontaneous and genuine. Hanne Schmidt barely even smiled in acknowledgment. She went back to her seat, picked at a patch on her orphanage dress, and seemed to be working on pulling out the stitching. Sister August did not move for more than a minute. She sat breathing in, out, in, out, as the children, the cabaret group, and even Hanne herself wondered if she was for the Turkish slipper.

"Thank you, Hanne," she said eventually, and swallowed twice in quick succession. "Now, would you invite the actors into my study for tea?"

The bruises that had covered Hanne's entire body when she arrived had long since faded. And although she was still thin, she didn't look consumptive anymore. But there were still dark half-moons beneath her pale blue eyes, and her chipped front tooth meant that she seldom smiled. It was the damage that you couldn't see, however, that Sister August worried about.

On the day she arrived, Hanne Schmidt, with dry eyes and a flat tone, had confessed that her father had spent the rent and bought her the clothes and the makeup and the shoes for a musical act, which she had performed in a local beer palace. But when the money didn't roll in fast enough, he suggested she perform little extras with the customers after closing time as well. When she refused, he hit her. Or touched her. Or threatened to tell her mother. Eventually her mother, who worked all day in a factory, found out anyway. Nobody slept that night. As soon as the trams started to run, her father packed his bags and left. Her mother, deserted, broke, and with four children to feed, drank a bottle of rye vodka and took the easy way out.

"How old are you?" Sister August had asked.

"Almost twelve," she had replied.

The girl had stood up and was on the point of leaving when Sister August suggested what might happen to her if she did. She spared her no details; she read out articles in the evening paper that chronicled murders, rapes, and dismemberment and then suggested that she should reconsider. Hanne Schmidt, who was by that time visibly flushed in her heavy coat, sat down again.

"What about my father?"

Sister August carefully folded up the newspapers before speaking. "God punishes the wicked."

Six months later, as the cabaret group, still in their costumes and greasepaint, filed out in the direction of her office, Sister August rubbed her face with her palms. She wished she still believed it was true, that the good were rewarded and the bad punished. That morning she had received a letter from the office of her order requesting that she come immediately to discuss her position. She had been at St. Francis Xavier's for seven years. She knew that in that time the orphanage had become a major drain on the order's limited resources. It was time, her Mother Superior wrote, to move on.

Hanne. Wernher Siegfried heard the name. So it was not her. He scanned the room once more. And then he saw a girl he had missed before, a girl in the back row with dark hair pulled tightly into two pigtails, her eyebrows clenched, and an expression that he recognized as matching the one on the face of the actress in the boathouse all those years before, when he had declared his undying love. This must be the girl who could be—he paused to check himself—his daughter.

"Please come this way," said the red-eyed nun who ran the place. "The tea will be getting cold."

As she poured him a cup of tepid English breakfast, the actor, writer, and occasional director offered to teach the children once a week, no charge. Sister August told him she would have to think about the idea carefully. She was not so naïve as to believe he wanted to do it out of the goodness of his heart. He must have another agenda. But when he went on to suggest that it could lead to a performance by the children, which could be the centerpiece of a fund-raising event, she saw that maybe this was just what she needed after all. If she could indeed raise a considerable amount of money, maybe this would prove to her order that her calling was there, in Berlin.

"But aren't you busy?" she offered. "You must have engagements, rehearsals . . ."

"Not every day," he replied. "I mean, I have a little time at present. You know how it is in the world of the theater. But we'll need a budget: nothing big, just about three hundred marks."

Sister August hemmed and hawed, she offered more cups of tea, but it was clear even to the actor that she had made up her mind. And so before she had even formally consented, he had fixed a date, the second Wednesday in January at four in the afternoon, to take the first class of a series in dramatic arts.

Wernher Siegfried smiled and slicked back his hair. He always placed a few coins in the box at the orphanage gate every time he passed on foot. Granted, it was not very often. But every time he took the elevated train along the river Spree, he thought of the actress and the baby she dressed in black and wondered how she had turned out.

His reasons for offering a class were, however, motivated mostly by self-interest. When he had gone to visit his mother that summer and found her dead and buried—he'd left no recent forwarding address—he felt suddenly and absolutely alone. He had been an only child with an elderly father, who had expired an inconsiderably short time after his birth, and a mother who had no interest in acquiring another husband or having any more children. The loneliness and longing he had felt as a child had come rushing back in one huge and engulfing wave. And then he remembered the orphan. Lilly Nelly Aphrodite could be the closest thing he had to a living relative. No wonder he had decided to seek her out, to befriend her, and then, if the circumstances were right, to unmask himself as her real father.

Tiny Lil had given up any fantasies of being claimed. Her anger had subsided but now she felt doubly bereft. Since visiting the general, Sister August had barely glanced in her direction. It was as if she had simply stopped noticing her, as if she had become someone not entirely there, invisible.

The night after the Christmas show, however, Tiny Lil recalled the effect Hanne's singing had had on the nun. She had watched the way Sister August's eyes fixed and observed the way her head rose and fell, just a fraction, to the melody of the song. Even though she tried to hide it, her brow was furled, her face was flushed; nothing could drag her gaze away from the girl on the stage; she was captivated, immersed, spellbound. And Tiny Lil lay and tried to imagine how it must feel to be at the very center of her focus.

At the other end of the bed, Hanne wasn't asleep. Tiny Lil could tell by her breathing.

"Where did you learn to do that?" Tiny Lil whispered. "To sing?"

"Can't remember," Hanne said.

To be a child is to be absolutely without power. At St. Xavier's, the children had no choice in anything, from the food they ate to the clothes they wore. The only capacity they had was in whom they chose to love. Tiny Lil's shoulders began to shake despite herself.

She sobbed silently into her pillow, her mouth jammed up against the cotton so that no one would hear her or tease her or tell on her.

"Don't cry," Hanne whispered. "She's only a nun."

But Tiny Lil wouldn't or couldn't stop. Hanne sat up, sighed, and blew her hair out of her face. And then she crawled up the bed and climbed in at the other end, Tiny Lil's end. At first they lay back-to-back, spine to spine, until Tiny Lil's sobs subsided. And then Hanne rolled round and laid her face against Tiny Lil's shoulder and her arm across her belly and almost immediately fell asleep. Hanne's cheek was warm and her arm was heavy. Tiny Lil lay as still as she could, aware that any movement might wake her and she would move away. And then, as she slowly succumbed to the rhythm of Hanne's breathing and the heat of the body next to hers, she, too, slipped into a dreamless, subterranean state. They woke early the next morning in exactly the same position, neither one having shifted even one centimeter.

On the second Wednesday in January, twenty children aged from seven to eleven waited patiently in a classroom. The Shakespearean costumes hung limply on a rail. The room was cold, as one of the teachers, a philosopher who had spent all day talking about Hegel, had insisted on a window being opened. Time ticked by. At half past four, they realized that the actor wasn't coming. Two bottles of brandy the night before with a dancer from Dresden had wiped clean his memory. He did remember three days later and made his way to the orphanage immediately with a scrawny bunch of daffodils and multiple excuses.

The following week ten children including Tiny Lil waited for the actor in the freezing-cold classroom. Although he was hungover, he was just ten minutes late this time. He looked at his possible daughter. She looked back.

"Well, well, well," he said. "Anybody read any Grimm? Or maybe we should do a few musical numbers instead."

It was soon clear that the cabaret artist had absolutely no experience in teaching children. Although he was a member of a troupe, he took no part in devising anything, either. They spent the first class learning a song called "The Major's Pants," which he only half remembered. It was no fun for anyone.

"I don't think Sister August would like us to sing about underwear," said his possible daughter.

She had a disarming manner, he noted. Her large gray eyes seemed to bore a hole into his skull.

"She might think it's funny," he replied, and laughed.

Judging by the children's response, that might not be so. He rubbed his chin with his hand. His possible daughter didn't seem to like him. This was something he hadn't foreseen.

"Well, if anyone has any suitable ideas, then please tell me," he said.

The next week Wernher Siegfried had an even worse hangover, caused, he had decided when he woke up, by the anxiety of the situation.

His possible daughter was waiting for him, clutching a sheaf of paper.

"I think we should do a play," she said.

"A play," he said in a patronizing tone.

"Yes. I've written one," said Tiny Lil. "But you have to promise me that it will be a secret."

The day after his first visit, Tiny Lil spent the afternoon in the orphanage library, a room under the stairs that had been set up in the last century and rarely visited since. She wasn't sure what she was looking for until she found it. But she did, at the back of a musty old volume, in a section where the pages had never been read and had to be torn apart with a finger.

And so he didn't tell Sister August that the orphans were not rehearsing a fairy tale by the Brothers Grimm, as she had suggested, and were in fact working on a play written by Tiny Lil. For his part, Wernher was baffled and yet charmed by his possible daughter's choice of material. And although he found her pious and uncooperative, stubborn and single-minded, he did his best to be helpful by donating props, suggesting staging, and even offering to play the part of the king.

It was also Wernher Siegfried who showed her how to use her face. Like her mother, she had high cheekbones and a small, determined mouth. But, unlike her mother, she had those eyes, eyes that could reveal everything, or nothing.

"Acting is a language," he told her. "A silent language. Speak with your eyes."

One stifling August afternoon eight months later, thirty dutiful adults sat on children's chairs in the gym hall. The orphans who were not in the play filed in and sat on the floor in front of the stage. Sister August stood at the back along with the director and another brand-new secretary.

"So, which one of Grimm's tales is it to be?" asked the secretary.

"I'm not sure," the nun replied.

"You haven't seen it?" she asked.

"It's a secret. I wasn't allowed to."

Sister August stared at the red velvet curtain of the makeshift stage with only a little trepidation. She had grown to dislike the actor, but she had trusted him. Surely he wouldn't let her down. She had been so preoccupied with the coming battle with her order that she had spent her afternoons writing out invitations and had not set foot in the class for dramatic arts. Here was the chance to prove that what she was doing in St. Francis Xavier's was progressive rather than conservative, liberal rather than archaic, secular rather than religious.

The general and his entourage had arrived along with a delegation from the cathedral. So, too, had industrialists and businessmen, heiresses and minor politicians. A minute before the play was due to begin, a group of performers from the cabaret group hurried in and made a great fuss looking for seats. The general, much to his chagrin, was made to stand up and sit down three times.

In a broom cupboard that had been transformed into a changing room, Tiny Lil looked at herself once more in the full-length mirror. She wore a long flowing white dress, a pair of the actor's old boots painted gold, and a cardboard crown. Her face was painted white and her mouth was a deep, dark red.

"I think it's almost time," said the cabaret man.

Wernher tried his best to find something he recognized in the girl in the crown. She gazed up at him and for a moment he saw an intelligence in her eyes that he knew neither he nor her mother had ever had. Her eyes settled on his chin. Instinctively he covered it with his hand. Now he wasn't so sure she was his after all.

"Don't be nervous," she said.

But he felt extremely uneasy.

"In the absence of any printed matter that is the more usual means of presentation in the theatrical medium," announced Wernher Siegfried as he took to the stage, a section of the gymnasium recently delineated by white paint, "may I present the stage highlight of 1911: *The Miracle of Saint Wilgefortis*."

The audience, who had grown a little impatient in seats too small for their adult bottoms, sighed, squirmed a few times, and then settled down. They patted their checkbooks in pockets or bags and calculated the least they could get away with without embarrassment.

"Well, this is a surprise," whispered the director to the nun.

Sister August didn't appear to hear him. The curtains were pulled aside to reveal a painted castle wall. Tiny Lil took the stage in her crown and golden boots. For a few seconds she looked out at the blur of faces in the crowd and instantly forgot her opening line. What was she doing there? Why had she let the actor persuade her to take the lead part? And then the sun came out and a beam of light fell through the cupola above. Suddenly the actor's words came back to her: Acting is a language; speak with your eyes. And so she took a deep breath, stepped into the light, and lifted her eyes.

"Oh, Father, don't make me marry him!" she cried out. "He's old, he's ugly, and I am chaste."

"What d'ya mean, chaste?" roared the cabaret performer, now dressed in a long red cloak he had borrowed from a production of *Henry VI*. "I am the king of Portugal and you are my daughter. You'll do as I say."

Siegfried, an actor of only moderate ability, hammed it up so much that Tiny Lil had to take a moment before she could continue.

"I am a Christian, sire. And I am married to God."

The king laughed so long and loud that some of the younger orphans in the front row started to whimper.

"You'll marry him tomorrow," he replied after an overly self-indulgent pause. "And that's my last word on it."

The curtains dropped with a flump.

From the left side, a small band of orphans dressed in huge waist-coats and doublets, so long that they reached their ankles, skipped slowly across the stage, hitting cymbals and tambourines. A train on the S-Bahn passed outside the window so close that the whole hall shook along with the instruments.

When the curtain was pulled up again, the suitor had his arms folded and was tapping his foot. Since he could never remember any lines, the suitor hadn't been given any. The king sat on a throne that Sister August recognized instantly as one from the chapel.

"My dear daughter, Wilgefortis, will be here any moment to marry you," he said. "Ah, here she is now."

Tiny Lil was now wearing a long veil over her face. The suitor rubbed his hands. He was a foot smaller than his bride. They stood side by side. Tiny Lil whipped off her veil. The suitor jumped back in horror. Someone stifled a snigger. She wore a huge red fake beard, borrowed from a production of *Falstaff*.

"What have you done?" said Tiny Lil's possible father when the laughing from the younger orphans in the front row had almost stopped. "He'll never marry you now."

"It was God's work," she replied. "He answered my prayer."

"You'll pay for this," yelled the actor. "With your life."

The audience, as one, turned and raised their eyebrows at each other. Sister August closed her eyes and breathed out very slowly. Her fists were tightly clenched in her lap.

When the curtain was yanked up again by a child on the balcony above, Tiny Lil, still wearing the beard, was tied to a cross. She took two deep breaths and then expired. The king and the suitor clinked a couple of tankards and pretended to drink. Nothing happened for a couple of seconds, and Tiny Lil's eyes flickered open as she tried to catch someone's eye left of the stage. Finally a small boy walked onstage dressed in torn and dirty clothes, playing a Gypsy tune on a fiddle. He paused at the would-be dead girl's feet. She kicked off one of her boots. He picked it up. Wernher, who was proud of the fact that he never missed his cues, strolled onstage just at the right moment.

"How dare you steal my dead daughter's gold boot," he hissed.

"But she kicked it off," the boy replied.

"How could she? I had her crucified. I'll crucify you, too, I think."

"Let me prove my innocence," he pleaded. "Let me play again and show you."

The boy played. The actor glanced briefly at the audience. They all seemed transfixed—all except the nun, and that could only be expected. Tiny Lil let him play on, longer than she had done in rehearsal; and then, with all her might, she kicked off the other golden boot. It flew up and turned round and round in the air, toe, heel, toe, heel, and then sailed down in a curve, struck the general on the head, bounced up again, and fell straight into Sister August's lap. Finally the nun looked up.

"So you are innocent after all," the actor proclaimed. "And my daughter was right. There is a God."

Here he threw himself on the ground and started to sob noisily.

"She was a saint, Saint Wilgefortis. And you can keep the boot."

And with that, the curtain fell once more and the audience broke into a somewhat unconvinced round of applause. Still wearing her beard, Tiny Lil came out from behind the curtain and took a bow. A few of the actors whistled. One of the actresses had been laughing so hard all the way through that she had to run to the bathroom. The general stood up and proclaimed that he had to leave immediately for another engagement. The contribution plate was awash with ten-mark notes, but the damage had been done. Sister August had proved that she was everything the general had assumed. As she said good-bye and thanked the audience for coming, the nun's face was ashen. She still held the boot. Some of the gold paint had come off on her hand.

"Lilly," she said when the last of them had left, "I want to see you in my office immediately."

It was at this point that God's singularly effervescent light switched itself off in Tiny Lil's mind for good. A puff of dirty cloud blew across the sun and she suddenly felt a small black hole open inside. She didn't care about what anyone thought apart from one; she had written the play for Sister August, to make up for the textbooks. God, all-seeing, knew, so why didn't she?

"My office," the nun repeated.

By the time that Sister August summoned Lilly, as she was known from that day, from the bench in the corridor where she had been waiting, her fury had subsided. She had lost three hundred marks, but the children wouldn't starve. Her own battle, however, was looking increasingly like one she was going to lose. Still wearing her white dress and crown, Lilly stood for several moments before the nun noticed her. And when she spoke, it was not in her usual voice.

"You know," she said softly, "when I joined the order, I thought I could do some good, save some poor innocent children from the clutches of poverty and evil. But now I'm not so sure."

Lilly struggled for something to say.

"Apart from taking the bishop's chair from the chapel," she said eventually, "you made a mockery of the saints."

"She was real. I read about her in a book."

But Sister August's mind was already elsewhere and she didn't appear to hear Lilly's reply.

"You can go now," she said.

Lilly ran out of the orphanage and stumbled straight through the general's rose garden, scattering loose petals and string and bamboo stakes. She tripped on a root and grabbed hold of a briar. A drop of blood beaded on her finger. It ran down her hand, mixing with gold paint until it left a trail of sticky, gory glitter. How could she have been so wrong? She threw herself down on the damp black earth and let self-pity overwhelm her.

It was late summer. Autumn was in the air and she shivered as she lay prostrate in the rose patch. The sky was steel gray and punctured with stars. A motorcar passed on the street outside and blew its horn. A formation of wild geese flew just above the rooftops toward the river.

And then she noticed that many of the precious roses, the Schneekönigins and Gallicas, the Albas and the rare Damask Perpetuals, some grown from cuttings by the general himself, were headless.

"You've been stealing roses," she whispered to Hanne that night. "Sister August will find out."

Hanne rolled over until she was facing Lilly. Her lids were heavy and her lips were dark red in the moonlight.

"Why should I care?" Hanne replied.

"Because stealing is a sin," Lilly said automatically.

Hanne barely blinked.

"The more you pick, the more grow back," she said. "So how can it be a sin?"

For a moment the two girls looked at each other: Hanne, limp and always tired, her arms draped around her small blond head; Lilly, wound up, curled round and round like a spring, her eyes so large that she seemed closer, much closer than she really was.

"Don't you want to know what I do with them?" asked Hanne.

"What?"

"I go to bars and tingle-tangles and sell them," she said. "Men buy them for their sweethearts. I'm saving up. When I've got enough, I'm leaving this place and I'm taking the boys with me."

Tingle-tangle: Lilly repeated it over and over in her head. Even though she knew a tingle-tangle was just another name for a seedy bar with performing girls, the word itself somehow suggested someplace magical.

"Hanne?" Lilly whispered.

She stirred.

"What is it?"

"Can I come with you?" Lilly asked. "Can I help you sell roses?"

"Course," said Hanne. "Why else do you think I would have told you?"

Berlin, Alexanderplatz

Tingle-tangle

Every evening for a year, barring church holidays, and days off due to ill health, Arnold von Heidle and his wife, Hilda, attended the Union Movie Theater in Alexanderplatz, Berlin. Two hundred fifty films they witnessed, incognito, to assemble their extraordinary statistics. And this is what they saw: ninety-seven murders, fifty-one adulteries, nineteen seductions, thirty-five drunks, and twenty-five practicing prostitutes.

The von Heidles, upstanding members of the Catholic Church, darlings of the diocese, give well-attended talks to church groups on the newest danger to the nation: the cinema. Proposing a blanket ban on filth in word and picture, Arnold, his dear Hilda nodding, reveals that the urban masses are squandering their hard-earned cash on the creations of squalid minds. What we need, he tells them all, is censorship.

Censorship: to snip and cut, to shred and paste miles and miles of celluloid. Arnold's mind drifts: as smooth as black silk stockings, as slippery as a concubine's cunt pumping out of the machine in one unspooling lick. He feels a nudge. Wake up, dear, are you ailing? He clears his throat and then continues. Films, he utters to the silent assembled, are the devil's handiwork. For a second it is so still you can hear the stroke of strung pearl on pure cashmere. And then Hilda, her timing perfect, begins to sob.

Lilly placed one foot on the ledge that had once held her shrine to Jesus and the Virgin Mary and pulled herself up with her fingertips onto the top of the wall. Over the other side, a tram rattled past, its windows filled with golden light in the cool blue evening.

The bricks were mossy and damp underneath her skirt. She sat astride the wall and waited for Hanne to pass her up the basket.

"Hurry up," she whispered. "Someone might come."

She could see shadowy figures underneath the arches of the S-Bahn across the street. The clip of a gentleman's shoes approached from the park. A man walked below her, so close that she could have almost reached down and touched the top of his hat. When he had turned the corner, Hanne passed up the basket. Lilly took it and then let herself drop down softly onto the pavement.

Hanne appeared a few seconds later and jumped down. It was nine in the evening. The main door was locked, but they had climbed out of the bathroom on the first floor. Nobody, Hanne assured her, would miss them until the morning.

"You still want to?" Hanne asked her.

Lilly nodded. The air was charged. She trembled although she wasn't cold.

"Don't worry: she never goes out at night," Hanne said.

Since the night of the play, Lilly had avoided Sister August. If she ever heard the swish of her skirts approaching or the clank of her key chain, she would turn and walk in the other direction or duck into a dark corner. One day when she was heading to a class, however, the nun suddenly burst out of her room.

"Lilly," she had said. "Lilly?"

Lilly's steps slowed down and she stopped. Then she waited, her gaze fixed to the floor in front of her. Sister August had chastised herself over and over for not insisting that she see the play first. What had she been thinking of, to let a cabaret performer loose on her children? And now Lilly would not look at her. And she was suddenly overwhelmed with nostalgia for the little hand that had stroked her habit as she prayed for the kaiser on his birthday.

She had also noticed that Lilly had found a friend. And although she was aware of a lessening of pressure, like a belt loosened by a notch or the removal of an uncomfortable pair of shoes, she was also uneasy. Lilly knew too little of life outside the orphanage, Hanne Schmidt too much.

"I just wanted you to know . . ." she said.

To know what? Lilly had wondered, her face growing hot and her breathing faster. That God was still watching her? That He was everywhere? Or that she still despised her? The phone began to ring inside Sister August's room. She would have to answer it. But instead she took a few steps toward her and then awkwardly, clumsily, a little too roughly, embraced her. Lilly's body stiffened. She waited for more words to come, but Sister August didn't have any.

She answered the phone before it rang off. Lilly went to the bathroom, locked herself in a stall, and pulled out the postcard of the Virgin with Sister August's face stuck on, which she still carried in her pocket. She thought about ripping it into hundreds of little pieces and flushing them away. She thought about it but she could not do it. Instead she smoothed down the faded photograph on the dog-eared postcard and put it back in her pocket.

Since that day, however, she hadn't needed to avoid Sister August anymore: the tall nun rarely came out of her room except for meals and Mass. Sister August had been ordered to go back to Munich to discuss the play, the orphanage finances, and her next position. The actor, Wernher Siegfried, had pocketed the remainder of the three hundred marks and had never come back to pick up his costume. And so, in light of this, there had been suggestions of a return to administration, a noncontact post with less responsibility. Every day, however, Sister August paced up and down before her window, practicing lines of defense and calculating budgets. She did not want to leave the orphanage and go back to licking envelopes. She had made it what it was. This was her true calling; the children needed her, and she them. If only they would give her one more chance.

She did not notice the two girls that night as they appeared very briefly on the other side of the iron entrance gate and headed toward the city center. She did not catch sight of the basket of pale pink, deep red, and milk-white roses. Night had fallen and she hadn't turned on the lights. She closed her eyes and would doze fully dressed until waking stiff and cold the next morning at five a.m.

The tingle-tangle was on Oranienburger Strasse. From inside came the braying of laughter and the smell of beer and damp wool. Hanne and Lilly divided the flowers in half.

"Remember, always pick couples, and never men on their own. And don't bother with women: they never buy anything."

"What is this place?" Lilly asked. "Have you been here before?"

"My dad used to come here," Hanne said. "It was his favorite tingle-tangle."

Lilly watched as Hanne gazed distractedly along the street.

"Aren't you worried he might be here?" asked Lilly.

Hanne shrugged. She still couldn't talk about her father. The last time she had seen him, he had punched her in the face. If she saw him again, she would punch him back. She had grown two inches in the last year. She wouldn't be scared of him anymore. Not that he would even recognize her. Dressed in a shapeless orphanage dress, she felt almost safe, a girl still, even though her girlhood had been stolen two years earlier, when she was ten.

Inside the tingle-tangle, a woman started to sing and some of the chattering momentarily ceased. Lilly breathed in the smell of the night, stale beer, tobacco, men's sweat, engine grease, and the scorched metal of the tram tracks. The street outside was streaked with color: red, blue, and orange light blurred in the puddles. In the air was the peppery taste of possibility. And hanging above it all, making her giddy, was the soft green scent of the general's roses.

The bar was lined with men from the construction sites. In the middle of the floor were tables and chairs where courting couples drank hot chocolate or schnapps from tiny blue glasses. Girls dressed in white poplin and stripy stockings flirted with boys wearing braces and dust-covered boots. On a small stage at one end, a woman in a tightly laced dress played the piano. Hanne and Lilly moved quickly round the tables offering pink and white Perpetual Damasks or cream and scarlet Bourbons for fifty pfennigs each.

"Will you kiss me if I buy you one?" said one boy of about seventeen to a girl who wore a hat decorated with a huge silver feather.

"What, kiss a boy from Pappelallee?" she laughed. "What would my father say?"

The boy chose a dark red Bourbon, half closed. He pulled out five coins from his waistcoat pocket and slammed them down on the table. Lilly watched as the girl leaned across the table and kissed him slowly, softly, on the lips. She pulled back, stared into his face, and smiled. With one movement he reached for the seat of her chair and pulled the chair, the girl, the hat, toward him. She barely took a breath before she was encased in his arms, his kiss, the confidence of his adoration. As quietly as she could, Lilly picked up the coins.

At the next table, two girls and a soldier were having an argument. One of the girls stood up and swung a fist at him. Before it hit, the soldier reached up and grabbed her arm.

"Now, now," he said. "Don't you know that's a felony?"

"Let go of me," the girl cried.

"He was only trying to protect himself!" the other girl shouted. And then the two started to yell at each other instead of him.

The soldier glanced round and saw Lilly with her basket of roses.

"What have we here?" he said. "Flowers for my flowers."

It was then that Lilly recognized him as one of the soldiers from the garrison. She remembered him perched on the windowsill in the general's office with his cup of tea. He looked at her long and hard. Lilly stared back. She would deny everything.

"How much for a pink one?" he said at last. "My pretty."

She picked up a Damask, still wet with night dew.

"Four marks," she replied.

He pulled a face.

"So, this is no ordinary common or garden rose," he replied.

"No," she said. "It's a Perpetual Damask. Bred by a Frenchman called Nabonnand."

The soldier looked up. He had thick dark hair and a large mustache. His face was creased with laugh lines and blurred with drink. He pulled out a handful of change and leaned toward her.

"I'm always here on a Tuesday," he whispered.

She smiled as she handed him the rose. He didn't remember her after all. The two women were still arguing.

"Better make it two," he said, and gave her a handful of marks and pfennigs. "And you can keep the change."

"Thank you," she replied. "And give the general my best regards."

The soldier cocked his head to the side.

"Oh," he said. "So you know the general, do you?" And then he winked.

Lilly handed the money to Hanne in the cool street outside. As she did so, she glanced over her shoulder through the open door of the tavern. And there was the soldier, gazing after her. She gave him a half-smile. He raised his glass. It was almost too easy.

Hanne grabbed her arm and pulled her from the doorway.

"What are you doing?" she said.

"Nothing," Lilly replied.

Lilly gazed at her friend, her eyes wide with shock. Hanne's grip was so firm, it hurt.

"I didn't do anything," she said. "I charged him a fortune."

"Never smile at them," Hanne said. "Never. Don't let them think of you that way."

"Why not?" Lilly asked. "What way?"

Hanne Schmidt did not want to tell her about the men she had known, men who had sought out nipples on flat chests and hairless legs in high heels. Grown men who liked little girls.

"Because," she said emphatically. "Just because. Let's go."

The autumn of 1911 was especially hot in Berlin. Although cool forests stretched all the way to the Polish plains, the city baked in its long stone coat and the heat drove people temporarily insane. One man stole an army uniform, rounded up a bunch of soldiers, marched to the town hall, arrested the mayor, and made off with four thousand marks. One woman rode the Ferris wheel at the newly constructed Luna Park before taking all her clothes off and throwing herself naked from the apex.

In the orphanage, half a dozen boys ran away. Their beds were almost immediately filled by some Jewish children whose parents had been killed when the horse-drawn cart they were all traveling in was hit by a train. And then there was another outbreak of lice and all the younger children had to have their heads shaved.

Sister August's head itched. Her body underneath the thick brown habit ran with perspiration. She watched Lilly and Hanne walk in the shade in the garden. Although they still wore shapeless orphanage dresses, their bodies had been redrawn with the curves and hollows of puberty. Recently they had begun to wrap their arms around their chests and would not strip down to their petticoats like the younger girls. She noticed then that although Hanne had always been aware of her own prettiness, Lilly was not. At ten, she was taut as a rubber band. Her big eyes and sharp little face were always moving, always fluid, and what could be seen as potential insubordination in a child was restless and beautiful in a young woman. They were heading toward the rose garden. Maybe the general had been right after all.

She locked herself in the bathroom and washed her face with cool water. She rarely glanced in the mirror above the sink, but this time she paused and examined her eyes, her mouth, her nose. The skin across her cheekbones was smooth but three thick lines crossed her forehead. Her eyes were clear but the lids were wrinkled. She was thirty-seven. How could she have grown so old?

That morning she had received two letters. The first was from the convent. She was instructed to give up control of St. Francis Xavier's to a Sister Maria. The second was from her mother. Her father had died very suddenly of a heart attack. Sister August stared in the mirror, looking for any signs of Lotte. But they were gone. He was not her father, she told herself. Her father was in heaven already.

Sister Maria would arrive the very next day. Sister August knew that she had been sent to watch her, to report back, and to detail all her misdemeanors. News had reached the order about the children staging unsuitable plays and being taught by cabaret performers. They had also heard that the orphanage was in receipt of some very strange gifts. But her worst crime, as far as she could tell, was to accept Jews.

All the children, apart from the Jews, attended Mass once a day; on that she could not be faulted. The priest came every Sunday to take a service and spend a couple of hours listening to confessions. And whatever the children told him didn't seem to upset him unduly.

The children were mostly clean and well fed, and as well as being literate, they knew some German poetry by heart. But despite her rationale, despite her deliberate attempt to be realistic, unsentimental, and practical toward the children, she wondered now if she had failed them, if her approach had not equipped them well for adulthood at all. And it was at that moment, as the tap dripped and the sound of laughter drifted through the window, that the general's words came clanging back to her. What did she know of life?

Hanne kept the rose money in a tobacco tin underneath her mattress. Lilly didn't mind pooling the takings. After all, it had been Hanne's idea. The garden had been well planned and provided them with flowers almost all year round. They always started at

Bötzow's beer garden before heading back to the Friedrichstrasse, Oranienburger Tor, and the Unter den Linden. Occasionally they spent some of their money and went to a late-night showing in a cinema. There, in the blue, smoky air, they watched Charlie Chaplin films or Oskar Messter's newsreels. Men stared at them in the queue for the chocolate kiosk but they never returned their gaze.

That evening the heat of the day still rose from the bricks, the cobblestones, and the painted metal archways of the S-Bahn. It was still light when Hanne and Lilly paused on the top of the wall to let the cool breeze from the river lift their skirts. Many of the roses had been scorched or blown or would start to turn brown the moment they opened. Hanne had cut some rosebuds too early and Lilly knew that they would never flower.

"Maybe we should charge less for the buds," suggested Lilly.

"Lilly, the men don't care about the flowers," Hanne snapped. "Can't you see that yet?"

Lilly paused before she spoke. Hanne's moods could change suddenly and unexpectedly.

"Then they should pay more," Lilly said softly. "Let's charge them double."

It was then that they heard the regular tick of a woman's footsteps approaching. Both girls lay on top of the wall, their faces pressed against the baked stone and dried-out moss, and waited for her to pass.

The woman came round the corner from the direction of the orphanage gate and stopped to adjust her shoe. She wore an old-fashioned, high-collared blouse and a long brown skirt that hovered a few inches above her ankles. Her face was hidden beneath a large straw hat. Finally the shoe was fixed. She stood up, took a deep breath, and continued walking. She was unusually tall. The girls sat up and looked at each other. Even in a different outfit, they could not mistake her. It was Sister August.

They left the roses on top of the wall, dropped down onto the street, and followed the nun in woman's clothing. She paused at the stone entranceway of the Tiergarten and then went through, walking along the avenue that led to the Grosser Stern in the middle of the park. From there, she headed south toward the zoological gardens.

"She's going to the Kurfürstendamm," whispered Lilly.

"I know," said Hanne.

A tram rolled past them and swerved into the Grosser Stern. It pulled in at a stop and momentarily obscured the tall woman in the large straw hat. And by the time it drew away, she was gone.

"Let's go back and get the roses," said Lilly. "Before it gets dark."

When the man with the brown eyes asked her name, Sister August told him it was Lotte. He bought her a glass of white wine and she did not stop sipping until she felt the alcohol reach her fingertips, her earlobes, and her wide red lips.

"Do you want to come for a walk?" he asked after her third glass.

They walked back to Zoo and into the Tiergarten. It was now dark and the moonlight turned the leaves of the linden trees pewter. His kiss was urgent and soon his fingers were in her hair, in her mouth, on her buttons, on her bare white breasts. She reached down and lifted her skirt until she felt him push against her, hard and hot.

"Slow down," she whispered.

He pulled back for a second and they looked at each other. Sister August saw that he was young—much younger, in fact, than she was. Her fingertip rested on the nape of his neck. It was soft, soft as the skin of a child. He shivered and then he smiled.

"You're a real beauty," he said. And there, in her civilian clothes, with the moonlight in her hair and the taste of wine and sweat on her skin, she knew she was. When he entered her at last, she was far, far beyond any place she had been before. She was liquid, she was made of light, she was buzzing and blazing as she was pulled to the brink, to the edge of herself.

"Jesus," he said, and pulled out just in time.

Sister August gasped twice and then finally fell.

The next day Lilly watched Sister August closely to see if there was any outward sign of her transgression. But despite the fact that they had seen her enter the Tiergarten in civilian clothing, she was calmer, much calmer than she had been for months. She even introduced with a smile the new nun who, they discovered at breakfast, was to replace her.

The night before in the park, she had sobbed as she had buttoned up her blouse and straightened her skirt. Lotte, he whispered, what's wrong? And she had wiped her eyes on his shirt and told him the truth. My father died. My father died.

Sister Maria was middle-aged and sullen. A large brown mole on her nose sprouted thick black hairs and her hands looked red and scalded. She immediately dismissed all the lecturers from the university. Meals became more frugal and portions smaller. One morning they woke to find the Jewish children's beds stripped and empty.

From the moment she saw Lilly and Hanne, Sister Maria decided that they were bound to be trouble.

"Do you know the books of the Bible?" she asked them. "In order?"

They shook their bowed heads.

"Psalm Eighty-four? You must know that: 'I had rather be a doorkeeper in the house of my God than to dwell in the tents of ungodliness.' "

They stared at the floor.

"Just as I thought," she sighed. "I think we should split you two up."

They were moved to opposite sides of the dormitory and were not allowed to sit together at mealtimes. As for the rose garden, it was placed out of bounds. Sister August saw it all but did not intervene. It was as if she had lifted her hands. Sometimes, to Lilly at least, the night they had followed her seemed like a feverish dream.

"Maybe it wasn't Sister August," Lilly whispered in the bathroom as they were getting ready for bed.

"Course it was," said Hanne, her mouth full of toothpaste.

She gargled and then spat into the sink.

"You are coming out tonight? You haven't changed your mind?"

"Course not," Lilly said.

At just after nine, the girls met at the window of the bathroom on the first floor. For the first time ever it was locked.

"Let's try the downstairs," whispered Hanne.

They tiptoed along the corridor and down the stairs. It was too risky to try the main doors. They would be locked with several heavy bolts apiece.

"A window?" whispered Hanne.

The windows in the dining room were long and opaque. There was a single pane right at the very top that could be opened with a long pole. It was, however, nowhere to be found. Lilly balanced one chair on another, climbed up, and unfastened the lock. And then they heard the sound of heavy footsteps on the stairs.

"Just where do you think you're going?" Sister Maria shouted.

"Go!" shouted Hanne, and gave Lilly a shove from below. "Wait for me at the wall."

Lilly threw herself up and over the lip of the sill, balanced for a second, and then tipped and fell headfirst into a lilac bush. Through the window she could see Hanne, her hands flat against the glass, her face blurred as she climbed the chairs. Eight white fingers appeared and clutched the sill. One buckled boot was thrust through the open window. She was almost there, but not quite. As Lilly watched, Sister Maria's figure appeared below. Her hand grabbed an ankle and pulled. Hanne's boot slipped back, the fingers lost their grip, and Hanne and all the chairs went tumbling down into the dining room.

Lilly lay on the top of the wall and waited. Hanne might still escape; it wasn't impossible. The street below, now filled with fallen leaves, seemed hostile and dangerous. The trains on the S-Bahn wailed as they passed, and the shadowy figures beneath the archways seemed more numerous than usual. The air was charged. There was a storm coming. The sky pressed down on the city like a palm on clay. She couldn't go out alone. But she couldn't go back, either.

Hours later she was awakened by the rain. The street was dark and wet. Hanne wasn't coming.

Sister Maria was waiting at the main door when Lilly appeared, soaked through and shivering. The nun marched her to the pantry and told her that, in all likelihood, she was destined for hell. Before she locked the pantry door and turned out the light, Sister Maria suggested that the only thing that could save her were several hundred Hail Marys, but even then her salvation was doubtful.

By the tenth Hail Mary, Lilly's teeth were chattering so much that she could hardly speak. By the time she reached the thirtieth, her fingers and toes were numb. On her fiftieth Hail Mary, Lilly's head had begun to spin. Where was Sister August? And how could she have let this happen to her?

When Sister August discovered her the next morning, Lilly was delirious. She was taken straight to the infirmary, where she fell in and out of consciousness for three days. In her nightmares Sister August had a thick red beard and was kissing Hanne. Lilly knew that if she didn't finish the Hail Marys she might spend eternity in purgatory, but every time she started, the words tumbled out in the wrong order and her fate was confirmed.

One night she woke up to the taste of lemons and thought she was three again. She saw Sister August leaning over her with a glass in her hand and loved her unconditionally. But then Lilly remembered in glimpses what had happened and the world started to turn too fast and make no sense.

There was no one around when she finally opened her eyes one morning and knew where she was and why. The fever had lifted, and although she felt a little shaky, she made herself get out of bed and go look for the nurse. The corridors of the orphanage were deathly quiet; the classrooms were empty, the garden deserted, and the door to Sister August's room had been left open. The children, Lilly later discovered, had all been ordered to attend a daylong retreat.

She found the nurse in the kitchen making porridge. The nurse hurried Lilly back to bed and tucked her in. As she ate her porridge, the nurse answered her questions. Hanne had been expelled. Nobody knew what Sister August said to the other nun, but she had left suddenly and without explanation. Sister August's departure had been more recent. She had set off the day before, leaving her habit and veil on her bed. No one, not even the convent in Munich, had any idea where she had gone.

The girl's eyes did not leave the nurse's face as she recounted the news point by point, and for a moment she almost believed she had overestimated her patient's possible response. But then Lilly dropped the spoon into her half-eaten porridge and let out a low, thin cry.

"She'll come back?" she begged the nurse. "Won't she?"

Lilly's response was generated by sheer, blinding panic. The thought that she might never see Sister August again made it hard to breathe. And so she cried without inhibition, like a small child who realizes she has been abandoned. Although she had been angry with her, Lilly had never suspected that this would happen. Hadn't she loved Sister August enough? What had she done?

"Won't she?" she repeated.

The nurse pretended not to hear the question.

"She waited until she knew you were getting better," the nurse said softly as she stroked the girl's distraught little face. "You were one of her favorites, you know."

But this did not seem to offer her any comfort at all. The child was inconsolable.

The nurse cleared the porridge away and started to wash up. With so much to do, she couldn't waste any more time. There was another piece of news, which, wary of upsetting the child further, she had failed to mention. After Sister Maria's visit, the order in Munich had decided to cancel all involvement with the orphanage. On hearing this, the industrialist's descendants had decided to sell the building. St. Francis Xavier's closing had been determined, effective immediately.

„KRI KRI"
HIMMLISCHES LUSTSPIEL
VON
CARLSEN
LYA
MARA
REGIE
FRIEDRICH
ZELNIK
MARMORHAUS

The Blue Cat

Berlin: the opening of the Marmorhaus Cinema. Constructed of solid marble of the palest hue with only the whisker of a crease here and there, the walls seemed to glow in the twilight, as if lit up inside by candles. At the main door, a man with a reel of tickets was placed to collect overcoats and evening cloaks. And then, one by one, the hansom cabs drew up and carefully deposited their passengers into the rapid blinking of the photographers' flashes.

Inside, a Negress in a white dress mashed out tunes on a piano. A dozen waiters stood with trays of perfectly balanced glasses of Champagne. Although the light was soft and inviting, the décor was everything but: a screaming-red bar, silver sculptures of maidens and horses, painted monkeys swinging from the ceiling—as if, someone said, in the lines and colors, twisting and clashing, banging and clanging, racing and crashing, beauty herself was undergoing a radical reinvention. It's modernism, someone pronounced; Cubism, another argued, Futurism, Secessionism. No, it's Marguerite Carré from Bourgeois-Paris. The theater, for one night only, had been doused in French perfume.

The privileged invited took their seats in the auditorium; and then, as the lights lowered and a hush descended, they realized as one that the Marmorhaus, for all its glory, was only the portal. The curtains parted and a film started to roll.

Lilly saw Kaiser Wilhelm II for the first time on a Thursday in February 1912. A thick fog had been lying across the city all morning, and by mid-afternoon there was the taste of snow in the air. She heard the military procession long before she could see it. Marches played on brass instruments lifted above the rooftops, and drums, the distance throwing them out of beat, boomed along the gutters, sending handfuls of indignant pigeons into the sky. Lilly reached the Unter den Linden just as the kaiser's open-topped automobile was approaching. As the car passed, she glimpsed his face, his huge dark mustache, his withered arm, and the sweep of his pale hair.

Of course, Lilly had seen him before on the cinema screen, walking with the empress and Crown Princess Cecilie in the palace gardens, opening regattas and launching warships. Wilhelm II was so fond of "film art," as he called it, that he would turn toward the lens, give that famous smile, wave that informal wave, or tousle a child's already tousled hair at the smallest prompt. That afternoon there were no cameras to focus on his smile, but he smiled nevertheless: at his subjects, at the huge crowds, at his city. Beside him, on the soft gray leather seats, sat a dignitary with white whiskers and a slightly morose expression.

"Hooray for the kaiser," a young man shouted from a lamppost. "And hooray for Franz Josef, the Emperor of Austria and King of Hungary." The applause was spontaneous, the noise almost earsplitting, the emotion palpable, as both men reached up, touched their hats, and set their decorative feathers aquiver.

A few seconds later, there was a small explosion, followed by the skittering somewhere close behind of horses' hooves. The royal car slowed down and stopped. The kaiser and the emperor both turned and peered back. But it was nothing. A child with a firework, that's all, the whisper went through the crowd.

Franz Josef had come to Berlin to talk to the kaiser. He was worried about the Balkan states' plans to form a league with a view to taking on the Turks over Macedonia. And so, when Lilly stared into the face of Wilhelm II, as if she could make him return her gaze by willpower alone, his mind was most likely on politics. His eyes glided across the blur of a thousand citizens and the flutter of a hundred flags and he did not see the face of Lilly Nelly Aphrodite, now just eleven, even though in his later years he would have given anything—well, almost anything—to catch that gunmetal gaze just once.

The brass band began another tune and the royal parade, first the kaiser in his brand-new Daimler, then the mounted infantry, and finally the goose-stepping cavalry, moved on and headed toward the Brandenburger Tor. As the car approached the stone arch, the procession slowed—this time on purpose—and stopped. On the top of the arch the Goddess of Victory rode in her chariot. Down below, the once king of Prussia, now ruler of Imperial Germany, stood up in his seat. A pair of guns fired. A clutch of swans honked. A horse farted. For a fraction of a second Berlin held its breath. And then Wilhelm cleared his throat twice and saluted. The crowds cheered until they could cheer no more. Dozens of hats were thrown up into the white sky and many were lost forever.

It would be six years before Lilly saw the kaiser again, in a train station at midnight. He missed his chance to meet her gaze at that moment too. His eyes, you see, would be too full of tears.

The parade ceremoniously processed into the park until, soldier by soldier and horse by horse, it gradually dissolved into the fog. On the Unter den Linden, the people watched until their eyes strained, until there was nothing more to be seen. And only then, when the procession was finally over, were the barricades pushed aside, the flags rolled up for next time, and handkerchiefs that had been waved used to wipe the faces of overtired children. Couples hurried home, their backs hunched in their coats, the smoke of their cigarettes floating behind them in dirty halos. Along Wilhelmstrasse and Dorotheenstrasse, the streetlights buzzed on, bright pink globes in the dusk. And with just a slight darkening of the sky, it started to snow, first a light flurry and then heavy flakes as big as five-pfennig coins.

In the months following Hanne's and the tall nun's departures, a lull had descended on the orphanage. The building had been put up for sale and every day a new batch of prospective buyers wandered around, taking measurements or trying to visualize the dismally appointed dormitories as luxury hotel rooms, perhaps, or swanky new apartments.

The orphans, suddenly released from all religious routine, never quite fell into a state of godless anarchy as was expected. Instead, out of respect for their beloved Sister August, the older children kept order, tucked up the younger ones at night, and stuck faithfully to the schedules and rules that she had devised. It was true that several packed up their nightgowns and made their beds for the very last time, but the majority decided to stay until the bitter end. The gates were open wide but there was nowhere, they realized, for them to go.

Of the ones who stayed, nobody talked about the future. Nobody mentioned the coming sale. It was almost as if they could stave off the inevitable by just pretending it wasn't going to happen.

Since her spell in the infirmary, Lilly had seemed to have completely recovered. Back then she had grieved copiously and without inhibition for Sister August, for her friend Hanne, for the mother and father she couldn't remember, for herself, until eventually she couldn't cry anymore. And now she felt dried up, numb, barren. Tears would sometimes creep up on her unexpectedly, in the middle of reading a fairy tale to the younger children or cleaning her teeth, but most of the time she appeared, at least outwardly, to be fine. She rose in the morning, she ate her meals, and at the end of the day she fell asleep.

One night, however, she woke up in the bed she used to share with Hanne and suddenly remembered the tin of rose money under the mattress. Most of the money was gone, but not all of it. Hanne must have expected Lilly to follow her. But the nights were so dark, the orphanage wall was so high, and the city outside was so huge that the idea of leaving of her own volition filled her with terror. She put the tin back under the bed and lay awake for hours, going over and over the old frames of her life until they became distorted, worn-out, drained of color, and finally she closed her eyes and prayed for the courage she so obviously lacked.

In early December, after morning Mass, an old-fashioned hansom cab drew up at the gates. Three nuns climbed out and began to walk toward the orphanage, their black shadows spilling behind them. Lilly felt her heart start to race. Her temples throbbed and her knees felt as if they might buckle. The nuns must have found out how she had stolen roses and stayed out late. These were serious crimes. What would they do to her this time?

But when the nuns' gaze, taking in the gloomy orphanage and dripping overgrown gardens, happened to fall across a white-faced girl at the kitchen window, there were no thunderbolts or lightning strikes. She did not read disapproval in their eyes but pity.

That morning, a special Mass was held at ten o'clock. At the end of the service, the children remained kneeling while they were informed that the orphanage had been sold. The buyer, a young man who had inherited his money from his family and was to blow the entire lot in one-tenth of the time it took to make it, planned steam rooms in the chapel and a row of treatment rooms where the classrooms were. The children looked around at the dark green walls and the greasy cupola and tried to make themselves believe that they would be leaving. Most of them couldn't remember living anywhere else.

The health spa man had bought the orphanage on the condition that he start work in two months' time, and since his had been the only offer, the nuns were in no position to negotiate. Twenty babies and toddlers were to be shipped to America, their passage paid for by a Catholic charity. Of the rest, it was decided that the youngest would be sent to the St. Catherine's Orphanage in Munich, while the others would be handed over to a charity, The Adoption Society, which would place the children in households as farm laborers or domestics.

Hanne's brothers were five, six, and nine, with white-blond hair and big blue eyes. They still waited for their sister every day at the front door and had to be coaxed to meals with promises that, were she to return when they weren't there, she would be sent straight to them. Lilly had assured them that their sister would come back to fetch them. But as the days turned to weeks, she gradually stopped believing it. And so, on the day of the nuns' announcement, she had gathered Hanne's brothers together and made them a promise: despite the dark, the high wall, and the ever-expanding city, she would try to find their sister and bring her back.

The nights were darker, much darker than she had expected, the wall higher, and the city far bigger than she remembered. But the rose money helped to make her bold. As she took one tram and then another, rode the S- and U-Bahn back and forth, walked for miles through cavernous streets, Lilly learned that St. Francis Xavier's was as calm, as perfectly still, as the dead center of a wheel. All around, Berlin was in a state of flux. You could sense it, taste it, smell it, from the mannequins in shop windows, whose outfits changed for the morning rush hour and again for the evening promenade, to the omnibuses, the cars, the bicycles, and the taxicabs, which raced round Potsdamer Platz from dawn until dusk. Nothing was fixed anymore. Nothing was nailed down. You could never guarantee, absolutely, that the spot in which you stood would look the same from one day to the next. Streets would be dug up practically overnight, landmarks demolished, and classical façades covered with tarpaulin, only to be unveiled a week later faced with bright new advertisements for chocolate or pianos or perfume.

In shops and department stores, on street trolleys and street corners, Lilly examined faces and asked questions. She found dozens of girls with pale gold hair and bare arms that they casually wrapped around themselves. And they all knew a Hanne Schmidt—it was a common name—but only old ones, fat ones: a Hanne Schmidt with five children or a medical condition, a layabout husband or an invalid mother, never Lilly's own fair-haired, rose-selling Hanne.

Sometimes Lilly wondered if she had walked past her friend in the street and failed to recognize her. Sometimes she imagined Hanne in the poorhouse dressed in rags, her eyes red-rimmed from weeping, her long white legs blotched with sores. And sometimes she would dream she found her lifeless and blue, her body lying limp beneath a railway bridge, or propped up on the backseat of a tram, a knife pushed into her heart. The mornings after the nightmares were the hardest. The city she walked through seemed filled with dark corners and cold basements, places where a girl like her could disappear. But if anything happened, who would look for her?

On the day of Franz Josef's visit, the day when the kaiser had been informed of Russian involvement in forming the Balkan League and was concerned enough to call a meeting of the Grosser Generalstab, but not concerned enough to cancel the military parade, Lilly turned and walked through the crowds back up the Unter den Linden. She glanced from face to face as the people poured past her. She peered under hats and into car windows, she paused at cafés and stared through the glass, and occasionally she approached total strangers from behind and tapped on their unsuspecting shoulders.

A blond girl in a red jacket and a hobbled skirt came out of a music hall and sauntered through the snow. With her handbag swinging and her heels clacking, there was something about her that looked familiar. Lilly followed her. For three blocks they walked one behind the other until the girl slowed down.

"It's fifteen marks," she said over her shoulder.

Lilly stopped abruptly. The girl turned round. For a moment they stared at each other. Neither was what the other expected. The girl, despite the lipstick and the swagger, looked about her own age. She composed her face and started to shout in an accent so thick that Lilly could barely understand a word.

A man stepped out of the shadows. He was dressed smartly in a hat and a loosely cut suit. When he saw the two girls standing face-to-face in the snow, one shouting, one silent, he shook his head and lit a cigarette.

"I'll take you both for twenty," he offered.

Five blocks later, Lilly slowed to a walking pace. The streets were emptier now that it was getting dark. She passed a bar, a baker's, a pawnshop. And then there was nothing, nothing but locked doors and shuttered windows. Snow swirled and raced and landed gently on her narrow shoulders, her eyelids, and her lips. The secondhand coat allocated to her the year before was too small. She pulled the sleeves down over her knuckles, held her arms crossed in front of her, and kept walking, but still the icy Berlin air slipped through the gaps.

She had planned to walk until she came to a tram stop and then take one or probably two trams back to Bellevue. A horse and carriage, a droshky, approached and she had to stand back, to push herself against a wall to let it pass. As it disappeared into the whiteness of the storm, she looked around and realized that she had no idea where she was. On both sides were wooden fences. Behind them were construction sites where heaps of bricks, mountains of sand, and stacks of metal pipes lay under a layer of snow. A little farther on, a vacant lot had been converted into a bicycle track, its circuit a perfect lozenge of untouched white surrounded on all sides by piles of black earth.

Lilly turned left and came to a boarded-up alleyway. She turned right and right again and finally reached a wide boulevard that had once been lined with sycamore trees. Most of the eighteenth-century villas and majestic gardens that had once stood there had gone. In recent months, the cobbles had been torn up, the trees had been felled, and there was a huge trench in the middle of the street. The noise of iron striking iron and the intermittent boom of rock imploding came from deep within. Lilly walked across the mounds of frozen mud and peered over a barricade into the hole. A hundred feet below, she saw a shower of sparks and the dull glint of iron rails. They were building another subway line.

She kept walking. There were no tram stops here. The wind howled and blew snow into her face, her eyes, her mouth. She was growing scared now, scared of the approaching night, scared of the cold. But nothing would make her look for shelter in those dark corners or basements, and so she kept going, her eyes tearing, her teeth clenched, her fists in balls. How would she ever get back? How could she go on?

Lilly didn't see the man until the top of her head hit the second button of his railway man's coat. When he bowed and begged her pardon, she momentarily forgot the snow, she forgot that she was lost, and she forgot her search for Hanne Schmidt. It was Otto, Otto Klint. But before she had the chance to say a word, he had nodded, stepped aside, and continued walking. He didn't recognize her.

He could have kept on going, he could have faded into the weather, but he stopped and turned. Maybe he was aware that he could hear only one set of footsteps on the freshly muffled cobbles, and they were his own. Maybe he could feel her eyes on the nape of his neck, which his upturned collar didn't quite manage to cover. Maybe he felt some tiny jolt of recognition, a yew tree, a shrine, a photographer's lens.

"Otto," she blurted out. "Don't you remember? It's me. Lilly. From St. Francis Xavier's."

He frowned. The snow still came down but more softly now.

"Tiny Lil?" he said. "Is it really you?"

She nodded twice. And then she rushed toward him and threw her arms around his railway man's coat. It was his face, a familiar face among thousands, and his voice, his voice saying her name or the name that she once had; it was Otto. For a moment she just breathed in and out as the warmth of his body began to seep through the coarse blue wool. It was Otto.

"What on earth are you doing here?" he asked.

In fits and starts she told him about Hanne.

"I've been looking everywhere . . . in every café and bar in Berlin. And now I . . . I don't know where I am. . . ."

Her voice trailed off. She couldn't trust her mouth anymore.

"Well, you had better come with me," he said. "Before you catch your death."

Lilly cradled a glass of hot wine in both hands. The walls of the tavern were hung with tarnished mirrors and heavy wooden carvings of hunting scenes. As the snow melted in her hair, it dripped down the back of her neck and she shivered.

"Cold?" Otto said.

She shook her head. She was warm. Otto sat opposite her. If she half closed her eyes, she could have been back in St. Francis Xavier's again, back in the days before he had left with the promise that he would visit, back in the days when Sister August had loved her, back before Hanne had arrived and everything had changed. Like hers, Otto's hands, cheeks, and ears were scarlet. As the spitting log fire lit up his face, she guessed he was now about eighteen.

"Why did you never come back to see us?" she asked.

He sighed and took a sip of his drink. He had no excuses, no answers, no reason.

"Tell me again," he said. "About your friend."

"Hanne? I think she may have been kidnapped," Lilly said.

Otto paused. "There are millions of people in Berlin," he said eventually. "If you haven't found her by now, maybe you never will. There are some things, some people, some places, that you just have to forget."

"But I could never forget her," Lilly rebuked him. "Not Hanne."

"Well, maybe she wants to forget you. And her brothers."

Lilly felt a wave of fury rise up inside her. But Otto did not notice the quickening of her breath or the slight jut of her chin.

"Why on earth would she do that?"

"Well," he said, "I think I have an idea."

"Go on. . . ."

"All right," he said. "I will."

He leaned back, ran his hand over his short blond hair, and, catching the waitress's eye, ordered another couple of glasses of wine.

"For some people, coming from the place we both came from means that we will never amount to anything," he said. "We're bastards, illegitimate, unplanned, unwanted. But I see it another way. We have no history, we have no roots, we have no past, so I suppose . . . we can choose to invent one. Every day, we can start all over and reshape ourselves."

Lilly looked at him. His eyes were bright and his lips were moist.

"Sister August said that God shapes us."

Otto let out a sigh.

"Come on, Tiny Lil. What shape did He give us? The destitute orphan shape? Admit it: you don't really believe all that stuff, do you?"

"Why, don't you?"

"No," Otto said. "Not anymore. And neither do you. Let me tell you a secret: I am the son of the kaiser and his mistress."

Lilly stared at him. Had he gone mad?

"Tomorrow I will be the son of Czar Nicholas of Russia. Can you see the resemblance?"

She looked. And for a second she could.

"Nobody would believe that," she said.

"But I did," he replied. "And you did too. For a second or two, anyway. But it's harder for a girl. You have to pick a man, Tiny Lil, a rich one, who'll support you. Tell him that both your parents died in an automobile accident and that you were swindled out of your inheritance by a wicked uncle . . . something like that. You could do it. If you believe it, they will."

"I don't think so," Lilly said.

"They'll want to hear it, Lilly. With a pretty face like yours, they'll want to believe it."

Otto watched as Tiny Lil blushed, the color spreading upward from her neck until it reached the tips of her ears. She had certainly turned out well, he thought suddenly. But when she felt his eyes on her, she glanced up at him with such a piercing look that for an instant he was sure she could penetrate his thoughts and he felt his own face begin to flush.

He pulled a bent cigarette from his pocket and placed it in his mouth.

"In years to come, when you're some baroness with a house by a lake," Otto continued, "you'll thank me. You will, you'll thank me. Lilly, you don't want to end up on a street corner. You've seen those girls, the ones who wear the lipstick and the high heels when they've barely lost their milk teeth."

He struck a match and sucked in the flame. And then he told her what had happened to him since he left the orphanage. First, how he went to work in the underwear factory and then, after a year of military service, how he had found a position in the railways through one of his captains. It was a good job, he said. He checked the rolling stock. And then, in great detail, he explained the science of locomotion with diagrams scribbled down with the stub of a pencil on the margin of the previous day's newspaper.

"One day," he said, "I'm going to drive the royal train." His nails were rimmed with engine grease. His mouth was full of the taste of journeys he had yet to make.

Lilly inhaled the alcohol that evaporated from her glass and let the warmth spread across her chest. The royal train. She had not even known there was such a thing.

"How is Sister August?" he asked.

"She left," Lilly replied.

"Of course she did," Otto said. "We rip up our pasts and move on. This is the modern age."

Otto had grown. His shoulders were broader; his feet were bigger. He was much taller, the product of a late growth spurt at seventeen. His face had lengthened and his chin was blurred with short fair prickles. As Lilly looked at him, she tried to see the baby who had been left on the doorstep in a milk crate, or the boy with a shaved head and patched boots who used to jump over the orphanage wall and disappear into the city for a few hours. But they were gone. Otto was now a young railway man with the kind of easy smile that prompted many a female passenger on the steam trains to Paris or Rome or Calais to pause before they boarded and wonder if their destination was the right one after all.

For a while neither of them spoke. It was already evening and the tavern was full of people. In the corner, a man was playing an accordion and a few couples had started dancing. Lilly had been to better taverns than this one, taverns with piano players and stained-glass booths where ladies drank Goldwasser from Danzig and smoked tiny dark brown cigars. But she had never actually sat down in one before.

"Shall we dance?" she asked. "Are we allowed?"

Otto laughed, a big, open laugh that came from the waist up.

"Of course it's allowed," he said. "This is Berlin, the capital of the world."

He took her hand and she stood up. Beneath her coat, she was wearing one of the gray cotton orphanage dresses. Noting her hesitation, Otto turned to a young girl who had just come in from the cold with an armful of roses, bought one, and pinned it to Lilly's chest. It was a pink dog rose, uncultivated, wild.

"Now you can take off your coat," he said.

As thick-waisted women laid their heads on the threadbare shoulders of thin old men, as drunken whores swirled their clients round before consummating their transactions in the shabby rooms upstairs, Otto and Lilly danced, if you could call it that. The whole of her hand was not much bigger than the size of his palm. The top of her head barely reached the bottom of his chin. And when she stepped on his toes or turned the wrong way, Otto laughed. When he backed into another dancer or led her into the corner, she laughed. And when they spun too fast and Lilly's face accidentally brushed the cotton of Otto's shirt, he leaned down and kissed her.

"Tiny Lil," he said. "What a surprise."

When they noticed the time, it was after two in the morning. The tavern was closing and the barmaid was sweeping the floor. The door had been wedged open with a brick and an icy draft raced around the room.

"I think the last streetcar left at eleven," Otto said. "And won't the gate be locked?"

"I climb over the wall like you used to do," said Lilly. "If you could just point me in the right direction . . ."

They both glanced through the open door at the darkened street. Lilly shivered.

"Why not stay with me," Otto said. "In fact, I insist you stay with me. I live very close."

Otto held her by the hand. Her head was full of wine. Was it such a bad idea?

"I have to go to work in five hours anyway," he said. "I'll sleep on the floor. I'd worry about you all night if you didn't."

Otto boarded with a widow who lived in a four-room apartment on the top floor of a five-story building on Dragonstrasse. They crept into the parlor and, as Otto instructed her, carefully stepped around the Turkish rug. You weren't, he whispered, allowed to step on it because you might wear it out. He led her up a narrow flight of stairs to a tiny, low-ceilinged attic room with a window that looked out across East Berlin. There was a single bed made up with a green blanket, a rickety wicker wardrobe, and a washstand with a cheap metal bowl and pail. The only evidence that Otto actually lived there at all was a set of tools in a leather holder on the floor and a pile of books on the table.

They sat side by side on the bed under the bare electric bulb with their coats on. Then Otto pulled down a box of chocolate cherries from the top of the wardrobe.

"My landlady gave them to me," he whispered. "She went to see an American moving picture with a man she met on the S-Bahn. He gave her these chocolates and led her to the back row. She excused herself to the powder room before the film had even started."

"And left?" said Lilly. "An American moving picture? But why?"

Otto smiled but didn't explain.

"Take one," he said. "Go on."

The warmth of their breath and the heat from the bare lightbulb slowly began to thaw the ice that covered the glass on the inside of the windowpane. Otto's knee absentmindedly bumped hers as he tapped out the military tune that he'd heard that afternoon. Lilly unwrapped a chocolate. She bit through the hard, dark coating and cherry brandy exploded into her mouth.

"Good?" he asked.

Lilly couldn't speak, her mouth was so full of alcoholic sweetness. She nodded. Otto was staring at her lips, her nose, her eyes. She swallowed.

"What?" she said.

They both heard the creak of bare feet on the stairs. Otto leapt to his feet and instinctively pushed his hand through his hair. A trickle of cherry syrup fell from the corner of Lilly's mouth. The door opened and a woman in a red silk Chinese dressing gown stood in the doorway.

"Visitors, Otto?" she said.

In 1912, Olivia Licht was forty-two. At that time she had thick black hair piled up on the top of her head above her heavy-lidded eyes. Her smell coiled around her and was instantly recognizable—essence of lavender, which she sprinkled on her laundry, cold cream, and something metallic like old coins kept in a box. Although her features, taken individually, were even, her face gave the impression that too much pressure had been used, perhaps, in its making.

Maybe it was a direct result of her occupation. A doctor's widow turned abortionist by trade, she made a good income with a contraption that she claimed had been manufactured in Paris by a Viennese specialist.

"Frau Licht," Otto said with a bow. "May I introduce my friend?"

"It's past midnight. And this is neither the time," Olivia Licht replied, "or, more important, the place!"

Lilly stood up.

"Actually," she said, "I have to go now anyway."

Olivia Licht took in the girl with the sticky mouth and the coat two sizes too small. She was only a little surprised that she still had it on.

"You see, he's not allowed. It's a rule. I'm so sorry, my dear. But we don't want you getting into trouble."

"Frau Licht," began Otto, "she missed the last streetcar. And the snow . . ."

Olivia Licht placed a pale hand on Otto's arm. Lilly saw the way her hand lingered. She saw the way that Olivia Licht gazed up at her lodger.

"Such a kind boy, always thinking of others," she whispered. "But sometimes kind acts can lead to unkind consequences."

Lilly suddenly felt very sober. She pulled herself up to her full height, which wasn't very tall. Otto shrugged and let out a short, mirthless guffaw. It was a reaction neither woman expected.

"I know the way," said Lilly.

She fiddled with her coat buttons and adjusted her boots. The moment seemed to stretch. Come on, thought Lilly, say something. Finally, as she was stepping down the stairs, Otto called after her.

"Wait, Tiny Lil," he said. "I'll walk with you to the corner."

Lilly protested, but Olivia Licht protested louder. She pointed out that he might be late for work, fall asleep on the job, and get the sack.

"I give you a special rate," she whispered. "But if you can't pay the rent, you know I'll have to lose you."

The landlady reached out her arm and her robe fell open, very slightly, revealing the long white slope of her breast. Lilly saw Otto's eyes slide down. But he already knew what was beneath the red silk. She knew he already knew.

"We had an agreement," she whispered.

Lilly coughed. Otto turned.

"Well, if you insist," said Lilly, "then I will accept."

Otto smiled his broad, generous smile and buttoned his greatcoat.

"Won't be long," he said.

The clouds above the snowed-up city were a hazy pink. A chemical plant several miles away was pumping out black smoke and the air was heavy with the taste of sulfur. And yet the streets of Berlin were all white, whiter and cleaner than either of them had ever seen them before. By morning they would already be trampled and soiled, the snow pockmarked with thaw and a dusting of soot. But for the moment everything was pristine. Otto walked her to the first corner, and the second and the third, until he decided he might as well walk her all the way home.

"What are you doing living in a place like that?" Lilly teased.

"It's cheap," Otto replied. "And she's not so bad . . . once you get to know her."

"She's a dragon," Lilly whispered. "A monster, an ogress, a witch in a wig."

"It's not a wig," Otto said.

They passed a couple kissing against a wooden fence, their arms and legs, hands and faces struggling, grabbing, pushing, and rubbing. They passed a group of old men and an elderly prostitute huddled round a fire on a construction site. They were taking it in turns to warm their hands between her thighs. They passed a man pulling four children behind him on a sledge. The children wore no shoes.

"Come on," Otto said, and, reaching back, he took her hand. "Let's skate."

Otto and Lilly ran and skidded, ran and skidded along the road on the thin strip of packed snow and ice where the automobiles and droshkies had driven. Every so often they heard a car approaching and jumped aside to avoid being hit by the arc of dirty snow that flew from the wheels.

A taxicab drove by. Inside, they glimpsed a lady in pale blue and a man in topcoat and tails. They were arguing loudly. At the end of the street, just as the cab turned the corner, a shower of cards flew out of the window. When they reached the spot, Lilly plucked one from the snow. Otto picked up a couple more from an icy puddle.

"Tingle-tangle cards," Otto said. "Quite a collection."

They couldn't have known it, but the man in the cab was a minor count who was having a scandalous affair with an actress. In the following weeks, he paid a friend to film his lover taking off her clothes. She ran away with the friend, the film fell into the hands of his wife, and he ended up with an alimony problem so severe that he had to go into business. He started to import pornography from France and made a handsome living for around a year until he was caught and imprisoned. But that night, the future was still blank. The film had not been shot, the bromide was still in its brown glass bottle. Nothing had been fixed.

"Can I see?" she asked Otto.

Otto handed her the postcards. On each one, a girl wearing underwear posed against a curtain. Lydia, Colette, Sophia, Masha. Another cab was approaching. Lilly slipped the cards into her pocket and stepped into a doorway.

They reached the orphanage just as the sky was turning milky. Otto scaled the wall, cleared it of snow, and then pulled her up in one swift move. They sat opposite each other on the damp, mossy stone.

"Well, at least I found you," she said.

"You'll never find your friend," he replied. "Promise me you'll give up or I'll never take you out and dance with you again."

He took both of her hands in his. He stared into her face.

"I can't do it," she said.

He laughed and shook his head.

"But I'll teach you," he said. "I'll teach you to dance."

Not dancing but looking for Hanne: he had deliberately missed her meaning. She let it go. On the tracks nearby, the first S-Bahn of the day thundered past, its carriages lit up pale electric yellow in the dawn.

"I should be getting back," Otto said at last. Suddenly she didn't want him to leave. She didn't want him to go back to Olivia Licht. She didn't want the evening to end.

"Not yet," she whispered.

She swung her legs over the wall and jumped down into the undergrowth.

"I am the Queen of Sheba," she said. "And I order you to come here."

As she stood in the near dark, surrounded on all sides by yew trees and moss-covered brick, every vein throbbed with unfamiliar energy, every nerve jangled. Even at that early hour, even under a blanket of snow, the city hummed and buzzed, its locomotions revolving quicker and quicker, its hammers hammering faster and faster. It was Berlin. It was a city with an appetite for energy, for thrill, for sex. How could it not fail to affect you?

Otto looked down at her and for a moment he was tempted. The only woman he had slept with was his landlady, when he was woozy with wine on payday. But then he looked again and saw that Lilly's large gray eyes hadn't turned opaque like so many girls her age; she didn't know men. Or the damage they could do to her.

"I have to go, Little Sister," he said. "Or I'll be late for work."

"Don't you believe me?" she said.

"Of course I do," he replied. "And you should believe it too. Remember, nothing less than a house on a lake."

A tram was approaching on the street. Otto blew her a kiss, jumped down, and climbed aboard.

Later that morning, snow was still falling, and the world was so quiet it seemed to be holding its breath. Lilly lay in bed and listened to the muffled clatter of a coal cart. When she was sure she would not, could not sleep, she reached down and picked up her crumpled gray orphanage dress. The dog rose had wilted and lost most of its petals but it was still pinned tight.

In her pocket was the corner of newspaper Otto had drawn on—and something else, something bulky. And then she remembered: tingle-tangle cards, a dozen of them at least. She glanced through them. Masha, Sophia, Marlena. Hanne. She looked again. Wearing a huge hat festooned with roses was Hanne Schmidt, her Hanne Schmidt, gazing over a barely clad shoulder. The name of a tingle-tangle on the Tauentzienstrasse was on the back: The Blue Cat.

At breakfast, Lilly served porridge and poured tea for the younger children. Everything, superficially, seemed the same as before, the stewed black tea in its huge black pot and the vat of porridge with a raw potato stirred in to soak up the salt. But the room was darker; a wooden fence had been erected around the orphanage by a team of workmen. Architects and builders came and went freely through the main entrance. The month of notice was almost over. But she had found Hanne when she had almost given up looking. Finally she had found her.

"Who'd like sugar?" she asked them all. "Today it's allowed."

From the street, The Blue Cat looked so dark inside that most people assumed it was shut. Behind a nondescript marine-blue shop front, long purple drapes hung across frosted windows. It was the kind of place that opened early and closed only when the very last customer was so inebriated he had to be carried out. It was, in short, a fairly typical lower-class establishment. The drinks were diluted with tap water, the girls were all either under eighteen or over forty-five, and the entertainment was organized by a Bulgarian who played the clarinet and the piano, sometimes at the same time.

The Blue Cat was always quiet in the early evening. Most of the regular clientele were home with their families or eating boiled beef and noodles in one of the many steamed-up restaurants on the Tauentzienstrasse. As Lilly waited for her eyes to adjust to the dark, a couple of men glanced over at her. But when they saw she did not greet them with a willing smile or a flash of ankle, they turned back to their drinks or tried to catch the eye of the endlessly obliging waitress instead. Lilly stood at the bar and studied the ceiling until the waitress had finished serving. And then, only when she had swiped the counter with a dirty rag, lit a cigarette, and poured herself a glass of ale did she nod in Lilly's direction.

"The manager's not hiring," the waitress said. "Come back in a week. And next time, use the back door."

"I'm not looking for a job," Lilly said. "I'm looking for Hanne Schmidt. I think . . . she works here."

The waitress's eyes narrowed.

"And who are you?" she asked.

"I'm . . . I'm her sister."

"Friend" didn't seem appropriate somehow. The waitress let out two streams of cigarette smoke through her nose. She looked Lilly up and down and then raised her eyebrows.

"Really," she said.

Lilly was directed to a door behind a curtain and then to a row of cramped clapboard cubicles beyond.

"And tell your sister that she's ten minutes late for her shift already," the waitress said.

Hanne Schmidt, tingle-tangle artist, was putting on her makeup. She wore a ratty old dressing gown and a hairnet. She was drawing on her eyebrows with a black pencil. One was finished and one was not, giving her an expression of ironic perplexity. She wasn't particularly surprised to see her former friend from the orphanage standing behind her in the low light of The Blue Cat's changing rooms. She had been expecting her. She was surprised only that she hadn't come sooner.

"Are my brothers behaving themselves?" she asked.

Lilly nodded. She couldn't speak.

"I made them these. I meant to send them . . . months ago."

Hanne pulled a paper bag from under her mirror. Inside were three hats and three pairs of mittens, all knitted with scarlet wool.

"Tell them to be good boys and to keep warm," she said. "And tell them that I'll come and get them very soon. Now be a dear and let me finish."

Lilly watched as Hanne Schmidt drew in the other eyebrow. She saw that, apart from the makeup, she didn't appear to have changed at all: she had the same pale hair and circled eyes, the same frail arms, which she wrapped herself up with. But as she observed her, Lilly began to notice subtle differences: a waist so tiny that she must have pulled her corset laces quite brutally tight; a red mark, a burn maybe, on her arm; and something else, something newly sober in her manner.

In fact, in the six months since she had been expelled from the orphanage, Hanne had been engaged to a Greek millionaire who had given her diamonds one night, only to take them back the next; her heart had been broken by a soldier who had sworn undying love on the carousel at the Luna Park and broken her nose on the ghost train; and she had to leave the family she had been boarding with when the father came into The Blue Cat "accidentally." And so she had taken the only place she could find with no notice, a damp little room in a run-down pension in Kreuzberg. In six short months, she was beginning to suspect that she was the kind of person who attracted terrible luck, unstable people, and unwanted advances. And she was right.

Her time at St. Francis Xavier's seemed to belong to another, kinder life.

"Well, sit down," she said to Lilly's reflection in the mirror. "And take your coat off."

Lilly laid her coat on the back of the chair and sat down. Hanne guffawed. She threw her hand across her mouth and for an instant she was the same old Hanne, the one whose eyes glimmered in the dark of the dormitory.

"What are you wearing?" she asked.

Lilly's face fell. Her skin prickled. She was wearing a dress that had come to the orphanage in a bundle of donations. It was thick green serge with a high lace collar, a little girl's dress, the only thing that would fit her. She stared at the floor, at the mouse hole in the skirting.

"I'm sorry. Are you in trouble? Is that it?" she asked. "I know a lady."

Lilly was suddenly furious.

"Hanne, I've been looking for you," she said. "For months. I thought you were dead. I found your card in the gutter. . . ."

"But I'm fine," she replied with a smile. "As you can see. You needn't have worried."

Lilly took a deep breath.

"And I have some bad news," she said.

Hanne turned back to her reflection. Lilly caught her eye as she lined it with kohl. And in that single second she saw that makeup couldn't disguise her apprehension. Whatever it was—and Hanne could think of a dozen awful things that could have happened—she did not want to know, not then, not yet.

It was at that precise moment that the Bulgarian shouted out Hanne's name round the curtain. She took a deep breath and turned.

"Then stay," she said as she took Lilly's face in her hands. "Stay and tell me after." And with one cool kiss on the cheek, she was gone.

"I knew a man with a great big . . .
Dick was his name. . . .
And I could say that he hung
With the crowd like the best of them
Forget the rest of them
My great big Dick had a great big . . .
Heart. . . ."

Hanne barely moved onstage. The hat from the photograph was on her head, her shoulders were bare, and she wore a short pink frilly dress, a pair of suspenders, and pale pink striped stockings. At first her voice was a mere whisper. And while her body appeared moribund, her knee twitched at twice the tempo of the song. At her side, the Bulgarian was pumping out the tune on an old piano with a huge grin pasted on his face. A trickle of sweat fell down his cheek. He threw Hanne a look, his eyes wide, his teeth bared. Hanne's face blanched beneath her powder and her voice trailed away. She looked out at the audience and spotted Lilly. And then something seemed to click. The knee stopped vibrating. Hanne narrowed her kohl-rimmed eyes, she stuck out her somewhat meager chest, and she formed her mouth into a perfect O. The Bulgarian whooped. Hanne winked and began to sway her narrow hips. And then, with her chipped tooth and her low voice, she started to sing again.

"If you want to tickle my fancy, take me down to Wannasee . . .
If you wanna see a little action, that's the beach for me. . . ."

I can't take them," Hanne said. "It's impossible."

Lilly stared at Hanne in the mirror as she reapplied her lipstick. Her face was flushed and feverish.

"I could sneak them out," Lilly suggested. "We've got a week exactly. You could find a place to live, for all of us. I could sell roses. At least we'd all be together. Hanne, I'm sure it could work."

"You're not listening," Hanne repeated, pressing both lips onto a handkerchief, which she then used to dab her eyes. "I can't take them. I can barely look after myself."

"Hanne, you're all they have," Lilly said. "Couldn't you take them for a little while? You're old enough now. You're fourteen."

Hanne Schmidt drew a large breath and stared at her reflection. The makeup is a mask, she told herself, no one can read me. It had been her mantra in the years when she had sung for her father. It still worked.

"It's impossible," she said, and stood up.

Lilly stood up too. And then she took Hanne by both shoulders and shook her, just as the nurse had shaken her all those years before.

"Listen to me. They might be split up."

For an instant, Hanne leaned into her grip. Lilly stared into her face, daring Hanne to look back at her. But when she did it was with complete impassivity.

"I have to work now," she said quietly, pushing Lilly's hands away. "Tell them I'll send for them when I can."

Hanne brushed past her as she made her way back into the bar. She picked up a tray and started to stalk around the room. As Lilly watched, she paused beside an elderly man, produced a postcard of herself in a bathing costume, and tried to sell it to him for one mark. He wasn't interested. When he refused for a third time, she grabbed a glass of ale from his table and poured it over his head.

The Adoption Society was located in a large gray villa in Charlottenburg. It smelled of disinfectant and expensive scent, and was staffed entirely by the wives of high-ranking military men who gave of their time voluntarily. Their attitude was a curious mixture of benevolence and condescension, and they dealt out children to anyone who wanted them with little real regard for what happened to them afterward. The highlight for all concerned was organizing the annual fund-raising ball, which gave them a chance to feel saintly and dress up in the latest fashions.

Hanne's brothers wore their red hats and mittens and would not take them off. They held one another's hands and cuffs and arms, their legs and arms continually entwining. The eldest brother's eyes restlessly scanned the room when they entered. The youngest brother walked with the bowlegged walk of the child who has wet himself.

They had been told they were going on holiday to the country but only pretended to believe it. They had each been given a cardboard tag with a number written on it and instructed to sit on a wooden bench in silence until they were chosen. They did not have long to wait: boys were the first to go. There were plenty of farms in the surrounding countryside that had lost their sons to the city and needed as many hands as possible to pull turnips from the frozen winter mud or tug at the engorged udders of their dairy herds.

Two ladies from The Adoption Society wearing rubber gloves and white coats inspected Hanne's brothers for lice, fleas, and worms and then, when they were given the all-clear, gave them fresh sets of underwear and a new pair of shoes. The boys were predictably hard to separate, but the ladies from The Adoption Society had plenty of experience. Pulling hands apart and unlocking arms with sheer brute force, taking a good few blows and kicks in the process, they half dragged, half carried the boys out of the main hall and handed them over to their new guardians with a parcel containing a Bible and a loaf of black bread.

"I'll pass on your addresses and Hanne will write," Lilly had promised each one earlier. But in all the commotion, nobody had bothered to record them.

Later, Lilly stood on the stone steps with the cardboard suitcase that every orphan over the age of ten had been given. She, too, had been allocated a pair of ugly brown working shoes, a few sizes too big, which she had laced so tight the tongue creased. *Can't I take the boys?* she had begged over and over. The ladies hadn't even bothered to reply.

It had stopped snowing but the ground was icy underfoot. A woman was running across the road toward the villa, a woman in flimsy shoes and a large hat. A car hooted, the driver swore loudly, a bicycle swerved and almost hit her. As she came closer, Lilly realized that it wasn't a woman at all but a girl dressed as one. It was Hanne Schmidt: Hanne, with her ripped stockings, chewed lips, and a kohl-streaked face.

"I'm here," she called out. "I can manage. I'll take another job. I'll work days and nights. I went to St. Francis Xavier's and they told me to come here. I missed one streetcar and had to wait an hour for the next. But here I am."

Her pace slowed as she reached the entranceway and she saw Lilly's face.

"Where are they?" she asked.

Words formed in Lilly's mouth but she could not say them. She swallowed and tried again. Nothing came.

"They kept them together?"

Lilly looked away. Hanne's eyes crumpled. Her hand flew to her mouth. The hat tipped back and fell from her head. And then with a whimper she sank down to her knees and plucked something from the snow. It was a single red knitted mitten.

The Countess

Mathilde changed her name to Maisie and began to drink afternoon tea. She traded in her dachshund for a beagle and took English lessons every Sunday. Why? Because Maisie had fallen for an Englishman. Stuart Webbs, eagle-eyed detective, screen heartthrob of the day, wears a deerstalker hat and tweed plus-fours. No thief can outsmart his deductions, no crime scene can fail to offer him that vital clue. And no woman—and here's the clincher—can as yet resist his charming manners and his doleful smile.

Arrest me, arrest me, breathed Maisie in her dreams. To be handcuffed and led away, to be charged and convicted would be worth any prison sentence. She could warm up his cockles, she would turn his frigid heart red-hot. She would commit a murder to be seized and held in custard, she tells her English teacher, who, purely for his own sadistic pleasure, fails to correct her.

Walking her beagle one day, Maisie wrapped leads with a man with a dachshund. She turned and was about to keep walking when she noticed something familiar about the sausage-dog owner's face.

"Good afternoon," she cried out in English. "I am thinking I am in love with you."

Ernst Reicher stared at the pretty, rich girl with the ridiculous dog. "Pick up your mutt's poop," he said in German, "or I'll report you to the police." The very next day Maisie changed her name back to Mathilde, gave away the beagle, and took up horse riding.

Hanne Schmidt, who had arrived an hour too late on the day that the children of St. Francis Xavier's had been "reallocated," did not hang around. The light was fading in the winter sky. The rush-hour traffic was beginning to jam. She smeared her eyes with the back of her hand, replaced her hat, and then, without a word, turned and walked back the way she had come, her high heels dragging on the cobbles and her shoulders, in a coat that was too thin for the weather, hunching against the cold.

Lilly could have gone to Leipzig. There was an orphanage with a space for an older girl. And then, if she had wanted, if she had the calling, she could have eventually moved to Munich to the Order of St. Henry. Suddenly memories of Sister August, the swish of her robes on the linoleum, the clank of her keys against her hip, flooded back. Lilly shook her head.

One of the Adoption Society ladies had a sister-in-law who—and here she raised her eyebrow—needed a domestic urgently. Since Lilly was too young to start work in a factory, she had been given directions and an address and told to present herself as soon as she could.

Earlier that day, another of the Adoption Society ladies had put herself in charge of the huge mound of paperwork that remained and, in a fit of domestic zeal, decided to give it away or bin it. Her overefficiency meant that dozens of children were permanently denied the details of their genealogy. This led to untold heartache, such as an episode years later when one mother tried to stop a man she was convinced was her own son, by the likeness to her former husband and the birthmark on his arm, from marrying her daughter. Because of the lack of paperwork, her appeal failed and all her grandchildren died before they were four.

And so, just as she was about to leave, Lilly had been handed a tatty cardboard file. Her full name and date of birth had been scratched out in fountain pen on the top left corner.

"Let's have a look," said the Adoption Society lady whose sister-in-law she was being sent to.

"No," Lilly said before shoving the whole unread file into her suitcase. "It's private."

Eyebrows were raised once more and doubts registered. But there was still so much to do, the leftover children to be dealt with and reports to be written, that nothing was said.

After a ride on a tram and a short walk, Lilly arrived at a detached house in the southwest of the city. It was dark and a single lamp burned on the porch. She checked the address and then rang the brass bell. A man wearing evening dress and a top hat opened the door. Loud sobbing could be heard from behind him. He excused himself and stepped back inside, and after a few minutes the sobbing stopped.

"Thank you for waiting," he said when he returned. "Your arrival couldn't be better timed. I'm Dr. Storck. Please do come in."

Number 34 Klausestrasse was a mess. Almost every inch of floor was covered in discarded newspapers. A grand piano stood in the corner, with piles of sheet music held down on the stool by a book; a wind-up record player hiccuped on the window ledge; dead flowers languished in half a dozen vases. As they passed a room off the hallway, the doctor pulled the door shut, but not before Lilly had had time to glimpse who was inside. A woman lay facedown, completely naked, on a table. Her back was covered in glass bulbs. The doctor smiled but did not comment as he led Lilly down a set of stone steps, through the kitchen, and past the scullery.

"This is where the last girl slept," he said.

He opened the door of a room just big enough for a bed, a small wardrobe, a chest of drawers, and a sink, and switched on the light. A single barred window looked out onto a wall.

"The last girl?" she asked. "What happened to the last girl?"

"Oh, don't you worry your pretty head about her," the doctor said. "Did you bring a uniform?"

"Was I supposed to?" she asked.

He frowned and then started to open the drawers of the dresser. Eventually, from the bottom drawer, he pulled out a creased black dress and a stained white apron.

"These should fit. . . . What did you say your name was?" he asked.

"Lilly," she said.

"Anyway, Lilly," the doctor went on, "the kitchen's at the end of the hall and the servants' washroom is off the pantry. Is there anything else you need?"

However, he didn't wait for a reply.

"I'm sure you'll do just fine."

And then he left, pulling the door shut with a small but final click. Lilly put down her suitcase. So much had happened that day: leaving the orphanage for a final time, arriving at The Adoption Society's villa, the "reallocations." She lay down on the bed fully dressed and felt herself fold up inside.

Time passed. A door slammed. The telephone rang. And then, as if emerging from deep water, Lilly sat up and began to take in the room. A couple of metal coat hangers clanged together in the empty wardrobe, a pair of starched sheets bristled beneath a coarse wool blanket on the bed, three black pipes on the skirting whooshed and gurgled, and the tap on the sink dripped. At least she hadn't been sent to the factory with a printed list of boardinghouses and women's hostels in her hand. At least, she told herself, she had a place to sleep and a job, even if it was as a servant.

Finally she opened her suitcase. Apart from the box that contained the photographer's lens and the postcard of the Virgin Mary with Sister August's ghostly face glued on, there was the cardboard file. Inside was a birth certificate and a newspaper cutting. Under the title "Young Mother Slain in Love Triangle," the article reported how a former debutante had fallen, first by joining a cabaret group and being disowned by her family, second by conceiving a child out of wedlock, and finally by finding solace in the arms of a student five years her junior. And then, blow by blow, it described the fatal shot that killed her outright, the debate between her two lovers, and the second bullet that the student had fired straight into the Bavarian's temple.

The cutting was yellow and curling. The victim's and the perpetrator's photographs, which before reproduction had been of a reasonable quality, were so faded that it was almost impossible to make out the features. Lilly read the piece three times. If it were indeed evidence of her parentage, her mother's name had been Emilie Moes, her father was Baron von Richthofen. She tried out the names in her mouth several times over, as if they should have some ring in their tone that she would recognize. But there was nothing familiar about the names or the faces. And when she wept herself to sleep, it was for the other parents, the parents she had imagined and who now, it seemed, were much deader than her real parents, for they had never really existed at all.

"She's Jewish," Lilly's new employer said as soon as she saw her.

"She's from the orphanage," said the doctor. "She's not Jewish."

"She could be."

"She isn't," he replied.

"She looks it," said the woman. "Dark, big eyes, something about the color of the skin. Well?"

"I'm an orphan," Lilly said. "But I was brought up Catholic."

The woman threw back her head and gave out a shout of laughter.

"Where does my sister-in-law find them?" she said. "And how old?"

"I'm almost twelve," Lilly replied.

"Practically a child. Does she think I can't afford someone a little older? Jesus Christ!"

The woman was wearing a loosely fitting day dress made of blue silk. Although she wasn't much taller than Lilly, she took up the space of two or three people; she paced back and forth, she fidgeted, she shouted and cursed. Although her hair had been tied up in a loose bun, she had pulled at it until it fell in strands around her neck. But she did not let Lilly see her face; she kept her back to the only light in the room and kept her head turned away or covered up with her hands. Lilly glimpsed an eye, a pinch of skin, a corner of lip, but that was all.

"I pay ten marks a week," she said over her shoulder. "And tell her she can have every second Saturday off."

"Won't she need to go to Mass?" asked the doctor. "Seeing as she's Catholic?"

"She can go at Christmas . . . and tell her to stop gawking. . . . She's a gawker, isn't she, Doctor?"

"Now, Alice . . ." said the doctor. "Her name's Lilly."

"But she must always address me as Countess," the woman said. "And she can go now."

Lilly turned to go.

"And one more thing," she said. "I'll have no tittle-tattle, understand? Understand?"

" 'Judge not lest thou be judged thyself,' " Lilly replied.

The woman flinched.

"You know," she said, "I think I get sent these people deliberately. Aren't there any normal servants anymore?"

And then she laughed, a taut, atonal laugh that suggested hilarity but also desperation, depression, and insanity.

Lilly took off the uniform and carefully folded it. Her hand shook as she placed it back in the bottom drawer again and pushed it shut. Working for that woman, Lilly had decided, would be far worse than going to an orphanage in Leipzig or working in a factory. One day off a fortnight, she considered, just one day. How could she live for that one day? She couldn't stay. She wouldn't stay. She would walk out;

she would take a bus to the train station and go to Paris. And then maybe America. And when she got there, she would invent a colorful past, just as Otto had suggested. She was the daughter of a cabaret performer. Surely she must have inherited something of her.

She pulled on her gray dress again and adjusted it the best she could. As she stood in the maid's room, however, she looked down at the dress and suddenly noticed that the waist was too high and the hem was frayed.

The window rattled. Outside, it had begun to pour with icy rain. She hadn't brought an orphanage raincoat. She'd have to buy one. And then she remembered she had spent all the rose money.

Lilly had never had a successful response from God when she had asked for a sign or begged for a prayer to be answered. The dead mouse did not come back to life, Sister August had not returned, and her parents, whoever they were, had left nothing for her but a faded news clipping. Nevertheless, as the rain slashed the window and the wind shook the glass, she prayed, she prayed as hard as she could, with her eyes squeezed shut and her knees pressed together.

When she opened her eyes, it seemed at first as if nothing had changed. The rain was still falling. The wind still rattled through the cracks in the glazing. The cardboard suitcase still lay open on the bed. Inside were her old boots wrapped up in a copy of the *Berliner Morgenpost*. As she unwrapped them, however, an illustration caught her eye: a typewriter. *Learn to type,* read the caption. *Become a secretary, work in an office. Become a student at Pitman's Academy*. The price of the tuition was available on application, the class size was strictly limited, and the course had a rolling admission. And there it was. A sign.

Lilly pulled her uniform back on again. She would work for the Countess, but only until she had saved up enough money. And then she would become a student at Pitman's Academy. She would become a secretary like the women in the director of St. Francis Xavier's office. It was an easy decision. It was the only respectable occupation, other than nun, that she had ever seen a woman actually do. A bell just outside her door rang several times. Clearly she was wanted. She ran upstairs. The doctor was waiting for her in the hallway.

"Good, good. Alice needs a quiet, thoughtful maid like you," he said. "She'll try and push you away, to rile you . . . but underneath it all, Lilly, she's actually very kind."

And then he told her that the Countess wanted a cup of hot water to be left outside her room at midnight.

"But don't make a noise," he added. "Take it there quietly, leave it, and go. We don't want to aggravate . . . her condition. . . . Think of it as a game. Pretend to be invisible."

Over the next few months, Lilly came to understand that working for the Countess was indeed an exercise in invisibility. But it was hardly a game. In every room in the house apart from the attic rooms, blinds were kept pulled down, curtains drawn, and windows locked. From the outside at least, the villa looked unoccupied, closed up, as if the owners had left on some long, extended holiday. And although the Countess insisted she needed tidiness, hot drinks, and a wardrobe of laundered clothes, she refused to see or hear any evidence of it. Anything that made a noise, such as the laundry mangle, the whistle of the kettle, or the carpet sweeper, had to be muffled or operated behind as many closed doors as possible. Even the cracking of eggshells against the side of a bowl was said to be too much to bear. As for the ringing of the telephone, it nearly killed her.

"Make it stop," she would shout from her bed. "And call the operator and tell her to only put through calls if there's an emergency. A real one."

Notes started appearing attached to the laundry, fixed to the lip of a crystal glass, or in the middle of the polished floor. "Clean again! Not good enough!" "This is dirty!" The Countess complained about everything, from the sound of Lilly's footsteps to the taste of the tea. She claimed that Lilly breathed too loudly, she stepped too heavily, and she scrubbed too hard. And so Lilly took to wearing two dusters around her feet instead of shoes and crept around on tiptoe to avoid the squeakiest floorboards. As if I'm not here, she told herself as she peered through the silent murk. And eventually she did feel invisible, her body weightless and her presence just a whisper in her head. But then her reflection in a mirror would startle her and she would see what she really was, a maid with dusters on her feet and a mistress who was crazy.

The doctor came about twice a week at first, summoned from the opera, the surgery, and sometimes his bed by the Countess's phone call. And each time she would beg him for something to lift the fog from her head, for medicines, treatments, or cures, for anything that could keep the noise out. The doctor was increasingly powerless to help her. The skies above Berlin were often filled with the low, insistent hum of zeppelins. Planes whined through the clouds, trailing advertising banners. And if the wind was blowing in the right direction, you could hear the cheers that greeted military parades and staged maneuvers.

In spring Emperor Franz Josef visited Berlin again, and the streets around the center came to a standstill. He had come to talk about Serbia's rapid expansion and plans to annex Albania. On the Balkan Peninsula, Bulgaria, Montenegro, Greece, and Serbia had been at war with the Turks for several years. An armistice had been signed the previous autumn but had just expired. What Franz Josef was intending to propose was military protection so he could declare war on Serbia.

"I can't stand the noise," the Countess told the doctor when he finally arrived.

"Maybe you should go back to the country," he suggested.

"Impossible," she said. "I have nothing to go back to."

She was a real countess, Lilly was informed by the postman. She had come from the South with a huge fortune and a young daughter after her first husband had died of an infected tooth. She had brought a dozen cases of dresses and a hundred pairs of shoes, and after a summer during which she attended every party and danced with almost every minor count at court, it was clear she was on the lookout for a suitable new husband. And yet, after a couple of short relationships with eligible if dull bachelors that had been salaciously well documented by her so-called new friends, she had suddenly, inexplicably, married a penniless poet six years her junior.

Immediately after the wedding, her new friends dropped her and her original in-laws insisted their granddaughter be sent away to school. When Lilly arrived, the new husband had gone to a sanatorium at the seaside, temporarily, and hadn't returned. A lull had settled over the villa. Nobody visited except the doctor. Nobody called on the telephone except by accident. Nothing arrived in the post except bills. A monosyllabic woman called Maria came in every morning and cooked, but the household was not what was known as "staffed."

Behind the shades in a house where it was so quiet that you could almost hear the bricks shrink, Lilly spent hours silently buffing, ironing, and sweeping. The Countess's underwear was pressed and folded and her laundry sent out twice a week. The cutlery and glasses were always polished and the house was kept absolutely spotless. She gave the Countess no reason to complain. But when was her husband going to return? Where was her daughter? And what was wrong with her face?

One day Lilly discovered the daughter's room. The doctor had visited and Lilly had overheard him give the Countess a draft to make her sleep. On her way to clean the bathroom, she noticed a faint banging coming from a small room next to the Countess's bedroom. She turned the key in the lock and opened the door. As in the rest of the house, the shutters were closed and a single strip of light fell across the room. As her eyes adjusted, she saw a pale pink counterpane on the bed and a rocking horse. A row of dolls stared glassy-eyed from the mantelpiece. The window was open a couple of inches and a soft breeze rattled the pane. There was a narrow wardrobe against one wall and one of the doors swung on its hinges. Before she closed it, she looked inside; at least twenty dresses hung from padded silk hangers.

The Countess coughed in the next room. Lilly froze. But then she heard nothing more, nothing but the shiver of wind in the trees and the coo of a wood pigeon. A model theater sat on the window ledge. The stage was set up to resemble a drawing room with a grand piano and two tiny silk-upholstered armchairs. There was a switch on the side. She flicked it and one by one a series of tiny stage lights flickered on. Lilly found a line of puppets hanging from the back. She chose a princess, a king, and a queen and lowered them onto the stage. And here the baron and the cabaret artist met their long-lost daughter. Tears were shed, explanations offered, and apologies ruefully accepted.

The next evening, she noticed that her own door was ajar. On her bed lay three of the daughter's dresses in pale green silk, blue serge, and white poplin. The styles were out of date, but they were made by hand, not machine, and, as far as she could tell, unworn. Lilly tried them on. With a few little adjustments, they would fit. This is how I might have looked, she thought, in my other life.

Years later, when she thought about the newspaper clipping and how it might have changed her, she realized that the discovery of her parents' story had no immediate effect. Instead she grew into the knowledge, just as she grew into the dresses of the Countess's daughter, gradually filling out the facts, the dates, and the tragic consequences until she had absorbed the information and wore it in the carriage of her head, perhaps, or in the heavy black pools of her eyes.

"Thank you for the dresses," she said the following morning as she placed the Countess's breakfast tray on her side table.

"Just tear them up for rags if they're no good," the Countess murmured.

Lilly glanced at her face in the gloom. Maybe the Countess had noticed how hard she worked. And maybe the doctor was right: beneath the brittle surface was a hidden generosity.

"Are you feeling any better today?" Lilly asked.

But she had gone too far. The Countess simply ignored her.

Lilly had initially supposed that the job would get easier. But she was wrong. Every single morning when she woke up, the day ahead seemed so predictable, so stifling, so boring that she could hardly get out of bed. How could she stand another minute, let alone one hour, two hours, three? How could she bear to put on her uniform again and assume the shape of a shadow? How long would it take her to save enough money to be able to leave?

But the time did pass; spring came, and then summer. And every week she placed another ten marks in a white envelope, which she kept in her box beside the photographer's lens.

In the evening Lilly would curl up in bed with one of the books that lined the study and read herself to sleep. She read anything at first—Dickens, Ibsen, *Vogue*—and then she found Goethe, Heine, and Ernst Stadler again. She had studied German poetry at the orphanage. And once she had found it again, she didn't know how she had lived without it for so long. She carried a volume in her pocket to read whenever she was waiting for water to boil or an iron to heat.

On her day off, she would put on one of her new dresses and walk in the park or take a crowded train to the country. She wasn't the only one. City boys, drunk on cider and high on cheap tobacco, took off all their clothes and somersaulted into deep water from rickety jetties. City girls with dusty petticoats and Sunday hats pulled out their ribbons, kicked off their shoes, and danced barefoot on the grass. It was a summer when it was almost impossible not to feel as if you would be young and beautiful forever. The sun shone every day. The air was full of laughter and hilarity; nothing mattered, no one cared. You could do almost anything with anyone.

As Lilly sipped lemonade or gazed down at the ripples in the water of some pleasure lake or other, she thought about Hanne and wondered how she was. And sometimes she decided that she would go to her and beg her forgiveness. But judging by the way Hanne had looked at her the last time she saw her, Lilly considered it unlikely she would grant it. And so she would finish her drink, compose her face, and read German poetry. No wonder she looked so detached, so aloof, so much older than her twelve years. She did nothing to draw men to her, but they came anyway. Indeed, even without the come-hither gaze, men fell for her large gray eyes, the graceful angle of her shoulder, and her tiny alabaster hands. They broke off from their friends, offered her refreshments, and asked her to go for walks along secluded paths. And as they licked vanilla ice cream from their fingers or downed the last mouthful of sour local beer, they told her that they were in love with life, with Germany, and—although they had just met—most definitely with her.

And then, shielded by weeping willows or deep in small copses of pine, they would stop for a rest or to tie a lace, sit down, and blame the heat for their breathlessness. And without guilt, much ceremony, or procrastination, Lilly would sometimes let them slip their hand into hers or kiss her on the cheek. Although she knew it was not love or anything close, the birdsong seemed sweeter, the green buds brighter, and the sky a shade of blue much bluer than she had ever seen before.

"What's your name?" they would always ask.

"Lara," she would sometimes reply. Or Hanne, or Clara. If they asked what she did, she told them she was an heiress, a ballet dancer, or a singer. And some of them believed her.

"Can I see you again?" they would always ask at the end of the afternoon.

"It's best not," she would reply, and then she would climb aboard a train or omnibus without either an explanation or a backward glance.

That season was so beautiful and, since Lilly saw so little of it, so precious that in the years to come, she forgot the truth; she reinvented how she felt. While pairs of cabbage butterflies flittered past and tiny fish flipped in the river nearby, while the sun shone green through the lime leaves and she sat with her eyes shut, sun-soaked and adored, she remembered an intensity of feeling that had in truth never been there. And likewise, months later as they shivered in a trench, those men and boys convinced themselves that they would have given her all their worldly goods in exchange for another kiss. But in truth, if they had bumped into her a week later on a crowded corner of the Tiergarten, you could be almost certain that they would doff their hats and she would turn her cheek, and they would both carry on without the slightest sign of recognition.

So, years later, when Lilly read their names on those mossed-over memorials and wept, she did not cry just for those boys, be they German, American, or French, but for the fact that the only witnesses to her youth, the only ones who knew her as young and beautiful and pure, were gone forever. And with them part of her was gone forever too.

The papers had started talking about the possibility of a war. It was said that although royalty and heads of state from all over Europe had attended the marriage of the kaiser's daughter in May, Germany had no friends apart from Austria. It was also rumored that despite the pageants, the gala operas, the banquets and military parades, the girl would not come out of her room, so convinced was she that she would lose her brand-new husband on the battlefield.

There was no sign of the penniless poet, and Lilly had forgotten all about him until she found a photograph that had fallen behind the bookcase. In scuffed monochrome, a young man sat on a checkered blanket under a wide tree. His skin was dark and his eyes were long-lashed and so clear they seemed almost bleached. He looked like a poet; he wore a floppy necktie and a wide-sleeved Russian shirt. She had met plenty like him that summer, Russian boys on their way to America, Bavarians who talked about the special scent of the South, students who claimed they were passionate about trees. She placed the photograph back behind the bookcase again and it fell behind a pile of encyclopedias, where it wouldn't be rediscovered for twenty years.

And then, one day in late October, he appeared again. Lilly came across him sitting at the kitchen table with a glass of vodka in his hand. Since she wasn't sure if she was supposed to be invisible to him or not, she lowered her eyes, ran a damp cloth over the blackened stove, and then quietly wrung it out at the sink. She could see his reflection in the window; his thick black hair was now threaded with gray, his eyes a faded blue. He downed the last of his vodka before he spoke.

"You're new," he said. "What happened to the last girl?"

"She's gone," Lilly replied.

He paused.

"Obviously," he said. "What do they call you?"

"Lilly."

"Well, Lilly, I eat breakfast at six, so I should like you to bring some coffee and a roll to my room. I also like a morning paper, so if you could arrange that, if it's not too much trouble. . . . And I know it's inconvenient, but I like a bath every night, so if you could just leave a clean set of towels on my bed . . ."

He sighed.

"And I only drink tea from porcelain. Can you remember that?"

She turned around. What did he think she was, an idiot?

"Yes," she said. "I can remember that."

He sat back and seemed to take her in: the hateful uniform and her ugly brown shoes. But although she thought otherwise, he did not even notice what she was wearing. Instead, with the cold, acquisitive eye of a proprietor, he measured the tone of her voice, the angles of her face, the flash of her eyes. She was a white page, perfectly grained and artfully cut. And he imagined running his hands along the soft skin of her inner thighs.

"Good. What's that?" he asked. "In your pocket?"

Lilly's heart dipped. He would sack her. She had almost enough money saved, but not quite. She pulled out a book of poetry and placed it on the table. He raised his eyebrow and looked as if about to speak. Then he picked it up and opened it at random.

"You like Rilke?" he asked.

"Yes," she whispered.

He flicked back to the fly page. She knew his name was written there in violet ink.

"Was it your book?" Lilly asked. "I haven't stolen it. I found it in the library. . . . I suppose I shouldn't have taken it, but . . ."

"By all means. Read poetry . . . keep it," he said, tossing the book onto the table. "Does the job bore you?"

She turned back to the sink and started to run the cold tap. He waited for an answer.

She didn't reply. He should never have asked. Her shoulders heaved as she tried to concentrate on scrubbing the white enamel. She was suddenly aware that the penniless poet had come up behind her. She turned and he was there, too close, far too close.

"Porcelain," she said. "Porcelain cups."

"Very good," he said. "Very good indeed."

From the moment the penniless poet arrived, the house felt different. Although most of the shutters were closed and remained that way, windows were thrown wide open behind them, and the air, now edged with the chill of autumn, seemed sharper, cleaner. When it was fair, he went for morning walks or sat outside in the overgrown garden and smoked his pipe. Otherwise, he worked in his study or read in the library.

Lilly could always tell when he was at home. Apart from the smell of his tobacco, there was a change in the atmosphere, a thickening, a quickening, which was occasionally punctuated by small, sudden acts of violence: a fly was crushed, a door slammed too hard, some coffee dashed into a cup.

"I'm writing again," he would tell her if he passed her in the corridor. "I'll make you renounce your Rilke."

But when she tidied his desk every morning, all she found were white pieces of paper covered with hundreds of small stabs of the point of his fountain pen.

She wasn't exactly sure when she became aware that he spent much of the day watching her. He would come into the pantry for a glass of water while she was pressing laundry. He would stand by her while she spat onto the iron. And then he would ask her for a cuff link, a spare collar, a lost suspender. And while she looked for it, his eyes would travel from her ankle to the nape of her neck, up and down and up and down again as the iron cooled. After so many months of being invisible, she now felt dangerously exposed. He wanted to know her, her body, her face, even her mind. And although her face flushed and her hands trembled, it was as if she had just stepped from the darkness into the light.

"Here you are," she would say when she found what he had asked her for. But even though he smiled and thanked her graciously, there was always a tiny grain of disappointment in his voice.

Pig swill," the poet shouted at the cook. "This is muck. Absolute muck."

In the kitchen a dish of pork and cabbage steamed gently on the table. The cook, her chest heaving, stared at the food in between them. Her face was pink and her ears were puce.

"Your soup is like liquefied cardboard, your dumplings are as heavy as bricks, and as for your bread, it's positively prehistoric."

Lilly had come in from the garden with a bucket of coal. The poet winked at her. He was clearly enjoying himself.

"It's the cooker, sir," the cook replied. "It's electric."

"So what are you suggesting?" he replied. "We go back to using a wood-fired range?"

The cook stared defiantly at the plate on the table.

"After much thought," he continued, "and since my wife is convalescing, I have come to a decision. You're let go. Dismissed. Go on. Go. Go!"

The cook, whom Lilly had only ever heard mutter the shortest of words, pulled herself together and cursed him and his spineless wife for the rest of their fucking miserable lives before pulling her coat over her flour-dashed skirt and walking out.

Lilly and the penniless poet looked at each other. And then he started to laugh. Lilly smiled.

"Can you cook?" he asked her.

"Only porridge," she replied.

"Well, I suppose that leaves me," he said.

Lilly was sent to market. On his instructions, she bought Havel River trout with blood still in its eyes and a rainbow gilt on its scales. She chose squeaky winter cabbages and wild mushrooms fresh from the Tegeler Forest. The penniless poet came back from his morning walks with a handful of crayfish wrapped in newspaper or a chunk of meat seeping blood through its white paper wrapping. And in the afternoons, he rolled up his sleeves and chopped onions or reduced red wine; he seared fish and stewed veal and left huge vats of stock to simmer for hours. There were a few culinary disasters, for—just as the cook had suggested—the new electric cooker would either undercook or burn things, but the poet devised a system where the hot plates were always heating up or cooling down and pans could be shifted from plate to plate.

The kitchen was now always a mess. Dishes filled the sink and the stove was splattered with gravy. And so Lilly worked around him, washing and stirring and moving pans around the hob.

"Stop for a moment," he told Lilly. "And try."

She put down the dishcloth and turned to him. He was holding a spoon filled with soup.

"Go on . . ." he said. "I need a second opinion."

She was aware of his eyes on her lips, but he did not raise the spoon and she did not reach for it. There was a fraction of a second when neither of them moved. A bell rang. The Countess wanted her. He blew on the soup to cool it and then fed it to her as if to an ailing child.

"Well?" he asked.

"It's fine . . . except . . ."

"Except?" he asked.

"It needs a little salt," she said as she hurried toward the stairs.

He frowned and then threw a large pinch of sea salt into the boiling vat.

"Good girl," he said.

The poet, whose pen name was Marek Klein, had been taught to cook by his mother. She had made herself learn when her family had lost its fortune in the depression of 1870. When her husband, and the father of her son, left her within a week of this misfortune, she had been forced to find employment and took a position as a housekeeper to a reclusive prince with a small castle in the Black Forest. And so Marek had grown up in a castle, which he would never inherit, with a mother who taught him how to cook and how to suffer. No wonder he had become a poet.

Marek Klein had written his best poetry in his teens, when he was full of giddy anticipation and unfulfilled longing. He had a letter from Rainer Rilke stating that in his opinion the young poet could be "on the brink of greatness." He may have been on the brink, but he never exactly took the plunge. His poetry became less great over the years, and by the time Lilly met him in the Countess's kitchen he had written just one mediocre piece after spending twelve months alone in a hotel on the Baltic coast.

Of course, his failure was never his fault. At the slightest prompt, he would launch into a tirade against publishers and editors, journalists, and other, more successful writers whose status had been attained by nepotism, usually, and good fortune, occasionally. He rarely submitted any of his poems anywhere anymore, suggesting that they were too sophisticated for the readers of the day, and claiming himself to be invested with a special gift, a gift that had to be nurtured, pampered, and protected at all costs from the twin blades of indifference and rejection.

The only thing he really knew with any certainty that he was good at, apart from poetry, was seduction. Like many young men of his generation, the poet had learned his seduction techniques from Tolstoy's Vronsky. Alice, the widow of a man twenty years her senior whose addiction to Turkish delight had been the end of him, was fair game. After jumping from the stone balcony of a villa in Wilmersdorf to escape a dull party and persuading her to follow him, Marek had taken her for breakfast in a cheap café. And then over coffee and peasant bread, he had talked and she had listened. He looked down on both the bourgeoisie and the working classes. He laughed at the military and the kaiser and their ridiculous pomp. He was drawn to the free-spirited, to the unconventional, to the nonmaterialistic, to the beautiful people. None of the opinions he expressed, except the latter, came from his own head. He had read Nietzsche, Kierkegaard, and Marx, and he quoted them inaccurately and without credit.

And as he talked, his hands began to wander, first a light touch on the arm, then a nudge on the shoulder, and eventually a lingering caress on the leg. Their breath had quickened, their eyes had brightened, and they had left the café and taken a taxi to a cheap hotel. He had signed them in with a flourish while she paid, in cash, in advance.

It was sex that had been the deciding factor in his wooing of the Countess, sex that had oiled the wheels of her rusted-up heart, and sex that had made her feel adored, desired, and liberated. No wonder she fell in love and married him within the month. And yet the euphoria did not last; the emotion was not reciprocated. In the first few weeks after their nuptials his kisses became infrequent, his touch became a grip, his gaze lost all suggestion of tenderness. When he ordered her to strip and stand beside him in front of the bedroom mirror, it was not at her naked image that he gazed but at his own still fully dressed self. And later, when, still wearing shoes, he turned her this way and that way, backward and forward, up and down, it occurred to her that the dexterity of his sexual routine was not one that aimed to possess her in every way, as she first supposed, but more likely an act born out of multiple copulations with multiple partners.

In fact, he was a man who, when lying on his deathbed in a small musky apartment in the Fourteenth Arrondissement of Paris, France, finally realized that his gift had been his undoing. While succumbing to natural causes at the age of ninety-two, he had one of those flashes of clarity the dying are said to experience. And as he struggled to take his last few breaths, he wondered: If he had loved anyone else as fiercely, as passionately, as he had loved himself, would he have ended up alone, uncared for, and posthumously unmissed?

He had married the Countess because he believed that life as a poet would be easier if he were rich. It wasn't. In his cold-headed plan, he failed to predict the spite his act would provoke when the Countess became postnuptially depressed. He also failed to predict how he would feel when he discovered his new wife's health problems were all-consuming and taken far more seriously than his own occasional low-level hypochondria.

"I need to talk to you," he whispered to Dr. Storck. "My head feels stuffy and sometimes I feel as if I'm suffocating."

The doctor, his eyebrow arched, suggested peppermint oil.

He had not come down with any new symptoms, however, since he had arrived back from the Baltic Coast. He had a new sickness, he wrote down in his journal, a malady called maid fever.

One day, the Countess was resting and Lilly was spring cleaning, running up and down the stairs with polishing cloths and firewood. The poet was hovering on the stairs examining a picture, and he would have to move up or down, depending, every time she passed.

"You have a smudge on your cheek," he said.

She rubbed her face with the back of her hand.

"No, there . . ." he said.

She tried again.

"Let me show you," he said.

And before she could stop him, he had licked his thumb.

"Got it," he said. "Soot, I think."

She averted her eyes. In the kitchen, the kettle began to whistle.

"Would you like your tea in the drawing room . . . sir?"

He drew back.

"Yes," he said. "That would be fine . . . Lilly."

His voice cracked a little when he said her name. It sounded like a confession, like a secret. And although she knew that it meant nothing, that it had to mean nothing, he met her gaze and held it until she looked away.

A Poet's Soul

Her name spelled out in yellow bulbs on the façade of the Zoo Palast, her photograph lit up against the darkening westerly skies, her face two stories high on the silver screen. Germany's favorite star, a blaze of filaments sparking in the dark blue Berlin night.

It doesn't matter about plot or story or genre. Nobody cares who wrote the script or who told the actors where to stand. The whole world is in love with Henny Porten (and Asta Nielsen and Meg Gehrts) because whatever part she plays—the wife, the lover, the daughter, the queen—she will always be recognizably, unmistakably her.

In the theater and films from not so long ago, there were no actors, only players; no photographs, only programs. But from America came Motion Picture Story *and* Photoplay, *magazines filled with star portraits and plot synopses, photo opportunities and rated reviews. Here, in feature interviews, exotic pasts and intricate love lives are fabricated for the daughters of tailors or shopkeepers or farmers. Everyone knows it's all hearsay, gossip, fantasy, made up by publicists, but everyone carries the magazines in pockets and pastes the pictures to walls anyway.*

And now Germany's stars and their public are on first-name terms: Asta at home, Meg on set, Henny on holiday. But still nothing will ever match a big-screen audience: the darkened cinema a willing foil to the star's singular light.

The Blue Cat had changed. The door was wedged wide open and the old drapes had been replaced by red velvet swags. Lilly noticed that Hanne's postcard had been pasted in a brand-new glass-fronted sign along with three other female "artists." A new photograph had been taken in which she gazed moodily over a chair. Despite the beer-pouring incident, Hanne had been kept on. The client had been mollified with a bottle of sparkling wine and Hanne had handed him a letter of apology written by the Bulgarian.

Since she had lost her brothers, Hanne's career had taken an unexpectedly upward curve. She was increasingly petulant, undeniably tetchy, and openly hostile to her audience. But the more contempt she threw at them, the more the men began to adore her. Every time she sang, pulled postcards of herself from her stocking tops, or placed tall glasses of beer in front of her clients, it was as if it were for the very last time. And if they didn't do as she suggested and buy her a drink, give her a tip, or purchase a postcard, they were punished. Once or twice, in front of packed houses, she poured beer over a customer's head again, but now it was met by thunderous applause.

"The worse you treat them, the more they admire you," the Bulgarian used to say with a shrug. And in her case, at least, it was true.

Maybe her popularity was because she appeared on the verge of walking out forever. In fact, she believed it was only a matter of time. She had been spending the afternoons with a film producer in a small hotel that rented rooms by the hour. He was a man who wore spats, his hat tilted at an angle, and a Rolex watch. He was married, of course, and hadn't promised her anything except work as an extra in his next project. But he could be persuaded, cajoled, she was convinced of it. In the meantime, she blew her tips on fancy frocks and face cream from Paris and managed to ignore all but the most irresistible advances.

Hanne stared at her former friend from the orphanage in her dressing room mirror, but this time she didn't comment on her clothes. Lilly had been almost erased from her mind. Only when she was drunk, when she had been dumped, or when she was broke did she give in to memories of St. Francis Xavier's, the roses, her brothers, and her former friend. The feeling would pass, however, she would sober up and vow not to think about them again. But now that Lilly was here, she realized that she had missed her much more than she had allowed herself to believe. She blotted her lips on a rag before she spoke.

"How have you been?" she asked.

"Fine," Lilly replied. "I'm . . . I'm a . . ."

Lilly drew a breath and let it out again slowly. She tried to start again but the words didn't seem to want to come out. She stared at the gaslight fittings, as if they held the clue to her sudden arrival. She wished she hadn't come. She glanced at herself in the mirror. She barely recognized herself anymore. Her mouth was raw. Her face was puffy and her eyelids were red. Hanne turned in her seat and finally faced her.

"You're . . . ?" asked Hanne.

Lilly looked her in the eye at last. And her former friend's face softened as if the mask she wore had now fallen away.

"I need to see a lady," Lilly whispered.

Marek, the penniless poet, may have been destined for great things but never made it past relative obscurity. Only two poems from this period ever made it into print, in a short-lived monthly journal called *Spunk!* Both were musings on the fickle nature of love.

When the previous housemaid fell pregnant and pointed the finger of blame at her supposedly impotent husband, the Countess was devastated. But he gave as good as he got. She later admitted that it could have been her fault; she shouldn't have been standing in the way when he hurled the crystal vase, a present from her first mother-in-law, at the wall. And what is more, she should have gotten rid of the aesthetically offensive vase before he had picked it up in the first place.

The doctor stopped the bleeding but he could not prevent the scarring. Marek wept but the Countess could not. Instead she sat in the doctor's office, watched a train shoot past, and thought about throwing herself in front of it.

So when her husband returned with a huge hotel bill and one paltry poem, she did not greet him with the warmth of a wife's embrace. And when he sacked the cook and it was clear he was paying a little too much attention to the new maid, the Countess hired another cook, a lively mother of five who had an adequate mastery of electrical appliances, and ordered her husband out of the kitchen.

One evening in spring Lilly found a package with her name on it lying on the kitchen table. It was from Marek. Inside was a journal with thick blank pages and a fountain pen filled with India ink. She sat down and on the first page she wrote her name.

"Lilly Nelly Aphrodite," the penniless poet read out over her shoulder. He had come into the kitchen so quietly she hadn't heard him.

"Someone must have had high hopes for you," he said.

As she sat and he stood behind her, the ink started to drip from her pen onto the paper. Very slowly, he laid his hand on the crown of her head and stroked softly, so softly, down to the nape of her neck.

"Lilly," he said. "Nelly . . ."

She shivered.

"Aphrodite . . . a gift for my muse."

Lilly stood up very suddenly. She turned and faced him. Ink was still falling in drops as big as apple pips and splashed onto the kitchen floor.

"Well, good night," he said. And with a bow of his head he left the room.

The next day he strolled by as if nothing had happened. Maybe she had been mistaken. Maybe nothing had happened. How could it? She was a housemaid. He was the Countess's husband. And her face blushed as she scrubbed the table with baking soda and her eyes stung with salt. That night she looked at herself closely in the small speckled mirror above the sink in her room. In the twilight she pulled her hair loose from the band she used to tie it back, she ran her finger along the curve of her cheekbone, and she tried to see herself as Marek might see her. Could he desire her? Could he want her? Could he be in love with her? She was thirteen. He was in his thirties. A bell rang. The Countess was calling her, but she still never used her name; she never called her anything but "girl" or "you" or "she." And as Lilly quickly tied her hair back and became a maid with no name again, she insisted to herself that on all counts she was bound to be wrong.

After all those years at the orphanage surrounded by other children, the silence of nothing but her own thoughts was almost too loud to bear. And so when her name came echoing through the lower floor of the villa, long and low, no wonder it made her feel like someone again, someone who was worth something.

"Lilly," the poet sang one day. "I've brought you a peach."

He placed it on the window ledge behind the sink and for a moment they both looked at it.

"I want to watch you eat it," he whispered.

She wiped her hands on her apron as he sliced it into four pieces with a pocketknife. Inside, the flesh was heavy with juice.

"Go on," he said.

She picked up a piece. She raised it to her mouth. He was so close she could smell him: cotton dried in sunshine, lavender soap, and the sweet sourness of his sweat. She raised her eyes to his. He looked from her eyes to her mouth to the peach and back. A hot rush coursed through her.

"I can't," she said.

"Why not?" he said.

"I'm not hungry," she replied.

She looked away. He took her chin in his hand and turned her face around.

"Liar," he said.

She ate the peach. She sucked all the juice from it, and then tore the flesh from the skin with her teeth and swallowed it.

"There," she said, wiping her mouth on her sleeve.

"Well?" he said. "How was it? What did it taste like?"

Lilly turned back to the dishes piled in tepid water in the sink.

"Like a peach," she replied.

"Like a peach that was waiting for this very moment, this very second and not before, to be eaten," he added.

She could feel the heat of his breath on her neck. How could he say such a thing? She blushed with equal amounts of anticipation and shame.

"Lilly Nelly Aphrodite," he said below his breath. And then he strolled out of the kitchen, whistling.

The Countess's daughter was coming home from school for the summer, and for the first time ever, the Countess began to get up at eight in the morning and go to bed at nine at night. She opened all the windows, and the curtains tailed out in the breeze. She left instructions for Lilly to buy flowers and order sugared almonds and English tea. A portrait of a little girl in a white dress with a sailor collar was placed on the mantelpiece.

On the day of the daughter's arrival, the clock seemed louder and the minutes felt longer. At five o'clock her train would arrive at Anhalt Station. As an afterthought, the Countess placed her husband's publications on the table in the center of the dining room.

At exactly ten past two, the telephone rang. The poet answered it.

Lilly heard the tone of his voice shift. The Countess's former mother-in-law had decided it was preferable for her granddaughter to spend the summer in the country, given the unstable political climate in the city. She urged the poet to persuade her former daughter-in-law not to call her back; they were going out for a picnic.

The Countess tried to stab the poet with the letter knife. She missed his heart but hit him in the hand. The telephone was ripped from the wall and ended up in the garden. The poet's publications disappeared forever. The doctor, summoned by taxi, arrived at three and stayed until six. The cook had prepared a three-course dinner. It was all thrown away.

That night the poet came to Lilly's room. She opened her eyes in the darkness and there he was above her, his right hand bandaged and his face scratched. She had no idea how long he had been there.

"I'm sorry," he said. "I was looking for the water closet."

She sat up.

"I don't think you should be in here," she said.

For a moment neither spoke.

"She doesn't love me, you know. She doesn't understand me. Not like you do."

"But you don't even know me," she whispered.

Lilly could feel her face burn. Her heart beat so violently in her chest that she feared it was visible. And yet she felt paralyzed as she sat there in her white nightgown, her hair unbraided and her legs bare beneath the covers.

"But I'd like to. Should I go now?" he asked softly.

She nodded. He let out a short snort of laughter.

"Let me," he said.

But it was a statement and not a question.

It was true that she had imagined his kiss on her lips. It was also true that she had imagined the taste of his dark skin and the salt of his sweat. She had even imagined the caress of his hand on her breast. But she had never imagined this. He held both wrists above her head and launched himself upon her. His sudden weight was such that she couldn't breathe. He reached below and ripped the cotton of her nightgown; his knee wedged her legs apart. And then the bluntness of him forced its way into her resistance. She cried out but he muffled her mouth with his palm. And then he started to push; he pushed until she was sure she would split. Lilly closed her eyes and willed it to be over. And soon it was, with a groan and a hot wetness between her legs.

The blood on the sheets came out. She stood shivering at the sink as the tap water turned from red to clear. It wasn't me, she told herself again and again. I wasn't there. And as she washed all traces from her body with a damp cloth, she half believed it. In the middle of the night, when sleep still wouldn't come, however, she listened to the dark. Even though he was two floors above, she could hear the ratchet of his snore. And she started to shake and could not stop.

The next morning Lilly found the Countess slumped over her bed fully clothed. On the wooden floor below the bed was an empty medicine bottle lying in a pool of sticky dark liquid. For a few seconds Lilly simply stared. A shaft of morning sunshine illuminated the Countess's body. Even from the doorway, Lilly could see the jagged scar, the scar that ran from her left eye to the corner of her mouth. The pull of the pillow below her face dragged her lips into a tiny ironic smile. One slipper had fallen off to reveal a pale foot with long, evenly spaced toes.

And then Lilly noticed a shallow movement, the twitch of an eye: the Countess was still breathing. She hauled the Countess upright and slapped her face. The cheek was white and clammy. She slapped again. A small pink rose appeared.

"Wake up!" she shouted.

The Countess opened her eyes but did not focus. Her head lolled. Lilly rubbed her hands, her arms, her legs, and then, when there was no response, she shook her shoulders.

"Leave me," the Countess whispered through cracked lips. "I want to die."

She tried to lie down but two arms prevented her. She looked up into her maid's eyes and instantly registered that she would not be able to swoon into oblivion as she had hoped.

"You can't just give up," said Lilly.

Maybe the girl was right. Maybe she wasn't so sure she wanted to die anymore after all.

"Call Dr. Storck," the Countess whispered.

The doctor came immediately. The Countess did not die. The penniless poet went to the casino and spent two hundred marks.

You can't just give up. The bruises on Lilly's wrists gradually faded. The insomnia continued and never entirely went away. The poet left early every morning and came back after midnight. The house was filled with doctors, specialists and psychiatrists, healers, and even a couple of priests. There was talk of the Countess going to the country, to recuperate in a spa, but she refused. Then Dr. Storck was back again and one by one he drew the curtains.

It was weeks later when the poet sought her out again. This time he was brandishing a new anthology of poetry as if nothing had happened.

"Read it! You will agree that it is absolute drivel," he said. "Because you, my Lilly Nelly Aphrodite, have a poet's soul."

And with that he reached out and, with one hand on her waist, pulled her close to him, so close that she almost stumbled, so close that the smell of the cologne he had splashed on his face that morning was overpowering. He swallowed and then he ran his finger along the line of her cheek. His mouth was only an inch or two from her throat. His body was hard and hot as it pressed into hers. And then he caught sight of her face.

"Anyway," he said, letting her go. "Come and find me when you've finished it."

She knew he was sitting in the summerhouse at the end of the garden, smoking a cigarette. She could smell his tobacco; she could see a single pinprick of burning red. It was early summer, and although it was late and the sky was dashed with the black skitter of bats, the air was luminous. The Countess was drugged and resting. Dinner had been served and cleared. No visitors were expected.

The summerhouse was open on all sides but raised from the ground by three wooden steps. She took them one by one until she stood on the edge of the top step, directly opposite him. He did not appear to see her at first. He was reading an article about a new wine restaurant in Leipzig. She coughed and he looked up. A single newspaper page fell to the floor, where it rustled and flapped in the breeze. The poet leaned back, completely placid, the glow of his cigarette flaring up and dying down as he inhaled long and slow.

"I need to talk to you," she said.

"Don't move," he replied.

And then she noticed that beside him was a large black object on three long legs. It was a moving-picture camera, a Leica, a gift for himself after the paper-knife incident.

The film he took of his wife's maid was hugely underexposed; he had no idea about shutter speeds or flashbulbs. Against the darkening sky and the even blacker density of the summerhouse, a faint silver hourglass with a face on top shivers in the dusk. It takes a moment or two to work out that the shape is in fact a girl, a girl with long dark hair, which seems to vibrate around her head like static. And then your eye is drawn to her face; her lips are black, her eyes two black holes pinpricked with white. Despite the poor quality of the photography, Lilly looks unearthly, like a vision or a spirit summoned up from the night.

And when the poet watched it several months later, before almost destroying it in a projector that had not been set up correctly, he wondered quite seriously if he had been mistaken about his vocation. He persuaded several more girls to pose for him, but nothing he ever made again came close to the one-minute-and-twelve-second moving picture *Lilly in the Summerhouse, May 1914.*

The evening air was chilly. She could stand it no more. She turned her back to his camera.

"Enough," she said.

He stopped cranking and stabbed out another cigarette in a geranium pot. And then he started unscrewing the legs of the tripod. She took a step forward.

"Marek," she said.

He glanced up and could not hide the slight displeasure he felt when he heard her say his first name.

"What is it now?" he snapped.

"You shouldn't have done what you did," she said. "I'm in trouble."

The penniless poet sighed with irritation, as if she had just told him she had smashed a window accidentally or broken a dish.

"How inconvenient for you," he said, and continued to unscrew the tripod.

Lilly waited for him to go on. He didn't. And as the seconds passed, she realized that he would do nothing, admit nothing, contribute nothing.

"Shouldn't you be working?" he said eventually. "That is, after all, what you are paid to do."

As the bullets were poured and metal helmets forged, as rifles were oiled and the Schlieffen Plan presented to the kaiser, Lilly developed an insatiable appetite. And that was where the poet would sometimes accidentally stumble upon her, in the kitchen with her finger in the cake batter or dipped in newly poured jars of jam. He was formal with her now. He did not seek her out or ask her opinion on his poetry anymore.

"My tea was a little cold this morning," he would say. "Could you make sure the water has actually boiled next time?"

And she would nod, because her voice would only betray her. When he was gone, her tears would roll into the sponge mixture and it would spoil.

Es ist nichts, she would tell herself. It is nothing.

"It is nothing," Archduke Franz Ferdinand repeated as he lay bleeding to death beside his pregnant wife on the floor of his carriage in the middle of Sarajevo in June. But of course, on both counts, it was not nothing.

Lilly and Hanne met outside The Blue Cat on her next day off. In Lilly's pocket was an envelope heavy with notes, and the word *Pitman's* written on the front.

"I have two hundred marks," she said. "Will that be enough?"

"Should be," said Hanne.

They took a tram and Hanne pulled the chain when they turned into Dragonstrasse. When she recognized where she was, however, Lilly hesitated.

"I'm not sure if I can get off here."

"You have to. Unless you want to fly there. Come on."

Hanne took Lilly's arm and pulled her down the stairs. They paused at Otto's block.

"Come on," Hanne said, and pushed open the heavy wooden door.

"Wait a minute," said Lilly. "You know the lady, right?"

"I know her," said Hanne.

"What's her name, then?"

"Frau . . . Lindt . . . no, Lundt . . ."

"Licht?"

"That's it," said Hanne. "Frau Licht."

Lilly sank down to the stone step. She covered her mouth. She felt as if she were about to vomit.

"I can't," she said.

"You have to," Hanne said. "You're here now. Besides, it's nothing special. I know a girl who's had three in the last year."

Hanne had already had one abortion, the product of a short-lived but frantic relationship with the Bulgarian. Frau Licht gave her plum brandy to quell the pain, and she was so sick the next day that the whole episode took on the hallucinatory feel of a bad dream.

"It'll hurt and then it'll be over," said Hanne. "And then you'll be back to normal again. Go on. I'll wait for you outside."

Otto was a little surprised to find Tiny Lil at his door. He had just blown an entire week's pay packet on an American who missed her train and let him pay for her hotel in return for nothing more than a peck on her cool Bostonian cheek. And now he was waiting for Frau Licht to ask if he could pay double next week. He had some news that might back up his case. He was about to enlist in the military again, this time voluntarily. The kaiser was gathering his troops. Everyone said that the war, when it came, would last no more than six weeks. And as wave after wave of heavily armed soldiers marched through Berlin, the air was full of hope. It was common knowledge that the German naval fleet, financed partly by a tax on Champagne, was one of the best in the world. The army was well equipped with the most modern in combat machinery. Otto wanted to be part of it, to be issued a brand-new gray uniform and sent to a training camp on the Rhine. He was also going to hand her his notice.

They sat in the parlor and he poured Tiny Lil coffee. It was true he had meant to go back and see her at the orphanage, and several times he had found himself strolling in that direction. But something had always distracted him—a pretty girl, a bar he had not noticed before, a rainstorm—and he had put it off. And now, she told him, it had closed anyway. Tiny Lil was more sober, more somber, than he remembered. She explained that she had a job as a servant. He expected more. She didn't continue.

"So, you want to go out dancing?" he asked.

Lilly finally caught his eye.

"Not dancing in a bar but in the Tiergarten," he continued. "You can dance beneath the stars on a Saturday all night."

She swallowed and looked away. In the pale sunlight, her skin was translucent and her eyes were the color of granite. He took her hand and kissed it. And then he wanted to kiss her face, her cheek, her lips again.

"I've missed you," he said, aware that it was not completely untrue.

For an instant Lilly glimpsed another future, one with Otto. But just as quickly as it appeared, it suddenly vanished. The front door slammed. Otto pulled back just as his landlady walked in.

"Your friend said you were here," she said. "You'd better come through."

Otto looked from Lilly to Frau Licht. He knew what his landlady did, even though he pretended he didn't. He had never seen any of the women. But he had heard them.

Lilly felt her shoulders descend despite herself. Otto seemed to shrink back a step. And so she made herself look up at him; she made him look back at her.

"The Tiergarten?" she said.

"The Tiergarten," he replied. And then, with a closed smile, he shook her hand.

Olivia Licht performed her procedures in a small bathroom just off her bedroom. A narrow table was covered with newspaper. A white coat hung on the peg behind the door. The bottle of plum brandy stood beside a toothbrush and some tooth-whitening powder. She sprayed the air with eau de cologne and handed Lilly a stained cotton gown.

"How much?" asked Lilly.

"Three hundred," she replied.

"Will you take two?"

"If that's all you have," she replied.

Frau Licht knew she was an inexpert practitioner. She had already been indirectly responsible for three deaths due to infection, but as the girls were always desperate and her success rate was around sixty percent, a steady stream of women traipsed up Dragonstrasse for so-called emergency procedures. She did wonder if it was her young lodger's progeny that she went fishing for in Lilly's womb with her Viennese contraption. But the fetus slipped away from her grasp, just as Otto had, for he had stopped sleeping with her several months before. She charged the girl anyway; if the baby survived, she could always claim it had been twins.

In fact, Lilly lost the baby in the third month. She started bleeding long before it started to hurt. And then, as cloth after cloth became sodden with blood and the cramps began, she realized that she had wasted her money.

The cook found her curled up in a corner in the kitchen and called the doctor immediately. To his credit, Dr. Storck canceled a whole afternoon's worth of appointments to look after her. And while the Countess lay on her bed inhaling a new treatment, oil of bergamot, the doctor administered morphine by the spoonful and cooled Lilly's brow with his handkerchief dipped in ice-cold water. He did not let her see the bloody bundle he wrapped in newspaper for him to take away. She did not know that he gave the fetus to the faculty of medicine at his old university, where it was preserved in a jar and placed on a shelf in the anatomy department of what is now known as Humboldt University.

A week later, a note appeared on the dining room table: *Please clean my room.*

Lilly took a duster and a bucket of warm water and slowly made her way up the stairs to the Countess's room. Windows faced north and south. You could see as far as Viktoriapark in one direction and Museum Island in the other.

"I cannot divorce him," a voice said. Lilly jumped and swung round. She had thought the Countess was downstairs, in the drawing room. Instead she was sitting in the shadows. Only the line of her jaw was visible. Lilly was filled with apprehension. How much did she know? What had the poet told her?

"Because, like you, I am a Catholic."

Her voice was low pitched and steady. All the life in her hands was gone.

"He has asked me to sack you," she continued. "But you work hard. You are quiet, you do not gossip. But other people will."

She sighed and swallowed.

"I'm sorry, Lilly," she said. "Would you like me to write you a reference?"

War was announced in July. The kaiser decided to take Paris by force. In August, after marching through Belgium with no opposition, the German army reached Reims. Three men in an open-topped car, one bearing a white flag, another his grandfather's saber, and a third, who was an opera singer, a bugle, crossed enemy lines to ask the city to surrender. There had been some argument that it should have in fact been a trumpet, but the opera singer insisted that it was almost the same thing. A ritual is a ritual, insisted the captain with the white flag. In the end, however, when no trumpet could be procured, they agreed to compromise. And so, with the saber waving, the bugle gleaming, and the white flag fluttering in the baking sun, they drove toward the city.

The peace envoy had barely made it into the town square, however, when they were all arrested and charged with espionage. Spies with white flags and bugles, the Germans probably pointed out, spies who could sing all the tenor parts from Puccini's *Tosca*. Maybe the opera singer even gave a rendition to prove it. Maybe the soldier with the saber, in stuttering French, told the gendarmes that his grandfather had used the saber against the Danish. Maybe the authorities in Reims believed them but locked them all up anyway. But what happened there was immaterial. Outside the city, both armies had fortified their positions and had started to dig a system of trenches. The Battle of the Marne had begun.

The three Germans were imprisoned for several weeks. And then a halt was called to firing and they were brought to the front line and pushed over the brink of a French trench. Tentatively they made their way across what would soon be known as no-man's-land, with their polished boots and their shining buttons, the unsounded bugle and the rolled-up white flag, splattered and soiled by the freshly churned-up mud.

Lilly saw Otto once more that year, on a temporary ice rink in an empty lot in late 1914. He was wearing a uniform and holding the hands of a girl with red hair and a purple muffler. As Lilly watched, Otto turned and started pulling the girl round and round the rink. And the more the girl screamed and told him to stop, the faster he skated. And then, digging the blades of his skates into the ice, he came to a skidding stop and the girl, with skates parallel and cheeks aflush, flew straight into his open arms.

He was dead by Christmas. His boots were stolen from his body by a boy from Silesia who deserted and walked all the way home, only to be shot by his own father.

Große Ereignisse werfen ihre Schatten voraus!

Thunder Clouds

Kreuzberg. The Palace Movie Theater. November 1914. The frontiers are closed. All foreign films are banned. No more Westerns, no more Charlie Chaplin or Tontolini. Just German films. The newsreel has started when Greta and her mother take their seats. On screen, the soldier holding the gun somewhere in France is young and blond. He bangs the door of a whitewashed barn with his fist. Five French soldiers come out of the barn with their hands upon their heads.

And yet, and yet, the third French soldier looks familiar. "It's Philip," Greta whispers. "Don't you see?" Despite the uniform and the hands across the face, it's him, her brother. "Why would he agree to do such a thing?"

Why did he walk down that lane in France, ten miles at least from the entrenchment known as the Front. Why? Because there was no mud, no blood, no gangrene or other bodily fluids, no death, no pain, no fear. Just uniforms taken from French corpses buttoned over stomachs still digesting the extra bratwurst each of them received in payment.

Greta's tear-filled eyes hold on to the roll of her brother's shoulder, the stamp of his feet in polished boots, the back of his head clasped with those still-familiar hands, while the people in the audience almost cheer the roof off.

"We're winning the war," they shout. "Our boys'll be home before you know it."

Greta and her mother both leave before the feature.

Years later, Lidi's abrupt and unexpected exits were legendary. It was said that she could be halfway through a film or a dinner or a conversation, with a glass in one hand and a fork in the other, when she would suddenly hand them over to the nearest person and make for the door. And she would quite often leave without her coat.

But in the early days of the Great War, after being sacked for alleged infidelities with her employer's husband, Lidi's exit was anything but glamorous. She packed her cardboard suitcase, folded the maid's uniform, placed it back in the bottom drawer where she had found it, and put on the Countess's daughter's blue dress. And then she left all the books that the penniless poet had given her, except one, on the bedside table, opened the window with its view of a wall, and pulled the door to for the final time.

Lilly, as she was known then, walked away from the villa where she had worked for so many months and did not look back. If she had, she might have noticed that from the outside the house seemed so still, so rigid that it was almost as if it had been sent to sleep forever. It did, in fact, stand virtually unchanged until 1945, when it was blown to bits by Russian shells.

It was a hot, windless late-August day. In gardens full of blossom, women in pale dresses poured lemonade from tall glass jugs. The soft clink of croquet balls and the occasional whoop of drunken young men drifted from the far reaches of smooth grass lawns. An open-topped omnibus motored past, the top deck full of couples with picnic baskets and straw hats. A horse and cart from the country clopped along behind it, laden with baskets of strawberries. A distant church bell struck two.

The doctor noticed the maid as he passed in a horse-drawn cab, but he did not stop. Earlier that day, he had spotted the kaiser's motorcar racing through the streets to another meeting at the Reichstag. The German army had defeated the French on the Western Front. The whole city was full of flags. Dr. Storck's excitement was such that he, too, would also enlist only a few months later. His role as a physician to a small group of wealthy ladies, however, did nothing to prepare him for the field hospital in Poland on the Eastern Front where he was posted in January 1915. Faced with small wounds oozing with gangrene that would rapidly kill otherwise healthy men, daily amputations, and a never-ending stream of horrific and usually fatal injuries, the doctor sometimes sat down, wept copiously, and had to be coaxed back to work by one of the nurses with hot tea laced with Polish vodka.

On that hot summer day, however, when the whole country seemed to be on holiday as people sauntered and strolled and even promenaded, Lilly walked at a pace that suggested she was going somewhere, that she was even a little late. As she walked she tried to clear her head, she tried to work out what she would do and where she would go. First she would have to find a room in a boardinghouse. But that wouldn't be easy: the rental barracks, as they were known, were overcrowded with workers from eastern Prussia. And then she would have to find another job. She was old enough to find work in a factory. Now that so many men had enlisted, it was rumored that they had started to employ more women. But why even do that? I am free, she told herself. I can go anywhere, do anything, and be anyone. I have no past, only a future.

And then the idea occurred to her that she ought to try to find some of her relatives. And yet they had never tried to seek her out. They must have known she existed. They must have seen the newspaper article. The road surface changed beneath her feet from cobbles to twin tracks of dust. The houses were built farther apart here, and saplings had been planted in long lines along what would be the curb.

The smell of rye drifted in from the fields where migrant Russians and Poles were bringing in the harvest. Lilly realized that she had been inadvertently walking away from the city instead of toward it.

On a corner was a signpost. She was heading in the direction of Potsdam. On the horizon, anvils of gray cloud were looming up and rolling closer. The air was filled with electricity. The sun was too hot. Her shoes were too small. The suitcase was too heavy. And so there, just level with the signpost, as a pair of magpies flitted from fence to hedgerow and back again, she stopped. An image of Marek in the summerhouse came into her mind before she could prevent it. He had fooled her; she was indeed worthless, disposable. There was grit in her eyes, her mouth, her throat. No wonder she didn't hear the car approaching.

The Daimler convertible slammed on its brakes, its tires bit into the dust, but it did not stop in time. Lilly didn't even raise her arms as a wall of polished chrome and painted metal came skidding toward her. It hit her so hard that she flew up into the air and over the hood before coming to land, hard, on the rough surface of the soon-to-be suburban road.

When she opened her eyes, she was momentarily surprised that she was still alive. And then she noticed that she had lost her shoes. Her dress was torn and both stockings were shredded at the knee. The contents of her suitcase were strewn along the road. A drop of blood fell from her temple and landed on her hand. She sat up. Nothing seemed to be broken.

"My dear girl," a woman's voice said. "I didn't see you."

"You should have been looking where you were going, Eva," a man's voice scolded. "She could have been killed. Are you all right?"

A couple had climbed out of the car. Both were wearing driving goggles.

"Can you walk?" the woman asked Lilly.

"Of course she can't walk," the man interrupted.

He turned to her and held out his hand.

"I knew I should never have let my sister drive a car. I'm so sorry. Are you hurt?"

"I don't think so," Lilly replied.

But they didn't seem to be listening. Still arguing, they placed their hands under her arms and gently hoisted her up. The heat of the road burned her feet through her thin cotton stockings. Her head was spinning.

"I think I need to . . ." Lilly said.

"Sit down," the woman ordered.

Lilly sank onto the wide wooden running board of the car. Here, at least, there was some shade. And then the woman noticed Lilly's dress.

"Oh, you're at Luisenstadt." The woman pulled off her goggles, leaving two dark red rings around her eyes.

The Countess had given her maid the unworn uniform of the expensive private school that she had wanted her daughter to attend. The blue serge was dirty and the hem was torn but the style was unmistakable.

"Let me get your suitcase? . . ." She paused at the end of the sentence, as if expecting something else of her. The woman was only a little older than Lilly, with fair hair, a strong chin, wide cheeks, and small flint-blue eyes. She wore a gray linen dress with a hobbled skirt. She inclined her head. Finally Lilly understood: she wanted to know her name.

"Thank you," she said. "It's Lilly."

"Lilly. It's the least I can do," she replied.

While she ran back and forth collecting camisoles and other undergarments, dresses and stockings, her brother brought out a hip flask from the car and offered her some apple schnapps. Lilly hesitated. He pulled off his goggles and leather cap.

"Have some," he said. "Go on. It's nice and cold."

He was wearing tall boots, breeches, and a flannel coat. He had the same wide face as his sister but his features were in almost the opposite configuration. His nose was narrow and freckled with sun. His eyes were wide and startlingly blue. He was as handsome as she was plain.

Looking back, Lilly wondered why they had not interrogated her further. They did not seem remotely curious about what she had been doing in the middle, it could be fairly judged, of nowhere with a suitcase. Lilly took a small sip and the schnapps burned her throat and made her cough. And so she took another and felt better. And then, from the corner of her eye, she saw the newspaper cutting about her parents on the ground a few feet away. As she watched, a motorcar veered past, heading toward the city. Caught in the tailwind, the snippet of newspaper blew over a hedge and was gone. Let it go, she told herself, it doesn't matter. And she wiped the dust and the tears from her eyes. In response, the man clumsily sat down beside her and put his arm around her shoulder. He smelled of leather, French cologne, and alcohol.

"Don't worry," the man whispered. "It's the shock. My horse threw me last year, and apart from the bruises, I felt quite odd. I was filled with sadness when there was nothing to be sad about. Lasted about a week."

He glanced round at her as if he was suddenly aware that he'd given her too much information too soon.

"Anyway, we should be on the safe side. Let's drive back into town and call our doctor."

"No," Lilly replied. "Really, I'm fine."

"You're not fine," he replied. "And then, after you've seen the doctor, we'll drive you home. Apart from anything else, you're not wearing any shoes."

Lilly opened her mouth to protest. But it was true. She wouldn't get very far without shoes. And so they sat in silence for a few moments, the apple schnapps making its way straight into her bloodstream.

"Aren't you . . . ?" she asked.

"Going somewhere?" he asked. "If you call lost going somewhere. My sister can't read a map. That's why she was driving. We were going to see the fountains of Sanssouci before they switch them off for the season. Have you been yet?"

Lilly shook her head.

"Don't blame you. It was my sister's idea," he went on. "Anyway, we need to get back to the city. You know how it is, people to see, things to do."

The sunlight was as clear as a lens. He pointed out a bird, a lark that had settled on a wooden fence and started to sing. They watched it until it flew away, and then she turned and noticed that he had not been looking at the lark at all.

Just then, the sister came back with her arms full of Lilly's belongings.

"We have this too," the girl said, holding up the book of poetry. She hadn't found the shoes. Or the box with the photographer's lens and the postcard of the Virgin Mary.

Lilly rode in the backseat of the Daimler with a thick woolen rug tucked around her despite the heat and her suitcase strapped on to the luggage rack on the rear. The man had taken the wheel and the car roared as he turned a corner too fast and shook as it sped over tram-lines. Although his sister regularly turned and spoke, the noise of the engine was so loud that it was impossible to hear a word. Lilly sat back and tried to take it all in; it was the first time she had ever trav-eled in a car.

At the Unter den Linden there was a huge traffic jam. Crowds of people had crammed into the streets to watch the new army recruits parade past in their brand-new uniforms and spiked helmets. The men were heading to the railway station at Zoo, where trains were waiting to ship them to the front.

"Isn't it exciting?" the woman said. "My brother's an uhlan. He's leaving next week for France. He's in the Third Regiment; it was our father's."

Lilly had noticed the uhlans on the kaiser's march. They rode horses and carried lances. Their uniform was more ornate than the ordinary cavalry, with red horsehair plumes on their helmets and brightly colored cuffs and chests. But there were no uhlans in this parade, just factory workers and farmers, laborers and postmen in hastily stitched gray, waved off by their wives and children and girlfriends with flowers and flags, and kisses and whispers in ears to wish them good luck, and the chance to use the guns they carried so proudly on their backs.

They had arrived in Berlin only slightly ahead of the storm. As they waited for the crowds to clear, the air turned yellow and then darkened as thunder crashed and sheet lightning lit up the sky. And within a minute or two, it started to rain torrentially, the drops cascading down on the cobbles as if each one had been individually hurled. Everyone ran for cover. The uhlan and his sister leapt out of the car and pulled over the canvas hood. Only the men in formation did not change their stride. The procession went on and on, the soldiers turning their faces up to the sky.

The jam dispersed as quickly as it had formed. The storm passed. And then they drove south, past Viktoriapark toward Steglitz, where there were flowers in boxes on window ledges and polished automobiles lined up in rows along the side of the street. Maybe, she thought, Otto had been right. Maybe she could be anybody now.

The uhlan glanced over his shoulder. "We're home," he said. "And I don't think we even introduced ourselves."

The uhlan's name was Stefan. His sister's name was Eva. Their apartment was on the first floor. The front door opened onto a hall that was almost a block long. Lilly was ushered into a drawing room, a room filled with heavy mahogany furniture and darkly rendered paintings. A maid was summoned and brought tea, ginger biscuits, and a bowl of warm water. Eva produced a pair of soft kid boots, "bought in a sale, a mistake for my coloring," with low heels and two buttons on the side. They were pale blue. Although they were a little big, Lilly pulled them on, buttoned them up, and was surprised to find that she barely even felt them.

"Have them," Eva said. "That is, if you like them."

Lilly nodded. She couldn't speak. She hadn't known such beautiful boots existed.

"Good. The doctor is coming," Eva said. "I have just called him on the telephone. And then we'll drive you home or to the station, if that's where you'd like to go. Don't worry, we won't tell. And now, if you'll excuse me, I must go and freshen up. You'll have to talk to Stefan, I'm afraid."

Stefan sat down on the divan beside the schoolgirl they had run over on a small, rarely used road in the outskirts of the city. A single drop of blood had dried on her eyebrow. She had hardly spoken a word since they had arrived. She quickly glanced across at him and he realized with a jolt that he had been staring. He looked around at the drawing room, which had once belonged to his uncle, and was suddenly filled with the urge to tell her none of it was his, not the ugly furniture or the dismal paintings of his sullen ancestors. She seemed disapproving, somehow.

"Your suitcase," he asked her. "Have you run away from school before?"

She started, as if she was not expecting him to actually talk to her. And then she nodded.

"My sister used to run away all the time," he said. "She eventually got expelled."

He laughed. She didn't.

"You're going to France?" she said.

France? It was his turn to be startled. The war. For a moment he had almost forgotten about it. For a moment he had been a law student again. For a moment he had been a man alone in a room with a girl who was running away from algebra and geometry, from needlework and piano lessons. But now his mouth filled with the metal tang of adrenaline and his heart began to race. And he imagined the sickening yield of foreign flesh beyond his lance and was filled with dread. And so he forced himself to think of his father, who expected it of him, and his mother, a woman whose photograph was all he had to remember her by, since she had been dead for most of his life, and he tried to make himself believe that death would mean they would all be reunited and that the worst thing that could happen might also be the best. He cleared his throat twice before he spoke.

"It's what I've been trained for," he offered.

He intended to be gallantly reassuring, but his words sounded like an apology. And so he self-consciously poured two cups of tea, which he sweetened with honey. As he handed one to the girl, his hand shook so much the china rattled. She noticed—how could she not?—but she took the cup and steadied it in her saucer.

"To the glorious Fatherland," he said.

"I suppose," she said.

Through an open window across the room, a trumpet started playing a military waltz, badly. The uhlan offered a biscuit, then picked a speck of lint from his cuff.

"Oh, it'll be all over by Christmas," he said.

"So they say," she replied.

"In that time I'll be lucky to actually see any action. It's only a matter of months."

She glanced away.

"But some months," she said, "are longer than others."

He smiled, but his hands suddenly felt cold.

"What do you mean?" he asked, although he knew what she meant.

She raised the teacup to her mouth and blew to cool it a little. And then she composed herself, looked over at him, and held his gaze. Her eyes, he saw now, were gray.

"I mean," Lilly continued, "that time . . . time doesn't always appear to pass at the same speed. At least, not in my experience."

She smiled and glanced away. He could never understand how

every day that she had worked had stretched and stretched so much that time itself seemed to sag, while her days off raced by so fast that she felt cheated. He wasn't the type who had ever needed to work.

But if she were Stefan, would she run away or volunteer to fight, would she wait for the rent of bullet or blade through her body, or would she charge ahead, shoot, and thrust at the enemy without any regard for her own safety? She guessed that in her present state of mind it would be the latter.

"You leave next week?" she asked.

"Next week," he replied. And then they both turned away, raised their cups to their mouths, and each took a small lukewarm sip.

"Does it hurt?" he asked, indicating her head.

She pulled back a fraction of an inch.

"It really is nothing," she said.

"Would you mind if I . . . ?"

She shook her head. The uhlan moved until he was beside her. He dipped a clean white handkerchief into the bowl of warm water and very gently washed away the dried blood. The girl stared straight ahead. Her eyes were of the clearest gray, almost luminous in the pale light of the afternoon. In his mind he tried to frame her, to hold on to her image, to the here, the now, to the charged air after the storm, anything he could keep in his head.

"Do you have brothers in the military?" he asked. "Your father?"

"My father's dead," she replied. "And I don't have any brothers."

The girl's mouth twisted slightly to one side. The uhlan felt a lump rise in his throat. He and the girl had more in common than he had first assumed. Carefully he dabbed the cut with a dry corner of his handkerchief. And then his gaze moved from her eyebrow to her eyes, where it lingered just a fraction of a second too long. Suddenly the door burst open and his sister Eva hurried into the room.

"Where has she put my pearls?" she said. "Honestly, you'd think she hides them deliberately. It was either her or one of your girlfriends."

Stefan pulled back. Lilly turned away. Although Eva was oblivious as she bustled out again, they were both aware that the intimacy of the previous moment had been broken.

"My sister is at art school. She's going to join the Red Cross," Stefan said when she had gone again. "You could do the same. They're looking for nice girls like you."

"I don't think so," she said.

"But why not?" he insisted. "Don't you want to be part of the war effort?"

"I can't stand the sight of blood," she replied.

She turned and looked up at him again. He had none of the penniless poet's easy charm. He was awkward, stilted, in awe of her. Nothing of my past shows in my face, Lilly told herself. He has no idea.

"Sorry?" he said.

Her words hadn't registered.

"I can't stand the sight of blood," she repeated.

Lilly smiled. Finally, Stefan laughed. Then his sister called him not once but twice from the next room.

"I am summoned," he said. "Have another cup of tea."

Two or even three rooms down, Lilly heard Eva's voice. Stefan cried out in mock agony. Eva was teasing him, and although Lilly couldn't make out the words, his voice was full of indignation. The maid came in with a plate of cake. Her step slowed when she saw Lilly. They regarded each other. In his bedroom, Stefan hit his sister with a pillow. Eva hit him back. The doorbell rang. It was the doctor.

"Where is she?" Eva asked the maid. "The girl who was here with the cut?"

But the maid simply shrugged her shoulders and began to clear the plates.

Lilly could hear The Blue Cat long before she reached it. Inside, the place was busier than she had ever seen it. Groups of enlisted men were singing, drinking, and calling out for entertainment. The air smelled of damp wool and hair oil. Although they hadn't seen each other for some time, Hanne's eyebrow was only slightly raised when Lilly kissed her, as if she had left just five minutes before.

"What happened to your eye?" she asked. "Was it a man?"

"No," Lilly replied. "It was a Daimler convertible."

Hanne threw back her head and laughed out loud. And then she opened her arms and the two girls embraced, arms around narrow waists and cheeks pressed against cheeks. And as the men in the bar started to chant and as the Bulgarian, sweaty but demonstrably elated, played an opening trill on the piano, they held each other as tightly as they could. Years later, when the details of Hanne's face were fragmented and lost, Lilly could still recall that breathless, urgent clasp in the darkened wings of the tiny stage of The Blue Cat.

"Work here," Hanne said after Lilly explained what had happened. "They're hiring."

The Bulgarian, who was bringing up as many kegs of beer as he could carry from the basement, took on Lilly immediately and ordered her to put on an apron and mop the floor. She placed her suitcase in the broom cupboard, pinned up her hair, and started to fill up a bucket.

At almost fourteen, Lilly Nelly Aphrodite, despite her long brown hair and small breasts, could pass for eighteen in gaslight. It was something in her expression, perhaps the way she held her head. And if you caught her eye she would not glance away, all eyelids and lashes, but would return your gaze, unsmiling. And within a few seconds, unless your intentions were perfectly honorable—and, let's face it, you wouldn't be drinking in a place like The Blue Cat if they were—you would be forced to unfocus your eyes and order another drink. Lilly made the Bulgarian more money at the bar than did all the other girls put together.

That night she moved into Hanne's run-down pension in Kreuzberg, temporarily, and the landlady rather reluctantly supplied a pull-out bed. Lilly paid fifteen marks a week, a sum that, for all her bad grace, the landlady was nevertheless glad of, since two-thirds of her tenants had volunteered. She was, however, still fiercely patriotic. Cursing the French and the Russians, but reserving her crudest language for the English, she swore her allegiance every morning to the kaiser with a cup of coffee laced with schnapps.

The English had just begun blockading Germany's ports and the country's supplies of coffee, milk, butter, meat, and wheat were said to be dwindling. And so, although she had stocked her larder, her cooking, already poor, was tempered with frugality. The only other tenants, an elderly man and his sister, politely consumed what they were given without complaint. Sometimes a few slivers of gray meat were heaped on a plate of unseasoned cabbage. Or they were served a bowl of soup made of boiled carrots and a shaking of salt.

Their window looked onto a narrow airshaft. Down at the bottom was a pile of rubbish. Up above was a square of sky. In the morning, while Hanne lay in bed, Lilly often sat in the frame and read her only book. Sometimes the window opposite would be opened a crack and a young woman with black hair dragged into a bun would pull back the flimsy curtain and light a cigarette. Behind her a baby sometimes started to cry. The woman would cradle her head in her hands but would not move. And the poems would start to swim before Lilly's eyes and she would stare at the same page until the cigarette was smoked and the baby was shushed.

At first, they had eaten soft white rolls with butter for breakfast every morning, with large cups of milky coffee. But then the coffee was served black and the rolls were no longer fresh but yesterday's or those of the day before. One day there was no bread at all, and only watered-down coffee. Long lines had begun to form outside shops, and the landlady began to leave at six-thirty every second morning to make sure she didn't miss out. She was usually back by lunchtime with a loaf of K-bread, which was an unappetizing color and made of potato and rye flour, and a block of lard.

Hanne, whose film producer friend still took her out for dinner in department store cafés, smuggled pieces of cheese and white baguettes home in her coat sleeves; most mornings they ate bread and cheese in bed before breakfast.

"The kaiser eats K-bread," the landlady would tell them with her mouth full. "What do you mean, you don't like it?"

Hanne and Lilly forced down what they could, but the landlady became increasingly suspicious. How could the two girls survive on so little and still have a bloom on their cheeks and a shine in their hair? They tried to make sure, however, that she never found any crumbs.

By December, there was hardly any fresh bread to be had in the whole of Berlin. Or potatoes. Or pork. The army had to be fed. And the wives of soldiers and munitions workers were given priority. The government will provide, the landlady pronounced. But soon she could not afford even pork drippings to spread on her week-old bread. And one day she queued all day for jam, only to find it had doubled in price in the time she had been in line and she could no longer afford it. She stopped talking about the war effort after that.

The winter was long and cold and damp. It was dark by three-thirty. All the rooms were unheated except the landlady's parlor, so they kept their coats and boots on until they were ready to undress and go to bed. No wonder they spent as little of their time there as possible. On their day off, Lilly and Hanne passed the time in dance halls, where they were spun round and bought drinks by lonely soldiers on leave. Or they went to the movies and cried all the way through. And when they had no money left and they had to stay in, they practiced waltzing in their room, prompting the Frau, as they now called the landlady, whose bedroom was directly below theirs, to bang on her ceiling with a broom. When they finally went to bed, they would lie awake and talk, often until two or three in the morning, about the future, when they would both be famous actresses or dancers or singers and they would live together in a big apartment with Hanne's brothers.

One night Hanne admitted that she was in love with the so-called film producer even though she had doubts that this was what he really did. He still provided her with a steady supply of butter and chocolate and bottles of wine in return for meeting him twice a week.

"You'll know it when you feel it," she told Lilly. "It's down here, deep down in your belly. Like a hunger."

But hunger was an abstract concept to them both, at least at that point in time. Hanne's boyfriend's black-market gifts were so generous that sometimes they had to force themselves to eat them. And they grew careless. When the landlady found a stale cream cake behind the wardrobe and a piece of pork loin wrapped in brown paper in the pocket of Hanne's coat, she confiscated them both and threatened to inform the authorities unless Hanne passed the food directly to her. And so Hanne threw her things into Lilly's suitcase, told her she'd come back for her, and left Kreuzberg the very next morning.

The film producer was suitably horrified when he opened his front door on a weekday morning to find the girl from The Blue Cat on his doorstep. He gave her twenty marks, hailed a taxi, and subsequently broke off all contact. Hanne had no option but to return to Kreuzberg again. Lilly could tell what had happened just by the look on her face. She climbed into bed, fully dressed, and lay with the covers over her head. Lilly sat down on the edge of the mattress as Hanne's body, swathed in blankets, began to shake.

"Don't," she said. "Don't cry."

The shaking didn't stop but increased. And then Lilly realized that she wasn't crying at all but laughing.

"You should have seen his face," Hanne said as Lilly pulled back the covers. "It was the funniest thing ever."

And they laughed until they wept, until they were doubled over, until they were gasping for air. But at some point Hanne's hilarity turned and Lilly suddenly realized that her tears were real and her shakes were in fact sobs.

"I loved him," she said.

Hanne stopped eating and would have starved to death had not the landlady, who took her back without asking any questions, nursed back her appetite with looted Belgian chocolate that she had been saving for a rainy day. And when that was finished and there was no more, they began to feel hungry all the time and Hanne admitted that it was nothing like being in love after all.

Although most of the theaters and cabarets had closed in August out of respect for the war, it was soon perfectly obvious that it was not going to be all over by Christmas, as had been so optimistically predicted. People still needed to be entertained; in fact, it was argued in cafés from Potsdamer Platz to Savignyplatz, a little distraction was needed now more than ever before, and so one by one the theaters and cabarets opened again. The Bulgarian wrote a whole new show. Gone were the large hats, the saucy clothes, and the double entendres. Hanne's new costume was loosely based on a nurse's outfit and her songs were laments to her soldier sweetheart. Every evening finished with a rousing rendition of "The Gates of Paris Are Open (Just Like My Heart)," which always brought the house down.

Then beer production ground to a virtual halt. Most of the land used for growing hops had been turned over to growing edible crops, and nearly all the breweries in Germany were forced to close. A few still operated; the government had to make some concessions to the proletariat palate, but the beer was of poor quality and questionable alcoholic content. The Bulgarian had to buy his pilsner on the black market and put his prices up accordingly. Many of his regulars began to nurse a single drink for the entire evening. Business, which had always been a little shaky, as the Bulgarian was in the habit of getting so drunk he would hand out free drinks in the hope of "making the evening go with a boom-di-boom," was now precarious. Hanne and Lilly, he told them with a shrug, would have to make do with tips.

The landlady agreed to let them stay on for a reduced rent but wouldn't feed them anymore. And so began a time when they would leave The Blue Cat at midnight and head straight to the queues for the bakery or the butcher or the grocer. For four or five hours they would stand in lines with women, children, and boys too young to fight, and wait. Lilly would be swaying on her feet by the time the shop opened at dawn. And then, no matter how orderly they had been, the crowd would turn into a mob and surge forward as hundreds fought over a few overpriced seed potatoes or a pound or two of butter. Lilly, although she used her elbows and shoulders with as much dexterity as the next person, often came back empty-handed. Hanne, however, always managed to bring back something: a piece of pork, a jar of jam, or a newly baked loaf.

"How do you do it?" Lilly asked her. "It doesn't matter how long I wait, I always get pushed to the back. It's so unfair."

"There's always a way," Hanne said vaguely, "once you set your mind on something."

Christmas that year was eerily beautiful. The streetlights had been turned off months before to save on electricity. There were no festive decorations or brightly lit shop windows. Instead, stubs of candles were tied with wire to the branches of a large tree that had been placed on the Auguste-Victoria-Platz outside the Kaiser Wilhelm Memorial Church, and the tiny flames were tended so that they flickered for the whole of Advent. It was here that Lilly would sometimes find herself, drawn to the lights like a moth. She was not alone. Hundreds of hungry people hung around the fringes, eyeing the plates of cakes and hot wine that the church handed out after every service. But she did not join the queue. Instead, she stood as close as she could to the tree and inhaled, as if the smells of Christmas alone were enough to sustain her.

In February 1915, Germany's dwindling petrol supplies were allocated to the military. Trolley cars would be stopped at random by the police, to save on fuel, and all the passengers would have to get out and walk. Lilly's soft kid leather boots didn't last out the month.

She pushed cardboard and newspaper into the soles but every night her feet would be wet and blistered. New shoes were well beyond most people's means, even if you could find them. Boot makers were working day and night to produce boots for the army. Hanne had several pairs of stage shoes, a pair of rubber galoshes, and a pair of heavy leather boots bought before the war, but her feet were three sizes bigger than Lilly's.

Lilly would soon have to endure the shame of asking for a second-hand pair from a benevolent society. Despite the weather, she had already seen hundreds of people without shoes, or with shoes in such poor condition that they might as well have not been wearing them at all. She knew that those without shoes would be the first ones to fall ill should the city be struck by an outbreak of influenza or diphtheria. And so one day, as the wind howled down from the river Spree, she lined up outside the Brides of Christ, a church hall near Potsdamer Platz. Whole families also waited in line, with barefoot children and babies in knitted socks. But then word reached her that they had only men's shoes left and she reasoned with herself that her boots might last another week after all.

It was around this time that a policeman started drinking in the afternoon in The Blue Cat. That time of day was always busy, even though the winter light fell through the windows and lit up the peeling paint on the walls and the scuffed, unsanded floor. With snow thick on the ground outside and the air filled with dozens of burning cigarette ends, the bar gave the impression of warmth if not the real thing. Only those with the steeliest resolve would leave after one drink. The rest would linger on, counting up their coins for another—until, that is, the policeman appeared—and then, with a communal shiver, they would finish their drinks, stamp the water out of their boots, and pull on their coats.

Despite the food shortages, he was fat, with greasy blond hair and a permanent film of sweat on his upper lip. Berlin was full of policemen, in plain clothes or uniforms, men who were said to be on full alert for any signs of civil disobedience. The Bulgarian instructed Lilly to give him a black-market beer on the house and, if he asked, to tell him it was old stock.

"Old stock," he'd said with a guffaw. "Funny, I'd have sworn it tasted Polish."

One day he came in with a pair of small, shiny black boots. He handed them to Lilly.

"Here," he said. "Special delivery. The soles are only cardboard, but they were all I could get."

"How much? I don't think I can afford . . ."

"They're paid for," he said.

The policeman's eyes ran up and down her body. They lingered on her breasts.

"By whom?" Lilly asked.

"Who do you think?" he said. "Your friend, Hanne."

Lilly's face flushed. Hanne had no money for new boots, or at least none that she knew about. Then the policeman started to laugh.

"And she earned it, by Jove, she really did. That Hanne's worth every penny, lads."

He raised his eyebrow, glancing around at the remaining crowd to make his meaning clear. And then, furtively, he reached out and with one hand he cupped her breast. Lilly swung her fist straight into his fat face. It wasn't the force of the blow that made him fall from his stool but the sheer surprise. He fell straight back and hit the wooden floor with a rounded thump. Laughter erupted from the regulars. Lilly came out from behind the bar to find him lying quite still, his eyes staring at the dark blue cornice. And then he sat up.

"If you were a man, I'd kill you for that," he said.

Hanne, summoned from her dressing room by the Bulgarian, suddenly appeared at his side. She looked from Lilly's face to the policeman's.

"He was telling lies about you, Hanne," Lilly said.

"Was I? Ask her," the policeman said. "Not many girls want to get paid in boots. You're a couple of tarts. I should bloody well arrest the pair of you."

He started to get to his feet. Lilly moved instinctively and, with one shove, knocked him into a table. Once more he lay sprawled on the ground, this time covered with spilled beer and broken glass and cigarette ash. No one laughed this time.

"Put them on," Hanne said as he lay there. "Like he said, they're paid for."

The Bulgarian was given no choice in the matter. Either they went or he was under arrest.

The landlady did not take pity on the two girls this time and gave them a week's notice. Their room was to be rented out to a war widow with a baby who came with a ration book and a guaranteed income, albeit small, from the government. On the following day Hanne left Lilly in a coffeehouse with the understanding that she was going to secure a room for them both from an old contact. Night fell, the coffeehouse closed, but Hanne didn't return.

It is claimed by some analysts of human behavior that the pattern of a relationship, be it with friend or lover, is thrashed out within the first few weeks of meeting. It could have been true that Hanne set the pattern very early on. Maybe, no matter what she said or did, Hanne was always going to leave Lilly when she was least expecting it, and Lilly, for her part, instinctively knew it. Hadn't she done it once already? And when Lilly returned to Kreuzberg that night, she wasn't surprised to find that Hanne had already been, gone, and taken everything that belonged to her.

Sister August, who was now known as Nurse von Kismet, did not recognize the teenage prostitute immediately. The girl, who was about sixteen, was suffering from malnutrition. She had been sent to the military hospital after collapsing outside a garrison near Ypres.

"We can't admit you," she said. "There's no room."

The girl had claimed she had come to France looking for her missing boyfriend. But that's what they all said. None of them ever bought a return ticket. Brothels were tolerated near the front lines. The men preferred German girls to French. It wasn't only sex, they pointed out. In fact, sex was often the least of it.

In May 1915, Lotte von Kismet had been at the front for six months. Her organizational skills were soon apparent, and in addition to her nursing duties she was put in charge of admissions. No other nurse worked quite as tirelessly as the former nun. Even the doctors were in awe of her seemingly inexhaustible work ethic. And if she was ever blunt rather than tactful, direct rather than polite, her fellow nurses put it down to her height, a disadvantage that had given her a strength of character that did not waver when her modesty was compromised when she was forced to wear aprons that just and only just skimmed her shins.

"Name?" she commanded.

"It's me," she said. "It's Hanne."

Nurse von Kismet stopped filling in forms and looked up. And her weathered face softened as first joy, then disappointment, and then compassion washed across it. Something stopped her from reaching across and hugging her former charge. The years of servitude to the Lord had given her boundaries that she still struggled to break down.

"Hanne," she said. "Oh, Hanne. Look at you."

Hanne Schmidt wore a grubby dress and high-heeled shoes. Her arms and legs were so thin they looked as if they would snap under the merest pressure, like bread sticks. She said she had lost her coat. And yet her cheeks were smooth and her eyes were bright. Her spirit had not been broken.

"You look the same," Hanne said. "Even without the habit."

A doctor came in and whispered that Lotte was needed in the operating room. She didn't have much time.

"How's Lilly?" the nurse asked. "I think about her a lot. And you."

Hanne shrugged.

"We worked together in a bar. And then we got sacked."

"And now?" the nurse asked. "Is she . . . ?"

"Here? No," Hanne replied. "She's still in Berlin as far as I know."

The nurse placed a week's supply of dehydration tablets in an envelope.

"Nurse von Kismet?" the doctor called.

"Two minutes," she replied. "I'm sorry, Hanne, about what happened."

"How could you have let them expel me?" Hanne said. "I lost my brothers. . . . They split them up and sent them away."

Lotte held her head in her hands. What were the chances of meeting Hanne again? Not high. And yet, here she was. Maybe God was trying to tell her something. If only she could still hear him. She had nursed hundreds and hundreds of men, men with limbs missing, with metal in their heads, their hearts, their minds. And when the moment of death came, as it did more often than not, they all thought she was someone else, a mother, a wife, a sister. Yes, yes, I'm here, she would always say. And she would stroke and caress and, if no one else was around, she would kiss them. What did these little acts of intimacy mean? Nothing to anyone else. Everything to the men. But this morning, the man who lay on the trolley beside the latrine seemed to recognize her. What were the chances?

"Lotte," he had whispered through cracked lips. "Is it you?"

She stared at him. At first he was just another shattered body that she couldn't mend. And then his face seemed to come into focus.

"It is me," she said. "I am Lotte."

"I looked for you for weeks. I couldn't stop thinking about you."

She never cried. She never cried except this once. He died with his head in her arms and her mouth on his and this time she didn't care who saw it. And even though his papers said he came from Hamburg, not Berlin, and even though the man in the park was tall and he seemed shorter, it was he, her lover.

When she had arrived at the front, all she desired was to leave no traces of herself; there would be no one to miss her, she had no shared histories or entwined narratives. But now she realized that this was impossible, that she couldn't cut herself off completely and in fact she didn't want to anymore. And she felt elated and yet devastated and then filled with regret.

"Maybe it was God's will, Hanne," she said.

"There is no God," Hanne replied.

Nurse von Kismet smoothed down her face. There is no right and wrong anymore, she had decided, no good and evil. War, prostitution, love, sex, all the morality of the Church seemed meaningless, all the so-called values turned upside down.

"Come with me," she instructed Hanne. "Quickly."

They went to the hospital canteen and Lotte placed a bowl of thick meat soup in front of Hanne. A high-pitched screech followed by a loud boom came from a few miles away. It made the cutlery rattle and the china clink together. Hanne looked up at the former nun in alarm.

"The hostilities are coming closer," Lotte said by way of explanation.

Everyone in the room, the cooks, the soldiers, the nurses, stood with heads cocked, waiting for the next sound. And then from nearer, much nearer, came the sound of gunfire. They all relaxed. Germany was still fighting back.

"Eat it all," Lotte said. "And then go home."

But Lotte knew the girl was unlikely to do either.

In Arcadia

February 1916. The night is overcast, no moon or stars; only the roar of the Fokker E-type's engine as it flies toward France. Tonight there's an extra passenger on the airplane to watch the bombardment: a Film-Führer, *as he asks to be called, with his camera mounted so it points through the hatch and his pile of film, which he stores in a metal box. Below, when their eyes adjust, they can see the ammunition trains, the roads crawling with gray, the soldiers in formation moving toward the front, even the new artillery, the Minnenwerfers, which can, they say, toss a bomb as big as an oil drum.*

"Look!" the Film-Führer *shouts. "Below!"*

Like huge silent fish without eyes are the zeppelins. Heading toward Lorraine, toward Revigny, toward Verdun, they cross into enemy territory to chart British positions, their guns, their camps, their trenches. But then a shell, a shot, a shooting star of light, is fired up into the night. Two searchlights point their fingers into the mist, back and forth and back and forth again. The Film-Führer *begins to pray.*

The enemy catch a zeppelin in their prongs and start to fire. They hit. The airship tips, turns pink, and bursts into flame. Up in the Fokker they watch it fall through the sky below, a blaze of white, an arc of skeletal metal, a crumpled heap in a muddy field. The sky is lightening in the east. The other zeppelins begin to drop their bombs; the German guns begin to fire. The battle for Verdun has started.

The cart horse swayed and then sank forward to its knees. The boy with the reins in his hands and the sob in his voice started to shout, "Come on! . . . Gee up! . . . Move! Why have you stopped? Move! Please move?" He hit the horse's ridged brown back with his whip, once, twice, three times. The horse flinched, showed the whites of its eyes, and then with a small moan, a letting out of breath, of steam, of life, it slumped and collapsed into a heap of angular bone and sagging skin.

Lilly wasn't the only one standing on Mariannenplatz who was watching. No sooner had the horse's head hit the cobbles than a dozen women appeared from doorways and alleyways armed with knives and bowls and cups. They ignored the boy's cries, his tears, his laments, and began to butcher the carcass, sawing through bone and slicing through veins to let the spurt of warm blood flow into their bowls. One woman, her face splattered with red, tried to hack off a ragged haunch with a penknife; another pulled out the tongue. In minutes, what was left of the horse would vanish completely. Lilly pushed to the front. All she had eaten for months was turnip—raw turnip, since there was rarely any coal to be had. She looked down at the skin and bone that remained and tried to convert it in her mind into something edible. She forced herself to think of stew, of soup, of meat. It was so long since she had eaten any, she had almost forgotten the taste. And yet she tried to make the connection. Horse . . . food; food . . . horse. The thought filled her mouth with bile and she had to resist the urge to gag. There was someone pulling at her skirt. It was the boy. Tears were streaming down his face.

"My mother," he sobbed. "What will my mother say?"

Lilly crouched down next to the bloody remains of the horse. An old woman was pulling out the horse's innards. She had the liver in her hands.

"Give it to the boy," Lilly said.

The old woman, whose apron was already full, hesitated. Her eyes swiveled round to look at Lilly, to see if it was just a ruse. The sound of the boy's sobs was almost unbearable. Lilly held the old woman's gaze. And so, with much shaking of her head and cursing of the government, she pulled a piece of newspaper from her bag, wrapped up the horse's liver, and handed it over.

If anyone ever asked the silent film star Lidi—or Lilly, as she was known then—about the hardships in wartime Berlin, her eyes would glaze over and she would suggest that she had suffered, but not as much as most people. She would be vague with dates and places and specifics, so vague that it did indeed seem as if, like an accident victim, her subconscious had wiped her memory almost clean.

In fact, on that day in April 1916, she had been living in a hostel for unmarried Catholic women for a year. With only her orphan's allowance to live on, Lilly had been allowed to make up the rent in cleaning duties. Every morning she would sluice out the latrines with scalding hot water and scrub the floor with carbolic soap. And every night she would do it all over again. And no matter how well she had done it the previous time, how scalded her hands had become and how many new blisters she had acquired, the floor was always filthy when she went down on her knees with her scrubbing brush in hand and the latrines were always caked with excrement and plugged with soiled newsprint.

Her bed, one bunk in a room of four, was damp and full of fleas. Since many of the other women didn't believe in bathing during winter, the smell in the room at night was suffocating. There was a single stove for the whole floor, and when there was enough fuel, each woman was allocated fifteen minutes. But it was loosely policed, and as all cooking was prohibited after nine, Lilly often waited all evening for nothing. Nobody spoke to her and she spoke to no one. She developed a hacking cough and at night the other women begged the Virgin Mary to either let her die or get better but make it quick.

She was more likely to die in there, she assessed quite unemotionally, than recover. The price of food kept rising and the queues for food kept growing longer. Living on stale bread and raw vegetables, she had barely enough energy to do much more than simply get through the day. It was as if a large part of her had shut down and the only visible remaining part of her was the part that ached, that was always hungry, that would do almost anything to survive.

Lilly turned back to the horse. She pulled out her water pail and quickly began to pick up what she could find: a bone, a rib, a stringy piece of flank. And then she was aware that someone was watching her. She looked up. A woman was staring at her over the remains of the dead horse, a woman wearing clean white gloves and holding a camera. Without warning, she raised the camera to her eye and took a photograph.

"Don't," Lilly said, shielding her face with her hand. But it was too late. The picture was already taken.

"Still reading poetry?" the woman asked as she wound the film. The remark was so incongruous that Lilly barely took it in.

"You're the Luisenstadt girl?"

The woman seemed oblivious to the pandemonium around her. An old man squeezed in front of Lilly and started to spoon up the horse's spilled innards from the filthy cobbles with a battered ladle, splashing her dress with blood. Wash day wasn't until the weekend. Her eyes swam. She tried so hard to keep clean, to look respectable. What was the point?

"You don't remember me?" the woman continued.

The woman did look vaguely familiar. But most people had become ghostly facsimiles of who they had been two years earlier, and unless you were sure of someone's identity, it was better to glance away than to be mistaken. Without answering, she turned and began to make her way back through the crowd.

It was late afternoon and the rush hour had started. A tram was at a standstill behind the horseless cart and was blaring its horn. As a traffic jam began to grow in both directions and a group of women squabbled over what was left of the carcass, as the boy sat on the curb with a lump of bloody newspaper in his hands and watched as someone made off with the horse's head on his shoulder, the woman with the camera appeared at Lilly's side.

"My brother and I ran you over on the road to Potsdam," she said. "Don't you remember? It does seem such a long time ago."

Lilly stopped and stared at the woman's face, at the flint-colored eyes and the wide cheekbones. Now she remembered her.

"I gave you some boots, which I see you're not wearing. Not that I blame you: they were an unfortunate shade."

The woman smiled at her expectantly. As she stood there with her filthy dress and her pail full of warm horsemeat, Lilly was ashamed: ashamed of how she looked, ashamed of what she had done, ashamed of who she was.

"Can I take your portrait?" the woman asked suddenly. "We could do it at the apartment. I'm putting together a series."

For an instant Lilly thought she was making fun of her.

"I don't think so," Lilly replied.

"I'd pay you," the woman quickly countered. "I haven't got that much, but if you name a figure, I'm sure we could come to some arrangement."

Lilly felt her cheeks begin to color. She had heard those words many times before, always from men. A figure, she could name a figure: ten marks, twenty. She could do it, she would tell herself, what did it matter? Hanne could. Thousands of other women could, so why not her? Think of the money. Just think of the money. And yet, as soon as the decision was made, she would remember the clatter of metal instrument on metal bowl, the suffocation of a hand across her mouth, the memory of her body starting to split and bleed, and she could not.

"No, thank you," she said, and started on her way again.

"I'll make you dinner, then."

Dinner: the word was as foreign as "picnic" or "luncheon." Large white plates and linen napkins; plates of peaches and purple figs; legs of lamb and roast potatoes. She was dreaming; she often drifted away like this, her mind filled with images and tastes that she hadn't even experienced firsthand, generic memories she didn't even own. The woman's small blue eyes had widened and she had reached out, almost touching her on the arm, making her stop.

"A deal?" the woman offered. "It's Eva. My name, in case you forgot."

The jam had cleared. The tram finally trundled past. All that was left of the horse was a large black stain on the cobbles. Finally, Lilly met Eva's eye.

"I'd say it was the least you could do after last time," Eva said.

And then Lilly remembered: She'd left suddenly, without thanking them or saying good-bye. Their maid knew; their maid could tell by the reddened chafe of her hands and the cast of her eye that she was not, as they had assumed by her dress, one of them.

But the war had changed everything. The social boundaries, which had seemed so watertight at the time, had become permeable. Lilly inclined her head, the tiniest nod.

"Wonderful. We'll have to walk, I'm afraid. No more gas for the car."

Eva took Lilly's arm and folded it over her own, as if it was a natural thing, as if she did it every day. Nobody had touched Lilly like this for months. She had been jostled, pushed, shoved, and elbowed but never treated gently or affectionately. Instinctively, however, she pulled away.

"I have to be back before ten," she said. "I mustn't be late."

The hostel had a strict curfew. There were, Lilly had been informed, a dozen women turned away every night, a dozen women who would and could take her place. And Lilly believed it. During that winter the first corpses started to appear on the streets. At first it was children and old people. But more recently she had seen girls her age. She could not lose her bunk.

Eva Mauritz had been on the tram on the way to the park when the horse had collapsed and died, blocking the road and forcing her, like the rest of the passengers, to climb off and investigate. She recognized the dark-haired schoolgirl immediately. She was thin but not hunched, skeletal and yet not pinched. Her face had been hollowed down to the bone, but it made her gray eyes seem bigger and more prominent in her face. In fact, she was even more striking than she had been on the day they had run her over two years earlier. Although she had grown a few inches, it wasn't just a new maturity: there was something both vulnerable and strong in her that Eva had not noticed before, a translucency of spirit but an opaqueness of will. Poverty, Eva ruminated, seemed to suit her. And she wondered what terrible misfortune had befallen her.

The cherry trees were in blossom early that year, and pale pink blew in gusts over the off-duty soldiers who slept on park benches and around the ankles of the widows who solicited on the corners. It was a clear, cold day with an endless blue sky and just the occasional race of white cloud.

"Underwear," said Eva. "Blossoms always remind me of thousands of tiny pairs of bloomers."

And she laughed again, a free, easy laugh. As if it didn't matter what anyone else thought; she was funny, she knew she was. The sun was on her face. The parks were still full of flowers despite the fact that there was no one employed to tend them. It was the kind of day where you could pretend that all was well, that all would be fine in the end.

It took an hour to walk to Steglitz. By the time they reached the apartment block, Lilly was exhausted; she had no energy to spare, few calories to burn. Inside, the apartment looked much sparser than she remembered. Some of the furniture had been chopped up for fuel and the rest was covered up with dust sheets. Eva explained that she often slept on a divan next to the fire in the kitchen.

"There's only me," Eva explained. "And it's warmer this way."

Eva had lost her maids, her cook, and most of her friends. People did not stay on in Berlin if they could help it. People did not want to fight for food or pay black-market prices if they had people they could stay with in the country. Her father, who had remarried, insisted that she come and live with him on his estate. Eva accepted but then postponed and kept postponing until he stopped inviting her. She could not bear the provinces, she said, the gossip and the rumors. But most of all, she couldn't bear the new wife.

Eva brewed coffee with a mixture made from ground walnut shells. It was bitter and black, but at least it was hot.

"Is your brother all right?" Lilly asked. "It's Stefan, isn't it?"

"He's stationed in France, next to a river called the Somme," Eva said. "He says it's rather beautiful, all rolling hills and meadows."

The uhlan. Lilly had often wondered what had become of the handsome young uhlan. With their red and blue uniforms and plumed hats, they had been easy to spot in the first few months of the war and sustained heavy losses. By Christmas, what few were left had been issued new brown uniforms and guns instead of lances. They were uhlans now in name only.

In her mind she saw him in the drawing room with a cup of tea balanced on his knee. As far as she knew, they were winning the war. But if that was so, why didn't they bring it to a close? How long did the kaiser think they could go on like this?

Lilly picked up the coffee with her thumb and forefinger, careful not to let the hot cup touch her palms. Eva was watching her, her face tilted into a question.

"Do you have any ointment?" she asked. "I have a few blisters."

"Jesus Christ!" Eva whispered as she dabbed the blisters with salt water and iodine. But she could tell by Lilly's expression that it was better not to ask how she got them or where.

"Didn't you join the Red Cross?" Lilly asked.

"Got kicked out," Eva said with a sideways smile. She didn't explain, either.

By the time Lilly's hands had been washed and dressed, it was dark outside. Eva lit a gas lamp and piled up the grate with coal. The room soon filled with heat. Lilly felt her whole body start to relax. She had joined the queue outside the baker's at five that morning. She struggled to keep her eyes open.

"Don't let me fall asleep," she said.

"I wouldn't dream of it," replied Eva.

When Lilly woke, for an instant she had no idea where she was. And then she saw Eva reading and remembered.

"What time is it?" Lilly said.

"It's just gone eleven."

Lilly leapt out of the chair and pulled on her coat.

"No," she said. "Oh, no! Why didn't you wake me up?"

"You looked so peaceful, I didn't like to. Never mind. I was late every day for school. Didn't do me any harm."

"You don't understand," Lilly said with a hint of hysteria in her voice. "Why didn't you wake me?"

"I'm sorry!" Eva replied in a voice that suggested that she was not. "What about the picture? And dinner? Your meat! Come back tomorrow and eat it. I'll expect you at seven-thirty."

It was several miles back to the hostel. Lilly ran most of the way. By the time she reached it, her bunk had been taken and her suitcase had been tagged and stored in the office.

"We have rules," the warden told her. "I'm sorry."

Lilly spent most of the night walking. Even in the middle of the night, the city streets were busy. Thousands of people got up in the dark to queue for food. Lilly joined a queue outside a bread shop and waited for four hours with the smell of fresh loaves in the air. There was none left by the time she reached the front, so she spent a week's allowance on a couple of rock-hard rye rolls instead.

At seven-thirty exactly that evening, she rang Eva's bell. No one answered. An old woman with a dog came out of the flat opposite.

"Are you expected?" she asked. Lilly nodded.

But she was aware that the woman was watching her, taking in her cheap boots and stained dress. She rang the bell again. Maybe Eva had assumed that Lilly would assume that the invitation was nothing more than a platitude. Or maybe she had changed her mind. The dog started to bark. The woman began to tap her keys against her palm. Lilly turned and started slowly down the steps. She had hidden her suitcase in the basement of the building. But now, with the woman watching her, she wouldn't be able to retrieve it. Her situation was getting worse and worse. She had spent all day wandering in the park, lingering for hours over one cup of so-called coffee, taking a tram from one terminal to the other and back, and now she was so tired she couldn't stop shivering. She would have to go to the hostel and wait until a bunk was free. That might take days, or even weeks. Her breath started to come quicker. Just walk, she told herself. But her feet were leaden and her head felt light.

Eva opened the door above, dressed only in a thin silk gown.

"Oh, it's you. I was in the bath," she explained. "I left the door on the latch. Didn't you notice?"

Lilly stepped inside the apartment and closed the door behind her. Pools of water led from the front door to the bathroom. She listened as Eva climbed back into the water. And she realized that she had been slowly counting the hours, the minutes, the seconds, until this moment.

"I didn't fancy horsemeat after all," shouted Eva from the bathroom. "So I threw it away. I hope you like turnip?"

She threw away the meat? Was she mad? Lilly's eyes filled with tears of both relief and sorrow: for the horse, for herself.

"I made it into a stew," Eva said. "But I had no idea what I was doing. We were taught to draw and dance and play the piano and read poetry, but nothing practical. I can't even darn a sock. Oh, and I had a little sausage that I added." And then she laughed.

That night they ate sausages and turnip in broth. Although it was watery and the sausage was mostly gristle and fat, Lilly ate every last scraping. Eva produced a small pat of butter to go with Lilly's rolls.

"I've been saving it," she said. "I'll cut you a large slice. It'll go off if somebody doesn't eat it soon. Go on. Have some."

Lilly hesitated and then took the knife. She put the knife blade in her mouth, closed her eyes, and let the butter melt on her tongue. Few things would ever taste as good as that slice of yellow butter in Eva's kitchen. The week before there had been riots in Wedding and Friedrichberg over the price of butter. Shopkeepers were tripling or even quadrupling the price. "You can't afford butter?" one grocer was said to have quipped to the women in the queue. "Then spread shit on your bread."

It wasn't only the dairies that had their windows broken, it was the butchers too. Hundreds of women had started to protest on the streets to demand butter, bread, meat. But Lilly knew that Eva had no need to queue for food. She had money. And although all food was rationed, it was well known that shopkeepers weren't averse to a little manipulation of the scales for "regular" customers. And there was always the black market.

"I queued for it," Eva insisted. "Like everyone else." But judging from the size of the slab and its freshness, Lilly knew that was unlikely.

It was already nine o'clock. She stood up and began to pull on her coat. If she hurried, she would reach the hostel before the curfew. She didn't let herself think further than that.

"Why not stay here tonight?" Eva said. "I have plenty of room."

As soon as Eva said it, Lilly realized that it was what she had been longing for.

"That's very kind of you," she replied. "But I can't."

Eva must have sensed that her reply lacked conviction. And so, to reinforce her invitation, she moved herself squarely in front of Lilly, blocking the doorway.

"You're not leaving," Eva said. "Listen, it's not altruistic. It's a purely selfish act. Since we dismissed the maid and Stefan went to France, I've been living in this huge place all on my own."

"But you don't know anything about me," Lilly said.

"I don't know what's happened to you, Lilly," she said. "It must have been bad, since you are still here, in the city, whereas everybody else left months ago. People like us should stick together."

Lilly took a deep breath in, out, and in again. Should she tell Eva the truth: that she was not like her at all, that she had nothing, nowhere to go, that if she left she would probably have to spend another night on the streets? And yet, maybe, she told herself, they were more alike than she had first realized; her own father had been a baron. But why was Eva doing this?

"Stay," Eva said. "Please?"

She reached out and touched Lilly very gently on the arm. Lilly glanced up and in an instant read her and knew what it was she wanted from her after all.

Eva Mauritz had discovered she liked girls one summer at the family estate when she was fourteen. Although her neighbor, a young officer with floppy blond hair and bad skin, swore his undying love for her at a midsummer party, she fell for the stable manager's daughter, a spry sixteen-year-old who had kissed her in exchange for her pony and then promptly told everyone. The indignity took some time to fade, but the knowledge of her sexual orientation did not. She was expelled first from school and then from the young ladies' division of the Red Cross for so-called inappropriate behavior.

Of course, she could have had no idea at that point that the latest in her series of ill-advised and rash invitations would inadvertently save Lilly's life. A month later, there was an outbreak of typhus in the Catholic hostel and more than half of the women died. That night, however, as the fire lit up Lilly's face and turned her lips a deep, dark red, Eva leaned over and kissed her, a firm kiss on the cheek, a sisterly, nonsexual kiss. But her hands shook and her heart was full of sparks.

"I'm so happy," she said. "Aren't you?"

A question hung in the air, unanswered. But it was not the one she had voiced.

Later, Lilly peeled off her clothes and climbed into a bath at Eva's insistence. Her last bath had been in thirdhand water in a tin tub a month before. But here she lay with her whole body submerged, apart from the circle of her face, as steam curled up into the cold air. On the porcelain rim sat a dish with a bar of French soap. Lilly sat up, covered herself with lather, and scrubbed her hair, her skin, her feet, until she felt as if she had rubbed a whole layer of herself clean away. But even though her skin was raw and her body naked, she was still cocooned inside. She could sense Eva's desire for her, but it left her untouched. Sooner or later Eva would sense her reticence and suspect she had been misled, but until then Lilly would offer what she had, even though she knew what she had would never be enough.

Eva had laid out some nightclothes and a spare toothbrush. Lilly dried herself quickly and then cleaned her teeth. A blurred face in the mirror looked back at her. She had almost forgotten what she looked like. As she wiped away the condensation, her reflection gradually appeared. She tried to smile, but her face, she noticed with a jolt, was one that had become configured for tragedy.

The next morning Lilly woke at five and lay awake as the room lightened. Eva had looked at her in the same way that Marek had, with the same hunger and giddy slide of her eyes. And once more she hadn't resisted it; she had been complicit.

And so she got dressed and started to clean the apartment. There were balls of dust in the corners of the corridors and the rugs were gray with soot. As quietly as she could, she dusted, polished, and washed floors. Eva rose at ten-thirty. As soon as she saw the mop in Lilly's hand, she tried to take it away.

"You don't have to do that," she told Lilly. "I've been meaning to get a lady."

"But now you've got me," Lilly replied. "Please, I'll only stay here if I have something to do . . ."

Lilly's grip on the mop was unyielding. And they both knew that Eva's question had been answered.

"If you insist," Eva conceded with a laugh despite the dip of disappointment she felt inside. "But it's only because you want to. If you clean, I'll cook. And I don't know what happened to your wardrobe, but you're welcome to have as many of my clothes as you like."

"That's very kind of you," Lilly said.

"I'm a very kind sort of girl."

Within a week, Eva commented later, it seemed as if Lilly had come back to life from the dead. They ate together, they danced together, they talked until late: about school, about clothes, about their childhoods. Although Lilly would remain tight-lipped about her recent situation, she hinted that it involved a father who wanted to marry her off to a much older, very wealthy man. And if Eva was ever suspicious that she had read Lilly's anecdotes in a book or seen them on the cinema screen, she never let on. But Lilly always covered her tracks. While her tales about boarding school and balls and banquets were filled with convincing detail, she was always vague with places and dates. In fact, the only real person in her stories was her school friend Hanne Schmidt, whom she described with such affection that Eva became fascinated.

"Tell me again about your friend who worked in a tingle-tangle," she would insist. And so Lilly would describe her friend's shocking downfall from aristocrat to bar singer, and even sing a snatch or two of her songs, which Eva always found hilarious.

"I know a man with a great big . . .
Dick was his name . . ."

"It's like you've always lived here," Eva said when she had finished laughing.

And so they settled into a routine of sorts, with Eva cooking and Lilly cleaning up, Eva observing and Lilly letting her, a symbiotic relationship in which neither admitted what was happening or questioned how it would end. Sometimes, without telling Eva, Lilly looked for a job. She paced the city streets, from Zoo to the Cölln and from Potsdamer Platz to Mitte, looking for notices in shop windows or cards on notice boards. But the city was full of unemployed female servants and the middle classes were unwilling, it was said, to hire again until the war was over.

Eva's camera was put away and the portrait was never mentioned again. It was just one in a series of short-lived passions. The next was writing a novel. Every morning after breakfast, she set up a brand-new Remington typewriter on the kitchen table and stabbed out each word letter by letter, swearing loudly when she made a mistake.

"Is it difficult?" Lilly asked. "Typing, I mean."

"No. Yes, I admit it. It's bloody hard. You want to try?"

Lilly sat at the table and Eva stood behind her. Lilly slowly bashed out the alphabet, letter by letter. Sometimes she hesitated and Eva would lean over her shoulder and point out a letter. And when she had reached Z, she typed up a sentence: *Eva has Every Eventuality Evaluated.*

Eva smiled and typed out a sentence in return: " 'My Little Lilly is a Lovely Lass,' " Lilly read.

"I have a guide if you want to learn," Eva said. "I did a course, but quite frankly, I have no natural aptitude. Maybe you could pick it up, though."

Lilly ran her fingers very gently over the Bakelite keys. Maybe she could. The book claimed you could learn in a week. It took Lilly three. She followed the exercises without any ink, since typewriter ribbon was increasingly hard to get hold of and she didn't want to waste it. And then, when she could manage a page or two slowly and clumsily, she offered to type up the first chapter of Eva's book.

"Oh, no. It needs another draft," Eva said. "It's not finished."

"When can I read it?" she asked.

"Soon, soon," Eva replied.

The next day Eva burned it. The typewriter, however, remained.

Eva's status as a "regular customer" in her local shops was undermined by extreme food shortages. Although Eva and Lilly both had ration books, what was listed inside them was pure fiction.

"A loaf of bread a week," Eva scoffed. "And a pound of meat a month. You know what he offered me? A cup full of flour and a pound of wormy apples."

And so in June, Lilly and Eva decided to go on a foraging trip to the country. As they walked to the station, they noticed that the city was strangely silent. That spring, boys with ladders had climbed trees, raided nests, and then sold the birds' eggs they found for fifty pfennigs each. Others had rigged up nets and offered starlings and pigeons, magpies and swallows, at one mark a pair.

Every weekend the trains left the main stations packed with people. At country stations, where there was little more than a church and a couple of houses, at least two dozen old men, women, and children would disembark carrying baskets and sacks. They had all heard that some farmers would sell eggs and milk—at a price. Others would chase trespassers away with a stick. But they couldn't guard all of their crops all of the time, and so every potato field, vegetable garden, and grain crop was liable to have had some of its produce "liberated."

The police, however, had grown wise to this and they patrolled the main stations in Berlin, arresting anyone caught with what they assumed were foraged goods. And so the foragers knew it was better to eat what you could in the country than to risk the prospect of the food you gathered, by honest means or not, being confiscated and left to rot on the platform.

Lilly and Eva bought tickets for the next train leaving, the nine-thirty to Munich, and they climbed off about lunchtime at a tiny village. The fields around were planted with rye and the hedgerows were tangled with cow parsley and goosegrass. First they decided they would try to buy some eggs from a farm. Following directions from the stationmaster, they turned off the road and headed up a small grassy track. As they walked toward a long, low farmhouse, they passed a hen coop and a cow in a barn. A boy of about eight sat on the wall to keep watch. They smiled and wished him good day, but he simply stared at them.

They offered ninety pfennigs per egg, but it was not enough. The farmer's wife, a tired-looking woman with thick, graying blond hair, watery blue eyes, and several chins, wanted two marks. From the open doorway came the smell of freshly baked bread and smoked bacon. She folded her arms and watched their reaction.

"That's daylight robbery," stuttered Eva. "Before the war you could buy six dozen for that price."

"That's what they cost today," the farmer's wife said as she started to close the door. "If you want eggs, get your own hens. Otherwise, eat turnip like everyone else."

"Greedy lump," said Eva as they walked away. "Fat old cow. . . . Even if I had the money, I wouldn't pay that for an egg."

From the farmhouse, they heard the farmer's wife calling her son for lunch. Eva sniffed.

"I can still smell bacon in my hair," she lamented.

They walked along in silence for a few minutes.

"I think you can eat dandelions," Lilly said. "But is it the flowers or the leaves?"

It was Eva's idea to liberate some eggs. Before they had a chance to change their minds, Eva was dragging Lilly back along the road toward the farm.

"We'll leave some money," she said. "Ninety pfennigs per egg. Which is still outrageous."

The boy on the wall had gone. From what they had seen of the house, the kitchen seemed to be in the back. Quickly they slipped into the chicken coop. Half a dozen hens rushed toward them, expecting grain. Neither Lilly nor Eva had any idea where to look for eggs and so they floundered around, surrounded by a clutch of hens, searching in corners and under planks. They both heard the sickening crack when Eva stepped on two eggs by mistake. A child's high-pitched scream came from the house. Without a prompt, both girls jumped over the fence and ran. They reached the turn of the road laughing and gasping for breath.

"Do you think anyone saw us?" asked Eva.

"I hope not," said Lilly.

A squawk came from inside Eva's jacket. It was then that Lilly noticed the bulge. Eva undid one button. As soon as it saw the light, the rooster started to crow in hoarse, clucking rasps. A door slammed in the farmhouse.

"What have you done?" said Lilly.

"I just grabbed it," Eva said. "We'll keep it in the apartment. I'll send them some money. . . . How much do you think a hen costs?"

"It's not a hen," Lilly said. "It's a rooster."

"So?"

"They don't lay eggs, Eva."

"Oh," she said.

The rooster started to flap its wings, to peck at Eva's hands and face. She held on tighter.

"Let it go," said Lilly.

"Absolutely not."

Kickeriki. The rooster's crow was almost as loud as the steam train's whistle. *Kickeriki.* Eva pulled her jacket over the bird's head, but it was too late.

"The rooster's out," shouted the boy back at the farm.

"Let it go, Eva," Lilly repeated.

"Lunchtime, Chooki!" he shouted.

Eva giggled but it wasn't funny anymore. From inside her jacket the rooster clucked and its feet started to claw at her arms.

"I left three marks on the hen coop. I paid for it. . . . Ouch."

They could hear the rattle of the grain bucket as the boy walked slowly down the lane toward them.

"Come here, Daddy," he shouted.

The rooster stuck its head out and opened its beak. Before it had a chance to cry out, Lilly grabbed its neck with both hands. And with one swift turn, she broke it. Eva stared at her for a second, her mouth open. And then she looked down. The rooster hung limp in Lilly's hand.

"What have you done?" said Eva.

Lilly quickly stuffed the rooster's body into her basket, covered it with a cloth, and then, taking Eva's arm, walked as briskly as she dared away from the farm.

The land opened out into fields and then closed in deep, dense forests. The road was sandy and infrequently used. And yet, though they were forty kilometers at least from Munich, the countryside was full of people. They passed several families scanning the ground and the hedgerows. One woman sat on a stool beside a small, slow-moving river with a fishing rod in her hand. She looked up nervously when she saw them coming, and her hand instinctively flew to a canvas bag at her feet.

The rooster grew heavier and heavier in Lilly's basket, but she forced herself to carry it as if it were empty. If anyone they passed suspected they had something other than a few edible leaves in their basket, she was sure they would have no qualms about a little more "liberation." Neither Lilly nor Eva spoke until they reached a crossroads. The right fork headed back toward the village, the left into a wood.

"I've been thinking," said Eva at last. "I think we should bury it and go back to the city. I feel like a common criminal."

"What?" said Lilly. "It would be criminal not to eat it."

"But if we're caught with it in our basket . . . Lilly, if only you hadn't . . . killed it. What are we going to do with it?"

Lilly didn't respond. In the air was the smell of turned earth and wood smoke. She began walking again and took the left fork of the road. Eva followed a short distance behind. The smoke was billowing up from a small clearing on the other side of the stream. Lilly headed toward it.

"Where are you going?" called Eva. Lilly jumped the stream and scrabbled up the other side of the bank. She waited for Eva to follow and helped her up.

"Lilly," Eva scolded. "Now my boots are all wet."

The clearing was out of sight of the road. Sitting on logs around the small bonfire was a family of Gypsies, two men, a woman, and three children. They were boiling up a pot of coffee. Behind them a horse was tethered to a tree. A cart loaded with belongings lay upended nearby.

"Let's go before they see us," whispered Eva.

But Lilly appeared not to hear her. Instead she took out the dead rooster and held it by its feet. She walked slowly toward the fire with her arm outstretched. The whole family turned.

"We'll share it with you," she said, "if we can share your fire."

The men glanced at each other. Maybe, Lilly suddenly thought, they would attack them, or rob them, or even rape them. There were stories about Gypsies, about how they ate their babies and stole away small children. The wood on the fire cracked like a gunshot; she jumped and Eva let out a small, high-pitched scream. The men's faces broke and they started to laugh. The children joined in. Only the woman did not smile. Then they spoke softly to one another in another language.

After some discussion, one of the men stepped forward and, with a small bow, took the dead bird. While one prepared the rooster, first plucking it and then taking out its innards with a knife, the other man handed them small cups of coffee. It was as thick, sweet, and black as treacle. While they sipped it, the men argued. The smell, they explained in halting German, might attract attention. And so, after another long discussion, they began to dig a hole and fill it with the ashes and burning logs from the fire. The rooster was wrapped up in leaves and placed on top of the embers. Then the Gypsies scraped soil over it all until the bird was completely buried. Finally they collected the feathers and the bird's bloody insides in a piece of newspaper, swaddled them in a cloth, and stuffed the bundle deep into a carpetbag.

"They buried our rooster," Eva whispered. The Gypsy who had taken the rooster heard her as he came back to the fire.

"It will cook slow," he said as he knelt down and began to stoke. "No one will know."

Lilly watched him. He was aware of her eyes as he picked up one of the children and began to play with him, tickling and throwing him in the air. And she wondered if she had ever been loved so naturally, so unconditionally, so casually.

"Papa!" the child cried out. "Papa!"

The Gypsy laughed and kissed him on the belly.

"Hey!" a voice cried out from behind.

Two men had jumped the stream and were coming toward them. One was a policeman. The Gypsies poked what was left of the fire and stirred the can of coffee. Lilly sensed their apprehension. They had taken a risk, and now they might have to pay for it.

"Eva," Lilly whispered quickly. "Speak to them."

"Me?" she replied. "Why me? I don't know what to say to them."

"Please," she insisted. "Say you're looking for the baron's estate. This is the country, there's always a baron."

The policeman and the other man came to a dead stop right on top of the buried rooster. There was a sickening moment before Eva turned and spoke.

"Good day," she said.

"Are you all right, miss?" the policeman said, looking with some suspicion at the Gypsies.

"Oh, we're quite okay now," Eva replied. "These kind people saved our lives—I would have died without a coffee."

The men had been ready for a confrontation, but Eva's upper-class accent disarmed them.

"My friend and I came down from the city, from Berlin, this morning," she went on. "I'm a friend of the baron, and we were trying to locate his estate. Maybe you can help us?"

The Berliners the policeman had met before were sullen and monosyllabic. Sometimes their pockets sagged to their knees with stolen potatoes, and cabbage leaves sprouted from underneath their coats. But usually they revealed nothing: their loot had been either expertly hidden or already eaten. This young woman, however, was different. The policeman was a man who, despite all the power bestowed on him, could not help but defer to a higher class. His parents had been employed by the old baron as a gamekeeper and a cook, and he had grown up in awe of the family who employed them. Unmarried, past forty, and an ardent supporter of the kaiser, he still fantasized about marrying up.

"Well, if it's the baron you're looking for, you're way off track," he said. "His place is on the other side of the railway."

"Oh, no!" Eva replied. "I knew we must have taken a wrong turn. I have no sense of direction, you know. Not like you. You're a man who looks like he always knows where he's going."

The policeman smiled and nodded.

"But you do mean the young Baron von Richthofen, of course," he said conspiratorially.

His companion shifted from foot to foot and watched the Gypsies.

"Oh, yes," said Eva, "that's the one."

"Inherited the title from his uncle," the policeman told his companion. "After that terrible business in Berlin."

"Terrible," Eva echoed.

"One bullet through the temple," he added. "Over a woman, I heard."

"Oh, yes," she said. "I heard that too."

"Aren't they Jews?" his companion added, not wanting to be left out.

"The von Richthofens?" The policeman nodded. "Bestowed the title by the king of Bavaria a hundred years ago. Bankers."

"Bankers," his companion repeated, and sniffed. Then he pulled a rag from his pocket and blew his nose loudly.

"Well, you have been very informative," Eva said. "The other side of the train tracks . . ."

"Can't miss it," the policeman added. "We can escort you if you like."

"Oh, no," she replied. "I'm sure we'll find it now. When we've finished our coffee."

The policeman lingered, glancing over at the Gypsies, who, for the whole conversation, had remained silent.

"And give him—"

"Your regards. We will," said Eva. "Thank you."

"My pleasure," said the policeman. "Oh, and ladies, there are a lot of thieves around at the moment. A gang of them even stole this poor farmer's rooster. So if you should see anything . . ."

"We'll come straight to the station," Eva continued for him. "And ask for you."

"Ask for me, yes," he said.

The men jumped back across the stream, the policeman giving Eva one long last look before they turned the corner.

"Wave to him," Lilly whispered.

Eva waved. He waved back.

"Don't ever make me do that again," Eva said when he was gone. "What a horrible little man."

The Gypsies unearthed the rooster when it was getting dark. The embers were still glowing deep red in the pit. They peeled off leaves one by one. The rooster was charred on the outside but cooked right through. The younger man pulled the meat from the bones and began to divide it up onto a row of small tin plates.

"Good?" the younger Gypsy asked Lilly.

She smiled at him. "Very good."

Eva noticed the way his eyes lingered. But Lilly seemed oblivious. Eva thought about the way she had broken the rooster's neck. Her nerve was almost unshakable. But as Eva watched her, it was suddenly clear by the way she held her head, the curl of her mouth, the flaring of her nostrils, that Lilly knew she was being observed and did nothing to acknowledge it. Her face was a shell, her eyes ornamental; she was resilient, beautiful, cold.

Eva had known the truth from the first time she kissed Lilly's cool marble cheek, but she didn't want to admit it to herself. Maybe, the thought occurred to her, she was simply being used. Maybe she should ask Lilly to leave the apartment. After all, she owed her nothing. But the thought of losing her was almost too much to bear. Eva suspected she needed Lilly more than Lilly needed her.

Lilly was thinking about what the policeman had told them. If it was the same Baron von Richthofen from the newspaper cutting, then he had been her father. And if that was so, she was half Jewish. Although she felt no different and she knew almost nothing about Jewish culture, it seemed to make sense. Jews were integrated into German society, but they were still outsiders.

By the time they had finished eating, the children were asleep, curled up by the fire in a pile of blankets. The woman glanced over at Lilly and finally smiled. Both her front teeth were missing. Nothing is what it first appears, she told herself. Nothing is what you first assume.

"We'd better go," said Eva. "We don't want to miss the train."

Eva noted Lilly's hesitation. She decided at that moment that she would not let herself be rejected, not by a girl she herself had found on the street. She stood up, came over, and put her arm around her. It was a gesture of more than simple friendship; it was an indication of ownership.

"Next time I'll steal two," she said. "You'd like that, wouldn't you, Lilly, my love."

The Uhlan

Soldier, stand at ease and smile for the film crew. Holy cow, it's Kurt! Kurt Stark, the film director. How are you? It's been years. Tell me about your wife, the very wonderful actress, Henny Porten. I adored her in Das Liebesglück der Blinden. *What an actress—untrained too. How long have you been married now? How often do you write? Is it true it's every day?"*

Dear Henny,

I was filmed today for the newsreel. Maybe both of us shall appear on the same cinema screen. Me at the front. You in your latest film. Dear Henny, Henny dear, the night drags on beneath the cruel trench moon. And the beat of the bombs goes on. I don't think I can stand it. I long for the white light of the stage or the blank, white square of the projector. I long to be clean again.

A month later, many miles away, a hand-span across the European plain at least, Henny Porten stands on a film set with a telegram in her hand. And on the page, each typed letter looks as if it had been made with so much conviction the typist must surely have been history himself. Her fingers run over the imprint of the letters through the paper as if she were reading Braille: Kurt Stark, stop, killed in action, stop.

In August 1916, news started appearing in the papers about a major British offensive on the Somme. Thousands had been lost in just a few hours. And yet the British hadn't gained more than a mile. Germany was still winning.

A list of missing presumed dead was pinned up once a week outside the Reichstag. Huge crowds of women swarmed around the building, politely waiting their turn. And at regular intervals throughout the day, however, those unfortunate mothers, sisters, or lovers who recognized a name would start to scream and have to be carried away, their bodies limp, their hair undone, their eyes glazed. The others wasted no time in pushing into the space they had left. The pages were pinned high and the print was small.

It was so hot that summer that Eva kept the shutters closed all day. The apartment cooled down in the evenings, so they sat in the drawing room with the windows open. Eva often talked about Stefan, about how funny he was as a boy, about his plans to be a lawyer, about his favorite color, about anything that came into her head. Once or twice a week, however, funeral cortèges would slowly make their way along the street below: a single horse pulling the wagon, bunches of wildflowers scattered on the coffin. And Eva's words would falter and she would clutch her arms around her middle as if trying to hold herself together, as if trying to soften the blow she suspected might come any day.

"What would you like? A glass of water?" Lilly would suggest. But still, what Eva really wanted from Lilly was never offered.

One evening, there was a knock at the door. It was past nine. Eva blanched. It could only be bad news: a telegram, perhaps.

"Let me go," said Lilly.

She unlocked the door and opened it a crack. Outside stood the uhlan, fumbling in his kit bag.

"Lost my key," he said.

And then he looked up. The door suddenly swung open. Eva leapt onto her younger brother and hugged him so hard he almost fell over. He dropped his bag, smiled, and kissed his sister's hair. But his eyes never strayed from Lilly's face.

Stefan was so thin that his eyes seemed bluer and his hands longer. His face was tanned but it had an ashen hue. He told them that after his horse had been shot from under him and there were no more to be had, he had become a stretcher bearer. More than half of his regiment, he added, had been killed since the start of the war. He had two weeks of leave, fourteen days before he had to go back to the front. He ran out of words after this.

They brewed him coffee, which he only sipped. They cut him slices of K-bread, which he broke but didn't eat. They filled the bath with freshly boiled water, opened a new packet of French soap, and listened at the bathroom door as he climbed in. They could hear nothing but the faint slosh of water settling. It was so quiet that Eva wanted to go in and check on him. But Lilly held her back. Instead they sat in silence until they heard the cascade of water as he rose and climbed out.

On the first day he went to bed and slept for fifteen hours. On the second he ate everything he could find in the cupboard, then he went out for a few hours and came back with a bag of army provisions procured from a "contact." On the third day he fell in love.

That morning the air was stifling and the sky was cloudless. It was already late September, but instead of lessening, the summer heat remained, oppressive and harsh, scorching the linden leaves brown before they fell and turning what was left of the grass yellow. At Eva's insistence, they had taken the S-Bahn from Friedrichstrasse to Grunewald with a picnic blanket, a basket full of bread and jam, and a bottle of cheap wine. In the country the trees offered some shade, and they strolled along a leaf-strewn forest path with Eva in the middle, her arms linked through both her brother's and Lilly's.

For long moments nobody spoke. Then Eva started talking and kept talking about anything that came into her head, from the price of butter to the names of trees. At this point she attributed her brother's reticence to the presence of Lilly, the girl she had invited to stay in their house without asking his permission. She thought he was angry; she assumed that he wanted to be alone with his family, that he did not want to have to keep up some pretense of hospitality on his days of leave. Nothing could be further from the truth. And as soon as they arrived at the lake, Stefan sent Eva off to borrow some wine-glasses from the Swedish Pavilion. When she returned, however, with three tumblers and a flask of overpriced kümmel, her brother, Lilly, and the picnic basket were gone.

Eva was twenty-two in 1916. And she had never kissed a man except once, at a party in 1912, when she had been invited to dance by her tango tutor. He had strutted her out onto a terrace and, over-come with a sense of drama, had pulled her into a clinch. She politely obliged and returned the kiss. But the tastes of brilliantine and garlic were so overpowering that she pushed him away and canceled the rest of the lessons.

The only man she had ever loved was Stefan. Since the death of her mother, her love for him had grown until she had sworn to her-self that she would never leave him, that she would always live with him, that she would never forsake him for anybody else. And she expected nothing less from him in return.

When she went back to the spot in the forest where she had left the basket and found Lilly and Stefan gone, she was a little puzzled. At first she walked back and forth along the bank of the lake shouting their names. She looked for them for more than an hour and then walked back to the S-Bahn station alone. At this point she assumed that one of them had become ill and had had to return without delay to the city. She was not angry. It simply did not occur to her that they would hide from her deliberately.

Lilly and Stefan heard Eva's calls but didn't reply. They sat out of sight of the path in a small hollow that overlooked the lake.

"Sometimes I need complete silence," Stefan whispered. "And my sister, though I love her dearly, does go on so. . . ."

"STE . . . FAAAN!" Eva shouted nearby. *"LIII . . . LLY!"*

"We shouldn't be doing this," Lilly whispered.

Lilly was about to stand up when the uhlan took her wrist and held it.

"Please," he said. "Please?"

His eyes pleaded with hers. His grip around her wrist slipped down until he held her hand. He smiled, a half-smile that softened the sharp new angles of his face. Eva's calls grew more distant; she was walking swiftly back down the path, away from them, toward the station. Lilly stared out across the lake.

"Don't feel bad," he said. "I'll take the blame."

The schoolgirl—Stefan still called her that in his head, even though he knew she was no longer one—the schoolgirl brushed a strand of dark hair from her face. He had occasionally thought about her when he was at the front. When the enemy was firing and the barbed wire was snaking in the air above his head, he had found himself going over his life in minute detail. And he vividly remembered the way the car had spun around the corner as the figure of the girl in the middle of the road had come hurtling toward him; the way his foot had pushed into the floor as if pressure alone could prevent them from hitting her; and, afterward, the way she had looked up at him, shoeless, ragged, but still defiantly alive.

And now she was real, she was here, and he realized that he had barely taken her in at all. Her wrists, her lower arms, her tiny hands were so fine, so flawless. She was wearing a pale blue dress that, despite the fact that it had a high collar and long sleeves, clung to her, revealing the slender body beneath. As the occasional leaf began to drift down from the trees and the heat haze began to rise, she sat and stared out across the lake. He would not let thoughts of the war, of what he had seen, come into his head. He was alone with the schoolgirl with a whole beautiful day ahead of them. Nothing else mattered. Nothing else.

The uhlan stretched, a long, languid, glorious grasp of air and space. She had almost forgotten how men were: their different scale, their limbs longer and their movements more generous. He pulled the cork from the bottle with his teeth and handed it to her. She hesitated and then held the bottle to her lips and drank. And while she did so, his eyes never strayed from hers.

"Would you like some?" she asked. She handed him the bottle but he didn't drink.

"How is your eye?" he said.

Lilly was momentarily puzzled. And then her hand flew to her face.

"My eye? It was nothing," she said.

"Can I take a look?" He traced her eyebrow very gently with his little finger.

"You have a scar," he said.

"It's nothing."

"I never thought I'd see you again," he whispered. "But I came back . . . and there you were." She held his gaze.

"Kiss me," he said.

Without hesitation, trepidation, or guile, she kissed him. Stefan let go of the bottle and it rolled down the gentle slope toward the lake and began to spill its contents in slow dark gulps.

Afterward she pulled back and stared at the uhlan's face. Ever since he had come back from the front, she had had trouble sleeping. She felt as though she had helium in her blood. Ignore it, she had told herself. It won't happen. But it had. It was happening. She touched his cheek and ran her finger along the blue graze of his skin. His mouth was so, so soft. There was nothing hard about him, nothing brittle or flinty or cruel. He was not Marek or Eva or Otto. He was Stefan—a name that sounded like a secret, whispered.

The uhlan had come to the conclusion that his life would be short. He had decided he would never have children, become a partner of a legal practice, as he had once planned, or take his grandchildren to the park. When he looked up and saw Lilly at the front door of his uncle's flat, he was instantly sure that it meant he would die within the year. Why else would this young girl he had fantasized about be there—a girl who seemingly had no sweetheart, no family, no one. And he did not resist. He offered himself to his fate with an open heart and a distinct lack of guilt. He wasn't the only one. The city was full of the newly wed and the newly widowed, half dressed in white, the other in black.

Stefan slipped his hand beneath the arch of Lilly's back and pulled her down beside him. He could, he told himself, spend days, weeks, just looking at her throat; he was completely addicted to the clean, sweet scent of her; he was mesmerized by her voice. He wanted her so badly he ached.

"Stop," she said on the banks of the Wannsee. "Not yet."

Ten days later Stefan married Lilly in a private service in the side chapel of the Church of St. Michael near the Oranienplatz. He had found a Catholic priest who would marry them without notice. In the registry she signed her name in full. She was almost sixteen. He was twenty. Although he had sold a painting to a jeweler for a pair of simple gold wedding rings, they had neither the right forms nor their birth certificates. The priest ignored the paperwork: the soldier was returning to France first thing the following morning.

The rain started during the ceremony and didn't stop. It streamed down the gutters and pooled in great floods on the street. Outside Stefan's window, the leaves turned overnight. In shades of gold and amber, red and orange, they blazed briefly before being blown away by gusts of sodden wind.

As Lilly and Stefan lay naked in the reflected light from the window, their bodies seemed to be drawn with water, their skin shimmering with drops and rivulets and tiny tides. Stefan kissed Lilly's face, her eyes, her ears, her neck; she was so fragile, so lucent. It was as if, at that moment, the rain that cascaded down outside was inside, too, in his room, in his bed, in his blood. He reached down and ran one hand along the inside of her thigh while the other found her breast.

Lilly's body stiffened; she had to fight a rising panic in her chest. The last time, she told herself. Don't think about the last time. She kissed his face, then found his ear and whispered.

"Teach me. Teach me how to love you."

Stefan's hands stopped. He was momentarily puzzled. Did she mean the emotion or the actual act itself? Although he would never admit it, he had no experience of sex; he only knew the bare mechanics from the filthy talk of the other men in his barracks. At the front he had been issued with a book of coupons, each of which he could exchange for ten minutes with a prostitute. He had waited in line, but when his turn had come he had taken one look at the elderly whore from Hamburg and lost any inkling of desire. And now Lilly was staring up at him, her breath fast, her eyes alight with expectation. He pulled back and sat up.

"I don't know what you mean," he said.

Not Marek but the Gypsy. Lilly focused on the Gypsy and the way he had loved the child. It had looked so easy, so effortless. But now, as the rain poured down and the hours slid past too fast, her limbs, her hands, her heart felt as though they were made of wood. Although she had shed a skin with Eva, unwrapping herself on the inside was much, much harder.

For a moment neither of them moved. Then Lilly took a long, deep breath. A swell of sadness rose and then fell away. She focused on the back of Stefan's neck, the nape, where the curve of his perfect head met the line of his spine. She reached up and touched him. He shivered.

"There," she whispered.

She picked up his arm and ran her finger along the inside of his elbow.

"And there."

But he still wouldn't turn.

And so she took his large hand and held it within her two small hands and pressed it to her chest, to her heart, until he finally shifted round and faced her again. Speak with your eyes, the actor's words suddenly came back to her. I have fallen in love with you, her eyes said. Believe me. And he understood and something within his face opened, capitulated, released. Without losing his gaze, she placed the hand over her breast. Then she reached and cupped her hand around his neck again, and slowly but firmly pulled him back down until he was lying beside her.

"I just need to learn you first," she whispered. "All of you."

In the half-light of the rain, Lilly explored Stefan's body with her fingertips, from the tidemarks of sunburned skin around his wrists and his collar to the hair on his toes, from the pale angles of his shoulder blades to the conch curl of his ears. Finally she moved down the center of his body from his chest, to his belly, to his penis. Stefan's eyes opened; he reached down for her.

"Come to me," he whispered.

And then, with a rattle of keys and the moan of hinges, the front door slammed.

"I've got schnapps!" Eva shouted down the hall. "Three bottles of kümmel! A pint of Bavarian beer!"

She didn't do it deliberately, Eva told herself later. She loved her brother. She just wanted to celebrate. What is a wedding without a party, after all? And so, later, as the three of them sat round the kitchen table and Eva talked, Stefan started to drink, just as she knew he would. They carried him to bed at midnight. He was so drunk that he had passed out.

"Maybe if we'd had something to eat?" Lilly had said as she began to unbutton his shirt.

"I'll do that," snapped Eva. "He's still my brother, you know!"

The uhlan was reported missing in action in November 1916. Lilly saw his name immediately. Stefan Mauritz—that was all: no details of his regiment or on what front he had been fighting. Her eyes ran over the list again just to make sure. But there it was: Stefan Mauritz. She would have to turn and tell Eva. Her heart thundered and her hands clenched and she could not. And then she felt a hand on her arm.

"There. There," said Eva. "Didn't you see it?"

They had come to the newspaper's office for a first edition. The newspapers printed up the casualty lists before the Reichstag posted them. "You have to pay for bad news now," somebody said. Every morning at seven, the pavements outside the *Berliner Morgenpost* office were thronged as people queued to buy their copy before the paper reached the newsstands. Eva took the newspaper out of Lilly's hands and they pushed their way through the crowd. She headed across the Königsplatz and they walked west through the Tiergarten to the radiating circle of the Grosser Stern. One solitary motorcar chugged around the huge fountain and veered back toward the Brandenburg Gate. And then it was only delivery boys on bicycles, their baskets piled high with newspapers and brown paper packages, whistling or shouting out to each other as they sped along side by side.

Eva marched down the Siegesallee toward the zoo, and Lilly walked a few steps behind. Neither broke down. Neither wept. Neither spoke. They passed a small beer tavern, locked up for the war, and stopped a little farther on, on a bridge over a lake. They listened to the sounds of the animals from the other side of the perimeter wall of the zoo; the distant screech of parrots and the low blare of an elephant, the bark of a sea lion and the hollow howl of an ape. Then Eva picked up a rock from the ground. She hurled it into the water, where it shattered the smooth surface.

"Down with this war!" she shouted into the thick winter air. "Down with the government! Down with the kaiser!"

Lilly did not respond. Instead she started to shiver. She shivered as if she had been the lake's surface, shattered by the trajectory of a rock. A young woman pushing a pram walked toward them. Her baby started to scream in huge drawn-out sobs. A lump rose in Lilly's throat, and she concentrated on taking air into her lungs and letting it out again, on breathing. The young woman passed and the baby's screaming gradually receded.

"It's not certain," Lilly said. "He might be wounded. Mightn't he?"

"Why do you care?"

"He's my husband, Eva."

Eva let out a small exhalation of derision. And then she turned away. Lilly watched the slow flight of a swan above as it flew toward the river Spree. They had been married for six weeks, and in that time they had spent just one night together. What Eva clearly suspected was true: the marriage had not been consummated.

At first Eva felt that she had hidden her true feelings remarkably well. When her brother and Lilly had eventually come back from Wannsee, their faces flushed with the cold and their clothes covered in fragments of leaf and bracken, she had looked from one face to the other and immediately guessed what had happened. Although she insisted that she didn't mind when they confessed where they had been, Eva felt, in fact, as if she had been garroted.

Of course, Lilly asked to borrow a dress for the wedding, and of course Eva obliged. But as she watched "that girl," as she had now started to call her—that girl whom she had found scooping up entrails from the street like a beggar—marry her very own brother, wearing her very own favorite blue dress, she felt enraged, betrayed, heartbroken. How dare Lilly steal away Stefan? And how dare Lilly give away so easily the one thing she had withheld from her for so many months? Eva had loved her; she loved her still. And one by one she bit every single fingernail right down to the quick.

"Congratulations," she had said with a forced smile after the ceremony. "You go home. I have something to do. I'll be back later."

When Eva had revealed what she had in her purse, she became a "regular customer" once again at the butcher's. She was invited into the back shop, where she swapped her mother's diamond engagement ring for the alcohol. And then she hurried back through the rain, against the wind and the falling leaves that danced in the air like huge pieces of dirty brown confetti, to spoil her brother's wedding night with smuggled Polish schnapps.

Two weeks after they had seen Stefan's name on the list, a package arrived through the post from the war ministry. It was stamped with the insignia of his regiment. Eva opened it. Inside were a bread bag, an identity tag, and an army watch.

"He's not dead," Lilly said.

Eva's eyes were sharp with tears and spite.

"What did you say?"

Lilly held the package up to her face and inhaled.

"His wedding ring—where is it? This is just an identity tag. Maybe he lost it. It's a mistake."

Eva left it all lying on the kitchen table and went to her room. Lilly pulled out the Remington typewriter. She would write to the war ministry, to his regiment, to prisoner-of-war camps, to all the hospitals that took injured men from his division. She inserted some paper and started to type.

Later, Lilly was stirring some potato soup, the last of her rations for the week. A stack of letters lay on the kitchen table. Eva hadn't come out of her room all day. The soup was ready.

"Eva?" Lilly said as she knocked softly on the door. "Are you all right?"

For a moment no sound came from the room, and then the door swung open. Eva was standing there, her face fixed.

"No," she said. "I'm not all right. How can you make soup?"

"How can I make soup? We have to eat, Eva," Lilly said. "And I've written letters."

"You wasted your time."

Was Lilly's work futile? A temporary respite from what might be the truth? She wasn't ready to believe it yet.

"What else can I do?" Lilly said. "I have to do something."

As Eva watched, Lilly's eyes dulled, but her skin was still aglow. She turned to go back to the kitchen but Eva placed a hand on her shoulder and stopped her.

"What else can I do?" she repeated.

Eva gazed at her mouth, her eyes, and then her mouth again. And then, very suddenly, she pressed her lips to Lilly's. Lilly was momentarily taken aback, but she wasn't surprised. The kiss, however, was tempered with anger; if only, Eva told herself, Lilly hadn't been so attractive—if only her lips, her ears, her neck hadn't been so desirable—then this wouldn't have happened; she wouldn't have felt angry with herself, angry with Stefan, angry with the whole world, in fact, and everyone in it. It was her fault: it was all Lilly's fault.

Lilly could almost smell Eva's misery; she could sense the wetness of her palms and the cantering of her heart. She stiffened but she did not pull away. How could she? She had lost a husband but Eva had lost a brother. Maybe this would help her, comfort her, calm her. But Eva took her stillness as compliance. Her kiss grew steadily more insistent; her tongue probed into Lilly's mouth; her hand slipped down onto Lilly's breast. What had begun as a gesture of comfort had become something else. Lilly pulled back, but Eva would not let her go.

"Eva," she said, "you have to stop."

"I wanted you first," she whispered. "I found you first."

Lilly's face started to burn. Was this how Eva saw her, as something to be claimed? And her heart seized up.

"Do you feel nothing for me?" Eva continued.

"Not like that. Not like I loved . . . love . . ." she corrected herself.

Stefan. The unspoken name hung between them like a sheet of lead. Eva's shoulders started to heave, not with sadness, but with pure hot fury. Lilly had used her, misled her, duped her. Finally Eva let her go, wiping her mouth with the back of her hand. Lilly turned, but Eva could see that her eyes were cast downward and her arms hung limply at her sides. At last Eva had her. And so she played another card.

"The day we ran you over," she said, "you were wearing a uniform. You never went to that school, did you?"

"Why do you ask me now?"

"Tell me!"

"No," Lilly said. "I didn't."

It was at that moment that Lilly realized that Eva had maneuvered her into a corner with the skill of a champion chess player. What she had lost, however, was not immediately evident.

Eva stopped talking. For three long days she did not say a single word to Lilly. On the fourth day Lilly could stand it no longer. She opened her suitcase and started to put things inside it. She made a semblance of packing, folding, sorting, closing, but as she put on her coat she realized she had no idea what it was she had packed. Eva would change her mind, wouldn't she? She wouldn't let her go. Lilly found Eva sitting at the kitchen table with a cup of hot water in front of her, her body taut, her eyes impassive.

"I suppose . . . I suppose I should go," Lilly said.

Eva nodded. Lilly was so taken aback that she felt physically winded. So she had been wrong.

"Will you at least see me to the door?"

As Lilly stepped across the threshold, she turned and her eyes met Eva's. Lilly swallowed twice. "If . . . when . . . he comes back . . ." she said.

"I'll be in touch," Eva said.

When the door closed, Lilly did not walk away. Her head slowly dipped forward until it was resting on the dark wood paneling. On the other side of the door, Eva pressed her ear to the wood and listened, waiting to hear the sound of footsteps going down the stairs. When she heard nothing, she pulled away. Her fingers ran along the grain of the wood, back and forth. She traced a face, a mouth, two eyes. And then she balled her hand and thumped it on the door.

The footsteps were neither hurried nor slow. Eva listened as they receded down the stairs and out onto the street. And then, room by room, she bagged up any evidence of her former friend and threw it all down the garbage chute.

Lilly found a job in a munitions factory and lodgings in Rixdorf with a widow called Gudrun, who also worked at the factory. Lilly slept behind a blanket partition in a tiny attic room and shared a communal bathroom with seven other families. After twelve-hour shifts, she and Gudrun would take it in turns to queue for food. But no matter how exhausted they were, they had to remain alert at the factory. One woman fell asleep on the production line and lost her hand. Another dropped some powder, caused a small explosion, and killed three of her friends.

Lilly's job was to secure washers around the metal casings of howitzer shells. They were covered with thick black grease, grease that ingrained itself into her palms and made them itch. The machinery around her stamped and whined with such intensity that Lilly's ears rang for hours afterward. All she thought about when she worked was to put the washers in the right place. All she did was count the number of shells—one, two, three, four—and when the clock struck the hour, she started over again. She did not think about the war or about Stefan and Eva. At least, not during the day. At night, despite herself, her dreams took place on the sun-soaked banks of the Wannsee or in the Steglitz apartment as torrential rain fell outside.

"My life," Lidi was later quoted as saying, "in the later years of the war? I was not there, I was an *Ersatzmensch*, a fake person."

It was true that Lilly still wore her wedding ring and talked about her husband as if she had recently heard from him. But there were plenty of others who were living with untruths: plenty of wives who were not really married and mothers whose children looked like the French prisoners of war who were imprisoned in Spandau. Nothing was real, nothing was what it said it was on the box: the dried egg and dried milk from the market were really just white and yellow powder made of washing soda, starch, and powdered paint; the substance sold as flour was three parts ash, and the coffee was made of ground-up bark. With food, as with everything else, you had to close your eyes and swallow.

In October 1917, just as Lenin had promised the kaiser, the Bolsheviks revolted. The czar was imprisoned along with his entire family and the huge country of Russia erupted into civil war. As the kaiser drank Herr Lenin's health in vodka for bringing the bloody battles on the Eastern Front to a rapid halt, the government promised jam. In the markets of Berlin, hundreds queued all day. At five p.m. the crowd that had waited so good-naturedly in the rain was told that the jam shipment had been canceled. That night Gudrun wept openly. Somehow the idea of jam, which in peacetime was called poor man's butter or children's food, jam made of purple damsons or blackberries picked from the side of the railway, had grown in her mind until she could taste it, until she craved it, until she couldn't eat another piece of so-called bread without it. It had come to represent hope, innocence, peace, and then, despite the promises, there was none to be had.

In November, a scandal broke when it was disclosed that government officials in the area of Neukölln had been buying up food at prices well above the regulated level. The black market, despite all the authorities had said, was now demonstrably the only market. At Alexanderplatz market, one woman walked up to a bread stall and just took what she wanted without paying. Others followed her example and within minutes several tons of overpriced bread, vegetables, and food substitutes had been liberated. Gudrun came home with a jar of a pale watery substance labeled applesauce and three loaves of bread. They ate it all in one sitting, without guilt. The next day, however, there were far fewer stalls at the market, and dozens of police.

Food demonstrations started to take place every other day. One woman hit a shopkeeper with his own broom and then, together with a group of her friends, chased him out of the neighborhood. The city was awash with rumors: The government had bought herring as a meat substitute, peace talks with the East had broken down, the herring had all been sent to Poland, the bread ration was about to be reduced again.

And still the war rumbled on. As spring began to crack the ice of the trenches, the German army launched another offensive on the Western Front. They drove the Allies back forty miles and brought in more troops for a final push. It was, in hindsight, a last burst of bravado in the face of defeat. Even across no-man's-land, the German soldiers could hear the smooth action of the Americans' newly forged artillery and see the flush of their well-fed cheeks. But worse still were the times they couldn't see their faces. Tanks, hundreds of them, rolled toward the German lines and broke through previously impregnable defenses. The Allies had eight hundred of them, the Germans twenty. At night the soldiers read about the riots in Berlin. Come home, their wives' and mothers' letters begged them. No wonder so many surrendered. No wonder so many of them deserted and began to walk the long way home.

There is a photograph taken in the early days of 1918. Around thirty women in heavy coats and mufflers march through Treptower Park. Some smile for the camera, but most of them clutch their handbags in their fists and look primed for a fight. If the picture had been in color, you would have noticed that most of the women's faces were tinged yellow. That's how you could spot a munitions worker; the TNT gave them jaundice. Lilly is third from the left. She was one of one hundred thousand women who had walked out at nine a.m. on the twenty-eighth of January and been on strike for three days.

Shortly after the photograph was taken, the striking munitions workers were joined by a group of Spartacists. Led by Rosa Luxemburg and Karl Liebknecht, this radical group read Marx and opposed the war. They had gotten their name when Liebknecht, on flyers that derided the kaiser, had signed himself Spartacus. They wanted nothing less than an uprising on the Russian scale. They wanted a revolution. In their ranks, handing out leaflets and shouting "Down with the war!" was Eva Mauritz.

Shortly after Lilly had left, Eva had met a woman in the Café des Westens. The woman was in her mid-thirties and called Lutz Ehren. She had made love to Eva in the ladies' toilet and then invited her to a Spartacist meeting. The relationship didn't last and Ehren left the party only six months later, but Eva joined the Spartacists and became a Communist.

As a channel for her anger, it proved effective. How she had longed to reject the comfortable mediocrity of her own middle-class background! What better way to liberate herself politically and sexually? But her newfound political convictions did not completely cure her. Over the previous year, she had come to regard the girl who had toyed with her and then married her only brother as manipulative and poisonous, her motives suspect, and her departure deserved. And so she had rewritten what had happened on the day that Stefan's possessions arrived. She had repeated it so often to herself that she practically believed it: how Lilly had torn up the letters that she herself had typed; how she had gone without leaving any way of contacting her, should Stefan's regiment be mistaken and he be alive after all; how she had abandoned her.

When they met face-to-face in the park as the placards waved and the crowds chanted antigovernment slogans, however, Eva was shocked. In reality the girl looked nothing like the image she had kept alive in her mind. She had a yellow tinge to her face and grease spots on her cuffs, and her nails were rimmed with black. But then Eva noticed that her eyes were still bright. She had forgiven her. And what was worse, she still had hope. At that moment Eva's heart was filled with such animosity that later she was ashamed.

"Any news?" Lilly asked. "Have you heard anything?"

"I have heard they have butter in Munich," Eva replied.

As the protesters began to jeer and the government forces began to approach, as the sky threatened snow and the wind blew in from the north, Eva pushed her hair away from her face. On her thumb she wore Stefan's wedding ring. Lilly had seen it, Eva was sure of it. Something in Lilly's eyes finally faded. Now Eva had made her believe it: she had made her believe that Stefan, her brother, was dead. Even though he lay not a mile from the park, in his own bed, with his discharge papers on the dresser.

The Last Train

The government has bought the film industry. Backed up by the German Bank, they've taken over the Tempelhof's Oberlandstrasse, those huge glass studios built for light, and renamed it Ufa. Now they need extra staff, canteen assistants, office cleaners, and wardrobe girls. The pay is peanuts, but as soon as word gets out they're hiring, they have to hire staff to hire staff.

Today the trees are covered in catkins as soft and tiny as mink coats for mice. Inside, there must be more than a hundred women waiting. The walls are freshly painted and the floor is newly varnished, and nobody wants to lean or sit in case they leave a mark. Although they wear their best dresses, their smartest hats, and their jazziest shoes, if you looked closer you'd see that their stockings are still full of darns and their hems are edged with soot.

Only the older girls get the jobs. Or the quiet ones or the ones who don't know the difference between Henny and Pola. The rest can't understand it. They weep and demand to see the boss, and when politely refused, they stamp and shout. And then they go back to their stone-cold apartments, where there is nothing to eat, and pace up and down with their coats on before running out to the Picture Palace or the Mozart Hall just in time to catch the last showing.

The trains from the Western Front usually came into Friedrichstrasse Station after nine in the evening. Most of the carriages carried coffins, coffins made of splintery fresh wood that still smelled of sap. These trains were always met by a few clusters of round-shouldered relatives who watched the disembarkment and then hurried from box to box, examining the names and rank numbers too casually scrawled in charcoal on the lids. And then, when they found their own, their lips would tighten and they would haul the coffin onto a handcart and wheel it away. Only those who could pay for the transportation and whose son or husband or father was still relatively intact got the body back. The rest, the missing and the blown-to-pieces and the unidentifiable, were buried without ceremony in the fields of France.

It was late October 1918. Every night for the last week, Lilly had come to the station after her shift had finished. By this time it had already been dark for hours, an India-ink dark that seemed to saturate the night until the city and the sky blotted into each other. Inside the station, however, the light was a grayish orange color partly lit by the greasy filaments of the all-night café. Children, cocooned in blankets, lay top to tail in corners like nests of rats. Women as young as twelve and as old as sixty-five offered themselves without shame or reserve price, while on the street outside, or in Friedrichstadt, or in the city parks, hundreds of teenagers, so-called line boys, coolies, and doll boys, hung around dressed in sailor suits or morning coats.

"Going somewhere, miss?" they asked her.

Lilly averted her head and kept on moving. Sometimes she squinted deliberately up at the destination board and often she glanced nervously at the station clock, but if anyone had watched her, really watched her, they would have noticed that she never bought a ticket. Instead, she paced the marble concourse where it was most brightly lit, tried to avoid eye contact, and waited.

Someone at the munitions factory had a brother at the front. He had come back on leave with a story about meeting a girl with a broken tooth who had once been a ward of St. Francis Xavier's in Berlin. Her name was Hanne. He went back to the front with a letter. A letter came back three months later written in a hand Lilly did not recognize. It informed her that Hanne would be returning to Berlin in the last week of the month. As Lilly read the letter for a second time, she had felt a familiar swell of relief: she had found Hanne again. And now she was restless and agitated with waiting. She couldn't stand another day, another hour, without her. Hanne was coming home. Lilly was coming home, too, for Hanne was home, or the closest thing Lilly had ever known to it. But how could she tell her about Eva, about Stefan? Where would she start? And so she decided to wipe out the whole episode, just as Eva had wiped her out. It did not happen, she told herself; I was not there.

"Miss," a policeman called out. "The station is to be cleared. The kaiser is expected."

Beyond him, there was already the shiver of a disturbance. Shoulders jerked in coats and handfuls of damp jacket were pulled until their seams stretched and the cotton thread snapped. A man let out an angry yell, a woman swore, a baby began to cry. And then, although she couldn't see him, she could hear the clipped footsteps of Wilhelm II and his entourage approaching.

The war still pounded on in the East and in the West. Lilly read in the newspaper that negotiations with the Russian delegation had broken down when Trotsky had walked out. At home, a million workers in twenty cities had gone on strike, and the Spartacists were said to be plotting more demonstrations. Street battles between the reds and the whites were a daily occurrence. And then there was the influenza, the so-called Spanish flu, which came not at all from Spain but from the U.S.A., brought over by farm laborers turned soldiers. At first it was the old who died, or the very young, or the very poor. But then another strain took hold, more aggressive than the first, and wiped out scores of the young and previously healthy. At this point it had been put to the kaiser, in terms less delicate than he was used to, that the army was collapsing, that the men could no longer be trusted, that Germany was losing the war. Wilhelm II, however, would not give up. He suggested the German naval fleet might save the day and secure the country's honor. And he insisted on a final push, another stab on the Western Front. Join the army, then, his increasingly skeptical advisers advised him. See for yourself.

Although Lilly may not have guessed it as he bowed his head and pressed a handkerchief to his eyes against the filthy air, Wilhelm II was close to breakdown as he climbed aboard the royal train, which was bound for Spa in Belgium. He did not see the young woman who watched him from behind the raised arm of a policeman. He did not know that his hasty departure from Berlin would not be brief, as he anticipated, but would in fact be permanent. And as he settled himself into the royal compartment, the train started to move forward, and he poured himself a cup of English breakfast tea, he felt a little better. He watched the blackened city hurtle by and wondered if his valet had brought biscuits. This would, however, be the last time his silver train would ever glide above the silver Spree, past Museum Island, Zoo, and Charlottenburg, and down through the Grunewald. Only a few months later, eighty wagons headed to Holland loaded up with his furniture and pictures, photographs and movies, helmets, and, in a carriage all to themselves, his three dachshunds.

Another coffin train had just pulled in on Platform Three, filling the station with steam and soot and the sour smell of hot metal. A few passengers disembarked: a couple of officers, a half-dozen white-faced nurses, and, right at the back, without a coat, Hanne Schmidt.

"Tiny Lil." Hanne's voice cracked and she started to cough. "Don't kiss me, I've got a cold."

When her coughing had subsided, Hanne looked around, at the squalor of the station, at the homeless, at the coffins. But she did not seem to see any of it.

"Berlin," she said. "I've missed you so much."

Lilly gave Hanne her coat, took her bag, and then guided her to the S-Bahn. And as they sat on the train as it rattled its way through the city, Lilly could not stop looking at Hanne, the way she sat with her eyes closed and her face angled toward the dull, dirty compartment light. Hanne turned and gave her a half-smile. But Lilly did not look away. If she stopped looking even for an instant, she suspected, Hanne would disappear again.

Gudrun was not pleased to see Hanne. She took in the heeled shoes, the scuffs worn almost through, the bulging carpetbag, the silk stockings, and the dress cut above the knee. She noticed the way Hanne stood with her weight all on her left leg, her right turned out just a little so the light stroked the inside of her thigh. It was obvious she was not a nurse, as she so casually claimed, but she did not take in the flush of her cheek or register its significance.

"You can stay for tonight," she told her. "But that's all."

Hanne glanced around the tiny room divided in two with a blanket.

"I wasn't planning to," Hanne replied. "Is there anything to eat?"

"No," said Gudrun.

Hanne sighed. And then she put her hands into the carpetbag and brought out a package wrapped in brown paper. Inside was a loaf of rough bread, some real coffee, and a couple of bashed tins.

"What's in the tins?" Gudrun asked.

"Pâté de foie gras de Strasbourg," Hanne replied.

"Where did you get it?" Lilly asked.

"Don't ask," she said as she opened the tin with a penknife. "Don't ask."

And so Lilly didn't ask about her time at the front. One day, Hanne supposed, she would tell her how it had been, how she had risen quickly through the ranks to become the highest class of whore, servicing officers and generals for hard currency instead of coupons. It wasn't unusual. She was young, she had been certified free of venereal disease by a doctor, she could carry a tune, and, after a few weeks of decent meals, she had started to put on weight. Look at what would have happened to her if she had taken Sister August's advice, she told herself. She would have looked like Lilly and Gudrun: starving, jaundiced, poor.

But she did tell her one thing without prompting.

"I met Sister August," Hanne said. "At the front. In a hospital. She asked about you."

Sister August. The name gave Lilly a jolt. How long had it been? she wondered. Five years? Six? A vivid memory came back to her, a clumsy embrace in a corridor, the nun's arms encircling her, a searching glance that seemed to read her inside and out. And she suddenly longed to see her again: her face framed by the wimple, her feet in men's shoes. She longed to smell her clean almond smell and meet her blue-eyed gaze.

"How is she?"

"Well, she's not a nun anymore," Hanne said. "Now she's just plain old Nurse von Kismet."

Lilly tried to see Sister August in a different outfit, in civilian clothing. She remembered the night they had followed her to the Tiergarten. She had seemed like another person entirely then: an impostor, a sinister doppelgänger. But the world had turned upside down. Now Sister August didn't exist, and the other woman did.

"The last thing I heard was that she was working on a hospital train. Somebody said it was bombed."

Lilly's eyes widened and two spots of color appeared in her cheeks.

"Bombed? But she's all right, isn't she?"

"People just disappear and you never know." Hanne shrugged. "That's the worst of it."

And then she sneezed twice and spread the pieces of bread with pâté. Lilly claimed she had already eaten, but the truth was that she had lost her appetite. Gudrun and Hanne ate one, two, three, four slices, until there was nothing left but the empty tins and the inedible crust.

"That was the best meal I've had since my wedding day," Gudrun said. "What did you eat on yours, Lilly? You must have had a decent meal when you got married." And then she cleared her throat and wiped her mouth with a torn napkin, aware that she had said something she shouldn't have.

"You're married?" Hanne said, and looked around the room, almost as if expecting a husband to suddenly appear.

"When? Where? Who?" she asked. "And why didn't you tell me?"

Hanne was staring at Lilly, waiting for an explanation. The room was quiet but for the small clink of plates as Gudrun began to clean up.

"He's dead," Lilly said simply.

It was the first time she had said the words aloud. But now that she had, there was nothing more to say. There was no body, no funeral, and no gravestone. There was nothing left but a cheap gold ring and a sharp twist of sadness. It was a marriage that had been over almost before it had even begun.

Hanne lit a cigarette, a strong, filterless French cigarette from a packet she had in her pocket.

"What was his name?" Hanne asked through curls of bitter gray smoke.

"Stefan," Lilly said.

"I'm sorry," said Hanne.

But it was clear by her face that she was not. Hanne had become numb to death, anesthetized to loss, hardened to stories of tragedy and misfortune. And if she ever cried for a soldier, a friend, or a lover who had lost his or her life, it was because this new bereavement stirred up memories of old, and she would find herself crying for herself, for the little girl who had lost her mother at the age of twelve.

"I'll make the coffee, shall I?" Gudrun whispered.

Stefan Mauritz's position as a stretcher bearer had been filled by the time he returned to the Somme. Instead, he was sent to what was left of a small French town called Beaumont-Hamel as a reinforcement. The British bombardment of German positions had been relentless. Over a million shells had been dropped. The number of known dead on the German side was already more than half a million. His commanding officer hadn't looked him in the eye when he gave him his orders. They both knew it was practically a death sentence.

When Cavalry Officer Mauritz arrived in September 1916, torrential rain had been falling on France for two days. It had comforted him at first: the memory of the rain on his wedding day was still fresh in his mind. But then when his uniform was soaked through and could not be dried, when everything—his clothes, his face, his food—was covered in mud, when the trenches, no-man's-land, the world, was sliding with filthy water, he began to curse the rain and believe that it had become deliberately malicious.

One day, in the middle of the afternoon, the rain stopped and the sun came out. A blackbird started to sing. The churned-up fields, the pools of mud, the rubble of the town looked almost polished. And he noticed that the broken stones sparkled with particles of quartz. Maybe, the thought crept into his head, maybe I will survive this war and return to Berlin, to Lilly, to my wife.

"Attention," the commanding officer hissed. "Enemy advancing."

He could hear their whispers and the click of their guns. He could smell their fear, their sweat, even the oil they used on their rifles. He picked one, a small man with a strange loping shuffle, and set him in his sights. And then he saw that the soldier's uniform was faintly steaming. He happened to glance down and realized that his own uniform was doing the same. The sun was drying out the rain, the mud, the recent past; they were the same, weren't they? He knew he should shoot, he should pull the trigger when he had the chance. Instead he started to pull off his uniform, his identity tag, his helmet.

Stefan heard the whistle of the bullets in the air, but he had no idea what they could be. He woke up in a hospital in Strasbourg. Six months later he was transferred to Mainz in Germany. He had been hit in the face. His nose was smashed, his cheekbone was shattered, and he had a hole below his left eye. It took him months to summon up the courage to look in the mirror, and when he did he did not recognize himself. His face had become distorted, stretched, bent. Only his eyes—still startlingly blue, still clear as clean water—suggested what he once could have been.

Lilly, however, had been right: the personal effects were not his. In the carnage that had followed the British assault, most of the men in his trench had been killed. His identity tag was found in the mud and attributed to a mutilated corpse. It was only months later, when he could open his mouth wide enough to speak, that he could confirm his identity. He was discharged in May 1918, officially unfit for duty.

"I'm so proud of you," Eva cooed. "My brother. A hero."

Stefan didn't say a word at the station or on the journey back to Steglitz with Eva in a taxi. He knew he had done nothing heroic. He had been a coward from the first moment he had heard the beat of the bombs. And yet he didn't contradict her. In fact, only when it was clear that the apartment was empty and there was no evidence of the wife he had left behind did he finally speak.

"Where is she?" he asked. "Where's Lilly?"

Eva took his hand in hers. She took a deep breath and then finally looked up at him.

"I'm sorry," she said. "I'm so sorry. It was the Spanish flu."

Tears welled up in Stefan's eyes and rolled down over his broken face. He had rehearsed dozens of possible bad outcomes—that she might not want him looking how he did, that she had found another man, that she had fallen out of love with him—but not this one.

"You still have me," said Eva. "I'm here."

But Stefan barely heard or saw her as he stumbled toward his room. How could it be true; how could his beautiful Lilly be no more; how could God have made him live through so much pain only to hit him now with a far worse torment? He eased off his wedding ring, the ring he had fingered and spun for so many months, and left it lying on the hall table.

In Rixdorf, Gudrun sipped the coffee in silence. Hanne opened her bag and pulled out a leather pouch of tobacco and some papers. Then she started to roll a tiny cigarette. So, Lilly was a widow. Hanne suspected that it wasn't unusual anymore. She had heard stories about couples marrying practically on the same day as meeting. People fell in love almost instantly, then swore they would remain faithful and dutiful to total strangers. The proximity of death increased the libido. But how long would these marriages last in peacetime? Maybe Lilly had been lucky: she had lost him before she had the chance to really know him. Or maybe, it suddenly occurred to Hanne, it was she who had been lucky, first found by Lilly's letter and then reminded of who she used to be. And her face flushed and her hands trembled as she lit her cigarette, as she realized how close she had been to being lost too.

Lilly was woken up at five a.m. Hanne couldn't stop coughing; she moaned, she yelled, her temples were burning hot. But it was the rattle of her chest that was most frightening.

"I can't breathe," she gasped. "Don't leave me, Lilly."

Gudrun stared at the young woman lying on her lodger's bed. The papers had reported that the illness didn't kill, that the death toll in Germany reported by the foreign press was propaganda. But when she tried to call the doctor from a corner shop, she was told that the lines were down: all the operators were sick.

Hanne seemed a little better later that morning. Her cheeks were still scarlet and her lips had a bluish tinge, but she sat up and drank a cup of water boiled on the stove. Lilly carried Hanne's bag and slowly they took the steps one by one. The hospital was a short tram journey away. When no trams came, they walked, Lilly's arm around Hanne's waist to stop her from falling. Hanne stopped every third step to cough. It took them several hours to walk a mile.

"I'll pay," Lilly offered. "Just make her better?"

The hospital had no room for any more patients. The morgue was full. Hanne was given a blanket and a space on the canteen floor. She lay down under the blanket without taking off her clothes, told Lilly to leave her there, and fell asleep. Back in the attic room, Gudrun had developed a fever. She didn't want a doctor, she insisted. Lilly nursed her with cool washcloths and cups of hot water. Gudrun sometimes called her Karl and wanted to hold her hand. But most of the time she tossed and turned as her head burned and her body sweated.

Hanne, despite developing double pneumonia, recovered. Gudrun died just before dawn three days later.

Lilly did not hurry as she made the journey with a borrowed handcart to the cemetery. She was tired: tired of grief, tired of war, tired of misfortune. And when the striking miners marched past on their way to the Reichstag, she paused and let them wash around her. Only the bare foot that protruded from beneath the blanket gave any hint as to what was beneath it. But nobody wanted to know, nobody wanted to see. The dead were everywhere. Corpses lay piled on the side of the street, black blood oozing from crusted bullet holes. Machine guns rattled overhead and occasionally a figure would fall three or four stories and land with a thud on the cobbles.

That day Lilly's body seemed to float within her skin as if it had become too large for itself. Her hands seemed huge, her mouth too small. If she hadn't brought Hanne back to the flat in Rixdorf, would Gudrun have lived? The outbreak of flu had become an epidemic, but Lilly hadn't so much as sniffled. With every breath she took, her heart felt like a fist. In, out, in, out; it clenched and unclenched itself over and over again.

That morning she had tried to sleep. She couldn't. She had tried to forget. She couldn't. She had tried to ignore the insistent roar of the blood in her head, but it was impossible. And so round and round she spun in her bed until eventually she lay immobile, completely enshrouded in a damp sheet of sorrow.

But although it seemed unbearable, intolerable, sometimes nonsensical, life in Berlin went on. On every pillar or boarded-up shop window she passed, a poster posed the question *Who has the prettiest legs in Berlin?* Hundreds of shops had been forced to close, but new cabarets and nightclubs were opening every day. The soldiers and revolutionaries, the troops and bands of workmen had lost their appetite for bread long ago. Their bodies ran on adrenaline and they swelled and ached with fear and sexual frustration in roughly equal measures.

Meanwhile, the German navy had mutinied and returned to port. The strikes spread south from the cities of Kiel, Bremen, and Hamburg. The king of Bavaria had been overthrown and a Socialist Republic of Bavaria had been announced. Even the policemen were handing over their weapons now and joining the demonstrations.

The gates were locked at the munitions factory. When Lilly returned to Gudrun's room, the landlady was waiting.

"The kaiser has abdicated. I think the war is almost over," she said. "I need this room for my son."

Two days later the armistice was signed in a railway carriage in the forest of Compiègne. All fighting ceased. The monarchy was in exile in Holland. In Berlin, on the banked-up seats of the Circus Busch, an assembly elected a new Republican government. Friedrich Ebert, a Social Democrat, was appointed chancellor.

It was almost impossible to find new lodgings: in addition to the returning military, Berlin was filled with Russian refugees—some, it was said, still with their jewels plaited into their hair. You needed pay slips, references, deposits. And so Hanne took a room in a boarding-house on Motzstrasse near Nollendorfplatz and paid up-front in cash.

It was late afternoon when they climbed to the third floor and unlocked the door. Room 14 was actually two rooms divided by a curtain that smelled of mildew and cigar smoke. On one side were two saggy beds. On the other, a straw-stuffed sofa and a cracked sink with a mirror above it. The rest of the furniture—the tables, the side-boards, and the wardrobes—had been burned as firewood by a previous occupant two winters before. The fireplace had subsequently been boarded up. But there was a gas ring and kettle to brew tea, French windows, and a small balcony that looked out over a chestnut tree.

Lilly suddenly imagined taking rooms like these with Stefan. They would have pushed the beds together, undressed, and lain there for hours in each other's arms. She could remember the way he held her, she thought she could remember the smell of his body, she could still picture the way he had yawned and stretched on the shore of the lake, but she realized with a jolt that she had forgotten his voice. She tried to hear it again in her head but it was gone. This is how we lose people, Lilly thought: not in one go but gradually. And Lilly understood that she had not only lost Stefan but also the life she could have had with him, a ghostly parallel life of now unattainable happiness.

The midwinter sun lit up the room with a pale blue light. Lilly put her suitcase on one of the beds while Hanne opened all the curtains. Below, another march went by. Across the road a woman was standing in the window, brushing her hair. In the room above, a man paced back and forth holding a telephone.

Lilly had a tiny widow's pension, and although the hostilities were over, Berlin was on the brink of civil war. What would she do now? How would she survive without a job? As Hanne stood on the balcony and smoked, Lilly had a sudden and vivid memory of Sister

August and the way she used to march along the corridors of St. Francis Xavier's with her keys swinging at her hip. She would rather have died than given up. It was up to Lilly to do the same. And so, as she unpacked her few threadbare dresses, she decided that no matter how hard it would be, she had to make herself forget about Stefan; she would stop grieving for another life.

"I can't believe the price of this place," Hanne said as she chucked her cigarette butt into the sink. "It's such a dump."

"Tomorrow I'll try the East," Lilly said. "I've heard there's still cheap lodgings in the East. And then I'll try all the factories. But with all the men returning . . ."

"Lilly," Hanne said. "We can stay here for a while. Don't worry about it."

"But I can't afford it, Hanne," Lilly said.

Hanne sighed.

"I've got something to show you."

She started to pull everything out of her bag. At the bottom, beneath the underwear and soiled stockings, the cold cream and combs, was a long, flat canvas bag. She threw it into Lilly's lap.

"Open it," she said.

Lilly undid the cord and opened the top. It was stuffed with foreign banknotes.

"It'll last us both," she said. "At least until we work out what we're going to do with the rest of our lives."

Upstairs, a man burst into song. His voice was strong but the tune was unfamiliar. His feet thumped, back and forth. He was dancing. At that very moment the door opened. A man in a white dress shirt without cuff links strode into the room. As soon as he saw Lilly and Hanne, he stopped abruptly. He looked from face to face, taking in the young girls, one blond and one dark, the suitcases, the afternoon light on their faces.

"Room twenty-five?" he asked with a heavy Russian accent.

"No, room fourteen," the dark girl replied. "Next floor up, I expect?"

"I most humbly and sincerely apologize," he said with a bow of his head. "You should keep it locked, you know. The door. Ah . . . I see you have a kettle also. I use mine to cook spaghetti, although I'm not sure it is allowed. Well, so nice to be acquainted. Good afternoon."

And then he turned and marched out again, pulling the door shut with a decisive click.

Lilly and Hanne looked at each other and started to laugh. The man was so formal, so polite, so courteous. Nobody had spoken to either of them like that before. Whether Ilya Yurasov, who had recently arrived from a POW camp, really did mistake the floors of the boardinghouse and barge in uninvited unintentionally is debatable. He was at that point running late for his new job as a piano player in the local cinema, and had returned for his wallet after leaving in a rush. But he had seen the girls earlier in the lobby, one blond girl, one dark, and he was intrigued.

"Be my baby," sang the man upstairs. *"You're the only girl for me."*

Although they could hear other boarders singing, laughing, sobbing, dancing, Lilly and Hanne only very occasionally passed them on the dimly lit stairs. And then they would all, as if by mutual consent, keep their heads down and mutter "Good day" without looking up. Sometimes droves of people stamped up the narrow stairs outside their room for an impromptu party in the room above at four in the morning. And then the girls could expect to be awake until dawn, when the party dispersed two by two into the rush hour.

The rent was collected once a week by a sad-eyed fat girl who would touch their money only with gloves on. There was a price to be paid for anonymity. There was a price to be paid for a blind eye turned. And so they lived from week to week in an establishment that catered to guests whose gains were probably ill-gotten, among people whose skin was the wrong color or whose talents would never be recognized by any professional body or whose papers were not in perfect order. And when the boardinghouse burned down four years later at two on a Sunday morning, nobody perished but the sad-eyed fat girl. Everyone else was working.

One night Lilly woke up suddenly and sat up. The room was filled with an artificial glow. Hanne was standing at the stove, making tea.

"What time is it?" she asked.

"It's midnight," Hanne replied. "I couldn't sleep. They've switched on the streetlights for the first time in years."

But even as she spoke, the filaments outside began to sputter and the globes that held them began to turn from orange to deep pink as one by one they lost their charge, until the only light left in the room was the pale blue flicker of the gas ring.

"For a few hours, anyway," Hanne added.

That winter there was a subconscious accord to assume a kind of collective blindness: you ignored the street fighting, you avoided the eyes of the starving or the crippled or the insane, and you did not contemplate the future, not even for a second. Instead, you found something to look forward to, something inconsequential, and you focused on it alone: the promise of a romantic interlude, for example, or a trip to the cinema or a skinned rabbit to turn into stew. Even Christmas, a festival that had so recently been infused with melancholy, grew and grew in people's imagination until it became all they could think about, all they could dream about, all they existed for.

And so, on that afternoon in December 1918, stalls had been set up on Potsdamer Platz selling indoor fireworks, gingerbread, and tinsel. For the first time since 1914, Christmas displays appeared in shop windows. Right in the middle of the square, propped up in a bright red metal bucket, was a small fir tree decorated with paper chains, colored glass balls, and a string of blinking electric lights.

Middle-aged men walked with a young woman on each arm, grandparents clung tightly to the hands of bright-eyed children, and the occasional sailor or revolutionary, with a strip of red cotton tied around his coat sleeve, strolled slowly from window to window, from painted snow scenes to piles of cakes and biscuits made out of clay, as if the last four years had never happened. A hurdy-gurdy player played "Deutschland über Alles." A group of schoolchildren sang Christmas carols. It was well below freezing and the slush in the gutters had frozen again but nobody seemed to notice. What manufactured magic there was—and it was more than just a sprinkling—was there to be treasured.

The German Bank was on the corner of Potsdamer Platz. Just as Lilly and Hanne reached the main doors, the sky darkened and sleet and icy rain began to hit the pavements. Everyone ran to find shelter in shops, in cafés, and under the wide canopy of the gingerbread stall. But nobody else climbed the three stone stairs to the wide dry porch of the bank.

Two armed doormen guarded the doors. One of them was about to grab Lilly's arm as she passed, to tell the girls that they had no business there, that soliciting was not permitted, that it was a bank, not a waiting room for the weather. But before he had even set his hand on her, Lilly turned and stared at him with such a look that he stood back and let her pass.

If you had seen a photograph of Lidi, as she was soon to be known, on that day, at that hour, at that minute on Potsdamer Platz, you would not have recognized her. She was almost eighteen. At that point her face was still unaware of itself. Her eyes, those half-moons of silver gray, were downcast and red-rimmed from the cold. Her chin, a chin that her co-star in *The Forbidden Depths* was to call the Helen of Troy of chins in an interview in 1924, was wrapped in a blue knitted muffler. Her lips—which, when sculpted in wax by the resident sculptor at the Movieland Wax Museum, were recorded as the most perfect pair of lips of any actress—were chapped and bitten. Her hands might have suggested what she was to become, hands that, though blistered and roughened, were full of language and expression. But without gloves or mittens, they were pushed down deep in her pockets and clenched tight against the cold. No, it was her carriage, the way she held herself, that made the doorman of the German Bank change his mind in an instant. In a city, a country, that had been crushed, she still looked decisively resolute.

On Potsdamer Platz, the sleet kept falling and eventually turned to hail. It collected in the dips of awnings and in the brims of hats. It rapped against automobile windshields and iced up the mirrors on an approaching omnibus. But it was warm inside the bank. A couple of large cast-iron radiators rattled beneath the window and a pile of logs smoldered in the fireplace in the manager's office. The teller was in his late teens. His face was pockmarked with acne but his gaze was steady. He wore a Boy Scout badge on his lapel.

"Can you change some money?" Hanne asked.

He nodded and held up his hands.

"This is a bank," he said, "not a cake shop."

He laughed and glanced around to see if anyone else had heard his joke. No one had. Hanne started to pull out the wads of cash from her canvas bag. There was so much of it that there was barely room on the polished brass counter.

The boy looked at the money in surprise. He had been expecting coins. The two young women gave no indication as to where the money had come from, but he had a good idea. One was fair, the other dark. His father, he strained to remember, was blond. He hadn't seen him for three years and now accepted that he probably never would again. If only his mother would stop writing letters . . .

The pile kept on growing, its size quite at odds with his expectation. Very little of it was German currency. He took the bundles of banknotes they pushed through one by one and counted them. As he did so, Lilly noticed his nose wrinkle. The francs and guilders, the rubles and pounds were filthy; they were sour with sweat and stained with smears of blood and grease. For years these notes had been rolled up and stuffed in boots, under armpits, in the linings of helmets. Each note was scuffed with hundreds, maybe thousands of countings. They had been won and lost, squandered and saved, stolen and given away for a song, or a smile, or a quick grope in a doorway. And eventually they had found their way into Hanne's purse.

"You want it all in marks?" the teller asked. "Why not dollars?"

"Because," Hanne replied, "I am not going to America."

The teller divided the money into four piles, shrugged, and pulled out a mechanical calculator. And then he counted out a stack of freshly printed notes, licking his fingers at regular intervals.

"Two thousand," he said emphatically. "And sixty-five marks, twenty-three pfennigs."

He patted the pile and then, after the smallest hesitation, pushed it through the slot. Hanne took the notes and laboriously counted them herself. And then she thanked him and stuffed them into her handbag.

"Good day," the boy said. "Maybe you'll buy me a drink?"

Hanne stared at him through the glass.

"Did we ever meet before?" she asked. "Were you in Ypres?"

The boy smiled and shook his head.

"I was in school right here in Berlin," he said.

"Maybe it was your father," she said as she snapped her handbag shut. "I never forget a face."

The teller was suddenly filled with a flush of mixed emotion; his throat constricted, his eyes watered, his teeth clenched. The next customer came up to his window.

"Do you have dollars?" she asked. "Excuse me? Hello?"

"How many do you need?" he replied, his voice barely audible through the glass and the metal grating.

Hanne paused on the top step. A Russian café on the other side of the square was already packed, although it was only mid-afternoon. From within came the strains of a small band.

"Come on," said Hanne. "I'm cold, let's have some tea."

The air inside the Café Josty was thick with cigarette smoke. While men in fur coats drank tiny cups of Russian tea, a couple of middle-aged ladies danced self-consciously on a wooden dance floor. Hanne led Lilly to a little table at the back. The waiter tried to suggest a place round the corner, a place more suited to their needs.

"Why?" Hanne asked him. "Do you think we're tarts?"

Hanne's gaze fixed on the waiter's face. Only the faintest hint of red appeared on each cheek.

"I think we should go," said Lilly.

Hanne pulled out ten marks and placed them beneath the sugar bowl.

"Bring us Champagne, the best you have," she instructed him. "And cake."

The waiter nodded and took the money.

They sat and waited. Neither removed her coat. The "Champagne" they were brought was lemonade laced with vodka. The "cake" tasted of frostbitten potato. The band in the corner started to play some jazz tunes, but with so much angst and sobriety that they were barely recognizable as jazz at all.

"Well, this is fancy," Hanne said.

And then on the street outside they heard the now familiar sound of a mob approaching; the footfall was irregular as boots shuffled or limped along the cobbles and over the tram tracks; its voice was a shouting, chanting, singing swell, with the occasional low belly boom of a rifle fired into the air.

The band kept playing. The women kept dancing. The door burst open and a portly middle-aged man and his whippet-thin driver burst in.

"Bloody Spartacists," the man exclaimed to everyone and no one. He shook out his umbrella, looked around, and then he saw Hanne.

The film producer had made a fortune during the war. What he imported, and where from, he wouldn't say. He now had a Daimler and a house in Charlottenburg. He had also started making films about sexual health.

"Well, that's the official line anyway," he said with a wink.

"And what are you doing?" he asked. "Still singing in a tingle-tangle?"

"Oh, no," Hanne replied. "I'm an actress now."

The film producer didn't even blink twice.

"Everyone I meet in this city is an actress," he said. "Or a cabaret performer, or a singer, or a dancer."

"And you?" He looked at Lilly. "I bet you're an actress too."

He gave Hanne his card, finished off their "Champagne," and ordered more, and more again. Outside, the Spartacists had passed on their way to the Reichstag. Ebert was being held hostage by a group of sailors.

"Call me," the film producer said as he was leaving. "Reverse the charges."

He did not, however, leave any money for the bill.

Then came the sound of marching: regular, real marching. The band stopped playing and the waiter put down his dish towel. Lilly and Hanne left another ten marks, drained their glasses, and hurried out. It was a division of the army, a few on horseback, most on foot, soldiers come home from the front to be demobbed. They still wore steel helmets, and some had limp bunches of flowers attached to their tunics, their helmets, or their rifles.

The streets were glassy from the winter rain. Across the square, a couple of damp red streamers still hung from balconies. A few bystanders clapped as the men passed. Some sobbed. Most simply watched in silence as the defeated platoons and regiments, their boots still caked with mud, their eyes empty with exhaustion, walked in the direction of the barracks.

"Come on," said Hanne.

"Not yet," replied Lilly.

And she examined every face, one by one, until they had passed by.

"I know it's pointless," said Lilly. "And I still can't help it."

As the soldiers were about to reach the far side of the square, however, a small group of factory workers came around the corner and started to walk directly across their path. An officer raised his arm and commanded his troops to stop. A man at the head of the factory workers, a man in a dirty apron with a bayonet slung over his shoulder and a red band around his arm, sauntered up to the officer. And then with one swift move, he tore the silver epaulet from the officer's uniform and threw it on the ground, leaving a small patch of blue wool of a particularly vivid color.

"Haven't you heard?" he shouted so everyone could hear. "All insignia have been abolished!"

The factory workers cheered. The officer's expression did not change. He stooped down and picked up his insignia, raised his arm, and commanded his soldiers to march on. The factory workers stood aside. Less than half of his regiment followed. The rest seemed to melt away into the side streets, alleys, or doorways, their uniforms already unbuttoned, all evidence of their military rank, all their useless decorations, their medals, and their insignia stuffed deep into their worn pockets.

The shooting broke out about ten minutes later. A grenade was thrown into a gutter and exploded next to a flower cart, filling the air with the smell of saltpeter and pollen. Hanne and Lilly ran for the underground station at the corner of the *Platz*. A few people clustered at the bottom of the stairs, not sure whether to continue Christmas shopping or come back another day. But down in the U-Bahn, everything felt strangely calm. The ticket booth lady took their money and handed out their tickets without a word. There were no delays, no cancellations to the timetable, no rerouting.

Trains in both directions were packed with people. Occasionally, as the train rattled under the city, the distant pounding of artillery could be heard above. But the atmosphere down there was restrained, with both shoppers and demonstrators giving up their seats to the elderly and studiously avoiding each other's eyes.

It was only when they surfaced at Zoo that Hanne complained that her arm hurt from holding her bag so tightly. Lilly's head ached from the "Champagne." They were both damp with sweat yet shivering when they reached the main door of their hotel, and both, though they could not say it out loud, were filled with relief.

On the last night of the old year, the sky was lit up with gunfire and fireworks. Sometimes it was hard to tell the difference between the two. Lilly and Hanne sat in the dark at the window.

"To 1919," Hanne whispered. "It can't be any worse. And happy birthday, Lilly."

In the distance they could see figures running over the rooftops. Half the city, it was said, was controlled by the Spartacists, the other by the Freikorps, the government's troops. A machine gun was fired down into a street nearby and a man cried out. And then there was silence—not the opaque silence of sleepers or empty rooms but the transparent silence of insomniacs and the wakeful, a silence that listened to itself.

Straßenkämpfe in Berlin.
Zweifronten-Barrikade in der Schützenstraße.
Aufnahme
Berlin.

The Screen Test

The Berlin premiere of Carmen *was packed. Up onstage, Pola Negri, in a glittering silver dress, shook the hand of the director and blew kisses to her fans. The orchestra began to play the Toreador song and the audience took their seats. "But why," she whispered, "do they open the Champagne now?" The orchestra played louder and a little louder still. "It's gunfire," someone explained.*

Afterward, at the reception, the Champagne bottles were finally opened—one, two, three, four—until there was a virtual symphony of bangs and whistles as the rifle fire drew closer. Later, nobody wanted to leave: nobody but Pola Negri, still dressed in glittering lamé; nobody but Pola put down her glass and pulled on her coat. "There are no taxis," she said in an accent heavy with her native Polish. "But the trains are still running, aren't they?"

They begged her, they implored her, not to risk her life, but Pola Negri had died on screen a dozen times and said she wasn't scared. And so she left the theater and, with her body pressed to the wall, edged slowly, slowly, along the empty block to reach the U-Bahn. A bullet ricocheted into the wall, a window smashed and showered her silver lamé dress with glass, but still she caught her train. Only later would she admit that she had wept all the way home.

It was snowing outside again and the electricity had been off all day. Even though it was strictly forbidden, according to the set of handwritten rules pinned to the back of the door, Hanne lit two dozen candles and placed them in saucers all around the floor. It was extravagant to use so many candles, but she had bought ten boxes full from a crooked churchwarden. With the snow coming down and the flickering light, the room was filled with dark shadows and reflected radiance.

"And now," Hanne said, bringing out a brown glass bottle, "let the conversion begin."

At first the peroxide felt ice-cold on Lilly's scalp. It trickled down the back of her neck and dribbled behind her ears. Hanne combed it through and then wrapped Lilly's head in an old towel. The smell made Lilly's eyes water. She held her breath but the taste was still in her mouth. And then it started to burn.

"It's supposed to hurt a little," Hanne explained. She had already bleached her own hair white, like a child's. Or an angel's.

The scissors cost twenty marks from a department store. They were clean and shiny and ever so slightly oily. Two hours later, after washing Lilly's hair in cold water, Hanne began to cut.

"There," she said eventually.

All around her chair lay little piles of yellow fluff. Lilly's head felt light. Her neck was cold. Hanne led her to the mirror above the sink with her eyes closed.

"Now look," she said.

Lilly opened her eyes. Instead of long and dark, her hair was short and blond. A golden curl fell over her cheek. Her fringe was swept over her brow in a brave yellow wave.

"You look a million times better," Hanne said. "But I haven't quite finished."

Hanne took out a stick of black kohl and drew on two arched eyebrows. Then she filled in Lilly's lips with dark red stain. Finally she pulled out a sour-smelling washcloth and covered her face with a cloud of white face powder.

"Now all you need is a new name," she said. "How about Lida or Lulu or Lidi?"

The film producer's "studio" was a glass conservatory in a villa in the west of the city. The previous owner had used the room to grow tomatoes and it still smelled of fresh earth and mold. The "set" was a flat white wall at one end and a faded green velvet sofa. The film producer stood behind a huge camera and introduced them both to the director, a tired-looking man in his fifties. He explained that they each had to do a screen test, to see how they looked on film. They weren't the only ones. Half a dozen girls sat in the hallway, every one an actress, every one, or so they claimed, "a special friend" of the producer.

Hanne sat on a sofa as she was told. Her face was rigid with tension. She clenched her shoulders and she bit her nails. She crossed her legs and uncrossed them again. And then they were ready. With several twists of his wrist, the director cranked up the motor of the camera. He settled himself behind the lens and made sure the film was threaded through the sprocket correctly. And then he ordered silence and his fabulously expensive Ernemann Kino started to roll.

Underneath a heavy winter coat, Hanne Schmidt was wearing her lucky dress, a white satin dress, which in her experience was always shed more quickly than any of her others. Her feet were in heels, her hair was in curls, her face was painted. But the camera ticked like a heart, like a heart beating way too fast. It was so loud that it seemed like the very sound of anxiety itself. Hanne's eyes darted from the film producer to the director and back again.

"Running," said the director. "Now strip."

Hanne's mouth fell open for a fraction of a second. And then she visibly relaxed. It was going to be okay. To sit passively was almost impossible for her. But to take charge, to perform, was something she knew she could do. She stood up and slowly took her coat off. And then her lucky dress. And then she started on her underwear.

"Very saucy. . . . Now give me a smile."

Hanne stopped so suddenly that she laddered her stockings, the stockings that had cost her five marks and she had bought only that morning. Then she wrapped her arms around herself and shook her head.

"What, you can strip but you can't smile?" the director said. "Is this how girls from Berlin are now?"

The producer knew a dentist who could fix her front tooth, but it would cost a lot. Hanne got a part anyway. She would play a police inspector's daughter who revealed one too many "secret" files to the hapless hero of the piece.

"Now you," said the director.

Lilly sat down on the sofa. She was wearing her old winter coat and a new blue silk chiffon dress, cut to the knee with a row of tiny pearl buttons down the back. An investment dress, Hanne had called it.

The bright lights had made the room at the back of the villa hot and damp. The windows were steamed up and the air was stale. But despite the trickles of perspiration that ran down between her shoulder blades, Lilly trembled. The director aimed his mechanical gaze at her and licked his lips. He checked the stock, positioned himself above the eyepiece, and once again started to crank.

"Rolling," said the director. "Okay . . . let's go."

Lilly's hands reached up and she began to unbutton her coat. Her hair fell into her eyes, yellow hair, shocking to her still, and she suddenly wished it was long again, long enough to cover her face. Her fingers wound around the last of the horn buttons and she pushed it through the buttonhole. Her coat fell from her shoulders. Carefully she pulled down her underpants and stepped out of them. And then, without looking up, she reached behind her back and began to unbutton her dress. The room was completely silent apart from the ticker of the camera motor.

"Beautiful," said the director.

Lilly stared straight into the camera lens. She could see herself upside down in its beveled surface, her blond hair and her face drawn in with lipstick and kohl. Was she beautiful? For a second or two she didn't move. As the lights blazed and the camera rolled, as time ticked through the sprockets and frame by frame her image was recorded, she took a breath and was filled with blue sparks, the same blue sparks she had felt all those years ago on the makeshift stage at the orphanage. As then, time seemed to slow down and every single second stretch; she was outside herself, she was free of herself, she belonged to the moment. Although the lights meant that she couldn't see them, she could feel the gaze of the director, the producer, the camera. And Lilly was suddenly aware of her own ascendancy; she was a temporary deity, momentarily immortal, a fixed point. But following swiftly came a rush of horror: at what had happened after her play, at what she was expected to do now, at how she had just felt. And her eyes began to swim.

"More?" she asked.

"Of course," replied the director. "Of course more. And make it swift."

Lilly swallowed and lowered her face. And then she dropped her arms and in a sigh of blue silk chiffon, the dress began to slip.

"I've got it," said the director. "I've got it all."

But he had spoken too soon. Just as the dress crumpled on the floor, just as her pale body, the swell of her breasts, the jut of her hips, and the dark triangle between her legs were unveiled, exposed, revealed, with a flicker and a small surge the illumination, all those hundreds and hundreds of volts and amps and watts, all those brand-new bulbs from Siemens, cut out, leaving the temporary studio in warm black darkness.

At first nobody moved. Only the camera kept turning. They all stood and listened as if the dark were masking something audible. Then the director shook his head at the producer. The producer tried the light switch, on, off, on, off, with increasing force, as if he could rectify the situation with willpower alone.

When it was clear that he could do nothing, Lilly reached down quickly, pulled her dress back on, and reclaimed her underwear. Without the lights, the room in the villa in the west of the city seemed nothing more or less than what it was, a back room in a shabby house in the suburbs. When a dog began to bark in the next garden, the fragile construct that it was a film studio at all was shattered. The girls in the hall swore under their breath, pulled on their hats, and began to leave. They guessed correctly that the power plant workers had gone on strike again. The whole city would be out for hours.

"What about my friend?" Hanne asked the director as he tried to pack up his equipment in the pitch-blackness. "Aren't you going to give her a part too?"

"Leave your name and a contact number," said the director. "I'll take a look at what we've got on film and then I'll be in touch."

Only three or four frames of the actress who would soon be known as Lidi, however, survived. The director burned out the first half of the roll of film when he accidentally opened the camera later that evening after three glasses of beer. In the film that was salvaged—the few seconds or so during which the director waited to see if the power cut was purely a temporary glitch—the image of Lidi is so underexposed that the almost nude girl in the almost dark could have been anyone. It was just as well, for the rest of his archive would eventually turn up in an auction room and be bought, duplicated, and sold under the counter all over Germany as *Girls on the Casting Couch*.

"I failed the audition," she said years later of that first screen test. "Thankfully," she added. When asked to explain, she politely changed the subject.

The fighting went on; the center of Berlin had been placed in a state of siege. On her way to buy bread, Lilly found the next street had been sealed off. Barbed wire and barricades had been erected overnight by both the Spartacists and the government troops, and for the next month they moved back and forth, a street or two at a time, a square, a park, a monument lost and gained over and over.

Hanne's first day of shooting was in another "studio" in East Berlin. The trams were erratic, so she had tried to walk; the streets were covered in masonry and the random stain of congealed blood, but they were still passable. But even Hanne soon decided that it was too dangerous. Bullets ricocheted across the Alexanderplatz and mortar shells bombarded the police headquarters. And the opposing forces didn't just focus on each other: passing through their checkpoints, pedestrians could be targeted at random for carrying the wrong papers, for offering the wrong answer, for giving the wrong kind of look. And so Hanne called the director from a café on the corner and he reluctantly agreed to send a car.

Hanne's filming schedule was usually nocturnal. The new tooth was taking longer to pay off than she had anticipated. But she never talked about what happened in the "studio" or where the finished films were actually screened. And Lilly could not help but notice the slow dulling of Hanne's spirit when it was clear that her new career was not what she had supposed at all but simply a repeat of her last.

And so, at Hanne's insistence, they both auditioned for revues, for cabarets, for theaters. The counts and princes of Prussia and Bavaria had come back from Mesopotamia, from France, and from Georgia and taken rooms in luxury hotels or reopened their villas. Nobody could ignore the barricades, the bloodshed, and the gunfire, but life went on. People drank, they ate, they drank, they danced, they wanted to be entertained. Together with hundreds of other young women, all dressed in knee-skimming skirts and with short, bobbed hair, Lilly and Hanne waited in dusty back stages or hung around in the stalls until, called one by one to sing, dance, or strip, they would take the stage and do their best.

Lilly, who could not sing or dance or even strip with any real sense of conviction, was never called back for a second audition. Hanne was recalled once to the Chantant Singing Hall in Oranienburger Strasse but was not chosen for the final lineup.

Although Hanne knew she was spending far more than she was making, she had become more extravagant than ever. She bought a wind-up phonograph and a stack of recordings. She had her dresses altered to make them shorter, sexier, more revealing. French fashion was now filling the department stores again, and Hanne bought them each a pair of buckled shoes with small heels from Paris.

"Take them," she had said when Lilly protested. "I can't go out dancing alone, and you can't tango in a pair of boots."

"I can't tango in a pair of shoes, either," she replied.

"Just put them on, for God's sake."

Hanne was tired of taking the lead, of presenting Lilly with solutions that she never took advantage of. And the worst thing was that she still thought she had a choice. Lilly put them on.

"There," said Hanne. "They're a perfect fit. And I'll teach you to dance. You must be the only girl left in Berlin who can't."

In winter 1919, the new republic had banned fishing in lakes with hand grenades and social dancing, or *Tanztaumel*. Five dance halls had been raided and closed down. But the fact that it was illegal only made it more attractive. Since the war had ended, dancing had become more than just a craze in Berlin: it was a mania, an obsession, an addiction. In secret halls and private clubs, in parks and even in the streets, workers and boys, soldiers and war widows and businessmen and whores danced the tango, the fox-trot, the cakewalk all night to the syncopated tunes of Scott Joplin or James Reese Europe.

The boarders in the room below eventually gave up banging the ceiling with a broom. For three hours, as Hanne played "Broadway Rose" or "Tiger Rag" over and over, they counted steps and spun around, they raised their knees and threw back their heads, they clasped their arms around each other and narrowed their eyes with concentration.

"I think you've got it," Hanne said eventually.

Hanne, who had learned it all from another actress while waiting for their scene, was a competent teacher. With each new dance, Lilly grew in confidence. Dancing, she realized that night, was an anesthetic. It made her feel high, energized, sexual even. Like Hanne, she swung her arms and rocked her hips. She tossed her head and clicked her heels; dancing was all about movement, about how glorious the body is, about being alive and young and vital, about holding on to time by dancing every single beat out of it. And once you started, she now saw, it was almost impossible to stop.

Just off the Friedrichstrasse, above a former restaurant, the Bad Boys' Ball was packed. When they arrived, a black jazz band from New Orleans was already playing in the corner. The slide of the trumpet and the giddy beat of the drum were infectious, rhythmic, undeniably erotic. Couples moved together, rubbing faces and bodies. One woman, frustrated by the restriction of her skirt, leaned down and ripped it up to her thigh. Not to be outdone, another girl ripped hers up to her waist, revealing her garters, her stockings, and her lack of underwear.

Although the music, the so-called devil's music, had come from the slave songs and rhythms of the marching bands of the Deep South of America, in Berlin in 1919, jazz had taken on a whole new meaning. It was everything the kaiser's empire had condemned. It was the sound of liberation: from starvation, from grief, from virginity, from conformity.

"What did I do after the war?" Lidi responded to an interviewer years later. She laughed as her face lit up with memory. "I danced," she said. "For a whole year, almost all I did was dance."

At three a.m. at the Bad Boys' Ball, the hall was raided. Four hundred arrests would be made, including the band. Everyone would eventually be released without charge. By October, the republic would reverse the law, making dancing legal again, and drop all state censorship. The ban on fishing with grenades in lakes, however, remained.

Hanne and Lilly joined the crush as the crowds swelled toward the back door of the Bad Boys' Ball. They all poured out into the clear spring night, their feet aching and their ears still ringing.

"Look," said Hanne. "It's the polite Russian from the boarding-house."

The Russian was with a big group of friends, both male and female, both Russian and German.

"Hey, Ilya," one young woman called. "Everyone's coming back to my place. You want to come?"

"I'm so sorry, I'm working early," he told her with a bow. "I most humbly apologize."

Ilya, so that was his name. Lilly took in his smart black suit and polished black shoes. The cuffs were beginning to fray and the style was prewar, but he had a way of wearing his clothes that made them look expensive. He was in his late twenties, she guessed, a man, not a boy. He caught her looking at him and she glanced quickly away.

"Come on," said Hanne. "Let's go somewhere else. It's only three."

But the polite Russian had left his friends and was coming toward them through the crowd.

"A very pleasant evening," he said to them both. And then his head tilted to the side. "I like it, your hair," he said to Lilly. "Extremely becoming."

"Thank you." Lilly smiled. "It's all Hanne's work."

He nodded and looked at Hanne. Her hair was bleached, too, but instead of softening her features, it hardened them. She lit a cigarette.

"I would like to invite you," he said with a bow, "to the Movie Palast on Nollendorfplatz. I play the piano there every night. Ask for me and you will be given free tickets at the door."

He was looking straight at Lilly, a smile playing across his face. When he caught her eye, he bowed. She blushed but suddenly felt gauche and unsophisticated, flat-footed in her new French shoes.

"Thanks for the offer," said Hanne. "Maybe we'll take you up on it."

Hanne linked her arm through Lilly's and suggested they both head over to a private club, a very exclusive club that admitted only women.

Before they walked away toward Friedrichstrasse, before they hailed a cab and headed over to the H-Lounge on Bülowstrasse, Lilly turned. The polite Russian was standing in a pool of streetlight, watching them go. On his face was an expression that Lilly could not read.

"Dosvedanya, dosvedanya," Hanne said as the cab swerved through the empty streets. "Those Russians are everywhere."

Like Ilya Yurasov, many of the Russians who had arrived in Berlin after the revolution had impeccable manners, learned as paying guests at the Carlton in Nice or the Ritz in Paris. Many were now doormen or waiters or bellboys. The others, well, they would be lucky to find a job at all. On any given night you could find dozens of czarist Russian officers in the cramped, dirty bunks of the homeless shelters, practicing their French as they sat it out until the Bolsheviks crumbled and dreaming of the day the czar, the Little Father, would come back to power and they could go home.

Before the war, Ilya Yurasov had worked as a director at the Khanzhonkov film studio in Moscow. On the Eastern Front he had been captured by the Germans and held prisoner in Lodz. In 1918 the armistice was announced and he was released. But instead of heading east like the rest of his regiment, he hitched a ride and ended up in Berlin.

From their first meeting when he barged into their room by mistake, Ilya Yurasov had seen something in Lilly's face that he recognized. It was a symmetry of feature, a tilt of the eye, a gradient of lip, all of which reminded him of another woman. Though the girl in the boardinghouse really looked nothing like Anya Gregorin, the Russian actress, her face had the same quality, the same striking gaze. But that night as he stood on the street and she turned and looked back at him, the upward trombone slide of Ilya's heart was quite, quite new.

That year cinemas were seldom less than packed. Some cinemas employed orchestras, but most recruited piano players to accompany the films. And when the lights went down and the piano started to play, as the red velvet curtains slowly parted and reopened on the cobbled streets of England or the mythic forests of Bavaria, the bathhouses of ancient Rome or the deserts of distant India, the audience laughed and gasped and wept as if enchanted by the play of light and shade and music.

The first film they saw was *The Golem*. At first Lilly watched the polite Russian as he played the piano in his shirtsleeves, his face illuminated by the throw of light from the big screen. But as the film progressed and the action unfolded against a series of nightmarish sets, as the music rose and fell in one crescendo after another, Lilly, like the rest of the audience, was drawn in. Would the golem catch the girl it had fallen in love with, or would it destroy the world instead?

They sat in their seats for long after the end titles had started to roll and the crowds had left. At the piano, Ilya rolled down his sleeves and pulled on his jacket.

"What did you think?" Ilya asked.

"It was quite terrifying," Lilly answered. "I loved it."

He laughed.

"Well, come again," he said. "Anytime."

Ilya Yurasov continued to give them cinema tickets. They were not, as they assumed, free: he paid for them by dipping into money put aside from his day job in the Afifa film-processing plant. And at the end of each film, when they thanked him, he bowed deeply and thanked them for being so kind as to come. But he did not ask either girl to come for a glass of wine or take a walk, as they both expected he might. The cinema tickets, he told himself, were purely a gesture of courtesy to two attractive young women. He could allow himself to go no further. He was a man of principle.

Hanne and Lilly saw all the latest films, often two or three times.

Costume dramas like *Madame DuBarry* and *The Eyes of the Mummy,* starring Pola Negri, and when the censorship laws were abolished, pictures like *Lost Daughters*, *Hyenas of Lust*, and *A Man's Girlhood*.

"That's where I want to be," Hanne breathed at the end of each film. "Up there."

The money that Hanne had made during the war ran out, but by this time the film producer's business was doing well: the market for cheap soft pornography was booming. Hanne was in increasing demand and was so busy having costume fittings, read-throughs, and screen tests that she gave up looking for more respectable employment on the stage.

Lilly found a part-time job as a cocktail waitress in the Kakadu Bar on Joachimstaler Strasse. It was a huge warren of a place with a dance palace, cabaret, vegetarian restaurant, and bar. Over every table in the dining room hung a parrot in a cage. To summon the maître d' or the waitresses or even just for the hell of it, the customers would tap their knives on their water glasses and, in an old man's voice, the parrots would squawk, "The bill, the bill."

At first the novelty of the parrots attracted huge crowds, who found the parrots hilarious. But when the parrots let their droppings fall into the soup or glasses of beer below, or when they contracted strange parrot diseases and feather by feather plucked themselves bald, the joke began to wear a little thin. By Christmas the bar would be populated mostly by tourists, foreign journalists, and whores.

Although they were both working, Lilly and Hanne still stayed out until five every night, dancing the tango with Greek millionaires, the fox-trot with politicians, and the cakewalk with sailors. And yet Lilly found herself thinking about the polite Russian from the boardinghouse, about the timbre of his voice, about the slant of his eyes. Her obvious preoccupation, however, did not put her dance partners off. They came back for more and each time danced closer and held her tighter.

"Tell them you're sapphic," Hanne said. "It works every time."

None of the men Hanne danced with were given so much as a second glance. None of them but one.

Kurt had lost all of the fingers on his left hand in the war: long, fine fingers, judging by the fingers on his right hand, with immaculate fingernails and sensitive tips. Hanne had spotted him at the Walterchens Dance Hall in Janowitz-Brücke. She said she noticed his eyes first: huge, dark pupils eclipsing the irises. And then she had become aware of his face. He was, she said later, the prettiest man she had ever seen. And she had never had anything pretty, she said, never, ever. She had walked right over and asked him if he wanted to dance. He had announced he did not know how. She tried to teach him but he wouldn't be taught. At the end of the night, however, he let her kiss his mutilated knuckle.

Kurt was addicted to morphine. A field doctor had prescribed it when he blew off the fingers with his rifle in late 1917, and when he returned to Berlin, his own doctor obliged him with repeat prescriptions. Kurt claimed he was in too much pain without it. It wasn't the fingers, or the space where the fingers had once been, but his entire body that ached and craved and hollowed itself out with longing for its previous completeness.

Besides, Kurt was in the Freikorps, the government troops. You didn't ask him what he did all day or where he had been. Sometimes you could tell just by his face anyway.

It was called White Terror. That spring the Freikorps, under a man called Noske, were said to have executed twenty-four sailors in Französische Strasse. Even though they had only come to collect some money from the paymaster's office. Even though they were mostly unarmed. By the time martial law was announced in March, the Freikorps were rumored to have murdered more than two thousand people.

Right from that very first evening when Hanne picked him up in the dance hall, Kurt spent every night in their rooms at the boardinghouse.

He would sometimes arrive at midnight, smelling of beer and stale tobacco. And then Lilly would lie in her bed and try not to listen to the regular beat of the bedstead banging the wall. She would try not to hear his muffled gasps and shouts, Hanne's laugh and her sobs; she tried not to notice the harsh words he uttered or the sound of Hanne's voice as she soothed him, the words inaudible but the tone unmistakable.

And sometimes he would turn up at three in the morning with pooled eyes and a hollowed-out face. And then, as soon as he was let in, he would fall asleep on the sofa, on the floor, even standing up, with his back to the front door. The next day he would sit on the divan with a blanket wrapped around his shoulders and his eyes would follow them around the room, back and forth, back and forth, until they both put their coats on and left.

"What am I going to do?" Hanne would say. "What am I going to do? I'll ask him to go. Tonight I'll tell him it's finished."

But even though she vowed over and over to end it, when she returned hours later filled with resolve and a couple of glasses of wine, he would disarm her with a kiss, a punch, or a harsh word.

"Help me," he would plead. "If you love me, help me."

Morphine could be bought easily on the street outside the police station on Alexanderplatz for a handful of change. And that would be where Hanne would head, to street corners or under the S-Bahn to buy small brown paper bags from young men in long overcoats. Kurt kept his syringe in the soap dish on the sink. He would be right as rain within the hour.

"I should move," Lilly whispered when he had finally passed out.

"Stay," Hanne begged. "I need you. I'll sort it out. Lilly, promise me you won't leave me."

Hanne's face started to collapse, and all her attitude and bravado, all that protective armor that had taken so many years to accumulate and that had seemed as impervious to breakage as Bakelite, began to crack.

And so Lilly promised.

Hanne's film parts gradually dried up. It wasn't that she had become unreliable, turning up hours late or not at all; something about her, the so-called director told his assistant, had changed. She had stopped pretending she enjoyed it. Instead she lay in bed all morning with Kurt and, until he sold it, listened to military marches on the phonograph. She spent the afternoon auditioning, walking from one theater to the next and from one back lot to another. She had told him she was a respectable actress. Now all she had to do was prove it.

On days like these, when Hanne was out and Lilly didn't start her shift until later, she was left alone with Kurt. At first he ignored her except to ask her, perhaps, where they kept the sugar or if she would like a cigarette. But sometimes, when he was high, he would tell her about himself, about how he had grown up on a small farm, about how, being the youngest child and only son, his father had expected him to be bigger, stronger, harder. And when he wasn't good enough, how his father would take him into the cowshed and beat him with a rake. But most of the time he would pace the floor in silence or stand at the door and sway.

And so Lilly began to go out for walks alone, to sit in cafés and read the paper from cover to cover, to go to the cinema—anything to fill up the hours until her shift started. The Kakadu became a refuge from the tension of the boardinghouse, and she would take her time tidying up at the end of the night, cleaning and polishing the bar twice over until even the parrots started to squawk "Time to go, the bill, the bill, time to go" at her. But then a new manager was hired and everything changed. He was a tall, wiry ex–army sniper with a nervous, twitchy manner. When he approached Lilly with his new business plan, she thought he was joking.

"All the girls who work in these places do little extras for tips," he claimed. "You think we make enough money from beer?"

He gave her a day off to decide. Lilly walked past barricades, past ruined buildings, past rows of "half silks," or amateur prostitutes who came out onto the street only after five p.m., when their jobs as office girls or shop assistants were over for the day. And then she found herself outside the Movie Palast.

The film was a romance about a blind girl and a war veteran. It called for lots of minor chords and a slow pace. Ilya Yurasov was aware of the girl from the boardinghouse in the audience. He knew that the other girl had a boyfriend now; he'd met him on the stairs. He was one of Noske's men, unfortunately, a thug with an insignia, a drunk with a truncheon. And so he wasn't surprised to see the girl on her own. At the end of the film, however, he was surprised by the girl's face. She had been crying. The film was a poorly acted melodrama. Surely she couldn't have found it that affecting.

"Excuse me for inquiring," he said, "but are you all right?"

The girl nodded and patted her eyes with a handkerchief.

"I'm sorry," she said. "I'm fine."

It was already eight in the evening, but the night was filled with shimmering autumn light. They walked west toward the boardinghouse, the horizon ahead streaked with red and amber, the clouds edged with the palest green. Ilya, the polite Russian, walked with long, loose strides. He had an easy laugh and dark eyes that tilted up very slightly at the corners. Although there was a tangible space between them, they both knew that they must look like a young couple out for the night. She thought about Stefan, about the way he had touched her. Find somebody else if I don't return, he had told her. And marry him. Why not this one? she asked herself.

As they walked, Lilly brightened up and they talked about films, about jazz, about Berlin. At one point Ilya turned and walked backward while describing the plot of a new film. His eyes widened as he reached the climax.

"The devil took his soul," he said. "And the girl died of a broken heart. Baboom."

Lilly laughed. He shrugged and smiled at her, the way he had outside the Bad Boys' Ball. And then he turned and they walked on in silence.

Lilly's pace slowed as they reached Nollendorfplatz. She didn't want to go back to Motzstrasse. She didn't want to see Kurt or hear Hanne's misgivings about him. Lilly couldn't help Hanne: only she could break it off with Kurt. And what about her job at the Kakadu? The thought of any of the customers touching her filled her with panic. She would not do it; she could not do it.

Ilya had noticed her change of pace and was suddenly nervous. If she turned and wanted him to kiss her, would he resist? Just being near her made him feel strangely exhilarated. He leaned forward to open the heavy wooden door of their lodgings, hoping she wouldn't notice the tremor of his hand.

"Ilya," she said.

He paused before he pulled the handle. Lilly stared at the buttons on his cuff and then slowly, slowly, she lifted her large gray eyes to his. He met her gaze. His whole body surged quite involuntarily.

"Do you know anyone who needs a typist? I need a new job."

He smiled and pretended to consider. So he was wrong about her. And although he felt a tug of disappointment, he was also relieved.

"In fact," he said, "I do."

Ilya Yurasov regarded himself as a man of substance. His heightened sense of honor, morality, and decorum came out of, he supposed, a visceral reaction to the irresponsible lifestyle of his parents. His mother had given him up when he was just two months old. He had been cared for by a succession of wet-nurses, nannies, and governesses while she was occupied by a series of increasingly passionate affairs with opera singers, minor royalty, and high-ranking military men. She had fulfilled her side of a bargain with her husband, one of the czar's advisers, and had produced a son, but she made it quite clear that that was all he should expect. He seemed quite content with the situation, however, and spent most of his time on his estate, where he had an ongoing relationship with the daughter of his manager.

Ilya grew up valuing justice above everything else, a quality that he had inherited from the women who had cared for him for long hours and little pay. They also instilled in him an aversion to rule breaking that never left him and that used to amuse his mother to no end. "Go on," she used to taunt him. "Steal an apple from the neighbor's garden. Go on, Ilya." But he would not.

And so, when Russia entered the war with Germany, much to the chagrin of his parents, he immediately enlisted. He never saw them again. They would eventually emigrate to Nice and live together in a small apartment near the Russian Orthodox church until the pressures of cohabitation proved too much and they split up, both rapidly remarried, and lost touch with each other and their only son.

The very next day Ilya made some inquiries on Lilly's behalf. Two days later a letter was pushed underneath her door: she was invited to attend an interview. It was only after she had read it twice that she noticed the company's letterhead was the Deutsche Bioscop, a film company.

Lilly took a train right out of the city, through the Grunewald forests to Potsdam, and then she took a tram to Stahnsdorfer Strasse in Neubabelsberg. The interview was brief. She was given a few pages of script by a matronly woman with unreadable eyes and timed as she typed. And then she was offered the job.

"When do I start?" she asked.

"Tomorrow," the woman said without looking up. "I'll get someone to show you round."

The Neubabelsberg film studios in 1919 had two huge areas with walls constructed from glass. That day, inside the larger studio, there was a horizon painted on the curved backdrop and a series of flats constructed to look like a medieval keep. A bank of lights was aimed at the set from up above and the floor at the edges of the space was thick with black cables. Nothing, however, seemed to be happening. And then, with a loud buzz, someone switched on the lights. A woman in a dressing gown stepped into the brightness and warmed her face in the light.

There was also a covered hangar for storing film stock, camera equipment, and props. Cars, real and miniature, models of skyscrapers, and papier-mâché trees stood beside cardboard gravestones and vases full of colored paper flowers. A moat, complete with drawbridge and portcullis, had been stored next to a plywood gallows.

Lilly was shown to a small hangar on the edge of the lot behind the main studio. The site had until recently been an airport and this hangar, she was told, used to house fighter planes. The ceiling was high and the only natural light came in from a dusty oblong window at one end. Strip lighting had been installed up above and the floor area was set up with about forty desks in rows, each with a typewriter. Twenty typists were already at work, and the clack of their fingers on the keys was almost deafening. Lilly was allocated a desk and given a sheaf of paper.

"I sat down and that was that; I felt as if I belonged there," she told an interviewer in 1926. "It was the first time in my life that I had ever felt that way. And the smell, I remember the smell, of ink and new paper and adrenaline. I sat down and just breathed it all in."

But didn't you dream about being a film star yourself, the interviewer asked, of being in the films you typed?

"Never," she replied. "I was given handwritten pages, I typed them, I handed the pages to somebody else. Sometimes I read the words, sometimes I didn't. Just by typing, I believed that I was helping to make something live, to make all these ideas and fantasies—those wonderful love affairs and heartbreaking tragedies—make sense, become reality. I loved films. Escapism? Yes . . . of course it was; everyone needed it then."

Lilly started work at nine in the morning and finished at six. The streets were peaceful around Potsdam, and it was, she admitted, sometimes hard to make herself head back into the city, to the fighting, the barricades, and the intermittent sounds of gunfire, to Hanne and Kurt.

"After I had worked in a factory, this didn't feel like work at all," she told the interviewer. "I wasn't paid a great deal, it's true. You know, I would have done it for nothing, if they had asked. My head was in another place when I worked."

Lilly had tried to thank him in person, but Ilya Yurasov had unexpectedly moved out of the boardinghouse. He had also resigned his part-time job at the Movie Palast. The sad-eyed fat girl mentioned something about him leaving a note for her, but she had lost it.

"Probably gone back to Russia," she said. "I would if I were him."

So that was that. He was gone without even a word. She should have expected it. There had always been, she realized now, something reticent in his manner. And although she started to see suggestions of him everywhere—the angle of a shoulder, a smattering of Russian spoken too fast, pale fingers below threadbare cuffs—she told herself that he was only someone who had helped her once. Everything else had happened only in her imagination.

The sad-eyed fat girl was right. Given the choice, who would choose Berlin? The city was still being patrolled by increasing numbers of government troops. The Spartacists had been gradually hunted down and imprisoned. And any revolutionary material, any pamphlet or magazine, that was found was confiscated, and those responsible for distributing it were shot. The fighting had stopped but the terror went on.

When Lilly saw a woman standing outside the station with a sack of several hundred copies of the Dadaist magazine *Die Pleite* that she was giving out to factory workers, she wondered if the woman was insane. Lilly was about to head down to the U-Bahn but hesitated at the top of the stairs. There was something familiar about her. She looked again. She was well dressed but a little unkempt; her hair was falling out of a loose knot, and there were holes in her stockings.

At that point, Lilly told herself to keep going. She could hear the rattle of a train approaching. They were not friends anymore; Eva had made that clear the last time they had met. And then, as Lilly lingered on the top step, blocking the path of dozens of increasingly irritated commuters, she saw what Eva could not see: the approach of three Freikorps from the street, their pistols drawn and their eyes shiny with excitement.

Of course Lilly used Kurt's name. They wouldn't shoot a woman whose friend was intimate with one of their own ranks. They took the magazines and regretfully let them both go.

Eva ate three bowls of dumpling soup while Lilly sipped a weak black coffee. The restaurant was small and cheap and rarely frequented by government troops. Eva looked over her shoulder to see if she could be overheard; then, when she saw that they were the only customers, she told Lilly she had been sleeping on a succession of floors for several months. They knew where she lived, she whispered, her small eyes wide. They had ransacked the flat in Steglitz and paid the neighbors to inform them if she returned. The door crashed open as another couple of customers came in. Eva jumped despite herself.

"It would be better for them," she said, "if I disappeared."

Lilly paid the bill and took her back to the boardinghouse.

Hanne was wearing a silk dressing gown that she had been given by one of her "directors." Her cheeks were red and the kohl around her eyes had smudged. Kurt, she mentioned with a wave of her hand, had just left. She sat down on the divan and her gown fell open over her leg. Eva's eyes dropped and Lilly saw her staring at five small purple bruises on Hanne's thigh.

"Thank goodness he only has five," Hanne said. "He lost the other fingers in the war."

Eva blushed and fumbled in her bag for a cigarette.

"It would just be for a few days," Eva said. "Just until I find another hideaway."

"Lilly is the only respectable person in the block," Hanne said. "I don't think a lady like you would like it here."

"I can assure you," Eva replied, "that I have stayed in far worse places than this."

Only Hanne laughed.

They left Eva with a cup of coffee and a saucer for her cigarette ash, and locked themselves in the communal bathroom.

"Just a couple of days," Lilly said. "I know there's no room. She said she had nowhere to go."

"It's all right," Hanne replied. "She can stay as long as she likes. I have Kurt. Why can't you have a guest?"

This wasn't the reaction she had been expecting.

"Are you forgetting what he does?" Lilly replied. "Hanne, are you forgetting who he is?"

Someone outside started to bang on the door.

"He needn't know anything. We'll just tell him the truth. She is . . . was . . . your sister-in-law."

And then she smiled, her false tooth a slightly brighter shade of white in the half-light of the open window.

Mord

The Studio

Light, shade, light, shade, the artist dreams of traveling in and out of tunnels on a train whose destination is unknown. His nightmares are set in rooms with tilting walls and dense black shadows. He is haunted by specters with white faces and malevolent movements.

He was an Expressionist painter, a member of the Berlin Sturm group. They did not believe in perspective or naturalism or representation. They did not paint landscapes or portraits or still lifes. They were employed by the film studio as set painters. It was a steady wage in unsteady times. Do what you will, the producers instructed. As long as it's cheap.

"Our vision is clear," they said. "Our style distortion. Films must be drawings brought to life. Here and only here can we truly externalize the fermentations of the inner self." And yet the critics missed the point entirely. Observing sets where the walls leaned in and the chimneys tilted, the windows sloped and the roofs collided, they derided their work as the hallucinations of sick brains.

But now the artist realizes that those sets were a premonition, not only of film noir and other later genres, but of the light, shade, light, shade of that train journey to nowhere that he would later make himself.

Kurt knew, of course. He knew as soon as he saw her. Her tattered clothes, a little out of fashion. Her good walking boots now worn down at the heel; her attitude, the way she talked to him with her contempt not exactly hidden but translated into the angle of her shoulder, the twist of her mouth, the slight narrowing of her eyes when he spoke. It was obvious.

But there was more. After just a few days, Eva began to find reasons to be near Hanne. She hovered around her, she put on her favorite record, she danced too close, she talked to her to the exclusion of all others, she touched her arm when asking her a question and stroked the stockings Hanne always left to dry over the backs of chairs. What was initially meant as a snub became an unspoken provocation.

"She'll have to go," Lilly said. "I'll ask her tonight."

Hanne, however, would not hear of it. In fact, she seemed to enjoy it.

"She's your sister-in-law," Hanne implored. "I won't let you do it."

Of course, although she claimed the contrary, Eva didn't have to stay; she had other options. The Spartacists still had hideouts all over the East where she could have lived in relative safety. And she had plenty of new friends. Eva had been a regular at a lesbian bar, the Verona-Lounge on Kleiststrasse, for the last few years. She liked blondes in dresses and not the women in men's hats and long fur coats who haunted the Verona. But Hanne was a different matter entirely. To be flirted with, to be toyed with, to be led on by a woman who was a Freikorps man's girl was so dangerously thrilling, she decided she would take the risk, whatever the consequences.

But there was more. She still thought about her brother, Stefan—about how, when he had returned from the front, he had withdrawn into himself so deeply that he had stopped speaking—and she was still angry. One day he had gone out for a walk and never returned. She had searched for him for a month or so, to no avail. He was never the same, she still told herself, since he had been stolen from her by

Lilly. And so when she looked at Lilly and remembered the way she had misled Stefan, she didn't feel guilty. Like so many of those hasty unions made in wartime, the marriage had been a sham, a desperate attempt to validate something fleeting and insubstantial. She knew it, Stefan knew it, his so-called bride knew it.

The situation in the boardinghouse grew increasingly difficult for everyone except Eva. All winter the radiator rattled and moaned, but it was never more than lukewarm. Lilly's bed was almost big enough for both of them, but Eva always seemed to end up with most of the covers. And so Lilly would rise in the middle of the night, put on all her clothes, make tea, and wait for the morning to come. It was too dark to read, so she went over the scenes she had typed during the day and, by taking on all the parts, she played them out in her head. Here the characters' motivations were clear and their resolutions deserved. The good were loved and the bad were punished. Happiness could be earned.

At work the pace suddenly increased. More films were in production than at any time after the war. When she arrived in the mornings a small pile of scripts to be typed was already on her desk, and she often had to work late just to get through them. Last-minute changes were standard. Her typewriter was old and some of the letters stuck. She typed until her fingers ached and her shoulders began to seize up. And then she would make a mistake and have to start the whole page all over again.

The first time Lilly fell asleep, she was woken gently by her supervisor, who brought her a cup of coffee. The second time she was given a formal warning and agreed to come in over the weekend to catch up. The third time she woke on the office sofa with her coat thrown over her and her shoes placed neatly on the floor beside her. It was a Saturday.

From that day onward, she began to notice the presence of a benign force. One morning a brand-new typewriter appeared on her desk. Nobody knew where it had come from. Another day she found a small bunch of winter roses on her chair when she returned from lunch. She looked around the office at the other typists and secretaries, but none of them gave any indication that they knew who had put them there. The studio had a huge staff: scene painters, electricians, wardrobe masters, and cameramen were on the move almost constantly from studio to studio and from country to country. One crew had just come back from Cairo. Another was going to the Orient. And then there were the writers and producers, who were always rushing off to endless meetings or first-day shoots, throwing rewrites at her or asking her to type up draft scripts, even though it wasn't officially allowed. It could have been anyone.

Back in the city, Eva would sometimes disappear for days. But she would always return, smelling of tobacco and railway stations, hysterical with reports of nightly raids and close shaves, but with a look of such unfulfilled longing on her face that the real reason she had returned was obvious. Lilly knew that Hanne encouraged her. She would let her gown slip over her shoulder and occasionally ask Eva to button up the back of her dress or ask her opinion on her hair. Once, when Kurt had passed out on the bed, Hanne dared Eva to draw him. She sketched a grotesque caricature of a young man whose empty eyes and hollow cheeks suggested that his insides had been sucked clean out. Hanne laughed at first and then, when Kurt shifted under the covers and began to wake, she promptly burned the page with a match.

At Christmas, Eva produced a couple of invitations to an artists' party that was being held in a school hall in Charlottenburg. It was a masquerade, a Silvester Ball to celebrate the New Year. There was only one rule: You had to wear a costume and a mask, which you couldn't remove until midnight.

"Do you want to go?" asked Lilly.

"I don't know," replied Hanne.

She lit a cigarette and stared out of the window at the blank white sky as the match burned between her fingers.

"Kurt has forbidden me to go dancing," she said softly. "So I'll have to go, won't I?"

The school hall was decked with garlands of silk flowers, paper snakes, and Chinese lanterns. A woman in a bathing costume played the bugle on the small stage. A jazz band all dressed as satyrs joined in for a bar or two and then broke off to drink wine or polish their instruments. A Spanish dancer was performing on a table. A Napoleon was trying to look up her skirt. On the dance floor, there were a handful of Pierrots in bright red costumes, a couple of Harlequins, a Scaramouche, and a few Columbines. Others were dressed as Chinamen with woolen pigtails, Arabs in turbans, and Negroes with blacked-up faces. Milling around the hall, drinking wine or smoking, were dozens more people in black evening suits. Some were men. Some were women. Some sported a monocle and a starched white shirt. Some wore nothing but the suit.

Lilly wore a black taffeta dress and a small cat mask. Hanne wore a red dress and a bird of paradise mask. Hanne had borrowed them from a friend who worked in a theatrical store. As they crowded through the doorway, a mermaid showered them with confetti.

"May I kiss the brides?" she said. And she kissed them both on the lips.

At that moment the girl in the bathing costume was carried offstage by a clown. The jazz band put down their drinks, stood up, and started to play. Everyone surged toward the dance floor, taking Lilly and Hanne with them.

"Hold my hand," shouted Hanne.

"I can't reach," Lilly replied. "I'll come and find you."

"Not if I find you first," mouthed Hanne.

And then they were both carried in different directions, passed from one person's arms to another's, from one embrace to the next, as the tempo of the music grew more insistent and the room grew warmer and warmer still.

"You look familiar," the first of Lilly's dance partners told her.

Her hair was still golden, her mouth was stained red, and she carried herself as if there was something precious in her breast.

"Are you on the stage?" he asked her.

"I work in films," she replied.

"I thought I knew you," he said.

And so the Pierrots, the Columbines, the clowns, and the satyrs tried to match her masked face with a memory they didn't have. But when they tried to kiss her or pull her into a dark corner, Lilly simply laughed, turned her face, and walked away.

As it approached midnight, some of the garlands were pulled down and worn around necks or over bare breasts. Lilly thought about Ilya, the Russian, and wondered if he was celebrating the New Year in Russia. As another man lunged toward her and she ducked and spun away, her heart struck a short note of regret. People disappear and you never know, that's the worst of it.

A Marie Antoinette and a Turkish dancer were sitting on the corner of the stage, sniffing cocaine through a rolled-up banknote. Heavy rain began to pound the skylight above. The roof leaked and water started to cascade down onto the dance floor. The air was blurred with alcohol and smoke. All the windows had steamed up. Nobody could tell if their partner's smudged kohl and lipstick were caused by rain or sweat or kissing another or by a mixture of all three.

After searching all over the hall, Lilly spotted Hanne in a clinch with someone in a black evening suit. A gong sounded: it was midnight. Everyone cheered.

"Lights off, masks off!" they all shouted. "Lights off, masks off!"

The room was pitched into sudden black as all the lights were switched off. In the dark, a man pushed past Lilly and the rough fabric of his jacket chafed her bare shoulder. And then she heard the unmistakable sound of a gun being cocked.

The crowd started to chant, five, four, three, two, one, and suddenly the lights were switched on again, brighter, much brighter than they had seemed before. And there was Kurt, standing in front of Hanne, Hanne who had her arms around the person in the suit, a person who still wore a mask. Kurt took a step forward and ripped it off. It was Eva. Of course. It was Eva.

Kurt was in full uniform. His face was damp from the rain and he swayed a little in his boots, as if they were too big for him. In his hand the pistol seemed to weigh heavily, but still he aimed it at the dyke in black. A woman screamed. A man told her to shut up. The room fell silent. But then into that silence came the most shocking sound of all. Eva's shoulders started to shake, and she started to laugh. In seconds, the rest of the room joined in. It was a joke, obviously. The gun was a fake, the soldier an actor. They laughed until they couldn't stand straight, until they wet their pants or got a stitch. They laughed at the actor with the mutilated hand (poor sod), they laughed at the government, they laughed at Germany himself, cuckolded by a woman. Kurt stared at Hanne. She did not raise her eyes to meet his. And then her mouth began to twitch, and although it seemed as if she could not help herself, the first inklings of amusement began to tug at the corners of her lips. As soon as he saw it, Kurt spun round; his shoulders hunched and his disfigured hand dragged across his face, wiping away the rain and the mucus and the tears. And then he seemed to collect himself; he pointed his pistol at the floor and fired once.

The woman screamed again and the crowd, suddenly unsure whether it was a stunt after all, began to panic, to disperse and scatter, out of the door and into the rain, trampling onto the stage and knocking over the drum kit. Kurt's gaze fell on Lilly. At first it was as if he did not recognize her, and then his eyes seemed to focus and harden. He turned back and, with more violence than was necessary, grabbed Hanne's wrist, pulled her to her feet, and marched her through what was left of the crowd.

That night Hanne lost her other front tooth as well as the shiny new false tooth. Three months later, in March 1920, a right-wing journalist called Kapp staged a military coup supported by Noske's troops. Ebert's government evacuated to Dresden and urged the workers of Berlin to stage a general strike. They obliged, and for five days there was no power, no transport, and no water. The city came to a standstill. The putsch collapsed. Noske and his army marched out of Berlin, singing. Hanne and Lilly stood at the window and watched them go. A small boy pointed and laughed at them. One of the soldiers drew out his gun and shot him in the head.

Mr. Leyer had a glass office. Mr. Leyer had a pile of scripts so high it was said to skim the ceiling, and a huge blackboard that could be extended across his window to block out the sun. Everyone knew him by sight. He was what was kindly termed diminutive but in other words small, with a large head and a habit of saying "Good morning" to everyone and anyone. He liked men, it was rumored, and was not like some of the other producers who held endless closed-door casting sessions from which dozens of would-be actresses would emerge one by one, pink-faced and flustered. So when Lilly had approached him in the corridor and asked if she could introduce him to a friend of hers, a star of cabaret and stage, he had simply nodded, admitted that they were always on the lookout for fresh talent, and carried on walking.

"Just make an appointment," he had called over his shoulder.

And now Lilly's lunch break was almost over. She and Hanne had been waiting for thirty minutes. The walls outside Mr. Leyer's office were covered in stills from the movies he had produced, many of which they recognized: a vampire disappearing into thin air, a pretty girl staring in amazement at a man in a top hat, a judge pronouncing sentence on a prisoner.

His newest movie, *Letters of Love*, was just about to be cast. Lilly had typed up the script herself.

"I am some sort of serving girl and my lover writes me letters," said Hanne. "Only there is a deranged postman who is in love with me and steals them. My lover comes back, he and the postman fight, my lover dies, and I end up roving the city streets in rags, quite mad."

"That's right," said Lilly. "And then you throw yourself in front of a train, a mail train."

Hanne smiled. After losing the other front tooth, she had decided to have all her teeth removed and have a set of false teeth fitted. She had read about an American movie star who equated her success with the purchase of dentures. Hanne's new teeth were porcelain. They were, however, poorly fitted and painful to wear. Her smile faded before it had a chance to hurt.

Ever since Kurt had left the city, Hanne's moods had veered between wild optimism and torpid depression. Some days she was going to be more famous than Asta Nielsen and Pola Negri put together. On other days she vowed to give up acting completely.

"I'm going to marry a rich old man, settle down, and have two dozen children," Hanne would say. "You can come and see me on Sundays and take tea. God, I'll be so boring you won't believe it."

"You will never be boring, Hanne," Lilly said.

"I never want to be poor again," Hanne replied. "I wish I'd listened to that bank teller. If I'd chosen dollars, I'd be richer than ever now."

Prices had been rising steadily since the end of the war. Lilly's pay had been increased twice, but still it didn't seem to go far enough. Bread had quadrupled in price. Coffee had become completely unaffordable. The Treaty of Versailles decreed that Germany had to pay reparations of two billion gold marks, in installments. Since Germany was virtually bankrupt, the reparations were to be paid in raw materials, in coal, iron, and wood.

Hanne had found a part-time job as an usherette in the Marmorhaus Cinema and managed to pay something toward the rent. It was only temporary, of course, she said. And besides, she could watch all the latest films for nothing. What she needed, she repeated over and over, was a way in, a break, a chance to prove herself.

Mr. Leyer's secretary had informed them that she had told Mr. Leyer that they were still waiting. Another ten minutes passed. Suddenly, Hanne stood up and began to pull on her coat.

"If I go now, I'll catch the two-o'clock train back into the city," Hanne said. "I have to be back for the three-o'clock show anyway."

Lilly did not knock and she did not apologize. On these two points Mr. Leyer was clear, when he told the story years afterward. As she stepped into the room, the sun momentarily blinded her.

"Mr. Leyer? We can't wait any longer," she said.

As her eyes adjusted to the light, she saw not one but four men inside the glass walls of Mr. Leyer's office. She recognized two. One was the small figure of Mr. Leyer; the other was Ilya Yurasov. They all turned and stared at her.

"Oh, hello," she said. "I thought . . ."

Ilya greeted her with a small incline of his head. In the letter he had written to her, the letter that the sad-eyed fat girl had lost, he had informed her that he had just been offered a new job. His prewar reputation had eventually caught up with him and he had been plucked from his lowly position as a negative cutter at Afifa and contracted by Deutsche Bioscop, a subsidiary of Ufa. In the letter, he had also explained that he had taken a new apartment, but he had given her his office telephone number and invited her out for lunch. As the weeks and then months had gone by and he had heard nothing from her, at first he had been bemused and then slightly angry and then relieved. He didn't want to get himself entangled; he didn't want any complications.

But he could not get her face out of his head. He had often wandered across to the typing pool and in all the frenzied activity had managed to watch her unobserved. He noticed that her typewriter keys stuck and it was he who had arranged for a new machine to be delivered. It was also he who had once found her asleep at her desk on a Saturday and had carried her to a divan and taken off her shoes. He had even mentioned her to his boss, the typing-pool girl who looked not unlike the actress Anya Gregorin, and might be worth considering.

Mr. Leyer, who was constantly being bombarded with casting suggestions by sisters, mothers, taxi drivers, had not bothered to follow up the lead. Ilya knew this and therefore was as surprised as Lilly was when she stepped into the producer's office unannounced.

"Oh. Anyway, it's about *Letters of Love*," she said. "Casting *Letters of Love*, actually."

Here, Lilly pulled Hanne out of the door frame, where she had been standing, and into the room. Mr. Leyer looked doubly surprised.

"Has the script been sent out already?" said one of the other men.

"No," Lilly said. "I typed it. I work in the pool."

"Well," said Ilya Yurasov, "you must have read a lot of scripts. So, do you like it?"

It did momentarily cross her mind that she wasn't supposed to admit that she read the work she typed. But Lilly did not pause before answering his question.

"Apart from the unoriginal ending," she said, "and the tendency to dwell on the melodramatic, it isn't bad."

Ilya laughed. His whole face softened. She noticed for the first time the color of his eyes: green—green with flecks of blue. He was in Berlin, after all. The elation she felt within, however, had to be put to one side. She was here for Hanne.

"My point entirely," he said.

The other men looked slightly dismayed. They were the writers. All four had met that day to discuss the script. Ilya had not been unforthcoming in his criticism.

"So, what do you suggest?" he said.

"Surely," continued Lilly, "surely in scene thirty-four she needn't actually pace up and down in front of her mailbox. A look would be enough."

"A look," he repeated. "A look?"

Without thinking twice, Lilly demonstrated. She knew how to use her face. The cabaret artist Wernher Siegfried, if nothing else, had been a good teacher.

Ilya nodded. Mr. Leyer nodded. The other two men folded their arms.

"So, what do you suggest for the ending?" Ilya asked.

Lilly glanced from him to Mr. Leyer. The blackboard was covered in writing.

"I really have no idea," said Lilly. "But since it's set in a city . . . maybe she throws herself from the top of a new apartment building."

Mr. Leyer looked at his Russian director.

"The typing-pool girl?"

Ilya nodded.

"Not bad," said Mr. Leyer. "Not bad at all. But I've never heard of any woman doing such a thing."

Outside, a couple of men were shifting scenery. As they passed, a painted flat of a forest momentarily blocked out the sunlight. At that moment Lilly glanced at Hanne with such a look that the two men could be in no doubt that she did indeed know of a woman who had done such a thing.

"So?" said Lilly. "Will you at least consider . . . ?"

"Indeed I will," said Mr. Leyer. "I suggest we do a screen test. . . . We could even do it now. We're casting this afternoon for that Lang film."

Lilly turned to her friend just as the sun filled the room again. But Hanne wasn't smiling. Instead, she was staring blank-faced at Lilly, at the short blond hair that she herself had cut and dyed and the large gray eyes accentuated as she had suggested with just a smudge of black. And it seemed as if she suddenly saw her afresh.

"Me?" Lilly replied. "Oh, not me. It's Hanne you want."

But it was not.

The Russian

"You are English citizens," the director tells the crowd through a megaphone. "It is the sixteenth century and you have come to watch the king's coronation."

They have hired four thousand extras, but they could have hired double or triple at half the cost. Nobody has a job anymore. Who can live on the government allowance? Everybody's an actor in Berlin now.

"Action!" the director shouts. "Take one."

They cheer until they're hoarse, and then they cheer more, until they've reached the nineteenth take without a break. It's the lighting, somebody says. It's the acting. It's Ebert, the president, on an official visit with his entourage. Ebert, the man they voted for but who has done nothing for them; Ebert, the one who cannot stop the strikes and shortages or the misery and the mayhem. From where they stand, it's possible to watch as he sips a cup of tea and nibbles a sandwich from the catering stand the extras have not been allowed to visit. They start to swarm, wasps in a nest.

"Down with Ebert!" somebody shouts. "Down with Ebert!"

Lubitsch, the director, keeps on filming. He catches their faces, shouting, flushed and furious, until they are on the brink of revolution, on the brink of tearing down his flimsy sets and stringing up the president on the cardboard flats of Westminster Abbey. And then he cuts. The film company has to abandon its schedule and loses a quarter of a million. The finished film, however, wins an award.

Lilly's screen test at the Neubabelsberg studio was short and functional. She was told where to stand, her face lit by a bank of lights, and she was asked to look left, look right, look straight into the lens. The script was handed to her and she acted out a scene.

"Have you done this before?" asked Mr. Leyer.

"Not with all my clothes on," she replied.

Leyer roared with laughter. Lilly barely smiled. And then she returned to the typing pool and stayed late to make up the time that she had missed.

On the way home, she went over and over what had happened that day. By the time she reached the boardinghouse, she had convinced herself that the whole thing was probably an elaborate joke. She would insist that they both go back to Mr. Leyer and try again. And yet, when she thought of the polite Russian and the way he had looked at her, she felt a jolt run straight from the top of her head to the ends of her toes. He hadn't left Berlin, after all. But why hadn't he been in touch?

Hanne was standing at the sink wearing nothing but an underslip and her French shoes. She was rubbing cream into her face with short, circular strokes.

"Did you get the part?" said Hanne.

"I don't know," said Lilly. "Hanne, I'm so sorry about this afternoon."

"Why not? That's what I always say. Why the hell not? If an opportunity comes along, then take it. I know I would."

Hanne spat on a tablet of kohl and then started to underline her lashes in black with a tiny brush. As she did so, her eyes reddened and her face set, but she kept going, never losing eye contact with herself in the mirror.

"Hanne?" Lilly laid a hand on her shoulder. Hanne turned and stared at it. Lilly removed it.

"I'm working tonight," she said, wiping two sooty streaks away and focusing on her cake of rouge.

"I've failed every audition I've ever done," Lilly said. "You know that."

Hanne smiled, but in the harsh light of the single bulb above the sink it looked more like a frown. And then she concentrated on trimming a small, blunt brush with a pair of nail scissors. It was already evening but the curtains were still open. Lilly drew them together, one at a time.

"Remember that play you wrote at St. Francis Xavier's?" said Hanne suddenly. "The golden boot. The beard. . . . Everyone laughed. You broke Sister August's heart. You ruined everything for her. And then the place closed and everyone was separated. . . . Why did you do it?"

Lilly felt the blood rush to her face. She stood, still wearing her coat and hat, and swayed slightly on her feet. Was it her fault that the orphanage had been sold? Was she the one to blame for the fact that Hanne had lost her brothers? It had never occurred to her before, but now Hanne's words seemed to have a horrifying kind of logic. And a weight descended deep into her belly that would never entirely rise.

"Is that what you think?" she said. "Is that what you've thought for all these years?"

Hanne started to buff her cheek with a powder puff, but underneath it was already flushed.

"I often think about my boys," she said. "I thought if I was in a film, if I was up there, you know, on the screen, they'd come looking for me—if they were alive, that is. . . . I'm late. If they offer you a part, any part, take it. We need the money."

And with that, she pulled on her coat, let herself out, closed the door with a click, and cantered down the stairs, her high heels echoing up the stairwell before they ceased abruptly with the sharp slam of the front door.

The next morning there was a note on Lilly's desk requesting that she go straight to Mr. Leyer's office. There were half a dozen people waiting in the corridor, but she was ushered straight in. The sun in his room was so bright that for a moment she was blinded again. A silhouette shook her warmly by the hand. As her eyes adjusted to the light, Mr. Leyer offered her the part of the servant girl and produced a contract from a drawer.

"We'd like you to play Hedda," he said. "It's not a huge role, but it's a start. Now, if you'll just sign here . . ."

He pulled a fountain pen from his top pocket and began to unscrew the top. Lilly hesitated.

"Sit down and read it through, if you like."

When she didn't take it, he put the pen down, sighed, and sat back in his chair. Behind him, outside, a rail of brightly colored costumes was being wheeled slowly by, sequins and crystals catching the sunshine.

"You're wondering, I suppose, at my motivation. And I must admit this is highly irregular. But it is not unheard of. The actress Molla Delusi was discovered working in a cake shop. The actor Gerhardt Dahl was once our postman. You see, the moving picture requires different qualities from what the stage requires. The rules of acting don't apply. In the theater it is all about the body, dialogue, words; on film, it is all about the face. And although, as you may have heard, I am inclined to fall in love with my own sex, it is clear even to me that you, my dear, have the face."

Mr. Leyer had watched her screen test several times over. In the flesh she was an attractive young woman—that was undeniable—but on film, her skin looked as smooth and flawless as a pearl; her eyes were invitations fringed with long, dark lashes; the arch of her brow and the curve of her cheek were gradients so perfect it was hard to resist the urge to touch. She was stunning. And what was more, there was something about her presence on screen that suggested that she wasn't acting. The script was trite and the characterization poor, but the girl made it all seem credible; you could see that, in her head, in her heart, in her whole body, she was there.

"I'm sorry," she said. "I can't do it."

Mr. Leyer was momentarily stunned. He was used to strange reactions from actors. One young man got down on all fours and kissed his shoes. One woman offered herself to him in nothing more than a raincoat and a pair of stockings and was politely rebuffed. But this, a refusal, this was something he had not experienced before.

"What?" he said. "Are you mad, my girl? Whyever not?"

What could she say? How could she explain about the play, about Sister August, about the closing of St. Francis Xavier's?

She shook her head.

"Well, if you're sure . . ." said Mr. Leyer. "But you're the one that everyone wants for this part, especially the director, Ilya Yurasov."

He started to screw the top back onto his fountain pen. The meeting was over. Just before Lilly turned to leave the room, she caught sight of her own reflection in the glass. She saw nothing extra, nothing special, nothing but her own ordinariness. But what would Hanne say? Hadn't Hanne told her to take it? Furthermore, Ilya Yurasov wanted her. He wanted her. She could hardly believe it, but there it was. And the willfulness that the midwife had spotted on the day she was born came flooding back. She turned to Mr. Leyer.

"Very well," she said. "I'll sign."

"That's the right answer," said Mr. Leyer. "Very good."

But even as she wrote out her name in full, her hand trembled and she was filled with trepidation. What would it cost her this time?

Since the budget was small and she was an unknown, her fee was modest. It was, nevertheless, ten times what she was being paid as a typist.

"You might be able to negotiate more for the next one," Mr. Leyer told her. "Congratulations. We start filming on Monday."

The next one. At that point, Lilly didn't really want to let herself believe there would be a next one. She was loath to give up her job in the typing pool and was given three weeks' unpaid leave instead.

Letters of Love went into production in late 1920. Lilly's love interest was also an unknown, a stage actor from Max Reinhardt's troupe. But while he beat his chest and waved his arms as soon as the camera started to roll, Lilly barely moved at all. And while all his impulses and emotions were acted out in semaphore, hers revealed themselves only in the cast of her eyes or the slightest tilt of her head.

"She is a natural," Mr. Leyer said when he saw the rushes. "She could convey her heart through the movement of her little finger."

The film took four weeks to shoot. Lilly lost her job in the typing pool.

As she had been filming from five in the morning until well after nine at night, she rarely saw Hanne. Occasionally they passed each other in the hallway when Hanne was coming in from a night out and Lilly was leaving to go to the studio, but they didn't talk. Too much had been said, too much was still unsayable, and all that shared history that pulled them together now pushed them irrevocably apart.

In the studio, however, it was decided that Lilly would become Lidi, and her history was rewritten. Her press officer, herself a would-be scenarist, claimed that Lidi was the daughter of a wealthy army officer who had died heroically in the first battle of the war. Her mother had, apparently, piled the rest of the family fortune into private acting tuition before succumbing to a fever of the heart and following the path of her late husband a tragic three months before her daughter was given her first screen role. The only truth, in fact, was her age, which needed no alteration. She was as old as the new century: twenty.

"You're single, aren't you?" the press officer asked. "That's good. All the girls say they are, you know."

There is only one photograph of the actress Lidi and the director Ilya Yurasov from this period. It was taken in February 1921, in a park somewhere in Berlin. They are both wearing ice-skating boots and long dark coats with beaver collars. Lilly, or Lidi, as she was known then, is laughing, her head thrown back and her eyes half closed. The Russian looks slightly uncomfortable and smiles as if he is unaccustomed to being photographed.

Some speculated much later that their affair could have begun on that first day, after her screen test but before she returned to Berlin. As the floodlights cooled and the sun began to drop, as the flats of medieval castles and circus tents and cardboard forests began to lose their colors, maybe, they imagined, he reached toward her golden head and then pulled her face up to his. But you can tell by the skating photograph that this was unlikely. No, right from the very start, Lidi's incredible presence on the screen was clearly not just purely physiological. Like millions of Germans at that moment in time, just after one war but less than two decades before the next, you can tell by her face that, despite everything, she is filled with longing, with feverish desire, with an overwhelming need for things or people she cannot have.

Ilya had been meaning to tell Lilly. He had, in fact, been on the brink several times. But when she looked up at him with those eyes, those eyes that told him something he both dreaded and treasured, he found himself disarmed, humbled, mute.

Ilya was engaged to a woman named Katya Nadezhda. Fifteen years his senior and widowed, with a daughter, Katya was beautiful, intelligent, and insecure. She had owned a flat on Nevsky Prospekt in St. Petersburg and an estate near Minsk inherited from her late husband, who had not believed in either fidelity or eating fruits and vegetables. Ilya had met her at a dinner party just after he had graduated from university with a first-class degree in classics. He had claimed he had no idea what to do with his life, and so she had hired him on the spot to teach her young daughter Latin. During the stiflingly hot summer of 1912, the textbooks remained resolutely closed while their affair blossomed. He was twenty-three and was filled with the heady sense of his own potential. She was thirty-eight and racked with the sense of her own decline. He proposed within a month but she politely turned him down for reasons that were obvious. She bought him a moving-picture camera instead and suggested he make something with it. Two years later he had made three films, two for the Khanzhonkov studio, and was about to make a fourth when he was drafted.

On the eve of his departure, Ilya promised Katya that he would return and marry her. They both knew their love was tempered with both gratitude and guilt. But it was still love. And so she accepted.

The war and then the revolution, however, kept them apart. He would have returned to Russia had her letters not urged him to go to the West, to wait for her there. She would leave St. Petersburg, she promised, when the time was right. And so he was waiting, working, saving up for the day that Katya and her daughter would join him. At first her letters came regularly, but then she told him that the situation in St. Petersburg had become much worse. She had decided to leave everything and head south, to the Crimea. From there she had heard it was still possible to buy passage on a boat and head West. And then, she promised, she would make her way to Berlin, to him, to her fiancé. The letters had then stopped.

And so Ilya had remained faithful to a woman he had not seen for five years. The camera, he told himself, was a membrane through which he could not pass. He could look, but the glass of the lens would always separate him from any woman. And that was the way, he told himself, it had to remain.

He worked nights to edit *Letters of Love*, and sometimes his assistant would find him asleep next to his splicer, Lidi's face caught in a glance over her shoulder, perhaps, or her eyes unfocused and her mouth slightly open. And yet, if he were ever challenged, he would hotly deny his feelings were anything but professional. But the evidence to the contrary was clear for all to see: it was in her eyes; it was in his cut; it was in every single frame of every single scene she appeared in.

Lilly continued to live frugally on a fraction of the money she had made from the film. The rest she put into a savings account. She worked on what she could, typing up scripts for writers she had met at the film company, but she knew this kind of work would barely cover the rent once her savings had run out. And although Hanne always seemed to be working, she never seemed to have any money. She should never, Lilly told herself, have signed that contract. Also, she hadn't seen Ilya since the last day of the shoot. He had taken her from the typing pool and dropped her again. She had been foolish, willful, vain. Sister August would have been ashamed of her. But despite all of this, she still felt the undeniable afterglow of blue inside.

And then, without a premiere and with the minimum budget for publicity, *Letters of Love* was released.

"Lidi's gift is such," said one review, "that she renders all others on the screen to cardboard. Her face is an instrument of a truly rare and unique substance.

"Even though this story of urban despair is a little slight," the review went on to state, "the results are spellbinding and the tragic climax heartbreaking."

Lilly had just come back from the studio, where she had dropped off a typed manuscript for a producer. She had picked up the newspapers on the way from the station. As she unlocked the door, she noticed that the air in the room was stale and smelled of perfume and something else, something that Lilly recognized but couldn't immediately place. Hanne was sitting at the window painting her toenails.

"My film got a review," she said.

"Any good?"

"Kind of," Lilly said. "Do you want to read it?"

Hanne shook open the newspaper and then, after crumpling the pages until she found it, scrutinized the review.

"Did you sleep with him?"

"The journalist? I've never even met him," Lilly replied.

Hanne handed the newspaper back. Lilly carefully folded it up again, smoothing it down.

"You won't be living here for much longer at this rate," Hanne said.

"What rate?"

But Hanne only snorted through her nose and looked out of the window.

"Listen," Lilly said. "It doesn't change anything. Let's go out dancing, let's go to the Café Josty and order Champagne, real Champagne, and then move on to the Friedrichstrasse. Let's dance all night just like we used to. Come on, Hanne."

"I'm working at the Marmorhaus," Hanne replied. "Late showing."

And then she pulled on her shoes and coat and left without another word.

It was a lie. There was no late showing that night. The smell that Lilly recognized but couldn't place was Eva's: her soap, her sweat, and her lust. She had spent the afternoon in bed with Hanne. Slowly, patiently, after many weeks of secret rendezvous over coffee, of small gifts, of longing looks, of pecks on the cheek, she had finally unpeeled Hanne's clothes. At last her fingers had lingered over her scars; her mouth had sought out the nape of her neck, her nipples, the triangle of golden hair between her legs. And after such patience, such sweet procrastination, the payoff was an incredible release for both of them.

Instead of working, as she had claimed, Hanne was going to meet Eva at her favorite bar. She wanted more, more of the wine that Eva always bought her, more of the kisses that, compared to Kurt's, were so soft they were barely kisses at all, more of the gentle adoration that she was under no compulsion to return. That afternoon, Eva had suggested that she move out of the boardinghouse and move in with her.

She still had some of her mother's jewelry to sell, she said; she still had limited funds.

Hanne Schmidt, like many girls of her generation who had survived the war, the flu epidemic, the food shortages, and the bitter Berlin winters, understood almost instinctively that when one avenue of opportunity closed, you had to immediately search out another. Leaving lovers, children, jobs, apartments, without apparent remorse—at least, not of the debilitating kind—they were perpetually moving on, casting off, starting out afresh, their eye on the as yet uncaught ball. There is always tomorrow, their actions seemed to say. There is always another way.

Maybe Hanne left the matchbox on the sink deliberately. Or maybe she did it subconsciously, taking away the potential awkwardness of an unavoidable confession. Certainly, although she had done so since the night of the masked ball, she didn't like deceiving Lilly, she didn't like lying to cover up her increasingly frequent meetings with Eva. Lilly picked up the matchbox and turned it round in her fingers. *Verona-Lounge*, it read, *The Love Domicile for Girl-Friends*. She opened it. Inside, a message had been hastily scribbled. *Until tonight*, it read. *Love, E.*

It had been raining and pavements were illuminated with the reflected scribble of electrified shop signs, traffic lights, and the headlights of passing cars. Lilly ran all the way to the cinema, splashing through pools of silver and yellow, amber and violet, only pausing once to let a tram pass. Hanne wouldn't lie to her, would she? Not after all that had happened, not after all they had shared. Lilly would find her there collecting tickets and selling chocolate as usual, and then she would explain that she had come to make up, to insist they go out dancing later, to show Hanne how much her friendship still mattered to her. Lilly's footsteps only began to falter when she approached the foyer of the cinema. The Marmorhaus was closed.

Lidi's first film made a respectable amount of money, and Mr. Leyer offered her another with Yurasov as director. They started shooting almost immediately. This time Lidi was given the lead role as a millionaire-turned-con-man's destitute daughter who is in love with a priest. She cries to order, Mr. Leyer boasted at the end of the first week, real tears every time. Ilya Yurasov nodded but did not comment.

Although they still lived in the same rooms, Lilly did not confront Hanne. She did not question her duplicity. Maybe it was because real life had somehow become unreal. Lilly had begun to feel that the only reality she could grasp was the reality of the film set. Only here could she make sense of who she was, what she was feeling, and why; only here could she follow a script. The rest of her life—the salary that she never had time to spend, the chauffeured drives to and from the set, the dressing rooms with their permanently fresh flowers that just appeared every day as if by magic—all seemed to belong to a dream life, to a sham that could collapse, like the German mark would do, almost overnight.

No, to Lilly, as she was still known by Ilya, the film set was home and the crew was like family, at least what she imagined a family would be. And every morning when she came onto the set, he would be there. And every day she would feel that phosphorescence inside. As he kissed her cheek and wished her good morning, she momentarily forgot that the world outside was chaotic and filled with the destitute, the starving, and the dispossessed, and she ceased to feel like a refugee fleeing from the scene of a disaster. And, for just a moment, she imagined he was hers.

After *Letters of Love*, Ilya Yurasov's name was regularly mentioned by the critics. His directorial style, so it was argued in Café des Westens, was mercurial, his technique deceptively simplistic. Pola Negri sent him a bunch of orchids and a card suggesting her people talk to his people. Asta Nielsen invited him to lunch. He failed to respond to either offer.

Years later, Ilya told a former lawyer in the next bunk at Dachau that he had loved Lilly the moment he first saw her. He described a young girl in a Berlin boardinghouse, the way her dark hair shone in the pale sun and her large gray eyes were shot through with silver.

"I loved her," he told the former lawyer. "I loved her for years but couldn't tell her."

"I know the feeling," the former lawyer said. "We went to the cinema a lot in those days. It was always lovely and warm in our local theater. She was one of my favorites, you know. Those films brought out this certain quality. . . . You must have had a hand in it."

"It was all there already," Ilya said. "And sometimes I wonder if we should have discovered her, exposed her, shared her. Maybe it would have turned out differently, for both of us."

"If you hadn't, somebody else would have," said the former lawyer, whose pragmatic style had been famous in the courthouses of Cologne. "And anyway, how could you have known then? The future is unwritten. You couldn't have predicted what would happen."

As the night stretched and ached with cold, Ilya lay on his bunk in silence and remembered a day in the spring of 1921. It was a time when the cost of making a film in Germany was the cost of a secondhand car in Paris or Pennsylvania or Perth and when the films he cut were filled with apparitions and mirrors and the sets were imaginary landscapes constructed out of wood and paint and paper.

"I had no intention," he whispered. "I never had any intention. All I wanted to do was make films and wait for Katya. That was my plan. And then . . . and then . . ."

Ilya's hands trembled beneath the thin louse-infested blanket as he tried to recall every last detail of the first night he spent with Lilly. It came back in glimpses and blurred images and scents: a certain shade of red, the sun on brick against storm clouds, the smell of pepper mixed with mimosa. It was saturation and intoxication, it was an appetite that was never fully quenched, it was both an ending of boundaries and a realization of an insurmountable isolation. It was pure joy tempered with absolute despair—the sense of loss, even as he lived it, of the moment, of himself, of her.

It was the evening of the premiere of her second film, *Girl of the Wind*. The Champagne was all finished and the cinema was closing and Lilly, or Lidi, was hovering on the stairs as if she were waiting for someone. But then, he had noticed, even in the most crowded party she always looked alone. She was, he realized only much later, waiting for him.

"Didn't your friend come?" Ilya asked her.

Lilly shook her head but did not explain.

"Shall we share a car?" he asked.

It was an innocent enough request. Only one studio car was idling on the street outside.

"I don't want to go home yet," she said as she climbed inside. "Let's go somewhere else for a drink?"

He leaned forward and told the driver to go to Kaiser Wilhelm Memorial Church. They climbed out and walked to a tiny bar he knew called the Cosy Corner. Of course she was recognized, but she was left alone. They were all actresses and directors at that time of night. Everybody was somebody, even if they hadn't happened yet.

A small band was playing jazz for tips. Lilly was wearing a red hat. He remembered that now. She took it off and placed it on top of his coat. And then they started dancing, to that band, to that song "Tomorrow's the End of the World."

The man who cut in had a huge beard. Ilya stood back and watched him dance with Lilly. But the song went on too long. The band, who knew only a few numbers, had not worked out how it ended. And as he watched her, she caught his eye and gave him the look he knew so well. But this time there was no lens to diffuse it and it hit him in the back of the throat, in the chest, in the belly. There could be no doubt, he knew at that particular moment, no doubt at all.

Afterward they had walked, aimlessly, or so it seemed at first, down one street and under the S-Bahn, along one avenue and over a bridge. Suddenly she paused at a block of apartments between the river Spree and the park.

"I used to live here," she said.

She ran her hand along the wall until she came to a small hollow just big enough for a foothold.

"This used to be my secret place," she whispered. "Behind this wall."

And then she told him about the orphanage, about Sister August, about Hanne. He knew it was somehow a gift, a gift of who she was. But it was more than that. For her, it was the telling of a story that she had never told before, a narrative that just through the telling could be reinterpreted, retold, reclaimed. They kept walking until they somehow ended up at his place near Alexanderplatz Station, and he didn't need to ask because they both knew that she was coming in. And then she stood in the pale, pale yellow of the streetlight that reached into his room from the street below and let her dress, her slip, her underwear, slide from her body like so many gossamer skins.

Tomorrow's the end of the world . . .

He thought she was sleeping. She lay motionless, her body curled into the crook of his arm. She had been there beside him for a whole night, getting up only to put a record on the gramophone. Several empty cups and glasses covered his bedside table along with a couple of books of poetry. Time, or so it seemed, had become unhitched, and they had slipped into a place where the incessant tick of minutes had been reduced to nothing more than the rhythm of the samba played in a basement bar across the street or the dripping of someone else's bathroom tap.

Her skin was flawless. He brushed his lips across the slope of her shoulder and kissed the base of her neck. His fingertips ran down her belly until they reached the downy silk of her pubic hair. She shivered and with both hands she pressed his hand hard against herself. He moved behind her, fitting himself into her curves. And she turned her head and her mouth found his again.

Hours later, he woke. Outside it was light again, the early-morning sun as bright as a four-hundred-watt bulb on the dirty gray tenement buildings opposite. Her eyes were open and she was staring at the sky. He suddenly felt incredibly sober, incredibly certain that despite everything, despite his promise to Katya, Lilly was the only woman he wanted. And his heart seemed to sound with a single note.

Lilly's memories of their first night together were played over so many times through the years that the premiere party, the bar, the band, the vodka, the walk past St. Francis Xavier's, and finally Ilya's apartment eventually took on the swimming confusion of a dream. Some images came back to her more clearly than others: his apartment, a place that looked hardly lived in but for the piles of books on the floor and the smell of black coffee; the way he looked at her with that long green gaze that seemed so penetrating she could barely stand it; his face in her hands as she kissed his eyes, his mouth, his lips; and then, as they lay down, the way the whole length of her fitted the whole length of him. The question that for so long had hung in the air between them had finally been answered. She could feel it in his body, in his warmth, in his voice, a voice with all its deep velvet resonance held back, turned into a whisper.

Yes.

When he gave himself away, he did it so completely that she believed that there was nothing between them, no deception or doubt or history. It was the first time, the first time she had so willingly yielded to anyone. After, when she lay with her head in the hollow of his arm, just listening to him breathe, feeling him wake just enough to find her hand and hold it, she finally admitted to herself that she had been starving for him, parched for him, craving him for as long as she could remember.

Lilly began shooting another film the very next day. If she was tired, she did not show it. Her eyes were so bright that the cameraman asked the director if he thought she might have taken laudanum. Without more than two coffee breaks, she worked for ten hours straight and filmed fifteen scenes. When Lidi and Ilya dined that night with other members of the cast to celebrate the first day of the shoot, some of them noted that she seemed particularly talkative while Ilya was strangely silent. Nobody, however, thought it was significant.

And as they lingered outside Kempinski's, and two by two the cast and crew of *Roses on My Pillow* climbed into a row of waiting cabs, there was a moment when either Lilly or Ilya could have gone home alone. But although the words were in his mouth and hers, her eyes kept straying into his and he knew that he would ask her and he knew what she would say.

Yes.

A 3264/1
Ufa
Foto Quick

The Inflation

The manager of the Ufa-Palast am Zoo stands on the lip of the front stairs and rocks back and forth. From here he can see that the queue stretches all the way to the station. "I'm sorry, we're full. I'm sorry, we're full." He has two thousand seats and all have been sold out at three daily film screenings for more than a month. Berlin may be hungry, but an appetite for the kinky or exotic or scary is stronger. "I'm sorry, madam, we're full."

The houselights lower, the audience settles, the curtains part, and Lupu Pick's Shattered *starts to roll.*

It's winter; the snow is falling gently in the middle of a darkening forest. Werner Krauss is a railroad trackwalker who lives in isolated monochrome with his wife and daughter. When a railway inspector arrives out of a blizzard, everything goes haywire. First the poor daughter is seduced and then spurned, and then the heartbroken mother freezes to death. Finally the railroad worker avenges the family honor by strangling the inspector. In the last and final scene he walks along the tracks and stops the express train. His lamp radiates a brilliant, hand-tinted red. The snow, the air, the night turn crimson. He climbs aboard the train and speaks his only line: "I am a murderer."

As the train speeds away from the dark forest still iced with snow, the audience, as one, lets out a sigh of satiation. What a trick, what an effect. A film with color, ingenious.

Lilly spent every night with Ilya, often lying awake until the dawn broke, talking, kissing, making love, unwilling to let sleep steal even a single moment. It was as if she could suddenly speak another tongue, a language of murmurs and moans and kisses that had been there in her heart all along but was incomprehensible until she met him.

"I'm so happy," she whispered more than once.

And he would reply with a kiss or a sigh or a caress.

I am weak, Ilya thought to himself as he lay beside Lilly. But the guilt that he felt always passed like a shadow. All he had to remember Katya by was a framed studio photograph. But when he looked at it, he found that her strong features and posed expression seemed to belong to another era, to another life he barely remembered living. Maybe she had fallen in love with another man? Maybe she had forgotten him? Maybe she was dead? He had taken her photograph down from his wall, but he found he could not throw it away.

Lilly went back to the boardinghouse only to fetch clean clothes or pay the rent. She didn't want to meet Eva; the situation was an almost exact reversal of what had happened with Stefan. She had been Eva's deceiver and she had subsequently been deceived. But it was more than that: she knew that she loved Ilya in a way she had never been able to love Stefan. The brief courtship, the marriage, the wedding night had seemed in retrospect to be nothing more than a charade played out by children. And in her head Stefan would always be more boy than man as he rode, with lance carried aloft, into the hail of bullets that killed him.

Hanne, however, didn't invite Eva back to the boardinghouse. They went to clubs or wealthy friends' apartments or, if neither was open or available, to seedy bars in West Berlin. Eva's invitation to move into an apartment together was rarely mentioned, and her small gifts had dwindled to almost nothing apart from the occasional bar of chocolate or pair of stockings. When Hanne finally brought it up, Eva admitted she had already sold her mother's jewels. She had no funds to speak of; in fact, she didn't have enough for a glass of wine, let alone a bottle. And then she laughed until her eyes watered and her side stitched.

"You still love me, don't you?" she asked Hanne when she had recovered her breath.

But Hanne, her face stony, did not reply.

Eva Mauritz's political convictions had waned since the heady days of the Spartacists' uprising. The revolution on a Russian scale had not happened. The leaders of the party had been murdered in police custody, their bodies unceremoniously dumped. The city seemed to have absorbed the dissent and then quickly forgotten it, with only the pockmarks of bullet holes on streets such as Karlstrasse to show there had ever been any conflict at all.

She had returned to the apartment in Steglitz but found it occupied by a group of refugees from Galicia. She would claim that she was a Communist and therefore was bidden to share what she had, but when faced with the reality of shared ownership she changed her mind and asked them to leave many times over. They refused, and so she chucked an old woman out of her room and slept there, only venturing into the kitchen for hot water. Apart from the bare floorboards, the iron bedsteads, and the few pieces of furniture that were yet to be burned, there wasn't much left in her uncle's flat anyway. The paintings once so loathed by Stefan, the typewriter on which Lilly had learned to type, the hand-stitched clothes, and the soap from France were all gone, all stolen by a member of the Freikorps who broke into the apartment by smashing the lock on the pretext of looking for Communists, or Kozzis, as they were known.

Eva had not seen her younger brother for more than two years. In the devastation of their flat, however, she had salvaged a single, posed photograph of both of them, aged nineteen and seventeen. And when she was feeling depressed or overwhelmed or rejected, she would look at it and weep. And so when Hanne Schmidt, her lover, her adored muse, her darling girl, did not return her devotions, her mind was drawn back to that image of her brother. He had loved her, she was sure of it.

At that point Stefan Mauritz was living in lodgings near the Anhalter train station. He had enough money in the bank to live on without working. If it was fair, he walked the city's parks. If it was cold, he would buy a cinema ticket and spend the whole day snoozing and watching the same film sometimes four or five times over.

One day he fell asleep in a matinee screening of a film he had not noticed the title of. He woke with a start and there she was, her face the size of a shop window, her eyes as large as the moon: Lilly, his wife. And his heart soared and then dived as he suddenly remembered. He touched his face and felt his changed physiognomy, so alien to him still. And then he thought about Eva, his sister, and he started to bang the armrest over and over with so much force that the couple behind him moved to another row.

Hanne dropped Eva in March 1921. After they had made love in the women's washroom in a tiny bar on Friedrichstrasse, she pulled down her skirt and fixed her hair as Eva pawed her body, wanting more.

"Good-bye, Eva," Hanne said as she unlocked the door. "It's over. I don't want to see you again."

"What are you talking about?" said Eva. "Come back."

But Hanne would not.

"Very well," she said. "Are you going to tell me why?"

"The truth? You disgust me."

Eva stared at Hanne, her mouth slightly open. And then she regained her poise.

"Me, I disgust you?" Eva said. "You are nothing, no one, worthless. You've got the street written all over your face. You're cheap, the cheapest I've ever had. Good luck, Hanne. But let me tell you something: you won't even get more than a few marks out there. All those dreams of being an actress. Take a look in the mirror. You look haggard, used up, old."

Hanne did not listen anymore. She walked out of the bar, her face blazing and her knees noticeably shaking. She should have expected it. She shouldn't let herself care. But still her throat thickened and she had trouble breathing. And without warning his name came into her head again. She hailed a cab and without even a moment's hesitation asked the driver to go to the barracks of the Freikorps.

Eva was shocked at herself. What was happening to her? Where was her private-school demeanor and well-read charm? The bar was full of young men with hungry eyes. She chose one and bought him a drink. And then she sat and talked until closing time about poetry and opera, about art and politics, until he grabbed her thigh and told her he'd do anything for the price of a loaf.

Lilly had come to collect the last of her things from the boardinghouse. The studio had insisted she move immediately to the Hotel Adlon, to a part of Berlin where their drivers didn't get their cars scratched and their headlights stolen every time they came to pick her up. She had packed a couple of suitcases, written a note to Hanne telling her that she had paid the rent up front for the next six months, and propped it up on the shelf above the sink. As she took one more look around the rooms, however, the door swung open and Hanne stood swaying, half in, half out of the door. Blood was smeared all over her face.

"You're here," said Hanne. "I'm so glad you're here."

"Hanne!" Lilly said. "What happened?"

Hanne said she had tripped and fallen down the U-Bahn stairs. She said that the stairs were wet and she would make a formal complaint, but with such little conviction that it was clear that none of it was true. Her stockings were ripped at the knees and there was a deep gash in her head. Her face, for so long kept composed, finally began to fold.

"My only pair of stockings," Hanne said. "To think I wasted my only pair of stockings."

"I'll buy you more," Lilly whispered. "They're only stockings."

But Hanne couldn't be comforted, and she cried without inhibition for the stockings that could never be mended and for Eva's insults that could never be taken back, and mostly for the man who could not forgive her and was so filled with hurt that he had held her with his good hand and punched her with his bad.

When Hanne's sobs eventually subsided, Lilly washed her cuts and dressed them. Hanne let herself be told what to do, be cared for like a wayward child, be mothered. Later, Hanne lay on the divan and Lilly tucked her in under a blanket.

"This place feels like the only safe place in the whole of Berlin," Hanne said.

Lilly stroked her hair. Hanne's forehead, she suddenly noticed, was lined, her eyes had started to drag at the corners, and the whites were yellow.

"Go to sleep," Lilly whispered.

"You always were my only real friend—you know that, don't you? Nothing's changed, has it?"

Lilly shook her head. "Nothing's changed."

Hanne sighed and closed her eyes. In a matter of minutes she was asleep. But it wasn't true: everything had changed, the world had turned, the stars had shifted.

The next morning Hanne was sober and silent. At eight-thirty there was a knock at the door. Hanne opened it. Outside was a porter from the Adlon.

"Hanne . . ." Lilly started. "The studio . . ."

Hanne glanced round the rooms. It was only then that she noticed the suitcases. She inhaled sharply.

"Just until I find a place of my own," Lilly added. "I can afford to buy somewhere now. For both of us."

As the porter picked up the suitcases, another man appeared at the door, a driver.

"There's a car waiting, ma'am," he said.

"You'd better go," Hanne told Lilly.

"We'll talk later," Lilly said as she pulled on her coat. "You'll come with me, won't you?"

Hanne smiled but she did not answer.

Lilly moved into a suite of rooms at the Adlon that evening. Although the beds were turned down every night, there was room service twenty-four hours a day, and all her laundry would be washed and ironed twice a week, Hanne refused to stay there. She said she hated the place; she claimed she was regularly accused of soliciting as she walked through the foyer. And so Lilly offered to pay her rent instead, but she would not accept it.

"I can earn my own money," she said.

"But you'll be all right?" Lilly asked.

"Of course I will," replied Hanne. "I can look after myself. I always have, haven't I?"

That morning Lilly started filming a script set in the Arabian desert. Several tons of sand had been shifted into one of the new studios, a silk tent had been erected, and a series of flats had been painted, trompe l'oeil, to look like a vast and endless wilderness. It was all lit with a mixture of natural light and electric. The scenario was simple: An English explorer falls in love with an Arabian princess, played by Lilly. Ilya would have been able to wrap it up in a few hours had it not been for the fact that the actor, who had come from the stage, insisted on detailed notes on backstory and motivation.

"Love can't be that complicated," Lilly laughed. "Can it?"

Ilya had not replied.

It was midnight. Ilya, beautiful Ilya, with his long eyes and his skin as smooth as water, was lying on his bed completely naked, completely open. But sometimes she still sensed a hint of his old reticence. Was he hiding something from her? The thought filled her with panic. All the people she loved—her parents, Sister August, Hanne, Stefan—had left her, and only one had ever come back. Maybe, the thought suddenly occurred, he didn't love her as much as she loved him. Maybe she would wake up one morning and he would be gone too.

"Ilya," she said. "Wake up."

His eyes were closed and his arms were around her waist. He moved closer to her so he could kiss her neck, her ear, her mouth.

"I want to marry you," she whispered. Ilya pulled back, opened his eyes, and looked at Lilly with a frown.

"What did you say?" he asked.

"Why not?" Lilly said. "If you have any reason why these two people might not be joined in holy matrimony . . ."

Her voice trailed off.

"I didn't have a family, I didn't have a childhood, nothing good ever happened to me until I met you."

"Lillushka," he said, "it's late. Can we talk about it some other time? We both have to work in the morning."

"No," Lilly said. "Let's talk about it now."

"Always so impatient," he said.

Ilya kissed her gently, pulled the blankets around him, and even as she watched him fell asleep.

But Ilya didn't sleep. Although his eyes were closed and his body was still, he lay awake until dawn. What have I done? he asked himself over and over. What have I done?

The next morning the phone rang once, twice, three times before Ilya answered it. It was Hanne. She wanted Lilly to meet her immediately for coffee in the Josty.

"I met a man," Hanne said as soon as Lilly sat down. "He is an art dealer. He said he'd been coming to the cinema for weeks on the off chance of seeing me. And I never even knew."

Her eyes were large and black and she could not stop smiling. At the next table a man laughed long and loud. Although it was only nine in the morning, at the bar a drunk started to sing.

"He wants to marry me," Hanne whispered for full effect. "When he has divorced his wife. And then we're going to live in his house in the Grunewald with a huge garden."

Lilly poured a cup of tea from the pot already cooling on the table.

"So he's married already?"

"What? Oh, yes," admitted Hanne. "He married young, forced into it by his parents. It was a mistake."

"Does he have any children?"

Hanne exhaled loudly. "He has two young daughters. Of course, I said they could come and stay with us anytime . . . and who knows, I might, you know . . ."

Lilly picked up the milk jug. It was empty. She turned to look for the waiter. Hanne's mouth began to twist.

"How can you be so disapproving? Isn't this what you wanted? To get me off your hands?"

"I've never thought that, Hanne."

Lilly took a sip of lukewarm black tea.

"What's his name?" she asked.

Hanne paused as if weighing up whether to trust her.

"Edvard."

Lilly looked at Hanne and they both started to laugh.

"It's not funny," said Hanne. "His mother was English. He has perfect manners. You won't believe it."

Hanne and Edvard invited her to an engagement party in September. The invitation arrived at the studio. It was addressed to Miss Lidi and partner. Ilya was editing the Arabian film, so Lilly went alone. Edvard welcomed her with both arms. He was a lugubrious man almost twenty years older than Hanne, with sad, baggy brown eyes, a head of thick white hair, a bushy mustache, and short, fat fingers.

"At least he has all ten of them," Hanne whispered when she

noticed Lilly's eyes focus on his hands. "And he has more money than he knows what to do with."

As Hanne led her by the hand to the drinks table, Lilly noticed that the room was full of artists and fellow dealers, writers and editors. She was Hanne's only guest.

"You're my only respectable friend," Hanne whispered.

The wife had insisted that the ownership of the house in Grunewald be transferred to her, so the betrothed had moved into the former family home, a large rented apartment in the west of the city. It had, as Hanne boasted later that night, a telephone in the bedroom and a shower with a head the size of a dinner plate. While most households had lost their servants to the war effort and had never reinstalled them, Edvard still retained a housemaid, a cook, and a driver. However, the cook had taken one look at Hanne and resigned on the spot.

Cinema, Edvard was fond of saying, was his undoing. From the first film he ever watched—Harry Piel in *Under a Hot Sun*, in a tent somewhere in France in 1916—to the films of Chaplin, Harold Lloyd, and Werner Krauss, the big screen rapidly replaced painting as his primary passion. While he was once moved by a well-placed brushstroke or a particularly vibrant shade of vermilion, he soon came to regard two-dimensional representation as nothing more than room decoration for the wealthy. Instead, he willingly succumbed to tales of cunning criminals, hapless heroes, and tragedies overcome just in time to finish with bright, trashy happy endings, twice during the week and four times at the weekend.

The first time he saw Hanne Schmidt, standing with her electric torch and ticket punch, he did a double take. He knew he had seen her before but couldn't place her. In fact, he had watched her "acting" three times over one hot day in July 1918, when his wife and children were in the country. In the murky humidity of a Saturday matinee, at first she thought he was asking her directions to the men's conveniences. But then she realized he was not saying "Do I have to go outside?" but "Will you go out with me?" By this time she was nodding fervently, which he took to mean yes even though she probably would have said no if she had heard him correctly.

He was waiting for her at the main doors at the end of her shift. He took her to the Romanisches Café opposite the Memorial Church. It was open all night, every night, and this night, like any other, it was jam-packed. They were shown to a table, a table that was permanently reserved for him alone, then he ordered a bottle of kümmel and chose a cigar from a box. And as the chess players silently battled upstairs on the balcony and the painters argued loudly at the bar, she looked at him and believed, for that moment at least, that he was just what she was looking for after all.

A month after they met, Rathenau was assassinated. The foreign minister and millionaire industrialist was gunned down as he drove to work in his open-topped car. The reason suggested was that he was part of a Jewish conspiracy.

There had already been three hundred seventy-six political assassinations since the war. Most of the victims were liberals; almost half were Jewish. More than three hundred fifty murders were carried out by right-wing groups; around twenty by the left. The average prison sentence for left-wingers, however, was fifteen years; the average for the right wing, four months.

And yet workers left their factories and took to the streets of every city in Germany to protest Rathenau's murder. The labor unions declared a day of mourning. His body was laid in state in the Reichstag. Over a million mourners were recorded on the streets of Berlin, several million more in Hamburg and Frankfurt. It was an outrage, everyone agreed, a travesty, a crime of cowardice and misguided prejudice. Two of the assassins were tracked down; one was shot, the other shot himself. Thirteen years later, however, Himmler laid a wreath on their graves.

Although his mother claimed to have English roots, Edvard was a German of Jewish descent on his father's side. Like Rathenau, he had fought in the war and been decorated. He was, however, heartened by the public's collective outrage.

"You see," he told Hanne. "It is a random act by schoolboy fanatics. Everyone knows that there is no such thing as a Jewish conspiracy. Germany is the Fatherland. I feel perfectly safe here."

And, sitting in his drawing room, where decorative paintings and Venetian-glass mirrors still covered every wall—where the heavy oak furniture looked as if it had been there since the beginning of time and the clock ticked the smooth, peaceful hours away—it was impossible to imagine that in one short decade, all of it would be gone and that, only a few years after that, Edvard would be dead from a hole he himself had fired into the soft, cultured recesses of his very large brain. It was impossible to imagine. But it would happen.

Berlin was swarming with foreigners; Americans, French, Swiss, and Dutch businessmen all bought up flats by the block or occasionally by the whole street. They opened hotels, started literary magazines, and bought paintings. Some relocated from New York and Boston just to live cheaply and luxuriously on black-market caviar and crateloads of gin.

In October, Mussolini marched into Rome with thirty thousand Blackshirts and was handed power by King Victor Emmanuel III. In Munich, Adolf Hitler, the man who had taken over the leadership of the NSDAP and renamed it the Nazi Party, watched and was inspired. Gone were the endless committee meetings, and instead a single strong leader, Der Führer, now led the party. The party newspaper, *Völkischer Beobachter*, increased its production to twice a week and would eventually be published daily. Membership grew from six thousand to thirty-five thousand in under a year.

In late 1922, when a shipment of telegraph poles failed to arrive in France, French and Belgian troops invaded the Ruhr Valley and took over the steel factories, the coal mines, and the railways. To retaliate, the Weimar government ordered the workers to go on strike. Nothing was produced or ran in or out of the valley for months, and 150,000 people were forced out of their homes by the invading armies. The government started to print money to pay wages and cover living costs. Businesses were also allowed to print their own banknotes, and soon railways, factories, even pubs, were producing money. It was, however, soon worth less than it cost to print. One day a cup of coffee in a café might cost five thousand marks. An hour later it would have risen to eight thousand. You soon needed a suitcase of money to buy a sausage. At one point a dollar was worth over four billion marks.

In a matter of months, wealth that had taken centuries to accumulate became worthless. A former bank manager withdrew all his savings, used it to buy a U-Bahn ticket, and traveled round the city once before returning home to starve to death. A family of four who were used to dining at their mahogany table on beef stew and apple cake burned the table to keep warm and then drowned themselves in a lake. A local director borrowed money from a currency speculator and bought his own theater. The show sold out every night but he still ended up with debts that would take several lifetimes of hard labor to repay.

But the film industry managed to weather the inflation. New cinemas were opening daily, and for the starving, the homeless, and the cold they were still a place of escapism, of refuge, of warmth.

One morning, a letter with a Russian stamp arrived in Ilya Yurasov's mailbox. It had come via the consulate. He looked at it for several minutes before he opened it. *My dearest Ilya,* wrote Katya Nadezhda.

I am living in the Crimea but now I am alone. Since my last letter, my life has been intolerable in so many ways. We left with nothing but the clothes we were wearing. My darling daughter succumbed to typhus a few months ago. So much sadness. So much torment. But how I long to see you again, my dearest Ilya. I have your photograph in front of me as I write. You are all I have now. All sailings to the West have now been suspended but I have heard that it is still possible to escape through Poland. I know we will meet again soon. Wait for me.

Until then,
your beloved, Katya

The date, written in the top right-hand corner, was May 1920. It had taken more than two years to reach him.

Dr. MABUSE
DER SPIELER
NACH DEM ROMAN DER BERLINER
JLLUSTRIRTEN ZEITUNG — VON
NORBERT JACQUES
REGIE: FRITZ LANG

Kinetic

Ina runs out from work two or three times a day to buy things, somethings, anythings: shoes that don't fit, a couple of glass eyes, a pipe, or a pound or two of salt. Someone will want them someday, surely?

Tonight she has a date with a man she met in a queue. They meet at the cinema to see Dr. Mabuse, *his choice, not hers. The curtains part and the show begins. Dr. Mabuse hypnotizes his victims. Dr. Mabuse is an evil tyrant, a megalomaniac, a cunning impersonator. Dr. Mabuse has gone mad in his basement workshop; his face is a white dot in a black background. Then, all of a sudden, that face rushes forward and fills the screen. Ina screams. She grabs the man's hand. It is damp and clammy. She instantly lets it go again.*

"Don't you like me?" the man says later.

A deal is a deal. He paid for the tickets; she should let him kiss her. A tram is approaching. He lunges, his face is in her face, as big as Dr. Mabuse's. The doors open, he grabs at her; he won't let go. Ina jumps onboard as the tram starts to move off, and watches him recede, smaller and smaller, still holding her handbag with nothing inside but a lipstick, two glass eyes, and a bag of salt.

By the end of 1922, Lidi had made nine films. All of them were directed by Ilya Yurasov. She filmed on location at the brand-new amusement park and the Berlin Winter Palace. She had also filmed on sets dressed to look like nineteenth-century Paris with flats of Sacré-Coeur and Notre Dame, deep, dark forests with cardboard rocks and fake snow, and claustrophobic interiors where staircases led nowhere and the walls leaned in at strange angles.

She had played a bank teller, a coquette, a trapeze artist, and a serving girl; she had taken her own life twice, once by drowning herself in a river and once by taking poison, and killed her wayward lover three times. She had been both the object of desire and the objectifier, the betrayer and the betrayed, the lover and the beloved. It soon became obvious that there was something about Lidi's manner that gave gravitas to even the flimsiest of plots.

"She is a pioneer," Mr. Leyer was fond of saying.

Mr. Leyer would later argue that cinema was as important in the development of interhuman communication as the printing press. From the moment the lights lower and we begin to watch a drama unfold, we observe, in huge close-up, the faces, the reactions, the emotions of our chosen heroes and heroines. Of course, these people are only actors and they are directed to provoke a given response, but this passive observation could be regarded as something that would fundamentally change the way we perceive ourselves and the way we relate to others. As Horace M. Kallen pointed out in 1942, "Slight actions, such as the incidental play of the fingers, the opening or clenching of a hand . . . became the visible hieroglyphs of the unseen dynamics of human relations."

In other words, a character's interior life could be revealed in a way it had never been revealed before; the gibberish of human emotion could be translated, transcribed, embellished; the potential of any given situation could be tested, played out, concluded, without any real emotional cost. It was as if, Mr. Leyer would note, we had accidentally stumbled on the medium of our dreams.

But did this change the way we handle real love affairs and moments of crisis? he would ask. Did it give us new vocabulary to deal with heartbreak and euphoria? Of course it did, he would claim. What man could be spurned by his lover without consciously or unconsciously mimicking Harold Kraus in *The Loveless Alley*? And how many middle-class women aped Elisabeth Bergner in *Husbands or Lovers?* as they stared out of the window at strangers on the street below?

In the era before the big screen, there was declamation, gesture, and dialogue. The camera would employ all these elements, certainly, but the intimacy of the close-up, the jump cut, and the zoom could act as a much more accurate mirror for our souls. And Mr. Leyer would argue that we would never experience grief, love, jealousy, or despair in quite the same way again.

As Lidi's popularity grew, at least three or four photographers would be waiting outside the studio. She refused to give interviews, but so many letters arrived every day that a secretary was employed part-time just to open them. And every premiere was met with rapturous applause and an increasingly hysterical crowd outside.

Stefan Mauritz always stood apart from the throng. He knew where she lived, he knew which route her drivers took to the studio. He knew which bars she went to on her nights off, and he knew that her best friend and former roommate was a lesbian. She had a lover, a Russian director, but she was still his wife. Why, he asked himself over and over, had Eva told him she was dead? Had Lilly asked her to? And if so, didn't she realize he would see her now? Her face was all over the city, on billboards, on cinema posters, on the front covers of fan magazines. It didn't make sense. But she had been dead and a part of him had died too. And now that she was alive, the dead part of him, his frozen, ugly part, still remained. He couldn't approach her; the problem was insurmountable. He would try to forget her, forsake her, erase her. And yet no matter how hard he tried to resist, he was always drawn back, to the cinema, to her neighborhood, to the orbit of her world.

Lilly had noticed him, of course she had, but although there was something familiar about him, she couldn't place him; he was only one specter or ghost from other, distant lives among many. Some of the young girls who sold themselves on Friedrichstrasse surely once were wards of St. Francis Xavier's; the extras with their carnivorous eyes and beery breath all looked like the customers from The Blue Cat, and some of the women who shouted and waved so voraciously from behind the barricades at premieres resembled the women who punched one another at the Catholic hostel. All of them made her feel deeply uneasy, all of them gave her vertigo.

She decided to move out of the Adlon: too many people knew her there, too many people who always seemed to want more than she was able to give. The apartment she bought was modest. It was just off the Kurfürstendamm near Savignyplatz and had belonged to a Jewish concert pianist. After the murder of Rathenau he had decided to take up an invitation to teach at a conservatory in Paris. Lilly declined to take it furnished and moved in with only a bed, a bureau, and a vase for flowers. The rooms were all painted white. The floors were of polished wood. It was a blank canvas, a new start.

Ilya still lived in the same apartment near the station. He worked hard, harder than he had ever worked before, directing one film after the next without a break. And on the weekends he spent hours working on the script of a new project, a reworking of the story of Mary, Queen of Scots, called *The Queen of Sorrow*.

Something of Lilly was always with him now: her scent, which lingered on his clothes, the echo of her voice in his ears, the ghost of her kiss. And the more he tried to push her out of his mind, the more he thought about her. Since he had received the letter, he had rehearsed what he would say to Katya, the sympathy and the reassurance. But how could he explain Lilly? He had once been a man of honor. Not anymore.

One weekend, shortly after she'd moved, Ilya took Lilly to a cabaret in the basement of the Café des Westens called Die Wilde

Bühne, or The Wild Stage. It was a dark, smoky, cavernous room where performers and writers such as Bertolt Brecht and Trude Hesterberg sang "Ballad of the Dead Soldier" and "Song of the Stock Exchange" on a small, cramped stage.

"Everyone drilled in liberty," one of the performers enunciated. "Liberrrteeee."

One of the acts was by Kurt Gerron, a man who would end up performing on a stage in a death camp. Dressed as a circus trainer wielding a whip, he sang about trying to tame "the beast humanity." This beast, apparently made up of anti-Semites and greedy capitalists, of politicians planning putsches and war-hungry generals, was eventually tamed and brought to heel.

Lilly laughed until she wept. Ilya barely smiled.

"What's the matter?" she asked him.

"It's not funny," he said.

That night they fought as they walked back to her new apartment. And as they passed beneath the linden trees whose black branches clutched at the orange light that streamed onto the night pavements, it was suddenly clear to Lilly that something had changed. He was angry with her.

"Don't you have any political views?" Ilya asked.

"Of course."

"Or are you a Jew-hater, like all the rest of you Germans?"

She didn't answer. The question was so clearly ridiculous. Most of their friends in the film industry were Jewish.

Later, Lilly would wonder what had gotten into her. Maybe it was the wine that had cost several million marks a glass. Maybe it was the inflation—of currency, of her public persona, but mostly of her feelings for Ilya—that made her act the way she did; she had offered herself to him unconditionally and he seemed not to have noticed. And so there, in the street, as the whores and pimps wandered by, as the taxis loitered and the last streetcars idled, everything suddenly unraveled.

"How dare you," she said.

The first blow hit him across the cheek. The second on the chest. The third he caught in midair. Neither of them would look away. Neither of them would concede. The alleyway smelled of urine and damp. Up against a wall pitted with bullet holes and encrusted with old paint, Ilya tore her dress open. His grip was firm, her clasp was firmer; they were a single entity, one breath, one skin, one intent.

And then it was over, the point lost, the hurt scattered, nothing healed, everything dispersed.

Lilly closed the front door of her apartment behind her. And the rooms, so fresh and white during the day, now looked like an empty stage set, spartan, cold, impoverished. Her dress was ruined, her skin was bruised, her lips were raw. She lay on the floor and wept.

Hanne was rich at first. Despite the fact that prices had been steadily rising since the armistice, she bought clothes imported from Paris and smoked Italian cigarettes. She spent afternoons at the movies or shopping or taking tea. But in the evening, while her husband was otherwise engaged, at the cinema, or visiting his daughters, she would wander along the Friedrichstrasse and the Tauentzienstrasse, the streets around the Kaiser Wilhelm Memorial Church and up and down the Kurfürstendamm. Here you could buy an envelope of morphine or pick up a tart. Young boys, their faces thick with powder and rouge, offered themselves to businessmen. Girls in school uniforms kissed each other in doorways or beckoned to passersby. The prettiest women were usually men, the ugliest were said to be the best in the sack, and everyone whispered the same phrase over and over, *"Möchtest du spazierengehen?"*—"Like to take a walk?"

One night at the Kleist Casino, the air heavy with the tickle of cocaine and the divans alive with the writhing of silk on bare flesh, as she placed her bets and took her chances, as the roulette ball rattled round with that low hum that promises everything, Hanne looked up and there, standing on the opposite side of the table with his hands in his pockets, was Kurt.

"Like to take a walk?" he whispered. By the time the ball had chosen its destination—zero, no winners—they were gone.

It was a Saturday in November, 1923. Every morning for weeks on end, a layer of ice had covered the city, frosting the rooftops and the threadbare branches of the trees. The freezing temperatures stilled the leaves, froze the grass into spikes, and glazed Lilly's windows opaque with white. A horse and cart made its way to the market, the horse's breath rising in plumes into the frigid air. A newspaper seller had set up outside the station and cried out, "Murder in Schiller, murder in Schiller, murder in Schiller Park!"

She rarely had visitors and that morning she wasn't expecting anyone. So when there was an assertive knock on the door, she ignored it. A hand knocked again, more insistently this time.

"Please," a man's voice pleaded. "A moment of your time."

Lilly immediately recognized Edvard's voice. She opened the door and he stepped inside. Two months had passed since Lilly had last seen him, and he was quite changed. He wore a suit cut for a younger, slimmer man, with a bright blue neckerchief bought for him, she guessed, by Hanne. And yet his shirt was stained and his face had a sunken look.

"Hanne wrote down your new address. I hope you don't mind?"

"Are you all right?"

Edvard nodded.

"May I sit down?"

Only there wasn't a chair. Although he didn't want to admit it, not there, not then, everything was not all right. The inflation had ruined him. Debts meant that he had been forced to sell his entire stock to a business acquaintance from New York who bought the lot for less than the cost of his return ticket. His former wife had gone to live with her mother and vowed she would never let him see his children again.

"I kept a record," he began, and brought out a notebook. "As her only friend, I think you should know."

He put on his spectacles and stated that Hanne had been incapacitated through drug use not less than a dozen times.

"I found her injecting," he said. "With a syringe. Morphine, probably. Or opium. She used my—our—money, until it ran out."

He snapped the book shut and took a deep breath, and his huge head slowly began to lower, as if the telling had sucked all the strength from him.

"I have been foolish," he said, more to himself than to her. "Lilly, do you know where she is?"

Lilly could guess. But she hoped it was not so.

"Would you like tea?" she asked him without meeting his eye. "I have coffee too."

He shook his head and stood up. He suddenly didn't know why he was there. He knew all along she would not say.

"It's him, isn't it," he said. "She's gone back to that filthy Brownshirt. . . ."

"I don't know," Lilly replied.

"I know what you're thinking. I know you think that she simply married me for my, my . . . and now that I am, now that I am . . ."

He blinked twice and his eyes glistened. He could not say the words.

"All you want is to be known . . . for someone to look right inside you and say, 'Yes, I can see to the bottom and it's clear and pure as water . . .' "

He was breathing heavily now. Lilly thought of Ilya despite herself: his face, his eyes, his voice, his body. She knew what Edvard meant. Hadn't Ilya once loved her like that? Or had she just imagined it? Lilly had been shaking when she finally plucked up the courage to make the call. It was a week since they had fought and she had managed to avoid him.

"Ilya?" she said.

"At last," he said. "You didn't return any of my calls. I was worried."

The telephone line between them seemed to stretch. His voice sounded as if he were speaking from very far away.

"Lilly? Are you still there?"

"Tell me," she said. "I know there's something. There is, isn't there?"

He paused. The silence hummed with static.

"Yes," he replied eventually.

She closed her eyes. She knew it. But how bad could it be? A child, perhaps; a debt; not a woman—she prayed it was not another woman.

"Lilly . . ." he said, his voice full of regret. And she knew. It was another woman.

"Just tell me," she said softly.

Ilya breathed deeply and in stops and starts he told her about Katya, about the last time he had seen her, about his promise.

That night Ilya had walked to the Cosy Corner and drunk vodka until closing time. But it had almost no effect on him. The weight of his secret had been lifted, but in its place he felt empty, drained, lost. She had broken off the relationship. He knew she would. He had another drink and then he went back to his apartment and lay on his bed, fully dressed, until morning.

Edvard seemed unaware of Lilly's tear-stained face. He seemed not to see the clothes and book-strewn floor. He talked on and on without pause.

"I've given up everything," he said. "And I tell you this. Love isn't worth it. Don't concede a thing. The more you give, the more you lose."

"I'm sure you don't mean that," she replied. "She'll come back, she always does eventually."

Edvard gathered his face into a smile. But it was more of a grimace, his baggy eyes struggling to stay in focus, the pleats of his face pulled only slightly tighter.

"And I would take her back, because . . ." he said with a short guffaw, "the trouble is, I can't remember the person I was before I met her."

"That's the trouble," Lilly said. "That's the trouble with love."

Hanne was at that moment in Munich with Kurt. He was one of six hundred armed men stationed outside a beer cellar where three thousand people had gathered to hear the Bavarian government discuss the current political situation. After marching into the meeting, standing on a chair, and firing his pistol, Hitler announced a revolution and proclaimed the formation of a new government. The euphoria did not last long, however. After a shootout with the police the next day, a dozen Nazis were killed, the putsch collapsed, and Hitler was arrested and sentenced to five years in prison.

And the German mark kept sinking. A day's wages, a widow's pension, a family heirloom, a lover's dowry, a virgin's chastity—it was all worthless, it was all meaningless. One writer sold his book for a sizable advance. By the time the check arrived it didn't even cover the cost of mailing the manuscript. The price of the cheapest seat in a theater was two eggs; the most expensive, a few ounces of butter. Factory workers were paid in bonds for boots instead of money. A young girl went to a party and swapped her clothes for a twist of cocaine. The man she ended up with had just sold his grandmother's pearls for a quart of cheap vodka. The cocaine was talcum powder; the vodka was cleaning fluid. Nobody was straight up; only fools were honest. Out on the street, in the squares and in the parks, all the statues were removed so they wouldn't be stolen by thieves. You came home from a night out and you couldn't get into your house, as someone had stolen the doorknob. Your roof started to leak and your phone didn't work; the lead from the roof was gone along with the telegraph wires. And for once every girl's mantra rang true: she had nothing to wear.

German films had begun to be shown in America. How could the American distributors refuse? The exchange rate reached 1.3 trillion marks to the dollar. They could have them for buttons. But the biggest market was still the home market. Despite everything, Germans still went to the cinema. Where else could they escape? Where else could they forget?

Most currency is pegged to the price of gold. Germany didn't have any. And so it was decided by the imperial treasury minister to peg it to the price of rye. In November 1923, a new mark, the rye mark, was issued at 4.2 to a dollar. The Americans, with their Dawes Plan, backed the currency but charged a high price. Nevertheless, the economy was stabilized. In the days and months after, the silence in the air was like the silence immediately following the last note of a symphony. It was a silence filled with reverberation, with an audible sense of something immense ceasing to turn. The world had finally done what Lilly had wanted. It had stopped.

Hundreds of businesses, however, went bankrupt. Nightclubs, small bars, cafés boarded up their doors and reneged on their debts. And then it appeared, to the displaced middle classes, to the ones who had lost pensions and savings and investments and who had to live like beggars instead of the comfortably retired that they were before, that many Jewish businessmen seemed to have weathered the hyperinflation, or even benefited from it. They owned property, and property was the only thing that kept some notion of value. And they noticed them, as if for the first time, buying food in the shops that they themselves could not afford, or attending the opera or eating out in restaurants. And they did not forget.

Margraf, the jeweler, led Lidi, the film star, and the Prussian count through two locked doors into his personal office. A few moments later his young female assistant came up from the vault carrying a tray covered in dark blue velvet. On this were laid diamond solitaire rings as large as wren's eggs, sapphires set in platinum, and pearls strung together like children's beads.

The count's breathing became more rapid. His large fingers hesitated over the tray and then fell upon a modest pendant of rubies.

"This one," he said. "Try this one, my dear."

The actress glanced up at him and sighed. She looked over the jewels, then picked up a diamond necklace, sat down in front of a mirror, bowed her head, and let the female assistant place it around her throat. Then she pulled back the fur coat from her shoulders and looked at herself. Her hair was dark again but cut into a short, sharp bob. It made her eyes look bigger and her chin more determined.

"It's thirty carats, madam," said the jeweler.

"I'll take it," she said.

The count flushed. He coughed and he stuttered.

"Aren't you at least going to try the pendant?"

He looked at her pleadingly, his pale blue eyes watering in the warmth of the jeweler's inner office.

"Buy it if you like," she said. "I can buy my own diamonds, you know."

The jeweler smiled and bowed his head graciously. Everyone knew that he had bought in bulk before the inflation ended and paid virtually nothing. A diamond ring could be had for a side of ham or two pairs of boots. A sapphire that had been in the family for generations kept that same family from starving for approximately a fortnight.

And now the actress was buying jewels that used to belong to families such as the Hollensteins, the Hapsburgs, and the Brandts; necklaces and tiaras and strings and strings of precious gems. She had no intention of wearing any of them—ostentatious flamboyance was not her style; she bought them as investments.

Lilly wrote out a check as the count fumbled with his wallet. She supposed that this wasn't the way he envisaged it; she suspected that she was humiliating him. And when he looked at her and smiled, she noticed a certain bitterness in the curl of his lips that she had not noticed before. Now that she had seen it, she would not be able to look at his face without seeing it, without feeling that same feeling in her gut. She suddenly knew that she would not accept his rubies, that she would return them in the box that same night and ask him most politely to stop calling her.

It's my fault, she would write on a card in old-fashioned calligraphy taught to her by Sister August, *not yours. You must be one of the most wonderful people I have ever met.*

Her driver was waiting outside with the automobile engine running. She kissed the count on his flushed cheek and thanked him profusely. And then without looking back she climbed inside the automobile and was driven away.

On the way to her apartment, several people stopped in the street and pointed. Her hat was pulled down over her face and she had pulled the collar of her fur coat up tightly around her neck, but still they recognized her. She picked up her driver's newspaper from the front seat, and there she was on page three with the count. "We lost our royalty," Mr. Leyer was fond of saying. "And now we have you."

Since she had broken with Ilya, she had been involved with a string of eligible men, and several women too. She had dated actors, actresses, writers, and numerous former aristocrats whose manners were impeccable but whose wallets were notoriously shallow. And after leaving them in varying states of mental anguish, she would always answer their pleas for a reason with the same words.

"Why? Because I'm not in love with you."

"What is love?" Lidi was reported to have mused at a party for the Italian pianist Ferruccio Busoni in October 1924. "It is never rational; there is no middle ground. Our hearts are extremists. They give either all or nothing." Although she always claimed that she had been misquoted, that she had never met a journalist at that party for Ferruccio Busoni and indeed wasn't sure that she had even attended, the words she allegedly uttered remained in the public consciousness in their simplified form: "Love is all or nothing."

As girls wearing panties embroidered with a single silk fig leaf served Manhattans and flirted with men in their evening suits, as Josephine Baker (yes, she was always there) danced naked and alone on the piano, and as jazz on the gramophone was played over and over until the needle was worn right down to a stub, Lidi took everything she was offered. Whiskey and Champagne, vodka and chloral hydrate, hashish and cocaine, she mixed and drank, smoked and snorted, all except one: Lidi wouldn't touch morphine. And as her head began to drift and spin, her body to thrum and tingle with liquids and powders and adoration, she sometimes wondered if there had been a point when she had inadvertently chosen her glorious life on screen over her real destiny. And once, when she had smoked too much hashish, she kissed the face of a man she had met on a staircase and was convinced for a moment she was kissing the face of another until the man spoke and she opened her eyes and saw that there was not even the faintest resemblance.

In the minutes or hours before dawn, however, when the men had removed some of their clothes and the waitresses had relinquished their panties, when the drinks were all finished or spilled or the glasses had all been smashed for amusement, when someone would be found limp and lifeless and rushed to the hospital, Lidi, like a blind girl, put out her hands until they alighted on someone's, anyone's.

"Love me," she would say.

But even as her lips touched the lips of another and she let their hands gather up her breast beneath her dress, as she slid her mouth across their skin and felt the unmistakable determination of their intent and the automatic surge of her response, she never gave herself completely; she couldn't. Close proximity only made her feel more distant; intimacy filled her with emptiness. And they would know. And they would pull away. And only the most brutal, the most cruel, the most narcissistic, would continue to rip and press, to tear and thrust in a futile bid to reach her, to have her, to possess her.

Ilya had turned down a number of films. Instead he spent his days working on his script for *The Queen of Sorrow* and writing letters to friends in Moscow, St. Petersburg, and Paris. Had they seen Katya? Did they know where he could get in contact with her? He received only one reply, from Katya's cousin, who was living in Paris. She had heard nothing about Katya for years. "But Katya is a survivor," the cousin wrote. "She's alive, I'm sure of it."

Lidi was half an hour late. She looked as if she hadn't bothered to dress for the occasion and wore a creased tea dress and a pair of scuffed shoes. Her hair was unbrushed, her makeup barely applied, and she lit up a cheroot as soon as she arrived and filled the room with bitter blue smoke. And then she pulled out a scuffed copy of the script and yawned.

"Shall we get this over with as fast as possible?" she said.

Friedrich Bernstein smiled. He liked her already.

"Forget the script, just take a walk," he said. "Take off your coat and walk up and down."

Lidi looked at him with frank disbelief.

"You want me to walk? That's it, just walk, like a cow?"

"Yes, that's it. Like a cow, a prize cow."

Lidi glared at Mr. Leyer, who was pretending to make a telephone call.

For a moment, she hesitated. And then she sighed, stood up, pulled off her coat, stubbed out the cheroot in the ashtray without having taken a single draw, and walked. No, she didn't exactly walk, as the room was too small and the request was ridiculous; she swanned, she loped, she ambled back and forth three or four times before coming to a stop right in front of him. And there she raised an eyebrow.

"You see, I'm not wearing a wig and I don't have a limp."

Lidi had been invited to audition for a German director who had been lured back to Europe from Hollywood with an invitation he could not afford to turn down, or so he wrote in his self-published memoirs, *The Magnificent Machine* (Bernstein Press, 1951). At that point Germany was flooded with American movies, some of them even directed by Bernstein himself. California financiers were buying up film companies in Berlin and even building their own cinemas to show their films. And so, in a halfhearted attempt to stem the flow, the Parafumet agreement was signed: in exchange for a loan of four million dollars, it was agreed that one American movie would be screened for every German film made. The agreement also ensured that any "suitable" German films would be distributed in the United States.

It was clear, however, that this could be only a temporary measure. The German film industry was in crisis. It needed more capital; it needed new momentum; it needed an international hit. Although there were dozens of filmmakers bashing out ideas in offices all over Berlin, Friedrich Bernstein, with his American tan and sanguine approach, was an obvious choice.

Elisabeth Bergner had been lined up by Ufa to play the female lead but had read the script and turned it down. Asta Nielsen was busy and Pola Negri had gone to America and had fallen in love with Rudy Valentino.

Bernstein knew Lidi only through the pile of film stills. He was so unimpressed that he hadn't bothered to thread the reels of the copy of *Letters of Love* he had been couriered the day before and watch the film in the screening room he had at his disposal.

"She's quite pretty," he said at the time, "but nothing more than you could see working behind the cosmetics counter of any department store. And what's more, I have heard that she hasn't worked for months."

And yet he had been coaxed incessantly by Leyer, who was one of the executive producers, into seeing her. He eventually agreed to an audition, if only to prove his point.

"She had exactly what I wanted," he told the now defunct cult cinema magazine *Movie Magic* in 1962. "There was something about her eyes that was arctic. No, that's not what I mean at all. She was warm; she had this way of looking, a kind of animal, no, sexual intelligence. It's hard to explain. It was as if she was both very young and very old, vulnerable and yet aloof. If I sound confused, contradictory, I am. I don't know what she had, but as soon as I saw it, I wanted her. She was the face, if you can imagine it, of Berlin at that particular moment in history."

Hanne had a tiny handbag in one hand and a cigarette in the other. She stood in Lilly's apartment, but would not sit down. She looked as if she had been up all night, and her eyes were smudged with black.

"It's been too long," she said. "I've been meaning to . . . I mean I've wanted to . . ." Hanne continued until she ran out of words.

"Edvard came to see me," said Lilly.

"Did he? Did he tell you?"

Lilly nodded.

"You know, I left him with the same as what I arrived with," Hanne replied. "Nothing."

She picked a strand of tobacco from her tongue.

"He used to give me books," she went on. "Great, thick books. Idiot. I burned them last week when we ran out of wood."

As the smoke rose from her cigarette in thin blue ribbons, Hanne laughed.

"He had no clue," she said. "He had no idea how to be poor."

She finally sat down on Lilly's bed and unfastened her shoes. The leather soles were sodden and the heels worn down. She pulled two pieces of cardboard and a couple of ten-billion-mark notes from inside and laid them to dry on the radiator.

"You know, when I was married, there wasn't a day—not a day—that I didn't think of Kurt."

She stamped out the butt of her cigarette and immediately lit another.

"He has gone into politics," she went on. "The Nazi Party. They gave him a job, unlike the country he fought for. He is a storm trooper now. You should see his uniform. It is so smart."

When Lilly didn't respond, she went on.

"What kind of a government treats its people like this? Did you know that they have decided to resume payments of war reparations to France? When the country is starving again? When no one can afford to eat anymore and the city is full of rich Americans buying anything and anyone they want."

"Hanne," Lilly said softly.

"This country is run by Jews," she said. "But not for long. We shall rid our country of them—of them all. The party leader is now Adolf Hitler. You should hear him speak, Lilly—he is so inspiring."

"Isn't he in prison?"

"Not anymore."

Hanne suddenly burst into tears. But when Lilly tried to go to her, to comfort her, Hanne pushed her away.

"You have everything," she said almost inaudibly. "Look at this place. You have the life I wanted. . . . Why you and not me?"

Lilly stared out the window, at the glazed empty sky above the skeletal trees.

"I don't have everything," she said.

But Hanne was oblivious.

"I need money," Hanne said. "In dollars. Don't look at me that way."

Lilly stared at her.

"What way?"

"I mean, why not?" she snapped. "Aren't you paid in dollars, in real currency, not rye marks? You know what I've done for you. You know how much I've given you."

Hanne was breathing rapidly but she would not look at Lilly. When Lilly didn't reply, she picked up the notes she had laid out on the radiator and ripped them into small pieces.

"A few years ago I could have bought my own brewery with this. Now I can't even buy a bottle of beer."

"If it's food and somewhere to sleep," Lilly said, "you can stay here with me. You know that."

Hanne finally looked at her. Her pupils were as black as billiard balls.

"Don't judge me," she said.

Lilly opened her purse. She handed her one hundred dollars. Hanne turned and walked out without another word.

All over the city, the Nationalists and the Communists were printing up their leaflets on the same thin gray paper. In the Reichstag they sang "Deutschland über Alles" on the right and "The Internationale" on the left; they waved red, white, and black flags on one side and red, black, and gold on the other.

Ebert, the president of the republic, was accused of treason by both sides for the part he played in the revolution. The Right insisted he had betrayed the kaiser, the Left that he betrayed the people. He decided to sue the accusers and, by the end of 1924, had nearly one hundred fifty legal actions in motion. Meanwhile several members of his cabinet were implicated in a number of well-publicized cases of corruption. Scandal followed scandal until Ebert was even being investigated on charges of seducing his secretary. When he felt a pain in his belly, he convinced himself it was only the pain of injustice. In fact he had acute peritonitis. Five days later he was dead.

All churlish resentment was forgotten on the day of Ebert's

funeral. As the cortège passed through streets where shopkeepers had once hung out their underwear in protest at his passage, wreaths threaded with black ribbons hung from balconies. The coffin was taken to Potsdam Station, placed on a catafalque, and covered in the Reich's flag. Outside, branches of pine were strewn all over the pavement to muffle the footsteps of the pedestrians.

It was pouring rain on the day of the elections. The polling stations were quieter than expected. Nevertheless, the next day it was revealed that the new leader of the republic would be the Right's choice, the safe choice, a former field marshal and veteran of several wars, Paul von Hindenburg, a man who had just celebrated his seventy-eighth birthday.

In the months that followed, life in Berlin seemed to settle down again. American loans to industry meant that factories could install production lines and start hiring. Workers and soldiers, who for several years had been fighting or begging or stealing, found steady jobs and were paid a regular if not particularly generous wage. To the high wail of the factory whistle, they fell in love, got married, started families, or saved for their day off, and politics didn't seem so important anymore.

To Lilly, Berlin had once seemed the very center of the universe. It had been, in fact, the fastest growing city in the world. But Berlin's streets seemed dimmer now. It wasn't just a government-decreed lower wattage for the streetlights. The war had changed everything; the spotlight had shifted, to New York, to Paris, to Buenos Aires.

And after the collapse of any generic notion of world domination came the collapse of almost every other well-buttressed conceit of the kaiser's empire. Lilly barely noticed the men masquerading as women, wearing lipstick, false eyelashes, and sock-stuffed brassieres, who walked the streets from morning till midnight without shame or inhibition. Or the women dressed as men in ill-fitting suits, who waited in the shade of the city parks to accost unchaperoned girls with their bare, hungry mouths. But the tourists stopped in their tracks, they gawped, they were visibly shocked. "You want depravity," a whore apparently shouted at an American couple one day. "Then come on in."

In the cabarets and theaters—Sound and Smoke, Nelson's, and others—political revues had been replaced by shows with titles such as *Berlin Without a Shirt*, *Everyone's Naked*, and *What Sailors Dream Of*, which featured naked women's bodies arranged into tacky tableaux. Critics labeled them *Fleischschauen*, or meat shows, but that didn't prevent them from being sold out every night including Sunday. Down in the Metropol or Wintergarden, the Tiller or the Hoffman, girls imported straight from the U.S. of A put on displays of coordinated high kicks fully clothed. Although the shows were slammed by the critics as unerotic, sexless, the routines like human machinery, with each component completely lacking in personality, the girls appealed to a latent sense of the military, their high kicks echoing and distorting a military march. German audiences adored them.

"Berlin, You're Still Berlin": the song was a hit and everybody sang it, even though everybody sensed it wasn't true.

It was supposed to save the film industry. It was to be the biggest film production Germany had ever attempted, part science fiction, part fantasy horror. Set in two worlds, one a romantic idyll, the other a brutal modernist underworld, the project was called *Kinetic*.

Friedrich Bernstein had already cast the male lead, Werner Gratz, a young actor with wide blue eyes and a whitened smile who he thought would appeal to a wider audience. His acting at that point had been limited to *Hamlet*, in a theater in provincial Saxony, but he had the arrogance and attitude of someone much more experienced.

Lidi was to play the Girl, a character who lures men to their deaths by making them fall in love with her and then inviting them to follow her to the underworld, a vast industrial city where they are immediately enslaved. When she eventually falls in love with the wide-eyed hero, she realizes what she has done and, filled with remorse, strikes the first blow in what will lead to the destruction of the city. It is only the audience who spots the irony, that the hero's father is in fact another industrialist who has plans of his own.

The plot was ridiculous, the costumes "archaically modern," and the sets suitably fabulous. The budget, two million marks, was the largest any film in Germany had ever been allocated, and Bernstein boasted that he planned to employ ten thousand extras and a menagerie of circus animals. Well-known artists were drafted to sketch the storyboards, and fashion designers from Paris were given the briefs for the costumes. A whole city in miniature made of plywood and cardboard would take up the floor space of one entire lot and feature staggeringly tall buildings and chasmed streets. The airspace above would be filled with balsa-wood airships and tissue-paper zeppelins that would buzz around gracefully until they exploded in the final few scenes. Whole forests made of papier-mâché would be set ablaze, and in one scene that was later written out a model train would shoot off the end of the tracks and smash catastrophically into a river.

And yet, at the heart of this lavish project was a conceit that Bernstein hoped would have universal appeal. *Kinetic* would be a simple love story with an epic resonance. Or, as the financiers stated more succinctly, it was the first film to be produced in Germany "on an American scale."

"It was either going to make my career," Lidi said much later, "or sink it. At that time I didn't care either way."

The Empty Chair

The camera is liberated, released, unhindered by the screws and straps, by the nuts and bolts, that once contained her. Once so passive, so patient, so static, so frigid, she has thrown off her chastity belt, the tripod.

In Babelsberg, Karl Freund straps his Leica Model 402 to his belly and hauls a pack of batteries onto his back for balance. The actor Emil Jannings, fresh from the previous scene, watches with a bottle of Scotch in his hand. And then, with camera rolling, Freund staggers and rollicks, he sways and trips, he falls and recovers. "The audience will get drunk just watching it," Jannings says at the end of the take.

Freund has mounted his beloved Leica on a bicycle, on trolleys, in baskets. In one scene the camera traveled for twenty meters from the ear of a sleeping actor to the mouth of a trumpet. In another, several suitcases were juggled on strings while the camera was lowered between them. The effect had the producer gripping the sides of his seat and claiming vertigo. But Freund isn't the only one to employ the so-called unchained camera. For Faust *they built a plaster ramp shaped like a wave. Up and down, the camera went, up and down over a landscape built in miniature. For those who'd flown only in dreams, the experience was unforgettable.*

It was the first film Lilly had ever made without Ilya. And from the first moment on the set, it was completely different. The pervading atmosphere on the set of *Kinetic* was one of adrenalized boredom. Her costume took three hours to put on, the makeup an hour. Gratz's face took less time, but after it was applied it was often immediately wiped off again with claims by Werner that he could not act "looking like a painted freak."

And yet when the light was right and the makeup was perfect and the scene was set, Werner Gratz would come to life and his face would express more than the script had ever hoped. The provincial audiences had been right to give him all those standing ovations.

"He is a genius," one critic wrote in a review in a local newspaper, which Werner carried around in his wallet. "One cannot help but weep with him over his beloved Ophelia."

Maybe he knew his intrinsic worth. Maybe that was why he insisted on top billing. Maybe that was why, when his request was turned down by the producers for the fifteenth time, he began to despise the actress whose name would always be bigger and brighter and, more important, higher than his.

If Lilly often looked vacuous as she played the coldhearted heroine, however, it was because she had been waiting around for hours, for days, for weeks, in full costume. Most of her previous films had taken around forty days to shoot. *Kinetic* would take three hundred ten. One day, however, it all became too much for her. They were filming a love scene and were on the twelfth take. The scene called for a secret tryst followed by a kiss. When Werner kissed her for the twelfth time, it was a clasp of such blatant distaste that he pulled back and looked her in the eye.

"Just kiss me like you kissed that Russian," he said. "You know, the one you had that sordid little fling with."

He kissed her again. This time she did not let him go.

"Bitch!" Werner Gratz shouted, and spun round toward the camera. The cameraman, unsure whether this was part of the script, kept rolling, as a thick, dark trickle ran down the hero's powdered chin.

"She fucking bit me!"

"Cut!" shouted the director. "Cut, cut, cut!"

"You can't get out of it, I'm afraid," said Mr. Leyer later. "You've signed the contract. But listen, it's not easy for anyone."

It was a shoot that, as many of the crew claimed, was living hell. The sets of papier-mâché, plasterboard, and painted fabric were enormous, the architecture monumental; the crowd scenes were hugely ambitious, with thousands of men, women, and children choreographed to move as one shifting mass; the lighting was theatrical and required numerous rehearsals and dozens of riggers to man the multiple spotlights.

Seven extras were injured when a plasterboard skyscraper fell on them. The actual wood and painted cardboard didn't crush them: five hundred of their fellow extras in a rush to get a cup of coffee caused a human stampede. The tiger that was to be tamed and befriended by the hero escaped, and even though it was entirely toothless and ate only minced chicken, it was shot by an ex–Spartacist sniper who had been given a job as a security man, and it ended up as a tatty rug on somebody's floor.

Everything that could possibly go wrong did. Explosives didn't detonate but set everything on fire; bulbs blew; scenic flats bent or fell over; models fell apart when the glue that held them together melted under the lights; cameras jammed; films came out underexposed, overexposed, or just plain blank; extras broke bones by slipping on stairs, on spills of paint, or on carelessly discarded fruit peels. Everything that could fail failed; everything that could break broke; the real world seemed to be conspiring against the synthetic reality of the film. Even the weather was appalling: torrential rain that followed unbearable heat, blizzards that piled the streets with snow and then melted, causing widespread flooding.

And Bernstein seemed only to make everything more difficult for himself, for the actors, for the audience. The script was locked off, or finished, before shooting started, but the actors were given new drafts every morning because Bernstein had been at it the night before with his pen.

"If I look permanently puzzled," Lidi said years later, "it's because I had no idea what was going on. My character went through so many rewrites that I had no idea who she was. And so I played it without any emotion, just in case it was the wrong one."

Without Ilya to direct her, Lidi's famously limpid eyes became cloudy, the perfect sweep of her cheek tensed, the curve of her eyebrows flattened into a frown. Anyone who had known Hanne Schmidt, however, would immediately have recognized her in Lidi's portrayal of the Girl. Her hair was dyed blond again and her eyes were smudged with kohl, just like her former friend's. And she wrapped her arms around herself and looked at the world with eyes half closed. To those who had never known Hanne Schmidt, however, Lidi simply looked angelically wrecked.

"I took uppers, I took downers," she admitted a few years later. "Quite often at the same time. I had incurable insomnia and yet I would fall asleep on my feet during the day. My dressing room was filled with glass bottles full of different-colored pills, some from the doctor and some from Bernstein. I'd take a handful and wash them down with Scotch. I have seen the film only once. And I did not recognize myself."

The film was released in 1926. It had taken two years to complete and cost five and a half million marks, almost three times as much as originally estimated. Even though it was launched with a vast party where girls dressed as robots handed out cocktails, and even though it was promoted with ten different movie posters that were pasted all over Berlin, it received a mixture of reviews ranging from the polite to the downright vindictive. In the first week of release, the queues outside the Ufa-Palast am Zoo were made up mostly of film extras with free tickets rather than genuine paying audiences. On the street it was said to be gloomy, ponderous, self-indulgent, patronizing. Lidi's performance was lambasted as wooden, dull, blank, the love affair as unconvincing. In contrast, Charlie Chaplin's *The Gold Rush* had just opened and would run for six months in Germany and take four million dollars at the box office worldwide.

Kinetic, film historians argued in later decades, managed almost single-handedly to ruin the German film industry. Anyone who had any talent and sufficient income moved away after making the film: away from Berlin, away from Germany, away from failure. Writers, directors, camera operators, electricians—dozens of them—sailed to New York and then took the train to California. "The *Kinetic* Effect," as it was sometimes labeled, flooded Hollywood with Germans. But it was also, many pointed out later, an ominous portent of what was to come.

Although Germany's film industry was losing twelve million dollars a year, a buyer was sought. The liberal press empire founder Rudolph Mosse was offered the chance but turned it down. And so Ufa in its entirety, which at that point included 3.5 million square feet of studio space, the production companies, the subsidiaries, plus one hundred cinemas, was bought by Alfred Hugenberg for less than a fifth of the amount of its value.

Hugenberg, a small man with a bush of white hair and shabby clothes, was an archconservative, a dabbler in politics who would later enter Hitler's first cabinet in 1933. He was also a tycoon who had created a media empire with a publishing company, an advertising agency, and a news bureau. Ufa was the final card in his pack.

The studios in Berlin kept producing low-budget comedies and documentaries. Ilya now worked constantly. He churned out melodramas with plot lines about warmhearted prostitutes and children and workers with irresolvable problems, low-budget horror films, and cheap thrillers to meet the quota of the Parafumet. Only one in five, however, were ever distributed to cinemas.

Lidi was still offered parts, but roles so small that it would have been publicly humiliating to accept them. She stopped going out. She fell into the habit of sitting at her window at night, where she would watch the blue spark on the wires of the streetcars recede. She had long since let go of her secretary and so her mail piled up until she threw it away, unopened.

It wasn't surprising that Bill Frame's invitations to dinner were never answered. As MGM's agent in Europe, however, he wasn't used to being ignored quite so blatantly. When he appeared in person in the lobby of her apartment building with a car waiting and a huge bouquet of hothouse flowers, she claimed she'd never heard of him and asked him to send her a card. He explained—as patiently as a man who was better used to saying the same words himself to the hundreds of actors, technicians, and dancers who would have licked his boots for the chance to sign with him—that he had done so already, over a dozen times.

"Oh," Lidi said. She looked up at him and his heart leapt. Even without makeup, she was lovely. And then, since she seemed to have run out of excuses and had nothing planned, she agreed to have coffee in a little place that she knew around the corner.

The café was shabby and the coffee revolting. Bill Frame, a six-foot Texan who had gone into the movies rather than the family oil business, adored her even more for it. As he watched her sip from her saucer all the coffee that the waitress had carelessly spilled, he tried to articulate—in the German he had been studying every morning for six months but was still struggling with—that *Kinetic* was a classic and her performance was groundbreaking. Lidi lit a cigarette and blew smoke into the air between them.

"Really?" she asked. "Even the director hated it. It was a failure."

"You're wrong," he replied. "I loved it. It was an epic."

Lidi looked at him and wondered if the flattery was simply a ruse. As far as she knew, it had never been released in America. But then he smiled at her with teeth so perfect that she suspected he had never suffered, not even from tooth decay, and she realized that he was guileless. He picked up his coffee, which had never been more than warm, and drained the cup. And then his eyes glistened with expectation as he leaned toward her.

"You must have thought about going to Hollywood," he asked conspiratorially. "Everybody else is."

She smiled and shook her head.

"My work is here."

"What work? You haven't worked for months. It's over in Berlin for you and you know it," he said.

She hadn't known it until he said it. And once she knew it, she wished he hadn't told her.

"But I don't speak English," she replied simply.

"You can learn," he said, his huge hands grabbing handfuls of air. "And, more than that, can you think of a single reason not to?"

Lidi considered. And a reason came into her head despite herself: Ilya Yurasov.

"No," Lidi told Bill Frame. "You're right, I can't think of a single reason."

At the next table sat a group of unemployed men in coarse brown trousers and stained yellow shirts. They smoked and spat and read a newspaper called *Der Angriff*, subtitled *The Oppressed Against the Exploiters.* Frame, whose attention was focused solely on the German actress, did not hear the dirty jokes they shouted or sense the way they took up more space in the room than their physical mass should have allowed.

At that point Frame had never heard of Joseph Goebbels, who had been appointed Gauleiter of Berlin the previous year. Dr. Goebbels, a small man with a deformed foot and a powerful voice, had been sent to introduce National Socialism to the middle classes of the city. In a year he had completely reorganized the party, recruited a private army, orchestrated a number of parades, and encouraged his bodyguards to fight Communists in the street to provoke agitation. He would become minister of propaganda but was at that point focusing on recruitment, opening up hostels for the unemployed with free food and board, but only for members of the party.

In the back of the steamed-up café in April 1927, as Bill Frame helped Lidi, the actress, with her coat, the men, who had recently been promoted to storm troopers, ordered another round of beer and argued over a bag of posters that the Gauleiter himself had handed to them that morning and that they were supposed to post all over East Berlin. And then one of them pulled out a leaflet and began to read.

"Each area or local group is to report all Jews living in the area, including as far as possible baptized Jews, with details on their persons, age, occupation, and address. This is necessary in order to develop reliable statistics on Jews in the whole population."

They glanced around the café, at the old Russian man in the corner who sipped sweet black tea with lemon, at the young boy with the long nose and brown eyes who was stacking bottles, at the young woman with gray eyes and a long coat who was on the point of leaving, whom none of them could place but all claimed that they had "poked." And then they all fell silent. Their division officer had arrived.

When Kurt saw Lilly, he froze. He would have to pass her to reach his men. She was with a large man, a man who spoke German with the rounded consonants of an American. Kurt raised his hand to hide his face. He had four deep gashes down his cheek.

"Kurt?" Lilly said.

She had seen him. Kurt started to crumple a Nazi flyer in his pocket into a ball. Her eyes were searching his, taking in his face and the fact that he couldn't raise his eyes and greet her.

"Are you all right?" she asked.

He shook his head.

"What's happened?" she asked.

Finally, Kurt let his eyes stray to hers. He tried to empty them of everything, the night before, the fight, the pain of her nails as they tore into his cheek, the coldness of the blade as it pressed into flesh. But she saw. She seemed to look right into his heart and see it all.

"It was an accident," he whispered, his voice as soft as a boy's.

Lilly left the café, the storm troopers, the American, and Kurt, and stumbled out into the road. Trams, cars, bicycles, careered past. She paced the curb, back and forth.

"Hey," said the American, suddenly appearing at her elbow. "What's going on?"

"I need a taxi," she said. "I need it now."

"Is there anything I can do?" he asked.

A taxi rounded a corner and came toward them.

"No," said Lilly as she hailed it.

"Well, don't leave it too long to get in touch," he said as she climbed inside. "I'll be leaving this crazy town of yours in a couple of months. And you should too."

As he closed the door, she gave him a look he would never forget. It was a look that was both question and answer.

The door to Kurt's apartment stood open a couple of inches. The main room was in darkness even though it was already midday. Light spilled around the closed shutters, throwing everything in the room into silhouette.

"Hanne?" Lilly said. *"Hanne!"*

As she stepped across the threshold she was immediately hit by the sweet, acrid smell of alcohol and stale cigarette smoke. She paused, listened, and was, she realized, suddenly, unaccountably scared.

"Lilly . . ." a small voice came from the bedroom. "I'm so glad it's you."

Hanne was lying curled up in bed, underneath a sheet. For a moment Lilly was so relieved that she sat down on the edge of the mattress and held her own face in her hands. From an apartment upstairs came the muffled sound of a gramophone playing the same song over and over, the tune audible, the lyrics muffled.

"I met Kurt," Lilly said. "Hanne . . . I was so worried."

She reached over and took her friend's hand. It was cold. Hanne had barely moved at all since Lilly had come into her room; there was a stiffness about her, a tenseness in her shoulders. And then Lilly noticed that there was another smell in the room, the metallic, visceral smell of congealed blood. Very slowly she lifted the sheet. Lilly clamped her hand over her mouth. Tears spilled from her eyes.

"You stay here," Lilly whispered. "I'm going to get an ambulance."

Hanne reached out and grabbed Lilly's wrist with surprising force.

"No," she whispered. "Don't leave me. I prayed to God that you would come, and here you are."

"But, Hanne, you need to go to the hospital."

"I'll go soon, I promise," she said. "But I'm so cold. Get in beside me. Please?"

Lilly took off her coat and shoes and climbed into the bed. Her body curved around her friend's from behind; her arms folded around Hanne's waist, her knees curled into the backs of Hanne's knees, and she held her, the way they had once held each other at St. Francis Xavier's.

"What has he done to you?" Lilly whispered.

"I forgive him," Hanne whispered. "Tell Sister August. Tell her she made a Catholic out of me after all."

Hanne's breathing was regular and deep. Lilly closed her eyes and impossibly, or so it seemed afterward, her breath fell in step, in, out, in, out.

When she woke up it was dark outside. The gramophone upstairs was silent.

Hanne's neck had been slit, her legs gashed open, her abdomen stabbed. Both eyes were blacked in with bruises and wept mascara. Only the calligraphy of her track marks remained untouched.

Kurt gave himself up without resistance. He was charged and sentenced within a month. He claimed reduced responsibility due to war wounds and gross provocation, and the judge, having looked briefly at Hanne's past record of employment, drug use, and marital infidelity, gave him a six-month suspended sentence.

The Sisters of St. Henry had just installed a telephone. The nun who answered it clearly didn't quite believe that her voice could actually travel all the way from Munich to Berlin without a huge amount of human effort.

"Can you hear me?" she yelled.

"Yes," Lilly replied. "I'm looking for Sister August. It's a personal matter."

"Just a moment," the nun shouted. *"I'll fetch her."*

In the long moments before Sister August was fetched, Lilly began to shiver. She had not wept for Hanne Schmidt. Not when she greeted the police and showed them the body, not even when she had packed up Hanne's possessions and taken them home. She had simply told herself that Hanne had done it again. She had walked out on her without notice, without a backward glance. But in that ache of time while the nun was being fetched and the silence of the telephone line wailed, she accidentally let herself realize that this time she wouldn't let herself be found again. This time she was really gone for good.

By the time the nun picked up the phone, Lilly was incoherent with grief.

"Hello!" the nun shouted into the chasm of the telephone line. *"Hello, hello!"*

It was not the right Sister August. The wrong Sister August explained patiently that Lilly's own Sister August, real name Lotte von Kismet, had left the order and then died years ago in the war, probably killed by a mortar attack on an army hospital. Her body lay in an unmarked grave somewhere in France, her long limbs bent to fit into a regulation-size coffin.

Edvard sent a bunch of white lilies. Hanne's brothers could not be traced. The ladies who ran the adoption scheme now spent their days raising money for aged pit ponies. And so Lidi, the actress, was the only mourner at Hanne Schmidt's small committal, apart from the Bulgarian who had once owned The Blue Cat, who came at the end and cried noisily into his sleeve.

Lilly sat alone in the cemetery as it grew dark. Few other mourners noticed her, a small figure dressed from head to toe in black. In the past few months she had felt not sad, not betrayed, but numb, so numb that she would often shake herself awake to find herself sitting like this, immobile, inert, with no idea how long she had been there.

Since he had bought Ufa, Hugenberg's dinners were not optional for any actor or high-ranking crew member. They were compulsory. And this one was no exception. The studio couriered a rack of dresses and sent a car.

The room was alight with crystal and scented with huge vases of freshly cut gardenias. Actresses, singers, and dancers in dresses shimmering with jet drifted from the terrace to the cocktail bar and back again. Joseph Goebbels held court in a corner. He was easy to spot with his limp and his overlarge head. He came to every premiere, every wrap party, every fashionable gathering, or so it seemed, in Berlin. His friends were American socialites and titled Germans. He was married but that didn't stop him from making advances at any passing starlet. His eyes, it was claimed, could strip you at twenty paces.

It was noted that the actress Lidi barely touched the food she was handed but drank several glasses of Champagne. "There's someone I'd like you to meet," somebody said. "There's someone I'd like you to meet." Her glass was empty so she took another. But then it was empty again and she decided that she must have spilled it. The room was too bright, the music too loud. She stood swaying slightly as man after man spoke to her, responding to him with a simple nod, a "Really," or an "I see." A fresh glass was placed in her hand and she drank it in one mouthful. And then she looked up, and although the diplomat with whom she was engaged in conversation repeated the question three times, she did not reply.

Dressed in a black dinner jacket with his deformed hand in his pocket, Kurt mingled among the financiers, the bankers, and the politicians as if he had been circulating in this kind of company his whole life. He had seen her, she was sure of that, but as he passed by he looked straight through her. Her glass was empty again. The diplomat had given up and been replaced by an executive. She smiled, made her excuses, and headed to the bar. There she picked up a bottle of Champagne, but the dark green glass was wet and it slipped through her fingers and landed on the marble floor with a loud fizzy smash. Everybody turned and looked, everybody except him. They were waiting, it seemed in that moment, for something from her, a word, a joke, a smile. It didn't come.

"Murderer!" she shouted after the former soldier as he made his way toward the French doors. "She loved you so much. . . ."

Even after years of elocution taught by Sister August, the second half of her sentence was swallowed in a sob. Kurt turned and looked back at her, and a single word slipped from his mouth, one word that he knew only she could hear.

"Jew," he said.

How did he know? Had she told Hanne? She couldn't remember. Lilly picked up a vase of flowers from the mantelpiece and hurled it, the roses, the water, the porcelain hitting the wall just to the left of him and showering the room with red petals and broken pottery. It was, some said later, so out of character that many had to do a double take. They laughed and wondered if it was some kind of press stunt. Then somebody took her by the elbow, covered her bare shoulders with a jacket, and tried to lead her to the door.

"No," she said. "No."

But it was not Mr. Leyer or Hugenberg or Kurt or even Joseph Goebbels.

"Ilya!" she cried. "Oh, Ilya."

"Lilly, let me take you home," he said.

But once they were outside, Lilly seemed to sober up. And the awkwardness between them returned.

"I'm sorry about your friend," he said.

Lilly nodded.

"Are you all right?"

He tried to look at her, to catch her eye. But she would not.

"Just put me in a cab," she said. "I'll be fine."

"Lilly," he said. "We have to talk."

Lilly looked up the street. A taxi was approaching.

"Let it pass," he said. "Get the next one. Please?"

"I'll call you," she said. "And thank you."

Ilya told himself later that he should have stopped her. He should have taken her hand and led her back to the place they had once been. He had loved her; he loved her still. Katya was a ghost, a figment from the past. Lilly was the one who was real, who was alive, who was there. But he let her go.

The taxi slowed as it approached the center of the city. In the middle of the street were a group of adolescent Nazis, boys as young as fourteen dressed in brown uniforms shouting, "Death to Judah!" As they marched past, Lidi saw that they had a girl with them, a girl whose head was shaved and who had a placard round her neck that read: I GAVE MYSELF TO A JEW.

Lilly had turned down a contract from MGM five times but agreed to sign it the day after Hugenberg's party. In truth, she hadn't even read the first offers; she had merely noticed the studio's stamp on the envelope and thrown them away. The deal she accepted was for three thousand dollars a week with a fully staffed house in the

Hollywood Hills. It was four times higher than the original offer and would cost Bill Frame his job.

The morning she left Berlin, the sun was shining. It promised to be the most glorious day in 1927. Wet shirts hung in courtyards would be dry before lunchtime, cats lay sprawled in the shade, windows that had been closed for months were finally yanked open to let the damp air of countless nights of restless sleep escape.

The grass in the Tiergarten was awash with black serge as bank clerks and businessmen stretched out their lunch break. Groups of students sunbathed on the beaches of the lakes in the nude. Long brown bodies lay side by side—the short, the hairy, the pale, the pink. Everybody who had a job could afford a beer in the Swedish Pavilion or a jaunt in a mildewed rowing boat. Even the city's landladies, the widows, the ones who'd lost their sons in the Great War and their daughters in the flu epidemic, came out onto their balconies, where their faces, painted garishly by gaslight, puckered in the sunshine.

The smell of moisture and decay, a smell that caught in the mouth, mixed with the scent of gardenia and honeysuckle, rosemary and lavender. If policemen and storm troopers, traffic wardens and train drivers unbuttoned their shirts and rolled up their sleeves, who could blame them? It was a day for forgetting sadness and forgoing judgment. Nothing mattered but the caress of your lover's hand or the midday sun on the back of your neck, nothing mattered but the effervescence of the beer in your mouth or the water as you swam, nothing mattered but the sense that you were at the moment in full illumination, in focus.

She had called him the day before she had arranged to leave. Ilya had agreed to come to the station to see her off. He had bought a couple of magazines and a bunch of mimosa wrapped in newspaper. At first he hardly recognized her: she wore a simple cotton day dress and a frayed coat. She looked uncomfortably like the girl he had found in the typing pool.

"You'll be a smash," Ilya Yurasov told Lidi as they stood shivering in the filthy shade of the platform. "A smash."

"Have you ever thought of leaving?" she asked.

"No," said Ilya. "At least, not yet."

Wait for me in Berlin, she had written. Katya's words were seared into his subconscious. He would wait. But when she finally arrived, he would meet her and explain what had happened. And then he would break it off.

The train was ready. The passengers were invited to board. Lilly stared at the green lights on the track but didn't move. If he had asked me to change my mind, I would have, Lilly admitted to herself later. At that moment, if he had expressed one single sentiment that suggested he still wanted me, I would have had my trunk removed from the train and ripped up my ticket. But why should he?

She didn't say much. And so he talked about the weather. And the bicycle race he'd been to the night before. And then he pointedly watched a large French gentleman argue with a porter about a tip. She climbed aboard her private compartment on the train to Le Havre and he slammed the door shut behind her with more gusto than he had intended.

"Lilly," he said suddenly through the window. "Forgive me."

Lilly stared at him. She thought for a second she had misheard him. How could he be this cruel? How could he bring up the past like this?

"What did you say?"

He didn't repeat himself. She must have been mistaken. The train whistle blew. How like a film, she thought in passing. He looked at the clock. This is the end. The end of it all.

"Write to me," he said. "Good-bye, Lilly."

"Good-bye, Ilya," she replied.

They had not kissed, or hugged or even shaken each other's hand. If you had seen them at this moment, you would have thought them distantly related or maybe employed by the same firm. There was a physical formality between them that was immediately visible.

She sat down in her compartment and stared out of the other window so he wouldn't see her eyes cloud over with tears. Ilya took it as indifference and his smile began to fade before the train even began to move. And then he watched as the locomotive blew a cloud of steam and began to slowly roll forward. It headed out of the station, with ever-increasing speed, toward the suburbs and then onward all the way to the flat fields of France.

I mean nothing to her, he told himself as he turned and walked away, still holding the crumpled bunch of mimosa. Everything we once had is lost. And so he did not see the figure that leaned out of the window at the very back of the train, the figure that had run the length of three carriages to try to catch one final glimpse.

Lidi, the actress, traveled incognito to the United States of America. There is no Lidi or Lilly Nelly Aphrodite on the passenger list of the SS *Sufren*, which left Le Havre on the fifteenth of October, 1927, and arrived in New York nine days later. There are two L. Smiths, however. One, we may assume, was Lidi. Onboard she avoided the endless cocktail parties and black-tie dinners. She ate in her cabin and spent the days sitting out on deck with a book. A few people tried to befriend her—an elderly couple from Vermont even offered to adopt her—but she politely and firmly turned them down.

She had not expected to be received like Pola Negri, who was Polish, with flowers and orchestras and the explosion of press bulbs when she arrived at Pier 27 in Manhattan. She was German, and Bill Frame had warned her that the bad taste of the war had not quite faded. And yet when she stepped off the gangplank with the address of a hotel that he had given her and a purse full of newly minted dollars in her hand, she was met by a dozen journalists, seven studio executives, and a translator.

"How do you like America, Lidi?" they shouted at her.

The translator hastily explained their question.

"I haven't seen it yet," she replied.

And when they heard what she had said, they laughed as if she were hilarious.

"Well, America loves *you*!" they yelled.

Before she could respond, however, she was rushed into a limousine and driven uptown to the Hotel St. Regis on Fifth Avenue.

"All the European movie stars stay here," said an executive who claimed he originally came from Frankfurt. "Is it true you only have one trunk?"

"I don't intend to stay here forever," she said. The studio executive, who would leave his wife for a Brazilian dancer, lose everything he owned in the crash of 1929, and eventually end up in Sing Sing, laughed.

"That's what I said," he said. "But once you've seen California, you won't ever want to go back."

Although she was barely known in the United States, two of her films, including *Kinetic*, had been released in the major cities and had clocked up respectable box-office returns. As the American economy boomed, people began to seek out new experiences, to wonder about the world outside their borders, to dream of foreign travel, and there was an appetite for the exotic, for the foreign, for the European.

"What do I remember of my first arrival in America?" she said later. "I remember the smell of roasting peanuts and flower stalls. I remember the light, which seemed a different color from what I was used to: cleaner, brighter, harsher. I remember the heat, which made the air almost too hot to breathe. And I remember the music. It seemed to be coming from everywhere, from people playing in the streets, from gramophones you could hear through open windows, from the band playing on the roof terrace of my hotel. You felt as if you were in a movie even when you walked to the corner shop to buy a coffee."

Lidi's arrival in America made the gossip page of the *New York Post*. The photograph was a little blurred and her left hand was raised and covered half of her face. Only one eye was visible but was in the process of a blink, and her mouth, which was open, seemed on the point of forming a word beginning with the letter O. The headline read "German Screen Vamp Takes a Bite of the Big Apple." From then on, it was decided by the studios to keep her out of sight until her first American feature was about to be released. She boarded a train for California the next day and, several days later, disembarked in Pasadena to avoid the waiting journalists. And then, or so it seemed to her American fans—of whom there were at least several thousand—she disappeared.

America

Ludwig's curls are dark and his eyes are the color of a bottle of bromide. He wears a white cotton coat and spotless white gloves. All the girls at the Afifa processing facility are in love with him. His room smells of seduction, hot celluloid, and damp silk.

Lang's new film Metropolis *has just arrived in a box from the censors. Since Hugenberg decreed that Ufa could "edit or alter the completed film as we see fit," some directors had walked out of Tempelhof Studios and never returned. Karl Grune, like others, wept when he saw what they'd done to his pacifist love story.*

But the girls and boys in white coats at Afifa are busier than ever before. Films are delivered by the vanload for cutting and slicing, for changes in subtitles and order of sequence and lopping of endings. And now Metropolis *is to be trimmed from 4,189 to 3,241 meters, from two and a half hours to a mere ninety minutes.*

Ludwig takes the first reel and threads it through his splicer. He holds his breath, he cuts. A tail, a curl, a spiral of film falls to the floor, scene after scene, gone forever. Afterward he will make love to the girl who works in the mailroom, in an attempt to soothe his conscience. And when it doesn't work, he will bring out the scissors. Cut it, he will insist, cut it all off. And then she will take a loose brown curl and snip.

The house that Lidi lived in from 1927 until 1929 came with a maid, a cook, and a gardener. MGM gave her a bank account with a balance of ten thousand dollars for her personal use. A tutor, a young woman who worked mainly as a voice coach, was hired to teach her English. The first day she woke up on Roxbury Drive, she lay and listened to the sound of the cicadas. Occasionally a motorcar would pass, its engine puttering and the driver calling out whenever it passed another automobile, "*Niceday, takecare.*" But despite this and the noise of the insects, she had never known such silence before.

From the terrace you could see the sea, and behind rose up the hills, hills cut into by Coldwater and Benedict canyons. In twenty short years, however, this barren stretch of coast had been watered and planted and then sold off as building plots for residential housing. Although the bricks and mortar gave the impression that the landscape had been tamed, this was only partly true. Out of the cracks in the patio came lizards and huge brown pine sawyer beetles. The green lawns had to be watered and weeded daily to combat the scorching sun. Wildflowers, yellow California buttercups, and bright pink Indian paintbrushes would grow back practically overnight, while the imported European blooms, begonias, and pale white lilies had to be coaxed into flower gently, with plenty of water and partial shade.

The autograph hunters and tourists who hung around the gate at Pickfair, the house built by Douglas Fairbanks and Mary Pickford, or who cried on the cold gray stone of Rudolph Valentino's grave, occasionally tried to catch a glimpse. But Miss Lidi, as she was called by her Mexican maid, never lay in the sun. They didn't loiter long; some of them had seen *Kinetic* and claimed she was cold and unfeeling. "She's German," they said, as if that explained everything.

America was the leading producer of film in the world. With five big studios and the so-called factory system, the industry could afford to sign up the most promising actors, directors, and technicians and keep them on long-term contracts. Paramount had Pola Negri, their European vamp. Now MGM had Lidi.

The party had been going on all day and most of the guests were pink-faced and salt-skinned, their gaze bleary with too much wine and the incessant wind. The red sun hung low and the wind whipped along the coast, snapping the striped awnings on the porch and blowing grains of sand into eyes and mouths and creases in clothes. The wide lip of beach was almost deserted. Only sandpipers stalked the wet strip where the sea advanced and then receded.

Over an open grill someone was cooking fish. A gramophone had been set up on a checkered blanket and a girl was hunched over a box of records, blowing sand from the grooves and carefully choosing a selection with exclamations to everybody and nobody in particular, that this one is hot, this one was done better by Fred, this one is inspirational, ohmylordy. Later she would dance on the spot on her own and then fall asleep on a lap.

Lidi's fine white silk chiffon frock, cut to float and flutter in the calmer climes of palm courts or dining rooms, clung to her arms and lashed around her knees. The straw bonnet on her head was pulled down tight and then it was gone, rolling across the beach before being whisked up by a gust and blown away to God knows where. Lidi took a drink from a tray, pulled off her shoes, and made straight for the water. And as she stood on the edge of the ocean, her toes sinking, just a little, into the soft surface of the sand, as a swell rolled over her feet in a rush until she was ankle deep in cool clear water, she looked, another guest said later, like an apparition, so pale that she was practically transparent, a shimmering, flickering projection from another, darker world.

Wafts of music reached her from the party behind. But she did not hear the famous actor approach. She did not smell the sweeter notes of his cologne above the barbecue smoke and the salt air. She did not catch, even from the corner of her eye, the presence that had been labeled remarkable by the *Hollywood Reporter* more than once.

"You came," he said in German, and placed his hand on the back of her waist.

Lidi jumped, then turned. The actor was in his mid-forties, with butcher's hands and an overlarge head. His eyes radiated creases all the way to his ears, which made him look as if he were smiling even when he wasn't.

"Thank you for inviting me," she replied. "You speak good German."

"My mother was from Saxony," he said. "But I grew up in upstate New York."

He moistened his lips with his tongue. Then he reached and tucked a strand of her windblown hair behind her ear. She looked away. It was an act so intimate that she found she could not return his gaze in case he thought that she condoned it.

"Can I get you anything?" he asked.

She had met the actor only once before, at a casting. She had not been given the job.

"A good part?" she replied.

The famous actor laughed and then he took her arm and guided her back up the beach.

"You're very witty as well as being very beautiful," he said. "Come and meet everyone."

Lidi shook two dozen hands and immediately forgot two dozen names. She drank four Manhattans and smoked a French cigarette. And although she made polite conversation, she was aware the other guests kept their distance. Only the famous actor remained at her side, filling her glass and trying to persuade her to dance. And when she yawned, he offered her his very own bed and she should have, she chastised herself later, known better.

"Sleep with me," the famous actor said in English as soon as the door was closed.

"I'm sorry?" she said, unsure if she had understood him correctly.

He repeated it in German. This time there could be no doubt. He moved closer and started to unbutton her dress.

Her shoes still lay on the beach and would be carried away by the mid-morning tide. The sun had dropped but would soon come up again on another perfect day. She walked up the driveway barefoot and found her car with the driver asleep inside. Her hand still smarted from the blow she had dealt the actor.

"You'll never work in this town again!" he had shouted in English, and she had almost laughed. She understood that without translation. Was that the best he could come up with?

After that, she rarely attended large Hollywood parties. She allegedly told the actor Emil Jannings, who had also moved to California, that she found Americans shallow and vacuous, their laws infantile and their food inedible, but this could have been a blatant attempt to cover his own tracks, as he was infamously rude about his filmmaking hosts. But even if this was true, it was soon immaterial. A bare two months after she arrived, she received a bad write-up in one of the most sycophantic gossip magazines, suggesting that she was stuck up. Go home, one of them suggested. And leave America to the Americans. Under her picture there was one word: *Nazi?*

Lilly was devastated. She lay awake all night and first thing the next morning called Bill Frame out of an important breakfast meeting.

"What should I do? I can't believe they would print such a thing. Can you ask MGM to issue a statement?"

"MGM won't do that," Bill Frame said. "But listen, it doesn't matter. They don't even know what the word means."

The next day she was sent a script; it featured a manipulative, evil, sexually driven woman. "This is the perfect vehicle for you," wrote the studio boss.

She turned it down.

From then on, scripts were couriered to her daily, but they all proposed she play the same kind of one-dimensional role: the adulterer, the seducer, the criminal.

Time passed, indigenous yellow poppies grew all over her lawn, and she instructed her gardener to leave them alone. The first sound film, *The Jazz Singer*, was released. And although nobody believed they would, films with sound effects, with songs, with dialogue took off. A new code was also in the process of being drawn up for American production by Will H. Hays that would effectively ban all eroticism and nudity from the screen and instead promote marriage, fidelity, and moral standards.

Lilly kept a packed suitcase at her front door and was on the brink of returning to Berlin every day. She dreamt about the city, about her apartment, about Hanne, about Sister August, and when she woke she would ache with sorrow. She had lost them and now she was lost. Scripts lay unread in piles, phone calls were never returned, and requests by mail went unanswered. It took three years for MGM to let her fall off the payroll. It was an understandable oversight. Dozens of actresses never made the transition from silent to talkie. Lillian Gish was dropped by MGM after the box-office failure of *The Wind*; Paramount used Clara Bow's thick Brooklyn accent as an excuse to cancel her contract; and although Mary Pickford had a hit with *Coquette*, she and her husband, Douglas Fairbanks, made a series of flops and would eventually both retire from the movies. The old silent stars were replaced by a whole raft of new ones such as James Cagney and Joan Crawford.

Lilly had invested her money, as Bill Frame recommended. She sold her diamonds and bought stocks and shares. In 1929, Wall Street crashed. America as a whole lost thirty billion dollars. Lilly's wealth vanished overnight.

Some said that after she left the house on Roxbury Drive she worked as an extra; they claimed that the back of her head or the turn of her ankle appeared in dozens of films, including *Tabu*, *Grand Hotel*, and *Trouble in Paradise*. Others, that she was supported by a wealthy Italian who kept her and funded her in return for a disdainful glance or the occasional kiss on the knuckle of her glove-encased hand. Someone else was sure she worked as a florist in a tiny kiosk on Sunset Boulevard and he bought roses from her every day except Sunday, when it was closed. She didn't deny anything. It was all true.

In fact, it was the letters that saved her. Just when she thought that she might walk into the Pacific with rocks in her pockets, the letters started to arrive, first one a month and then one a week. She kept them for decades, filed in order to plot out the slow trajectory of her heart.

It is so good to hear from you, wrote Ilya in a letter dated early 1930. *I think about you often and your new life in California. I can't believe that America has you and is not using your talents; that the directors and producers of Hollywood are not fighting between themselves for the honor of working with you. Their loss is more than they will ever realize. You ask me about the industry here and I have to admit that it is rather slow at the moment.*

My dearest Lilly, he wrote in 1931. *Yes, the lindens are in flower and the man on the street corner is still singing Wagner, badly. In some ways Berlin has changed. But in others it will always be your city. I start shooting my film early next year; the financing is in place and I have begun assembling my crew. The actress I have cast, however, is a dull electric bloom compared to your flickering flame. Yes, I am still considering the move to America, but not until I have sorted out my affairs in Berlin.*

It was on the way to the central post office on Spandauer Strasse, one cool bright day in March 1932, that Ilya came face-to-face with Katya Nadezhda. It wasn't surprising that he didn't recognize her: he hadn't seen her for years. That morning he had already passed dozens of old women who had come out to enjoy the weather, to sit in the parks and turn their faces to the cool spring sun. And so when he found himself staring into the face of a tired woman heading in the other direction, Ilya simply bowed and moved aside. But instead of passing by with a nod of thanks as the other women had done, she stared up at him with an expression he couldn't interpret.

"Excuse me, madam," he asked. "Is there something the matter?"

"You don't know me, do you?" she replied in a whisper.

There was indeed something familiar about her face. Straight white hair fell to her shoulders beneath a cloche hat. She wore a patched black coat and carried a battered clutch bag in one hand and a newspaper in the other. She glanced down, shook her head, and started once more on her way.

"It doesn't matter," she said in Russian.

He knew that voice, he knew that accent, he knew her after all. And his heart seemed to momentarily stop beating.

"Katya," he said. "Is it you?"

The woman paused. And as all the shopgirls out for a breath of fresh air and businessmen on their way to important meetings rushed past, she turned around slowly.

"Ilya," she said. "It's been so long."

And then her eyes filled with tears.

As Katya Nadezhda dabbed her face with a darned cotton handkerchief, Ilya was filled with so many conflicting emotions that he was momentarily mute. But Katya barely noticed. In a series of rapid assertions and corrections, recollections and half-remembered anecdotes, she began to talk as if words alone could dam the flood that threatened to overwhelm her. She had been living in Berlin for ten years. She worked in a private kindergarten run by the Siemens factory. Other than that, she led a quiet life, she said. She read, she went to the park, she liked the cinema.

"I saw your name a few times," she said. "It made me feel proud to think that you'd become such a success. Tell me, are you married?"

Katya looked up at him at last. Her eyes had dried. She had found her equilibrium. Ilya took one deep breath and then another and finally managed to articulate the question that had been threatening to choke him.

"Why," he said. "Why didn't you contact me, Katya? Ever since I got your letter from the Crimea, I've been waiting . . . just as you asked me to. . . . I wanted so much to . . . but I waited . . . because . . . I made a promise . . . and you were here all the time. . . . No, I never married."

Katya sighed and glanced away.

"The letter," she said. "I didn't know you got my letter. Those were awful years. . . . I don't think about them anymore. But surely, Ilya, you realized that it was a letter from another lifetime . . . didn't you?"

Ilya's hands, his mouth, his knees were all about to betray him; they were all on the brink of mutiny.

"No," he eventually replied. "I didn't."

"My poor boy," Katya whispered under her breath. "My poor, poor boy."

A newspaper seller passed by on his bike and threw the latest edition into a doorway to their left, a baby pushed by in a pram started to bawl, a group of children washed around them as they hurried to catch an approaching tram. Only Ilya remained static, only he remained inert. Katya reached out, covered his hand with hers, and gave it the smallest of squeezes. And then she readjusted her hat. She was going to be late for work, she said. But they should meet up sometime, for a coffee, for a glass of wine. She didn't, however, offer any way that he could contact her. And then, with an incline of her head, she stepped aside, moved off, and was immediately swallowed up by lunchtime crowds.

My dearest Lilly, Ilya wrote later that day. *I have been trying to write this letter for many hours. I met Katya in the street today. It is finally over. I am finally released. Part of me is filled with relief while another part weeps for my younger self, for my misplaced valor, for what I did to you and for all the time we have lost.*

The next letter was dated a week later and included these lines:

Your letter filled me with hope, Ilya wrote. *But I wish I could take back the last ten years and live them all over again. I wish I could do something to atone. You deserved so much more. And for that I can never forgive myself. . . . The production has been delayed. But as soon as I have finished this film, and as soon as I have the finances in place, I will come to you, Lillushka. I would come sooner but so many friends and colleagues are depending on the project: as you know it has been tough for the last few years. We must keep busy, we must keep working, and time will pass like oil. With all my love, Ilya.*

It was E. A. Dupont who spotted Lidi, the former German movie star, later that same month. While driving through the parking lot of Studio B at Universal, he glanced out of his window and looked straight into the eyes of his favorite actress of all time. Dupont had just arrived in Hollywood from Britain, where his films *Moulin Rouge* and *Piccadilly* had been box-office hits. He was casting his first American film, *Ladies Must Love*. Although it was a well-known fact, vouched for by several other witnesses, that upon recognizing her he immediately stopped his car and invited her into his office, he later claimed it was she who had approached him, looking for work as an extra.

The studio bosses were skeptical. Could she read lines? Yes. Didn't she have an accent? As soft as Garbo's. Only one German actress had ever made a successful transition across the Atlantic, and besides, they added, wasn't Lidi a supporter of Hitler? Dupont, whose moods oscillated between love of the Land of the Free and downright animosity to its half-witted population, responded indignantly: "She's a true icon, a huge talent. Just imagine the poignancy: a beautiful, destitute exile, saved by the love of an American man. And anyway, if she's a supporter of Hitler, then what the hell is she still doing here?"

And so Lidi was "rediscovered," with a double-page spread in the *Hollywood Reporter*, in which she was sympathetically interviewed and photographed. "America saved me," she was quoted as saying. "It is my home now." "Indeed her melancholy beauty has never seemed brighter," the editorial went on. "Now is the time for her star to shine again, American style."

I always said you'd be a smash, Ilya wrote in 1933. *I only wonder why it took them so long. Here, dozens of my crew have been sacked from the project. No one of Jewish extraction is allowed to work for Ufa unless under exceptional circumstances. I too have heard rumors about a camp near Munich for the so-called enemies of the regime. Yesterday they were burning books in the street. Can you imagine? Books!*

From June of that year: *No, it is not possible. Money isn't enough. You could pay the immigration tax but the paperwork is too complex and the quota has been tightened up to only around 160,000 immigrants a year from all nations, including Germany. Since Hitler was elected in March, it has become much harder to leave. Stay where you are. Please, don't even think of coming back. There is nothing you could do here.*

And there is another letter tied up in the bundle. But the writing is not Ilya Yurasov's. Written by hand on heavy white paper embossed with Ufa's letterhead is an invitation from Goebbels via Hugenberg's office. He had watched her films in Hugenberg's house in the mountains many times over. Anyone could tell by looking at her, he went on, that she was a true Aryan of aristocratic stock. She could be the future, he wrote, of the German film industry. As *Kinetic* was also a favorite of the Führer's, he would like to invite her to star in a German film.

I implore you to accept, he wrote. *For too long has the light behind your name been dimmed. Germany is your home and we are your people. I await your reply in earnest, Joseph.*

Ladies Must Love (1933) starred the vivacious and hitherto unknown blond June Knight. Although it was launched with a lavish party, it made a loss at the box office. E. A. Dupont worked for four American studios before he was eventually fired from *Hell's Kitchen* in 1939. Lidi's picture appeared in the *Hollywood Reporter* once more. The same word was printed beneath it as before. But this time there was no question mark. *Nazi,* it read. *Nazi.*

VOLKE

In Berlin

At first there is nothing to see, the film is black, the film is blank. But then it all comes into focus: a dark shape against the dark night, the Reichstag. Suddenly birds fly, stones fall, the ground seems to shiver. The main doors of the government building blow open to reveal an almost menopausal flush of heat. The cupola lights up, as if by a devilish filament, throwing into black relief the statue of Germania on horseback above. And as the flames break through the curves of the gilded copper and glass roof, they send shards of light up into the Berlin sky and down, in great sheets or arrows, onto the cobblestones below.

The Nazis immediately claim the arson is a Communist plot. President Hindenburg, a man so old his eyes rarely focus, agrees to the demands made by his chancellor, Herr Hitler, and signs Article 48 of the Weimar Republic. Germany is placed in a state of emergency. All civil liberties are suspended.

Forty thousand members of the opposition will be rounded up and imprisoned. Forty thousand Communists and liberals and journalists and writers and artists. The film, shot by an amateur who just happened to be passing, is taken out that night into a back court and set alight. It catches easily, burns almost as brightly as the Reichstag, cracks twice like gunshot, then turns to ash, and breath by breath blows away.

The train sped toward Berlin through cool green forests where the bright summer sun collected in pools. Bareheaded girls and brown-backed men rode bicycles along dusty lanes, with children stowed in wicker baskets or pulled alongside in little tin wagons. Some stopped and watched the train rattle past and waved, or bit into an apple or drained a bottle of beer. Others kept cycling, their knapsacks heavy with damp swimming trunks and a splaying novel, their heads giddy with too much sun or the wine they'd drunk at lunch.

The tracks drew alongside a highway, and for a minute or two a rider on a shiny black motorcycle matched the train's speed until his engine sputtered and with a shake of his head he fell back as the road curved away. And then there was just forest, forest hushed and heady, its eyes closed, its arms open, its dark mouth seemingly holding its breath.

All day the sun had streamed through the mottled glass of the first-class compartment window, kept closed, the conductor claimed, to keep out the heat. Now he had opened it with a key and gasps of air rustled the morning newspaper and the familiar smell of pinesap and acacia blossom replaced the fug of cigarette smoke and spilled coffee. It was June; it would be a beautiful summer.

As they approached the city, nothing looked too different: a few new buildings, a plot overgrown, a billboard advertising shampoo where once a church had stood. The suburbs flew past and occasionally Lilly strained to glimpse some graffiti scrawled on a wall or a shop front. And then the train was slowing down and the conductor was striding back and forth along the corridor shouting, *"Nächster Bahnhof, Potsdam! Nächster Bahnhof, Potsdam!"* A car was waiting for her at the station, but no one else: she had made sure of that. She tipped the porter and climbed into the car as the driver loaded her cases into the trunk. And then he started the engine, put the car into gear, and they were off.

Like anyone who has left one country behind for another, when

Lilly first arrived in America, she couldn't help seeing the old in the new. Main Street looked just like the Unter den Linden. Venice Beach reminded her of Wannsee. Now that she was actually driving through Berlin again, it was almost as if the Berlin she remembered had been replaced by another, meaner version. The avenues and public squares seemed narrower, darker, more oppressive than she remembered; the light sifted.

She had read about the boycott of Jewish businesses, but it was still a shock to see so many shops boarded up, their windows defaced with paint. And the graffiti, she could read it now, was always a single word: *Juden*. Then her eye was drawn upward; Nazi banners were hung from lampposts and balconies and flagpoles and draped across windows, the red background and the white circle emblazoned with a crooked cross, the swastika.

The cinemas of the Kurfürstendamm still looked the same: the strings of bright lights, the worn red velvet carpeting leading to the box offices, the names in lights three meters high. And yet although they could have been in Paris, London, or New York, there were no Charlie Chaplin films or Marx Brothers comedies. The Jewish boycott had censored any film that failed to meet the standards of "pure Aryan elevation."

Since the National Socialists had taken over the running of Ufa, dozens of actors, producers, directors, and technicians had either left of their own volition or had their contracts canceled. Elisabeth Bergner and Peter Lorre, both Jewish, had emigrated after being labeled "undesirable," and many more were about to follow. Some were accused of having Jewish blood and others of having a Jewish partner. But anyone could also be blacklisted for having so-called un-German views.

To stop the drain of talent, Goebbels had already tried to engage Asta Nielsen and Greta Garbo, but neither would return his phone calls or requests by letter. He courted Fritz Lang for a day or two, until the director secretly caught the night train out of Berlin to

France, leaving his wife, the scriptwriter Thea von Harbou, behind. Her relationship with Goebbels was more fruitful. Lang and von Harbou divorced a few years later.

Despite the weather, there were fewer people strolling in the streets or trying to catch the last of the sunshine than Lilly would have expected. Instead they huddled in groups, talking. At every street corner was a clutch of policemen. An army truck driven by a soldier in a green uniform passed by. And then another. She was suddenly apprehensive. Although the streets looked familiar, she didn't know where she was anymore.

"Where are you going?" she asked the driver.

He glanced at her in the rearview mirror, and in that fraction of a second that their eyes met, she could see that he was scared too.

"To the Esplanade," he said. "The Esplanade Hotel."

He swung right and she recognized the raised platforms of Zoo Station. In heavy traffic, the car inched across the busy junction and accelerated into the Tiergarten. She sat back and made herself relax; she knew where she was again. It would be fine.

"That's right," she said. "The Esplanade."

As they approached the burned-out Reichstag building, the number of military personnel grew larger. There was the smell of cordite in the air.

"Who are those soldiers?" Lidi asked the driver. He hesitated and glanced back at her over his shoulder before he spoke.

"The ones in green?" he replied. "Göring's men."

Whole streets were cordoned off and soon there were no civilians on the street at all, just soldiers and policemen.

"Von Schleicher and his wife have been shot," he explained.

"The politician?"

The driver nodded.

"In the back of the head," he added briefly.

And then he was silent, as if he had said too much and immediately regretted it.

"But you mustn't ask so many questions," he suddenly said, without looking back at her. "This isn't America."

The hotel suite was full of flowers, orchids and lilies in vivid orange and pale lemon yellow. One basket was from Goebbels, another from Mr. Leyer. The porter placed her bags beside the bed but wouldn't accept a tip. And then, just after he had closed the door, came the unmistakable sound of gunfire. She jumped, despite herself.

It was the last day in June 1934. Hindenburg, the elderly president of Germany, was confined to a wheelchair at his country estate. He would be dead in a matter of months. At Nazi headquarters, there were rumors of a left-wing plot to overthrow Hitler by the party's own army, the SA, or the Brownshirts. And so *Kolibri*, or Hummingbird, the code word had been given. Hundreds of men and women would be shot that night, half of whom had sworn allegiance to the Führer. Ernst Röhm, the chief of the storm troopers, was dragged from the bed he was sharing with a young boy, imprisoned for two days, and then shot in the chest at point-blank range after he refused to commit suicide. In Berlin, one hundred fifty of his deputies were rounded up and murdered by Hitler's personal bodyguards, the SS, at the cadet school in Lichterfelde.

And there were more. *Kolibri*. The names on a list were to be eliminated one by one: Gustav von Kahr, who had opposed Hitler during the Beer Hall Putsch of 1923; Father Bernhard Stempfle, who had taken some of the dictation for Hitler's book *Mein Kampf*; Gregor Strasser, one of the original members of the Nazi Party and formerly next in importance to Hitler; Berlin SA leader Karl Ernst, who was involved in torching the Reichstag building in February; Catholic leader Dr. Erich Klausener; and Dr. Willi Schmidt, a music critic who had no political allegiances with anyone but who unfortunately shared the name with someone who had.

But in the softly lit suite on the third floor of the Esplanade Hotel with its huge bed, marble-topped tables, and brocade-lined walls, as the day faded outside and the streetlights came on, humming with deep pink, Lilly picked up a card written in a familiar hand and opened it. And then nothing could have convinced her that she was not in the right place at the right time.

I will come at ten, wrote Ilya Yurasov. *Wait up for me.*

The deal had taken months to map out. She had employed an agent, and a lawyer recommended by Mr. Leyer. Finally, after screeds of correspondence by proxy with Ufa and the Ministry of Propaganda, she had requested a modest fee and a series of nonnegotiable clauses for one film with the option to make more.

While the two sides were battling out the deal, the days and weeks and months had dragged past until she could hardly bear it, until she would have signed anything if it had been offered. And then she could wait no longer and against her lawyer's advice she bought her train ticket, headed from California to LaSalle Street Station in Chicago, and then, after a wait of two hours, boarded another train for New York's Grand Central. But the trains, despite the fact that they were advertised as "express," took five days to travel from one coast to the other. To Lilly, they seemed to crawl inch by inch across the wide, flat plains of America, loitering at red lights in the middle of nowhere and languishing in dusty provincial stations, even though no one ever climbed on and no one ever disembarked, as if they had sensed her irritation and were conspiring to vex her. After another wait, another restless night, she had boarded an ocean liner and spent ten days watching the sea boil and counting the minutes as they slipped past, her body aching with impatience. And now, finally—finally—she was back in Germany with a special visa from the Ministry of Propaganda and a contract pending signature.

Berlin rolled out beneath her, the wide expanse of Potsdamer Platz, the newly constructed multistory department store beyond, the brightly lit avenues, and the wide *Strassen* that radiated so confidently north, south, east, west, into acres of shadow. And then it started to rain, lightly at first and then so heavily that it was almost as if the whole city had been thrown out of focus.

Apart from the crumpled bunch of mimosa, nothing about Ilya was the same. It had been more than six years. His beautiful dark curls had been cut close to his head and were now flecked with gray. His face was so thin that his cheekbones protruded and his lips seemed fuller. He had the stubble of a beard. And there was something static in his manner that was new, a kind of inner stillness. He was also soaked to the skin.

Lillushka—she was always Lillushka with him—was the opposite: she couldn't stop moving, as if all that traveling had left its mark on her and she was still in motion despite herself. She closed the door, took his coat, poured him a drink, took the flowers—which, compared to the rest of the blooms that filled the room, were embarrassingly modest—and started to rip off the outer leaves. Her hands, she noticed suddenly, had become wrinkled from the American sun.

"I've never seen such rain . . ." she started to say.

Ilya gently took the flowers from her and put them down. Then he cupped her face in his hands and kissed her neck, her throat, her mouth. And the years telescoped and meant nothing.

"Ilya," she said, and threw her arms around his neck. "Oh, Ilya."

To Ilya Yurasov, Lilly, his Lillushka, looked exactly the same. He experienced the same sweet note in the belly when she looked at him, the same cantering of his heart, and the same constriction of his chest. Her clothes smelled different, of soap powder and sunshine, but her skin, her lips, tasted just as they had all those years before. He pulled back and looked into her large gray eyes, the gray eyes that in recent years he had gotten to know so well from her films, the films that he had threaded up and watched over and over; and although he was an atheist, in his head he thanked God several times over.

"You shouldn't have come," he said. "You shouldn't have."

"I couldn't wait any longer," she whispered. "I can't wait any longer. But look at you, you're soaked right through. Take off your wet clothes."

"Always so impatient," he replied. And then he laughed out loud and she saw he had barely changed at all.

As Ilya lay in Lilly's bed and waited for her to join him, he hoped nobody had seen him in the lobby. The situation had changed since his last letter. Most of the Russians in Berlin had already moved on, to Paris, to New York, to London. Since the Nazis took over, he had been watched. He was an anomaly; could he be a Communist agitator? A militant Jew? He refused to join the Reich Film Guild, and when precensorship had been introduced a few months before, and every single process from screenplay to edit had to be examined, he had been given a list of conditions that he knew he couldn't meet. He had been dropped from his own project.

Without an income, he had lost his apartment and moved on to Mr. Leyer's floor. He had been offered work in Paris by the Alliance Cinématographique Européenne, but his exit visa had been denied. And then he received the telegram.

Coming home stop, it read. *Arriving on June 30 stop. Love your Lilly stop.*

His Lilly paced up and down that overblown, overheated hotel room still fully dressed. She was suddenly nervous. Had she aged? Was she still desirable? Did he still find her attractive? He was watching her with a look of such peace on his face that she never forgot it.

"I feel as if I'm dreaming," he said. "Prove to me I'm not."

She pulled her shoes off, unbuttoned her clothes, let them drop to the floor, and lay down beside him until there was not an inch where his body did not touch hers, and finally she was completely still.

"Welcome home," he whispered.

The next morning it was still raining, the sky the color of tin. As Ilya slept, Lilly listened to the sounds of the rush-hour traffic, of pneumatic tires on a layer of water, of the screech of the tram track and the whistle of a policeman overlapped with the rattle of a room service cart in the corridor. How could so many years have passed? It was inconceivable. But now, she thought, all that time seems no more than a blink.

"Lillushka, are you sure you know what you're doing?"

Ilya was awake now, his eyes open, his gaze serious.

"If you appear in their films," he whispered, "it will look as if you condone all they do, as if you agree with all their policies, all their sanctions. And all the work you have ever done will fade into insignificance. This will be what you are remembered for: the actress who came back from America for Joseph Goebbels."

"I'll do one. We won't come back."

"One is enough. Your reputation will be ruined. You will be a Nazi by association. And even if you never make another film again, you might be vilified, demonized, discriminated against. Think about it, Lilly. Is it really worth it?"

"Some things are more important," she whispered. "I've made up my mind."

As the rain fell outside, Ilya watched its liquid reflection stream down the brocaded surface of the walls. And although he wanted so much to believe that Lilly's plan could work, he found himself unable to. The Nazis were not fools. You didn't strike a deal with Goebbels and expect to win. But to dream of another future, to be so close to such faith in the impossible, was transcendent. She had come back for him. And that was all that mattered.

"Thank you," he said.

And then she kissed his tears away.

The marriage took place that evening in a tiny church in Schöneberg, a church that was blown to bits by a bomb in 1945. A record remains, however, in the registry in the city hall on Schlossplatz. Lilly wore a cream-colored satin dress; Ilya, a borrowed suit. Mr. Leyer was their only witness. After a swift glass of French Champagne, it was decided that it would be safer for both of them if they didn't see each other until it was time to leave.

The Hotel Kaiserhof was on Wilhelmsplatz, opposite the Imperial

Chancellery. She took the lift to the third floor. When the doors opened, a man was waiting for her with a clipboard. She was shown into a darkened suite at the very end of the corridor and invited to sit down. A pair of wooden doors with polished brass handles divided the rooms. The curtains were closed even though it was mid-morning. A white screen was hanging on one wall and below it there was a tray with tea and cakes. She poured herself a cup of tea but did not drink it. She picked up a cake but could not eat it. Within a minute or two she realized she was not alone. Suddenly the bedroom doors flew open and a small, dark man came through, adjusting his collar. There was something wrong in his gait and her eye was immediately drawn to his built-up shoe. It was Joseph Goebbels, Gauleiter of Berlin.

Goebbels had just heard that Hitler had personally commissioned two more films from the former actress Leni Riefenstahl, and Goebbels was in a cantankerous mood. She was going to produce and direct so-called film monuments recording the Nazi Party's conventions. He couldn't help feeling suspicious of the woman. Wasn't direction and production a man's job? And since he was minister of propaganda, why hadn't he been consulted? But now he was bringing back a German film star from America. This was something the Führer couldn't ignore. This would be his trump card, upstaging all Riefenstahl's expensive triumphalism.

"What a pleasure to meet you at last," he said. "Joseph Goebbels."

Even though they had in fact met before, the minister of propaganda held out his right arm and shook her hand. In his left hand he held a scrap of paper and a pen.

"Would you be so kind?" he asked, and handed them to her.

She was so taken aback—by his appearance, by his enthusiasm, by his request—that she held the paper and pen in her hand for a moment and did not respond.

"I should really say that it is for my daughters," he added with a smile when he noticed her hesitation. "But that's not the truth and I'm sure you'd suspect otherwise. I am, I confess, a fan. If you would . . . an autograph?"

"Of course," she answered.

Lilly was about to sign the piece of paper when he reached across and took her wrist. He turned it over and examined the white skin of her arm and her turquoise veins.

"You know, you look different from the way I remember you," he said. "You are dark, not fair. You have large eyes, a small mouth, high cheekbones."

Her heart started to race, her palms to sweat. And she was suddenly sure that it was a trap: that they knew she was half Jewish, that everything she had planned, all she had risked, was for nothing.

"I'll sign if you sign for me," she said softly.

Goebbels looked at Lidi, the actress who was a favorite of the Führer's, the actress who was going to consolidate everything he had worked for, with slight unease. Had he conceded too much? Could he trust her? Was she hiding something? And he decided with absolute certainty that she had to be brought down a peg or two. Although at that moment he had no idea how he would do it.

He dropped her hand, picked up the contract, and signed.

"I expect dinner," he said as he wrote. "À deux, of course."

Suddenly the door opened and a woman strode in, unpinning her hat.

"Ah, Magda?" he said. "What do you think of her? Isn't she delightful? In the flesh she looks decidedly . . . sultry."

Magda Goebbels shook Lilly's hand but didn't smile. She looked at her husband and the actress with a wariness prompted by her recent discovery that her husband was having another affair. This time it was with a young woman from an Alpine hotel whom he had "persuaded" onto the big screen. Mercifully, in some respects, she proved to be a hopeless actress.

"Pleased to meet you at last," she said. "We have a shortage of good people."

"Really?" replied Lilly.

"Yes, it was something of a coup to get you, I suppose," said Magda Goebbels as she opened the door to a maid bearing more tea. "But you will do rather well out of it, I hear. As well as two hundred thousand marks, half paid in foreign currency, you have asked for a return ticket to America for you and for your husband."

"The ministry will arrange all that," said Goebbels. "Just call them with your dates and times."

"I only just heard you were married," said Magda Goebbels. "Anyone we know?"

"I have the perfect script for you," Goebbels cut in as he stirred the pot of tea. "It's been in preproduction for a while. As far as I know, it was actually written for you by someone you once worked with."

"I've worked with quite a lot of people," Lilly replied. "I wouldn't necessarily remember a name."

"Of course," he said. "Anyway, we have had to rewrite some of it, but the basic conceit is good. It's called *The Queen of Sorrow*. More tea?"

Goebbels lifted the teapot, his wife offered milk, but they both noticed simultaneously that the actress's face had blanched. She shook her head.

"Well, then, maybe you'd like a cake?" asked Joseph Goebbels with a slightly strained smile.

Eva Mauritz, Communist agitator and sister of Stefan, had been released from the Moringen women's camp near Hanover sometime in spring. For two years she had been incarcerated in a converted psychiatric hospital where she slept ten to a cell with other Communists, Jehovah's Witnesses, and Gypsies on straw-filled sacks.

As a Communist, Eva had received the brunt of the "correction": she had been beaten daily by the camp commander until she admitted everything and more and cursed the ground that Karl Marx had ever walked upon. If she was physically scarred by the experience, she didn't let it show. But to those who had known her before—to the women she'd loved and left in Berlin's clubs, such as the Magic Flute Dance Palace and the Dorian Gray—to hear her echo Göring's words and encourage them to "take hold of the frying pan, dust pan, and broom and marry a man," it was patently obvious what damage she had sustained.

Her only visitor, her only confidant while she was in prison, had been her brother. In 1927, as her only living relative, Stefan had been informed of her whereabouts and had come looking for her. Something had changed in him and he seemed to have pulled himself together again. He had found a job as an insurance clerk and a comfortable room in a boardinghouse. Over the years they had come to a tacit agreement not to mention the war or the years that followed. And yet, one day just after her release, he admitted that he knew that Lilly, his wife, was still alive.

"I watched her, you know. For years I watched her. But why?" he implored her. "Why did she ask you to lie for her?"

Eva could not admit her culpability. In fact, she didn't admit anything.

"And now she has emigrated to America and I will never see her again."

"I'll make it up to you," Eva said, and reached up and cupped his broken face. "I promise. We can get a place and live together like we used to."

But Stefan pushed her hand away.

"I hate this city," he said. "I hate this government. I hate this country."

And he left without another word.

In 1934, one in three people in Berlin was unemployed. The Great Depression had already crossed the Atlantic well before Lilly made the trip. The new government had to take drastic measures: wages were cut, trade unions taken over, and the unemployed put up in tent camps on the outskirts of Berlin. But as the French politician Léon Blum pointed out at the time, while socialism represents a morality and communism a technology, fascism represents an aesthetic. All over Germany, cinema façades had been updated or lit up with newly installed spotlights. They had become government buildings in what would become known as a campaign of illusion.

Goebbels had high hopes for *The Queen of Sorrow*. The filming schedule had fallen behind and the budget had already gone to pot, but they were almost finished. They had left the climactic scene—the scene in which Mary, Queen of Scots, has her head chopped off at the order of her treacherous cousin, the queen of England—until last.

Anyone who saw the filming of scene 125 would never forget it. The setup had taken a week to perfect. Flats had been painted to look like a medieval English castle. Three spotlights had been positioned, at three, six, and nine o'clock, to throw the longest shadows. A mob of extras had been chosen for their strange physiognomies or physical deformities. The scaffold had been polished with butter.

They rehearsed the scene several times. Lidi, dressed in black velvet, her face as white as alabaster, her hands tied behind her back, whispered the words, "Into your hands, O Lord, into your hands." And then off came her black velvet gown, to reveal a chemise of brilliant crimson, and she placed her head on the block.

They filmed the scene in a single take. The sight of a young woman with her newly bleached fair hair pulled back and her gray eyes wide open as the ax came down was heartbreaking. Some of the extras even cried.

Goebbels was extremely irritated when he was informed that the actress Lidi had married the Russian director Ilya Yurasov in secret the day after she arrived. Yurasov had not been seen entering the Esplanade Hotel, as he had feared; it was only when the churchwarden in Schöneberg was arrested for sheltering a Jewish mistress and bartered the information in exchange for her that the marriage was uncovered.

Goebbels had met the director once years before at a party and found him charming. When Yurasov had applied to go to Paris, however, he had personally turned down his exit visa. The explanation given was a lack of correct paperwork, but the real reason was that Yurasov was a highly skilled filmmaker, a talented director, a writer of note: he was a valuable asset despite his defiant stance. And now he had inadvertently assigned him a visa and the German film industry would lose him.

But his irritation was more than merely professional. Three times since returning to Berlin, the actress had accepted Goebbels's invitation to dinner and then canceled at the last minute. Goebbels was a man not used to being rebuffed by women, not since his political ambitions had been realized, and as she had given him no indication to the contrary, he believed that an affair was just a matter of logistics. And now he saw plainly that the Russian director and the woman he had gone to some lengths to bring back to Germany had duped him. But what could he do? He had personally signed a contract with the actress. He didn't want her to go back to America and spread the word among other German actors on the point of returning that he couldn't be trusted. No, he couldn't get out of it without major embarrassment or scandal. A month before the date scheduled for the premiere of *The Queen of Sorrow*, however, Goebbels received an interesting phone call from the Berlin chief of police.

Lidi's contract stipulated that she had to attend the film's premiere. As the film was being edited, however, she grew increasingly restless. She was not alone. It wasn't just the endless military parades up and down the Unter den Linden or the public beatings, it was the sense that the city wore its new bravado with an underside of shame. Since homosexuality had been criminalized, many of the bars and cabaret clubs she used to know had closed down or had changed hands, while countless new decrees banned Jews from working, owning shops, even hiking in groups.

Mr. Leyer was taking care of Ilya. He had found him a job in the film-processing plant again, working the night shift as a negative cutter. It was a mundane and laborious task, cutting miles of film together in the order that he was instructed, slicing and pasting reels and reels of numbered frames. He would be safe there, Mr. Leyer told Lidi, until the time came.

The premiere of *The Queen of Sorrow* was held in February 1935. Lidi wore a gold lamé dress and a pair of diamonds in her ears that had been given to her by the minister of propaganda. He had seen the rough edit and had informed the Führer that it was a "singular triumph."

The night was cool and clear and the sky was overcrowded with stars. The cinema's façade had been draped with white cloth and was bathed in cool blue electric light. When Lidi arrived in a long black Mercedes-Benz, two dozen white doves were released from a series of birdcages. She paused momentarily on the stairs and smiled out at the crowds. Many photographs were taken by the party photographer. None is known to have survived.

One by one, more cars rolled up and dispensed their passengers. As well as party officials, the specially invited audience was made up of actors, journalists, and businessmen. At the welcoming reception inside were trays of French Champagne and English muffins. Dozens of jokes were made about the choice of refreshments. None of them was particularly funny, but they were symptomatic of an almost tangible anxiety that was in the air that night. There was a definite sense, it was said later, of foreboding.

As Lidi took her seat between the minister of propaganda and his wife, there was news of a delay. The film was so new, the rumor spread, that a final print had only just been completed. At first the film star made polite conversation about the weather, but then she lapsed into a tense silence. She closed her eyes and willed herself back into Ilya's arms, she tried to remember his softness, his laugh, the upward slant of his eyes. But the reality of her situation could not be ignored for long. There was not enough time: their plan had allowed for a fifteen-minute delay, but not for this. If she didn't leave soon, she would miss the train. Not long now, she told herself, not long now. But as the minutes ached by, she began to tremble with unease, with apprehension, with pure hot fear.

"Nervous?" asked Goebbels.

Lilly nodded. She couldn't speak. She couldn't trust her voice not to give her away.

It was then announced that it was a person they were waiting for, not a print: a rather special person who was late because of business of an official capacity. Goebbels took advantage of the lull in the proceedings to mount the podium and thank his leading lady. He praised her beauty, her purity, and her decision to support her country when it mattered. If there was something triumphant in his tone, Lilly didn't register it.

At the Ufa-Palast, at nine, an hour after schedule, the lights lowered and a single spotlight picked out the entrance of the small man with the black mustache. He marched to his seat, turned, saluted once to the assembled crowd, and then sat down. Hitler was a little put out to discover, when the houselights rose again before the feature, that Lidi was gone. He had been looking forward to meeting her. But the screening was already late and Goebbels pointed out that women were apt to make frequent visits to the lavatory in these sorts of circumstances. And so, when the orchestra launched into the overture, he sat back, relaxed, and waited for the red curtains to part.

Mr. Leyer met Lilly at the back door of the Ufa-Palast with her suitcase. A car was idling at the curb.

"It's a close call," he said, "but you'll make it as long as the traffic's light."

"Where's Ilya?" Lilly asked. "I thought he'd be here."

"Don't worry. He took a taxi from Afifa. The ministry made out a ticket for him in your name and left it at the ticket office. I've just checked and he's already picked it up."

"He was working tonight?" Lilly said. "How can he at a time like this?"

"He's been on night shift," Mr. Leyer explained. "We don't want to arouse their suspicions. Now hurry or you'll miss the blasted train and he'll go without you."

"Thank you so much," Lilly said as she squeezed his hand. "For everything."

Mr. Leyer's eyes glistened. He knew he was a sentimental fool.

"Good luck," he called out as the car drew away. "And give my love to that husband of yours."

It was only then that he looked down and found the pair of diamond earrings that Lilly had pressed into his palm the moment before she had climbed into the car. When an SS man found them several months later in Mr. Leyer's desk, he pocketed them and gave them as a gift to a girl from Hamburg. They were found in the rubble of a building near the Rathausmarkt in late 1943.

Of course, everyone stared at the film star as, still dressed in lamé, she hurried through the station toward platform 12, but nobody approached her for an autograph—not there, not then. They could see by her face that she would not have paid them any attention, that she was cutting it fine, that nothing or no one could detain her. There was a commotion at the ticket office—another random act of violence, another senseless beating—but she barely registered it.

The guard helped Lilly aboard the very last carriage and then blew the whistle. As the train began to move, she stood for a moment at the back of the train, watching the platform, the station, the city recede, her golden dress catching the reflection of a million streetlights. And then she turned and began the long walk to the front of the train, to carriage A, to compartment 14, where her husband was waiting for her.

Hitler was furious, Goebbels apoplectic. All press representatives were ordered to hand in their notebooks and swear never to write a word on the matter. The orchestra was sacked on the spot, the invited audience held for five hours without food or water and then released with muttered threats to keep the whole event quiet. They were lucky: the projectionist, the ushers, and the cinema manager were arrested and interrogated.

The actress had departed, not only from the Ufa-Palast and from Berlin, but also from the actual film. Not a single frame of her remained. Whole scenes were cut out, or cut in two, or edited down to remove her presence entirely. Other actors talked to closed doors, to themselves, to each other, but never to Lidi. Instead, the crowd jeered at nothing; Sir Thomas Bromley, played by Hans Albers, convicted an empty stand of treason. It was ridiculous; it was hilarious. No wonder so many at the premiere laughed into their handkerchiefs. They couldn't help it.

The producer blamed the director, the director pointed to the editor, the editor singled out the negative cutter—not the usual negative cutter, he quickly ascertained, but the one who worked the night shift, the one hired recently by Mr. Leyer: the Russian. The next morning, Afifa was surrounded and searched. The Russian, however, had gone.

One may imagine the moment Lilly reached compartment 14 of the boat train to Le Havre. Were the curtains closed? Was the guard still with her, carrying her suitcase, or did she carry it herself? Did she pull back the heavy glass door slowly or with an impatient wrench? And when she saw who was inside, did she wonder for a moment if she had the wrong carriage, the wrong reservation, the wrong train? Because, sitting in compartment 14, a man sat nervously fingering a newspaper: a man, his face now scarred, whom Lilly had believed for almost twenty years to be dead.

Stefan Mauritz had been sleeping when the SS came to look for him earlier that evening. His landlady showed them up into his room with a concerned frown. Herr Mauritz was one of her most respectable tenants, tidy, well-bred, and conscientious. The poor chap, she would say later, had had a difficult life, what with his face, but haven't we all? When they told him to pack, he was filled with panic. He had done nothing illegal.

"I'm not . . . Jewish," he said.

When they told him that his wife, the film star Lidi, had arranged for him to leave Germany with her that very night, he was overwhelmed with emotion. But the joy was short-lived. It didn't make any sense.

"How did you know about me?" he asked.

"We arrested your sister in a bar of ill repute last week," they replied. "In custody she claimed she was a personal friend, a relation, of the actress Lidi, real name Lilly Nelly Aphrodite. We investigated her story and found a record of a marriage at the Church of St. Michael near the Oranienplatz in 1916. She's a lucky girl, your sister. . . . You are Stefan Mauritz, aren't you?"

As they waited, Stefan packed quickly and was escorted to the station. The lady at the ticket office handed over the permits and tickets without hesitation. It all ran as smoothly as Goebbels had planned: his men had been working on Lidi's case ever since the chief of police's phone call the previous week.

And so, as the train compartment door swung open and his wife's face, the face that could express more than a whole page of dialogue, registered first surprise, then horror, and then agony, Stefan Mauritz knew that it was all somehow his fault. And he wished he had died in the war after all.

"I'm so sorry," he said. "I'm so sorry. I'm so sorry."

Lilly had looked at the man with the disfigured face and wondered momentarily if she was dreaming. His face was a flashback from her nightmares: he was a haunting, a malign spirit; he was her stalker. But when he spoke, time seemed to flip and all at once she saw beneath the contours of his ruined face; it was the uhlan. He was alive. The spark that she had doused and buried so many years before suddenly reignited; it was Stefan. As the emotion registered, however, it was swiftly followed by another. Her eyes left his face and took in the compartment.

"Are you . . . alone?"

There was no one else in compartment 14. And as she realized what had happened, what Goebbels had done, it was as if the dead had risen up to spite her after all. Lilly turned and opened the door; she was going to try to get off the train, to go back to Berlin, back to Ilya, to do anything but stay, when the two SS men who had been sent to accompany her to the boat blocked her way.

"Is there a problem?" they asked when they saw her face.

They looked at Stefan, the war veteran, and then back at Lidi, the film star. The train began to speed up as it left the suburbs, the express train that Mr. Leyer had encouraged her to choose because it did not stop until it reached the low French coast.

"You do know this man?" they asked when she didn't answer. "He is your husband? Because if he isn't . . ."

"Yes," Lidi, the actress, replied in a whisper. "He is. Everything's in order."

But according to the French count and his daughter who had taken the adjacent compartment, she closed the door, drew the curtains, and sobbed hysterically all night.

Lilly and Stefan Mauritz sailed from Le Havre on the *Ile de France*. Although they were issued temporary visitor permits in New York when they arrived, where they went once they had disembarked is unrecorded. It was possible to find work at that time without documentation and, like thousands of new immigrants, make a passable living in the so-called black economy.

Lidi, the actress, didn't return to her apartment in California to collect her belongings or contact any of her former acquaintances in

Hollywood. After the defacement on her door, her windows, and her walls had been washed off, the apartment was eventually let out, first to a screenwriter who lived there for twenty years before he was ousted from the industry by McCarthyism, and then to an aspiring actress who tried to kill herself with a mixture of barbiturates and Kool-Aid, but went on to become one of the most famous soap stars of her generation.

Ilya had arrived at Anhalt Station on the night of the premiere in good time. All he needed were the tickets, the exit visas, the paperwork. He was nervous, even though Mr. Leyer had assured him that he wouldn't be missed until the following evening. Mr. Leyer didn't know what Ilya had done.

The first cut was the hardest: the first slice, which scored the film just before Lilly's figure appeared, a silhouette against the light of the early-morning sun. But he was soon cutting faster; it was his script, and he knew where she would appear and for how long. Lilly's face caught in a smile, Lilly's figure beneath a window in a tower, Lilly's eyes closed as she was given her sentence. It was all exactly how he had written it, the way he had imagined it. In only a couple of hours, her entire performance was lying in curls around his ankles. The risk, he reasoned with himself, was worth it. They wouldn't discover what he had done in time to detain him. If something went wrong, however, it was a glorious epitaph. But in truth, he hadn't let himself seriously consider the latter outcome.

The staff behind the international ticket desk was slow to deal with his request; the ticket girl brought the bookings clerk, the bookings clerk brought the supervisor, the supervisor said he needed to speak to his superior. Ilya was waiting for the station manager when he saw Lilly, his Lilly, still dressed in lamé, hurry across the concourse toward the waiting train. He relaxed at last. It was going to work after all. How could he have ever doubted her?

The station manager arrived a little out of breath and informed

Ilya that the ticket left by the Ministry of Propaganda had already been collected in person. And no, the manager said, there had been no mistake. He'd even met the man himself. Ilya shook his head and politely asked the station manager to repeat what he had just said. Had he misunderstood? Had his grasp of German failed him?

"Her husband," the manager said slowly, his blue eyes bulging. "Lidi's husband."

"But I am Lidi's husband," Ilya replied.

The station manager frowned as he looked him over, a Russian with a thin face and threadbare clothes.

"You want a ticket?" he said, producing a rail ticket and waving it in his face. "Then buy one like everyone else, or stop wasting my time."

A whistle blew. The boat train was about to depart. Ilya snatched the ticket from the station manager's hand and ran: he jumped over suitcases, he pushed past commuters, he knocked over a newspaper stand to reach the heavy glass doors that opened onto platform 12. And even when the police appeared from all corners of the station and ordered him to halt, he didn't stop running. They caught up with him on the train tracks just beyond the signal box. As they handcuffed him and wrenched him to the ground, he didn't take his eyes off the nine-thirty p.m. to Cherbourg, as Lilly in her golden beacon of a dress, as the future he had finally let himself believe in, began to pick up speed and head at full throttle into the darkest night he had ever known.

Goebbels had no proof that Lidi had a hand in it, but as a precautionary measure after the hushed-up premiere, he recalled every single copy of every one of her films and personally watched as his assistant destroyed them. Pages were also ripped from magazines in libraries, and film magazines had their archives raided and trashed. Ilya Yurasov, negative cutter, who was in police custody for another offense, did not deny what he had done. As well as cutting Lidi out of the film, he admitted he had burned all the original footage. He was charged with "gross aesthetic vandalism."

Dozens of letters addressed to Ilya Yurasov arrived at Dachau from the United States, all written in the same hand. Only one was ever passed on to him. It was so heavily censored, however, that only a few sentences were legible.

My dearest husband, the letter read.

> *After months of inquiry, of writing to . . . I finally managed to track you down to the camp outside Munich. And although I have been informed that my letters are not likely . . . What you did filled me with both gratitude and with rage. . . . Our pasts conspired against us. . . . The first night we spent together . . . The taste of coffee on your lips and the whisper of your voice . . . poem by Rilke . . . "Be ahead of all parting, as though it were already behind you like the winter that has just gone by. For among these winters there is one so endlessly winter, that only by wintering through it all will your heart survive."*
>
> *With my love, your Lillushka*

Even though Ilya slept with it rolled up in his hand, Lilly's letter was eventually stolen and used either to wrap tobacco or to light kindling. Ilya did, however, manage to keep a single frame from the film *The Queen of Sorrow*. It was all that existed of their work together. Somehow he managed to smuggle that single square inch of film around with him until he reached Treblinka in 1940. One of the few men who survived remembered the way he used to look at it for hours.

"Who is she?" they'd ask.

"Hold it up to the light," he'd reply, "and you'll see."

The Final Frame

At seven in the evening all the lights in Berlin went out, every street sign, every advertising illumination, every traffic light and crossing beacon. They said it was an air-raid drill, a practice blackout. Everyone closed the curtains tight. Some people lit candles and played Puccini. Mussolini was coming on a state visit that very evening.

At nine the citizens were invited by loudspeaker to step outside, and to their delight they found another world. The streets were lit by giant lighting rigs on the backs of lorries. Four rows of painted white columns had been placed along the Unter den Linden, each supporting a massive plaster golden eagle. Banners had been hung over building façades, huge flagpoles erected, pedestals installed, and rows and rows of giant searchlights aimed upward into the night sky. And then the rumble of a cavalcade could be heard approaching.

Lit by a single spotlight, Mussolini and Hitler in an open-topped car motored slowly through the Brandenburg Gate. Behind them thousands and thousands of soldiers marched in lines that stretched forever. They all carried burning torches or banners or both. The spectators' cheeks flushed, their hands burned from the clapping, their voices grew hoarse, but they didn't care. No, that night was magical, electrifying, epic. Who could not believe at that moment in the heroic vision of our Führer? In one voice, they sang to the Swastika, a song of blood and destruction and tears. And when the final chorus faded and the last of the soldiers had passed, they heard it loud and clear—the unmistakable ticker of the camera.

Acknowledgments

My great-aunt Nina Schmidt, who worked in the marketing department of the German company Ufa in the 1920s, inspired this book. It was her scorn at my ignorance of this period that led to my initial research and the discovery of a wealth of fascinating material. I chose to tell one story, but there were countless others. What took shape is intended to be a parallel history, one that might have happened; although much of the novel is firmly based on fact, I have fictionalized events and invented films, characters, places, and plots.

I consulted dozens of books in the course of my research, among them: *Before the Deluge* by Otto Friedrich; *Berlin: Culture and Metropolis*, edited by Charles W. Haxthausen and Heidrun Suhr; *Berlin Cabaret* by Peter Jelavich; Baedeker's *Berlin and Its Environs* (fifth edition, 1912); *Berlin in Lights: The Diaries of Count Harry Kessler*, edited by Charles Kessler; *Berlin in the 20s* by Rainer Metzger; *Dietrich* by Malene Sheppard Skaerved; *From Caligari to Hitler* by Siegfried Kracauer; *Fun in a Chinese Laundry* by Josef von Sternberg; *The German Empire* by Michael Sturmer; *The Haunted Screen* by Lotte H. Eisner; *Home Fires Burning* by Belinda J. Davis; *Lulu in Hollywood* by Louise Brooks; *Memories of a Star* by Pola Negri; *My Years in Germany* by

Martha Dodd; *Nights in the Big City* by Joachim Schlör; *Reading Berlin 1900* by Peter Fritzsche; *The Roses of No Man's Land* by Lyn MacDonald; *The Ufa Story* by Klaus Kreimeier; *Voluptuous Panic* by Mel Gordon; *The War from Within* by Ute Daniel; *What I Saw* by Joseph Roth; and *Women and the Great War*, edited by Joyce Marlow.

For the images in this book, I thank Bettina Schulze-Mittendorf; the Bundesarchiv, Berlin; the Deutsche Kinemathek—Museum für Film und Fernsehen, Berlin; the Deutsches Historisches Museum, Berlin; the Filmmuseum, Potsdam; the Friedrich-Wilhelm-Murnau-Stiftung, Wiesbaden; and heimatsammlung.de.

I also thank Simon Trewin, Zoë Pagnamenta, and Jessica Craig at PFD; my editors, Sarah McGrath and Heather Barrett, Sarah Stein at Riverhead, and Nora Mahony at John Murray; my mother, who always had the right size envelope; my father; all my friends in Scotland and New York who traveled with me, listened, made suggestions, and read early drafts, including my sister Kate, and Lisa, Audra, Charlie, Alison and Greg, Rosie, Louise, Roz, Karen, Giselle, Sara, Andrea and Jon, Stephen and Frances, and Zoë. I'm very grateful to my first agent, Giles Gordon, whose favorable response to the first few chapters encouraged me to keep going, and to Tracey Howell. Finally, special thanks to my children, Theo and Frances, and my partner, Paul Harkin, for everything else.

The writer acknowledges support from the Scottish Arts Council toward the writing of this title.

The verses quoted on page 396 are from Rainer Maria Rilke's *The Sonnets to Orpheus*, Book 2, XIII, as translated by Stephen Mitchell, in *Ahead of All Parting: The Selected Poetry and Prose of Rainer Maria Rilke* (Modern Library).

List of Illustrations